Acclaim for Michael Lowenthal and

CHARITY GIRL

"Lowenthal's narrative style is perfect for a heroine who suffers but remains a survivor, striking just the right mix of dark and light, worldly and innocent."
— *New York Times Book Review*

"*Charity Girl* tells a deeply disturbing story with compassion and sly cleverness." — *Boston Globe*

"Lowenthal has created memorable women who deal in a variety of ways with a shameful moment. He does both literature and history a favor." — *Orlando Sentinel*

"*Charity Girl* establishes [Michael Lowenthal] as one of the country's finest authors . . . A resplendent, unforgettable novel." — *Bookslut*

"Well-told, finely detailed . . . [*Charity Girl*] manages to both illuminate and entertain. It's a real find." — *Buffalo News*

"Harrowing yet inspiring. . . . Rich in period detail, swift-paced prose, and deserved political outrage."
— *Kirkus Reviews*, starred review

"Captivating . . . a spirited and exciting story."
— *Library Journal*

"Engaging . . . Lowenthal captures the brash, unlettered, raucous, and messy spirit of the times vividly."
— *San Francisco Chronicle*

CHARITY GIRL

CHARITY ★ GIRL

MICHAEL LOWENTHAL

A Mariner Book
Houghton Mifflin Company
BOSTON · NEW YORK

First Mariner Books edition 2008

Copyright © 2007 by Michael Lowenthal

ALL RIGHTS RESERVED

For information about permission to reproduce selections
from this book, write to Permissions, Houghton Mifflin Company,
215 Park Avenue South, New York, New York 10003.

www.houghtonmifflinbooks.com

Library of Congress Cataloging-in-Publication Data
Lowenthal, Michael.
Charity girl / Michael Lowenthal.
p. cm.
ISBN-13: 978-0-618-54629-9
ISBN-10: 0-618-54629-4
1. Sexually transmitted diseases — Patients — United States — Fiction.
2. Women patients — United States — Fiction. 3. Sexually transmitted
diseases — Government policy — United States — Fiction. 4. Sexually
transmitted diseases — United States — History — Fiction.
I. Title.
PS3562.O894C47 2007
813'.54 — dc22   2005037775

ISBN-13: 978-0-618-91978-9 (pbk.)
ISBN-10: 0-618-91978-3 (pbk.)

Book design by Melissa Lotfy

PRINTED IN THE UNITED STATES OF AMERICA

VB 10 9 8 7 6 5 4 3 2 1

For my mother,
Janet Wyzanski Lowenthal

Charity causes half the suffering she relieves, but she cannot relieve half the suffering she has caused.

— *The General Need for Education in Matters of Sex,*
   published by the Chicago Society of Social Hygiene,
   circa 1907

One

SOMEONE HAS COME for her — someone is here! — and gossip speeds so readily through Ladies' Undergarments that Frieda, in a twinkling, is forewarned. (The elevator boy tells the stock girl, who tells her.) She grins, but as the newest-hired wrapper at Jordan Marsh she's still minded awfully closely by Mr. Crowley, so she struggles against the glee and keeps to work. She snaps a box open and handily tucks its ends, crimps tissue around the latest stranger's buys: a nainsook chemise, a crêpe de Chine camisole. But her fingers, as she's knotting up the package, snarl the string.

She's been waiting for him to come again, conjuring. Every day this week, she's woken half an hour early to wash her hair and put herself together. On the modest black shirtwaist required by Jordan's dress code gleams her only brooch: Papa's gold seashell. She's nibbled at tablets of arsenic to pale her face, rubbed lemon zest on her wrists and her throat: the pinpoints where her flurried pulse beats. A girl who can't afford to buy perfume finds other lures.

1

Now, at last, Felix has come, as he promised. She fills her mouth with the hum of his name: *Feel-ix*. The feel of his thumbs on her hipbones, hooked hard. The taste of his taut, brazen lips.

He's come for her at work again, for where else could he search? Their first — their only — time, they didn't use her room (the landlady would have kicked her out, and quick). Instead they went where he wanted, and afterward, in her fluster (her brain swirly with passion, with a fib she'd caught him telling), she neglected to give him her address. Her rooming house has no telephone.

Lou, who was with Frieda when Felix swept her off, predicted he would soon enough be back. Lou didn't speak to him but says she didn't have to; she knows from boys, knows all she needs. Frieda scans the department for her surefire companion, hoping to score a last bit of advice. But Lou is nowhere to be seen. She must be in the fitting room with a customer.

It hits Frieda that Minnie, the stock girl, said *someone*. Why not say *a man*? Or speak in code? The shopgirls have their secret tricks of talk. "Oh, Henrietta!" one will call, although no clerk goes by that name, meaning: That customer's a *hen*, not worth the bother. And if a cash girl whispers, "Could you *hand* me *some* of that?" she means, Don't look yet, but is he handsome!

Minnie didn't ask to be *handed* anything; all she said was "Someone's here for you." For an instant Frieda fears that the visitor is Mama; Mama's tracked her down and come to fume. Frieda is still six months shy of eighteen, so Mama retains parental rights. She could have Frieda booked on a charge of stubbornness. She could force her to go live with awful Hirsch.

Silly, no, the explanation's simpler: Minnie's just too new to know the code. She's worked at Jordan's less than two full weeks.

Frieda had her own missed-signal mishap, her very first Friday at the store. She was struggling after lunch to keep pace at the wrapping counter when Lou, her new pal, hastened by, tapping her wrist twice for the time. Strange — that very wrist was adorned with an Elgin watch — but Frieda's mind was cottony with fatigue; she said, "Ten past two," and went back to her bundles.

Seconds later, she heard, "Excuse me," and looked up. The man was gray-templed, enticingly tall, a crisp-rimmed homburg in his hands.

"Yes," he said. "Hello. What I need are undergarments. Corsets, brassieres, camisoles."

"I'm sorry, sir," said Frieda. "I'm just a bundle wrapper. You'd have to find a salesclerk for that. Try Miss Garneau" — that was Lou — "or Miss Fitzroy."

"No, no," he said. His gaze skittered oddly across her features, as though following the flight of a bug he hoped to swat. "*You* can help me, miss. I'm sure you can."

"I'm sorry," she repeated, nervous not only that her incompetence would be spotted (what did she know of boning or figured broché?) but that the clerks would be mad at her for meddling.

"But you see," said the man, leaning over the counter so that Frieda smelled his oversweet breath, "I'm aiming to surprise a lady friend. Naturally, I wasn't able to ask her size. But you look just about her dimensions. The salesclerk, if I may say, is a bit too saggy in the bosom."

He stretched *saggy* to sound exactly like its meaning, and Frieda couldn't stifle a rising laugh.

"Would you mind terribly telling me your size?" he said. "I lack any experience in these matters."

His voice was cultured, Frieda thought, the kind of voice that could get away with talking French — words like *amour* and *sonata* (or was that Spanish?). He had a moth-eaten attractiveness, his features clearly hand-me-downs from a previous, more vital self. His eyes were the color of tarnished pennies.

"Eaton," he said. "George Eaton. Would you help me?"

The first and last rule in the Jordan Marsh manual: *The customer must always be served.* Frieda told the man her measurements.

Soon enough she found herself wrapping a large package of their priciest hand-embroidered undergarments: fine albatross, in slow-burn shades of rose. Grace Fitzroy, who'd booked the sale, took the finished bundle and gave it, Frieda saw, to Eaton. But instead of heading left, toward the bank of elevators, he turned right and sauntered straight to Frieda. Atop the package sat his careful note: "For you, with the hope that I might see how they become you. Meet me out front. Six o'clock."

As soon as he was gone, Lou came rushing. "You batty, Frieda? Why'd you talk to him?"

"He's a customer. He asked for my advice."

"Not *him,* though. He's notorious! Why didn't you mind my signal?"

When Frieda professed ignorance, Lou had to explain that two taps of the timepiece meant *Watch out.* The store teemed with disreputable men. "Next time," she admonished, "tell him off."

Frieda couldn't fathom why the gifts should be returned — hadn't Eaton paid for them in cash? — but Lou and Grace said she had to do it. (Grace crossed herself: "There but for God.") Obediently Frieda gave them up, but kept as her secret where she planned to go at closing time. She exited as usual by the employees' alley door, then crept round, keeping in the shadows. George Eaton was waiting by the main glass-door entrance, whistling a nonchalant song. Whistling and waiting, just for her.

Frieda stood trembling — ten minutes, fifteen — studying this man who wanted her. Eaton placidly tipped his hat to passersby, now and again checked his pocket watch. She couldn't quite judge if he was dashing or disturbing — or if maybe there wasn't all that big a difference. How would it feel to ask so boldly for what you wanted?

She took two jittery steps in his direction, then scuttled back to shadowed safety. Her tongue turned edgy, sharp within her mouth. And her heart, by the time Eaton shrugged and loped away, thumped so hard she feared it might bruise.

Which is how she feels now, minus the doubt: Felix is no lewd lurker preying on the guileless; he's a mensch, a U.S. Army private, ready to brave the trenches Over There. (His uniform! Its manful, raspy feel.) Sure, maybe she's loony—they've kept company but the once, which ended with Frieda running off—but something tells her he might be a keeper. She knows it by the fierce, delicious tension in her joints. Her whole self is a knuckle that needs cracking.

From the skein, she snips off a prickly length of twine. She'll count to ten—no, twenty—then allow a quick peek up. By then, she thinks, he'll be right here. Here.

She's at twelve—doubting she can last eight further counts—when a lady's treacly voice says, "Frieda Mintz?"

Instinct almost makes Frieda deny it. She hates to hear her name asked as a question. In a tiny, grudging tone she says, "I'm her."

"Good, then. Wonderful. How easy."

Get on with it, Frieda wants to say.

Get on with it and get the heck away from my counter so I can be alone when Felix shows.

The lady has a damsel's braids the color of a dusty blackboard, as though her schoolgirl self was aged abruptly. Her smile shows a neat set of teeth. "I'm sorry to have come to your workplace," she says, "but it's all the information we were given. Is there somewhere we can speak more privately?"

Only now does Frieda see that Felix isn't coming, that her visitor is—who? How does this stranger know her name? The pressure in her joints pinches tight. "No," she says. "I've got to stay. I'm working."

"But I really must speak with you, Miss Mintz."

"I had my break already," Frieda says.

"Then I guess we'll just have to talk here." The woman shivers slightly, hunch-shouldered and indignant, like someone

5

caught suddenly in the rain. "I'm Mrs. Sprague. I'm with the Committee on Prevention of Social Evils Surrounding Military Camps."

The long, daunting name is a gale that buffets Frieda, dizzying, disorienting. *Evils.*

"You're familiar with our work?"

Frieda manages to mumble no.

"Well, we're trying to do our bit to win the war. For those of us who can't actually enlist ourselves and fight, that means supporting our boys in every way — isn't that right?"

Mrs. Sprague's churchy tone reminds Frieda of the man who came into Jordan's last Thursday to train a squad of four-minute speakers. (As if Boston needs another squad! At every movie hall and subway stop she's heard them, preaching in the same zealous accent.) When Frieda walked past the employees' room at lunch, she heard the speech coach's red-blooded baritone ("Whenever possible, address crowds in the first-person plural. It makes them feel invested, don't we think?") and the class's steel-trap response ("We do!").

"I said, isn't that right, Miss Mintz?"

Frieda stares at her twine-roughened fingers. "Suppose so."

"You 'suppose.' But do you really under*stand*?" The lady's smile widens, showing more tidy teeth. "Too many girls — too many pretty ones like you — get their desire to help soldiers all mixed up with . . . well, with desire itself."

How does she know of Frieda's longing for a soldier? Did she spy her with Felix at the ballgame? (The game was the only public place they went.)

"And here's something I bet you haven't heard," says Mrs. Sprague. "Have you heard that more soldiers are hospitalized now with *social* diseases than with battle wounds?"

Frieda, in confusion, shakes her head. How could a disease be something social?

"Most girls don't know that. Most don't *want* to. And if a soldier's hurt when he goes over the top, that's the price of freedom, and we'll pay it. But any man hit by this other kind of sickness — well, he's crippled in his body *and* his soul." The last word seems to trigger something in the woman; she takes one of her gray braids and twists it round her thumb, as if remembering long-ago pain. "A bullet wound can heal. Not a soul."

Frieda glimpses Mr. Crowley standing ten yards off, with the floorwalker from the Notions department. Can he hear? Does he see that she's not wrapping? Twice last week he scolded her for minuscule infractions (sitting before her break, excessive laughter). What would he inflict for this transgression? "You're scaring me," she says to the strange woman. "Would you please leave?" She grabs a slip of tissue to stuff within a frock, but her fingers only fold the flimsy paper.

"No," says Mrs. Sprague. "No, I can't. It seems that your name and address — well, the fact that you work here — were given by a soldier to the Camp Devens guard — and then to our Committee on Prevention — when the soldier was found to be infected."

"Infected?"

Mrs. Sprague colors and looks down, away from Frieda. She plucks a mote of cotton from her sleeve. "You might have heard the layman's terms. The pox. The clap." Despite her lowered voice, the consonants resound; the smack of them seems to make her wince. "The soldier has reported that you were his last contact. We have to assume you were the source."

But Frieda thought you had to "go the limit" to risk sickness — and she hasn't, not with anyone but Felix. (Well, and Jack Galassi, but that was long ago.) "Felix?" she says. "I don't . . . I can't believe it."

"I'm not at liberty to disclose the soldier's name."

Lou arrives with two piqué petticoats to be wrapped, and piles them onto Frieda's growing backlog. She taps Frieda's right shoulder: *You all right?*

Frieda nods, but the movement nauseates her. In the teeter of her panic she tries to summon Felix's face; haziness is all that she can muster. His smell, though, storms upon her — pistachios, spilled spirits — and the agitated rapture of his kisses.

7

"Okay?" Lou says, this time aloud.

Before Frieda can answer, Mr. Crowley sees them huddled and he scowls; Lou returns to her customers.

"You're lucky," explains Mrs. Sprague. "Because you met this soldier outside of the moral zone, we don't have authority to arrest you. And we can't *force* a medical exam." She peers at Frieda as if judging the future of a stained dress. Is it salvageable as rags, or just trash? "But here's warning: if you're found anywhere within five miles of Camp Devens — or any installation for that matter — believe me, you'll be head and ears in trouble. Stay away from the town of Ayer. Hear?"

As if ducking a blow, Frieda nods.

"Our hope," Mrs. Sprague continues, her tone a bit tempered, "is that you'll volunteer for medical care — and help us all by helping your own health. It's not too late to turn away from ruin."

But Frieda can taste the ruin already, a spoiled-milk acridness near her tonsils. She feels sweat — or something worse? — beneath her skirts.

Mrs. Sprague finds a pad and pencil in her purse. "Do you live at home? We'd like to reach your parents."

"They're dead," Frieda mutters. (Papa is; Mama might as well be.)

"You're adrift." The woman marks something in her book. "Then tell me where you yourself live."

"Harrison," comes out automatically, but she's quick enough to falsify the number. "Seventy-two," she says — Mama's Chambers Street address.

"Telephone?"

Frieda shakes her head.

Mrs. Sprague makes another note and tucks her pad away, looking saddened by the thought of such privation. One after the other she lifts her gray braids, which have fallen in front of her hunched shoulders, and places them back behind her neck. The gesture's exactness reminds Frieda of Jenny Cohn, the best-off girl in first grade; every day, Jenny brought her doll to

8

school and shared it, encouraging Frieda to pretend, but all the while would stand there watching every move, ready to snatch the doll away if Frieda played wrong.

"I know life is hard," says Mrs. Sprague, "for a girl like you. But be*lieve* me, it could get a great deal worse. I visit the girls we catch — we have a brig in the Ayer Town Hall — and I'll tell you, they don't look very well. Once they've *really* come a cropper, they're begging for their old problems."

"Excuse me, ma'am," says Mr. Crowley, fast upon them. Spittle wets his mustache at its twists. "Miss Mintz here has some purchases to wrap. If you need assistance, can one of the salesladies help you?"

"No," she says. "My business here is done." Then to Frieda: "We do this because we *care* — remember that. I'll hope to see you soon. It's not too late." She turns toward the elevators and disappears.

Frieda doesn't look at her, and not at Mr. Crowley, but at the mound of unmentionables on the counter. She folds two chiffon negligees — slippery, obscene — and boxes them as fast as she can manage, cutting string, tying stony knots.

Two

S HE MET HIM the day of the All-America Liberty Loan
parade.

The sky! The cloudless, godsent sky. The breeze that set flags
snapping like applause. There were flags hauled up church
spires and draped from windowsills, flags clasped in toddlers'
pudgy fists; a teamster's horse had stars and stripes inked on
its blinders.

Frieda carried a pint-sized flag glued to a stick, as did every
girl in the Jordan Marsh contingent. They waited on the Common, near the corner of Charles and Beacon, with the other de-
partment-store delegations. Nearby, a boy in a tweed reefer sold
frankfurters (though they couldn't, of course, be called *that* any
longer). "Liberty sausages!" cried the boy from his cart. "Take
a bite out of the kaiser. Profits to the Red Cross. Liberty sausages!" The meaty steam swirled and lifted and joined with the
scent of the eager, milling crowd. Gulping it all, Frieda felt a
glorious sort of hunger that had nothing whatsoever to do with

10

food (a want that deepened even as she fed it): hunger for connection, for this mighty communal motion, hunger stripped of all anxiety.

Normally by this hour she'd be famished. On eight dollars a week to cover groceries and rent, plus shoes and waists suitable for work — and with prices so frightfully war-inflated — she never had enough to make ends meet. Even with washing her own laundry at home, stringing bloomers on a line above the sink, something almost always had to go, and most commonly that thing was lunch. But Lou, an ace at scrimping and living beyond her means, had taught Frieda the gumdrop trick. Three gumdrops at noon — a penny each at the Milk Street sweetshop — and you could fool your stomach into feeling full; only after the break, too late to spend more, did hunger exact its retribution. (Seventeen cents saved of a lunch that would cost twenty, times six, was a dollar-plus per week. With luck, those savings paid for a Sunday at Revere Beach: some fellow would make good on her initial investment, treating her to ice cream and a boat ride. Or she might splurge on a picture show at Scollay Square — the new *Hazards of Helen,* in which Helen jumps her car onto a barge, was just colossal.) By day's end, Frieda was dizzy, and mere blinking taxed her strength, but this was how a girl on her own could make it.

Today, though, she was sharp, her vision magnified — amazing what a full hot lunch could do. Jordan Marsh, along with every other downtown store, had closed at noon in honor of the pageant, and employees were supplied with free meals. Frieda, who hadn't tasted meat this whole week, gobbled heaps of red flannel hash (each bite made more flavorful, as was true so often now, by her awareness of its not being kosher). Like the poster girl for Hoover's wheat-conservation plan, she downed three slices of Defender Bran bread.

During coffee, the floorwalkers distributed sashes for each Jordan's girl to wear: BRUNETTES AND BLONDES, BUY LIBERTY BONDS. "And to top things off, *literally*," said the head of operations, "we're also going to give you girls these." From his jacket he pulled a khaki trench cap. "Who says an army can't be pretty?"

Lou, sitting beside Frieda with their chums from the department, immediately began to grouse. If there wasn't money, as the bigwigs claimed, for any raise in wages, and no budget for overtime pay, where'd they found the dough for all this sprigging? Out of the girls' paychecks, that was where! And for what? For these idiotic sashes.

Frieda had never contradicted Lou — Lou, who'd been a better sister in the few weeks of their friendship than Frieda's real sister, Hannah, had managed in a lifetime. But now Frieda rose to her full sitting height, and she told Lou, "I'd proudly *pay* for mine." She said it not so much for the sake of patriotism (though she counted herself ready to do her part), but because there was no place she wanted to be more than with these girls, gaily parading, on display.

This Liberty Day, this first anniversary of America's entry into the great world war, marked for Frieda something more personal: a month since her arrival, her escape. Before, still living under Mama's heavy thumb, she'd have wasted this day caged in shul. (A parade on Shabbos? *Bist du meshuga?*) Then, after hours in the women's balcony, her head sore from the strident drone of Hebrew, she'd trudge with Mama back to their apartment. Mama would draw shut the drapes she'd sewn from castoff sheets and daven in the cabbage-stinking gloom.

What if Frieda hadn't fled? By today she'd be Mrs. Pinchas Hirsch. The deal he'd made with Mama called for marriage straightaway, before Sefirah, the weeks when weddings aren't allowed. Mama, without consulting her, agreed: Hirsch had piles of money, and his boys needed a mother; only a fool would let the chance pass.

Frieda, a mother? And wife to a man more than twice her age, whose ears sprouted curling gray hairs?

Thank goodness, no, today she wasn't Frieda Hirsch, nor Friedaleh, cooped up in Mama's rooms. She was Miss Mintz,

Ladies' Undergarments bundler. A girl who had chosen her own course.

Turning now toward the wind that poked litter across the Common, Frieda let it part her brown curls. She perched the cap on her head, then raked it left a bit, hoping to look as sharp as it made her feel. Lou donned her cap, too ("No sense spoiling the sport, I guess"), and pinned it to the hair she worked so diligently to keep blond. "Hup two three," Lou bellowed, mockmarching in place with an eye toward the leafless maple trees, which a dozen Polish boys had claimed as bleachers. One of the boys kissed the tight bud of his closed fingers, which then spread precociously to bloom. "Hey, *ksiezniczko*," shouted the boy on the branch above him.

"Hear that?" said Lou. "They adore you."

"No, *you*," said Frieda, wondering what they'd been called. But didn't everyone love everyone today? In a crowd like this, how could someone not? This was what she'd dreamed of when she ran away from home: the chance to adore and be adored by everyone, with no boundaries, no allegiance but to *now*. "Can't believe it," she said. "It's all of Boston."

"More," Lou called. "Papers say a million."

Frieda was wrestling with the notion of a million — the number of avid nerves within her skin? — when bugles sounded, and suddenly, with a whomp and roar of steel, came a tank: a real tank, crushing along. "Hail Britannia," called the crowd to the nobby British soldier who saluted from the tank's open porthole.

Next came Mayor Peters and the Sons of Saint George, the Woman's Christian Temperance Union. Frieda rose to her tiptoes and glimpsed a Mercer Runabout (she'd never seen one outside of the movies) with a sharp-jawed starlet at the wheel. Mabel Normand? Could it be? The one who raced speedsters on screen?

Then the floats, built on motor trucks and on horse-drawn wagon beds, all guided by drivers in costume: Lady Libertys, Uncle Sams, Minutemen. The Electric Supply Jobbers' float featured an effigy of Kaiser Wilhelm strapped into a genuine electric chair. "Electrocute Bill!" the men shouted. The crowd, in response, raised a din of vengeful screams, and a jobber, fist clenched, flipped the switch. Voltage arced greenly through the sky.

Frieda read the next float's banner: SHIPSHAPE WINS! EMPLOYEES OF THE FORE RIVER SHIPYARD. The men wore grime-encrusted jeans and sleeveless undershirts, their piston-like arms smeared with grease. With pneumatic guns they riveted sheets of bright steel: the bulkhead of an actual destroyer.

Lou pointed to the one with ginger hair. "How'd you like to be riveted by *him*?"

But Frieda was thinking of Papa and his ropy butcher's arms, burled with muscle from years of cleaver wielding. The skin at his elbow's crook, where she used to rest her head, and his smell: blood and sweat and reassurance. A year he'd been gone, but still she saw him in every strapping man. Would he have marched today? Yes, she could see him with a flag pinned to his apron. Or, if not—if Mama had demanded he stay home—at least he'd have encouraged Frieda's presence. "Let her," he used to say in his touchingly accented English whenever Frieda begged for scraps of freedom. "Did we sail across an ocean to raise our daughter in 'Smother Russia'?"

Finally the call came, and with a bustle of petticoats their division stepped onto Beacon Street. They joined just in front of the Navy Yard band, which played "The Marseillaise" and "Keep the Home Fires Burning" and a new song she'd never heard before:

What are you going to do for Uncle Sammy?
What are you going to do to help the boys?

None of them knew a thing about marching—they were shopgirls, they hadn't trained for this—yet somehow they squared into perfect formation, game pieces all in a row. Each wore her sash and her starchy trench cap and a sky blue dress with pleated skirts. Tubby, thin, tall: all the same. Frieda, without quite planning to, found herself in front, her smile the very first that people saw.

They clopped up Beacon past the stolid old mansions that today looked about to burst their walls: windows full of waving arms, roofs teeming. Topping the hill's crest, they came upon the State House, whose dome flashed in the clean April sun. A reviewing stand was festooned with eagle busts and miles of stripe. For Frieda, the stand called to mind a frosted birthday cake, with the dignitaries, in their top hats, like candles.

"He's staring at you," said Lou above the roar.

"Who?"

"The governor, there. Or is it Coolidge?"

He had kind eyes and a chin so cleft you could have hidden nickels in it. Frieda smiled at him, and he smiled back, and she sensed that an agreement had been sealed. He would deliver victory and peace and happiness as long as she maintained this fervent spirit: openhearted, burnishing, alive. *This* was what she'd do to help the boys.

Down School Street then, and the crowd tightened; their cheers made a hot breeze. Frieda cheered, too: "Buy a bond! For the boys!"

"I'll buy *that*," yelled a constable with huge tufts of sideburns.

"Hip hip for brunettes and blondes," said his partner.

Amid the passing blur, patches of clarity drew her eye: a man with raised arms, a rip in his suit exposed; a boy who grinned so wide she saw his molars.

And what did these spectators see of Frieda? The West End youngster with brooding tea-dark eyes, her shoulders pinched with fear and acquiescence? Or a new girl, made golden by the sun? Frieda felt expanded, stretched past her normal limits — a balloon that the crowd's breath was filling.

At thirteen, when her body began its changes, she had wanted to take flight from all that flesh. Would her hips and her thighs now thicken like Mama's? Would her chest be ballasted with weight? But her body's growth brought her, in these

15

subsequent years, to a shape nothing at all like her mother's, a shape of smirky curves, just shy of fullness. Was it the just-shyness that made men look at her that way — how they stared at her now on Beacon Street — as if wanting to give her something, to make additions? She felt their stares as a giddy, ticklish pull, as when the Atlantic Avenue El rounded a bend with extra speed. Something had been welling deep inside her for so long — something like liquid, like a soul; now it rose toward every inch of skin.

She saw the soldier then. Or he saw her.

He stood on the curb among a dozen other doughboys, and though they all sported the same uniform, his distinguished itself with a slightly different tint, as if the cloth were flesh and his was flushed with blood. He had a bowfront nose (like hers, but even longer), a puppy's unruly wet grin.

She stared a second. More. She wasn't sure if she was being dared, or daring.

His face seemed to say that he'd been searching for a phrase — on the tip of his tongue, driving him insane — and bingo! he'd remembered it finally: *her.*

Lou was asking something, trying to steal Frieda's attention — "Way, way up, geez, see how *high*?" — and Frieda, still gazing at the soldier, briskly nodded, for height was precisely what she'd gained: a mountaintop reached without a climb. This must be pure dreaming — a dime-novel folly (she'd read all of Laura Jean Libbey): *the moment I fell in love at first sight* — but did dream-love bring this gritty, fresh-kill taste? Frieda swallowed. Swallowed urgently again.

The soldier was still staring. Smiling hard. He pointed the gun of his hand and pulled the trigger.

The Navy band blared another chorus:

> *If you're going to be a sympathetic miser,*
> *The kind that only lends a lot of noise,*
> *You're no better than the one who loves the Kaiser —*
> *So what are you going to do to help the boys?*

The next verse was drowned out by a growling from above, a sound like anger caught in someone's throat. Frieda, peering up — half a mile, it must have been — saw what Lou had urged her to look at: an airplane, vulturing above them. She'd never seen an airplane flying and was surprised by its jerkiness. It teetered and swooped and righted itself again — a flaw in the diamond-face of sky.

Then, with a morbid cough of engines, the plane plunged, and a hatch opened, and out dropped the bombs. Frieda ducked. So did Lou. Desperately grabbing. Each trying to crouch beneath the other.

But the bombs dawdled, flitting on the breeze like outsized snowflakes. Paper! A shrapnel of propaganda. Frieda grabbed a broadside from the air. *Soldiers Give Their Lives. What Will YOU Give?*

Rising from her cower, she looked back at the doughboy. He had caught a paper missile, too; he crumpled it and tossed it straight at her. She wanted to say something — her name? a solemn oath? — but a whistle sent the column marching forward; the press of the ranks behind her forced her on. In her last glimpse, the soldier was extravagantly laughing — at her, it seemed, but also at himself — laughing because what better option was there?

Three

---★---

"ORGET HIM," said Lou, huffing hard with each step. "Plenty more fellers where he came from."

"You don't understand," Frieda pleaded. "He was so..." Somewhere in the distance from her mind to her mouth the explanation got utterly succotashed.

They were trudging up four flights to Lou's room. It was Wednesday — dance night — and ritual demanded that Frieda go home after work with Lou; that way they could eat and primp together. The routine: hike from Jordan's through downtown to the South End, straight to Schick's Delicatessen Store, where boiled dinner went for twenty cents a pint. (With corned beef and cabbage and carrots and potatoes, it was meal enough for two, plus leftovers.) Then a final block to Lou's rooming house on Shawmut and up the dark stairwell to her door: a hundred treads all faintly sloping leftward.

The climb wrung the breath from Frieda, too. Today the spring lines had come in, and on top of her normal duties she'd been called upon to stock and shelve displays. It was her first

18

decent chance to impress Mr. Crowley and notch a spot on his advancement list. Jogging between her counter and the brimful garment racks, she'd memorized the merits of the brand-new corset covers, of cambric nightgowns sewn with convent edges. She'd been raised believing that colors were simply colors —nature's own finite set of hues—but now she was instructed otherwise: she learned of a newfangled green known as Neptune; Romance, this season's lip-pale pink; and a white-on-white weave, labeled Virtue.

By midafternoon she'd been absolutely tuckered—so spent that she forgot Saturday's soldier. But then, on a washroom break, she passed the collection box to purchase "smokes" for "Boston's Own," the 301st. (Was that her grinning doughboy's division? If she gave, would it buy the luck to find him?) She hated thinking about him, because thinking would get her exactly nowhere. Forty thousand soldiers at Camp Devens, and all she knew of him was—what? The way he'd gazed at her: accomplices in an all-or-nothing heist. She also hated (hated it more) *not* thinking about him, for the memory might then chafe away like sunburn. The whole thing would have been just what Lou said: a kid's crush.

"And this boy of yours," added Lou, slumping hard onto her mattress so the iron bedstead clanged against the wall. "Think he didn't make eyes at every girl?"

"He was different," said Frieda, even as she doubted it.

"You want to go and *look* for hurt? Fine. Me, I got plenty as it is." Lou unlaced her shoe to massage a swollen ankle. "Holy mother of God, are my dogs barking!"

"Mine, too," said Frieda, and joined her on the bed. "Maybe we should take a pass on dancing? We could go see *The Open Track* again." They'd seen this latest *Hazards of Helen* episode twice already: a villain accosts Helen as she drives her touring car, but she pushes him out the door and speeds on . . . in time to save the railroad from marauders! Frieda loved it—loved anything with girls in fast cars.

"Kidding?" said Lou. "Skip *dancing*? It's the only proven cure."

19

As always, there was more than a bit of snarl in Lou's voice
—a sound, Frieda thought, that could scare a charging moose.
(Lou was from way up in Maine, a farm in Aroostook County,
and the name made Frieda picture moose and bears and other
beasts.) As the middle child of nine, Lou had told her when
they met, she learned early to hold her own "in English, French,
or elsewise."

Frieda found her pretty in a blunt, intrusive way: her face
had the sturdy elegance of a plow blade. She was twenty-one,
with bought-blond hair and a cocky, priceless smile. Men
couldn't keep away from her.

Nor could Frieda. Lou was a cliff to the edge of which she
was drawn, fearful not of any possibility of being pushed, but
of her own dark inclination to jump. Lou was unlike any other
girl that Frieda knew (so brassy, so lavishly alive), except perhaps—perhaps—the girl who hid within herself.

Lou's furnishings, in addition to the creaky bedstead: a gas
plate, a chest of drawers, a cracked full-length mirror; but she'd
tried her best to ornament the place. ("If you live in a dump,
what does that make you? Trash.") She'd papered the walls
with *Vanity Fair* tear sheets: Theda Bara in a vampish public-
ity shot as *The Vixen*, leggy beauties modeling mink stoles. On
the windowsill, a single, half-wilted geranium languished in a
rusted coffee can.

"Listen," Lou said. She had hoisted herself from the bed and
was spooning boiled dinner into two tin bowls. "Do you think
you're gonna find true love on the street? Course you're not! Besides, love ain't what you need just now. Have some fun—play
the field a bit."

Easy for her to say! Lou went through men like pairs of
cheap stockings. Frieda hadn't learned to do the same; she
wasn't positive she wanted to.

"What you *need*," said Lou through an overambitious bite of
beef, "is to get fussed up and out on that dance floor. Quit sulk-
ing and find someone new."

Frieda swallowed her own modest mouthful of dinner, her

first genuine food of the day. "Just like that? Snap my fingers, and I find him?"

Lou scoffed. "Haven't I taught you nothing? If you want to get any notion took of you, you gotta have some style."

After dinner, then, she made Frieda stand in front of her and she gave her a thorough studying, like an orchardist preparing to prune a tree. And prune she did: Frieda's eyebrows first, tweeze by ruthless tweeze ("Men like wildness, sure," she said, "but not between your eyes!"), then stray wisps of hair at Frieda's ears. She roped Frieda in a necklace boasting a single keen-edged rhinestone, as blatant as a swollen tooth. "Stop twitching!" Lou said, but Frieda couldn't help it. With a pencil smeared in residue from the blackened gas-plate burner, she painted a mole above Frieda's lip. ("Draw their eyes to a fake flaw, and they're more liable to miss the real ones.")

Frieda tracked her transformation in the mirror, uncertain if this catchpenny version of herself was closer to, or further from, the real thing. Mama had always made her feel that dolling herself up would be a sin — and worse, not worth the bother. (How Frieda might be both too plain and too alluring was a contradiction she'd only lately come to question.) Where the girls in Lou's magazines were pale and wasp-waisted — the fastidious end products of refining — Frieda was the raw, unmilled grain: brown hair that ripened in the sun with red highlights, cheeks that went to freckles after June. But she'd learned that some men — many men — had a taste for rawness.

At Jordan's men watched her. At the Liberty Loan parade. And most stunningly — the thought of it restored moxie to her muscles — at the grand halls where she and Lou danced.

Before she left home, the only dancing Frieda had done — the only dancing Mama had condoned — was at the Russian Emigrant Relief Fund Ball. To the wheeze of travel-battered, button-stuck accordions, pimply boys waltzed their rheumy-eyed aunts; Frieda'd had better times plucking chickens. But Lou showed her worlds as different from those flops as chickens are from swoop-necked swans. Dances at the Bowdoin Square

Ballroom, the Scollay Palace. Wednesdays and weekends at the least.

She fell in love with an orchestra's biting, full-tilt blare, with the flattering light of chandeliers. They danced the bunny hug, the grizzly bear, the Chaplin wiggle: twirly tough dances that loosened up her limbs as they loosened in her private late-night notions. Some folks, she knew, called such dancing scandalous, but if this was shameful — her lungs pumping, her skin rife with blood — then so, Frieda thought, was life itself. In shoes with lifted heels, on a wax-slick parquet floor, she could slide scot-free into her own future.

At the dances, Frieda met other wage-earning girls — shoe vampers and laundry feeders, stenographers — all of them making their way, making *themselves*. But the men! Fellows who strutted the tango, catlike, haunches taut; clunkers with two left boots but charm to burn. And every single one willing to treat. Sometimes she and Lou scraped together the entrance fee and met some fellows inside the hall. Other times they went first to the Keith's Amusement Centre or to a café beside the Bijou Dream; without fail, a pair of men would come and ask politely if the ladies wouldn't care to find a dance. Lou never blanched; she called it "picking up."

"We *all* play the game," she'd explained the first night, as she helped Frieda pin her hair into place. "We all play — ain't nothing to be ashamed of. Let the feller treat for your coat check, your drinks. Later, if you're hungry, maybe food." Lou transferred coins from her change purse to a clutch; she always brought the streetcar fare, in case. "How much you give back is up to you. Sometimes just your company, or a snuggle in the balcony, or . . ."

"What if it turns out I don't like him?"

"A boy's not going to spend all that money on you for nothing. Remember, you gotta be a good Injun."

So Frieda had doled out favors to a string of grateful men. One midnight, in the moonshadows of the Granary Burying Ground, a Sweepervac salesman groped beneath her dress;

she'd let a stevedore named Jim caress her neck. But she never allowed a man to go as far as Jack Galassi — for fear of getting pregnant, was what she told her dates, but the deeper truth was even more old-fashioned: she was waiting to find the one like no one else. She drew this line firmly in the sand of her self-will, like the other distinction Lou insisted on:

"Getting treated when you pick up boys is one thing," Lou explained, "and we're lots of us charity girls. But it's never just for money, straight out. If they think you're a common you-know-what who sells herself, then that's all you're ever gonna be."

Which wasn't to say that the spoils were wholly up to the man's design. Lou was a veritable robber baroness, profiting on the principal of her charm. "How d'you think," she asked Frieda, "I got this Elgin watch? Made a second date with this feller that I met — a looker, but his breath smelled like old eggs — and then I showed up fifteen minutes late. 'Ooh, I'm *so* sorry, but my stupid watch is broke! *Now* how'll I ever mind the time?' The very next night, lo and behold, he had a gift. 'Now you can check the time,' he said. I did: it was time for a new feller!"

Lou had employed a similar technique to get her newest hat (a toque of aqua tulle with chiffon roses), which a night watchman had given her last Wednesday, and which she now snugged onto Frieda's head. "Looks to me like you need a pick-me-up."

"Lou, you've never even worn it."

Lou leaned back to admire her handiwork. Her lips shaped a broad, soft-touch smile. "Save your breath. I'm not hearing 'no.'"

Two blocks from the Independence Ballroom, they sheltered under the awning of the Seaman's Credit Union. Trying to check their faces in the bank's plate-glass window, they were stymied by the paucity of glow: the city was under "lightless night" restrictions to save coal. So they served as each other's vanities: Frieda smoothed Lou's face powder with a nimble tongue-dabbed thumb; Lou fixed a smudge on Frieda's mole.

When they stepped out from under the awning, two men had materialized. "*La-dies*," said the shorter one with affable impatience, as though Frieda and Lou were their chronically tardy sweethearts. With casually deft fingers he rolled a cigarette, but his poise was foiled by his tall, skinny pal, whose fidgeting evoked a doomed man awaiting his final meal.

Fellow number one lit the cigarette. Through a theatrical cloud of smoke, he said his name: "Frankie Gallivan. And this here's Tip Gilooly."

Frankie was a jack-in-the-box of a man, Frieda thought — five feet three if he tipped his chin, maybe. His nose looked to have been broken in at least a couple of spots, the caricature of a lightning bolt. Tip, for his part, had a good foot on his friend, but by hunching seemed to use just half the space. His long, moon-pale face wore a slightly qualmish look, as if he was scared of heights and the view from his own eyes spooked him.

"So . . . ," Frankie said. The word trailed suggestively, like the slink of smoke from his nostrils.

Lou glanced at Frieda, then at the fellows, vettingly; you had to watch for rounders and cadets. But these weren't white slavers, Lou's wink to Frieda implied. They were just two lively Irish lads from Southie. Lou reached out, snatched the cigarette with a fly-swatting motion, and stole an indulgent inhalation. "So," she copied Frankie, her tone splitting the difference between mockery and flirtation, "we gonna camp here all night, or we gonna dance?"

"You're quite the little fizgig, ain'tcha?" said Frankie. He reached up and hooked his arm in Lou's. Off they went.

Frieda tagged after, Tip stilting along beside her, until they caught their friends and fell in step; she wasn't sure if she was the booby prize, or if he was.

In the quick hike to the Independence they exchanged their whats and whyfores. The fellows were linemen for Boston Edison. They'd been kept out of the Army — Frank for his height, he said, admitting the obvious; Tip for a reason that went unsaid — but were proudly engaged in war work: constructing new transmission lines ("Fifteen thousand volts of voom!") from the L Street station to the destroyer plant at Squantum.

"And you two?" said Frankie. "You got jobs?"

(Tip still hadn't peeped a single word.)

When Frieda named Jordan Marsh, Frankie's smile tightened. "Hear that, Tipper? A couple of downtown gals."

"We work in Intimates," Lou euphemized (Frankie's smile pulled even tighter), then she gave Frieda and herself quick promotions: "I'm assistant buyer. Frieda's our very best saleslady."

Lou was perpetually buttoning up her stories two or three holes above the truth. It unnerved Frieda. Wasn't it begging for exposure?

But then they reached the dance hall. The men paid their way, and as they swept all together up the ramp to the main room, Frieda's doubts burned off under the sizzle of all those bulbs. The hall loomed vast — the square footage of a whole wing at Jordan's — and was magnified to infinity by mirrors. Here was a world untouched by wartime thrift!

At the far side of the dance floor, on the streamer-draped stage, Professor Okay's Orchestra performed its alchemy. Frieda recognized the tune — "In for a Penny, in for a Pound" — she'd turkey-trotted to it once with a furrier from Brighton. The floor was packed with dancers: men with their hair slicked by sweat and petrolatum, girls with minxish, mounded pompadours. The girls' taffeta gowns had powder puffs and yards of ruffle, but Frieda, despite her own simple sateen frock (the best that Lou had managed for a loaner), didn't feel the slightest bit outdone. Her borrowed hat fit as firmly as a new conviction.

At Jordan's, Frieda always thanked her stars to be a bundler and not, despite the higher wage, a cashier girl. She watched every evening as the cashier girls rose from the dim, barren basement where they toiled, deprived of normal life but through pneumatic change tubes, by which they sent notes to upper floors: *Has it cooled off yet? Thunderstorms or clear?* Now, standing here in the ballroom's lucid glare, she realized that she was not so different. Her life until recently — until these bur-

nished, jackpot weeks — had been spent dungeoned, ignorant
of the weather; now at last, at last, she had emerged.

Their dates, who had beelined for the bar, returned with
drinks (Mamie Taylors and, for themselves, Rusty Nails). In
toast, four glasses met: a lucky clover.

"Gee," said Frankie, shading his eyes from the chandeliers,
"you'd think we built those power lines to *here*."

Tip said, "It'd be worth every volt." He lifted his face as if to
bask in sunshine.

Maybe, Frieda thought, he'd be all right.

Tip lit a cigarette and offered her a puff, which she took even
though she didn't smoke. To chase the rough heat, she sipped
her cool drink; her throat was dazzled, pleasantly haywire.

Professor Okay revved his orchestra to another frisky rag-
time, and the floor was deluged with new dancers. "Shall we?"
Frankie asked, and when Lou ardently nodded, they set down
their drinks and rode the wave. Tip and Frieda followed close
behind.

Dancing with Tip was an awkward affair. He pawed her
hips; she struggled for his shoulders. The whirligig of his long
limbs kept clipping her. "Sorry," he said. "Christ, sorry." Each
apology tore him further from the rhythm.

Tip had the faltering air of a mule sold too often, who can't
keep straight its new owner's orders. He stank of mothballs,
but Frieda would have sworn the smell rose from his pores
more than from his threadbare suit, as though his body itself
had long been stored away. Her own body, despite its entangle-
ment with Tip's, pistoned with the music's lubrication.

"Go easy?" said Tip. An offer, or a request?

She ignored it, fixing her grip around his neck. From this
close she caught a difference between his eyes: the left one
moistly bashful, the right blank. So *that's* what had disqualified
him! Now that she guessed it, the glass eye was obvious. She
stared into its marbly dispassion, and rather than evoke pity
or condolence, the defect roused an urge to dance rough. She
wondered why damaged goods incited further damage: Was his

misfortune a hedge against her own? Their feet jigsawed space in an outlandish one-step. Frieda pressed her cheek against his chest.

When the song ended, Frankie and Lou, who'd been lost in their own wiggling, announced that they were leaving the dance floor. "It's slam-bang here," said Frankie. "How 'bout some privacy." He cocked his head unsubtly toward the staircase.

The balcony was where, in quarter light, girls sat on fellows' laps, and hands roved in shifty, shadowed motions. At least that was how Lou had described it; Frieda, though she'd indulged in her share of dance-floor petting, had yet to stray above the ballroom level.

"Let's go," said Lou. "We'll have a bash." She turned and hoofed off with restless Frankie.

Tip was staring at Frieda, and his glass eye seemed to see right through her. Something had stiffened him to his full treacherous height — maybe the same force that inspired Frieda to clutch him. Together, leaning close, they approached the balcony stairs, Tip's camphor scent tart with potential, like gasoline.

She was stepping up when the sludgy sound of Yiddish made her stumble. To her left, her cousin Sadie — Mama's sister's youngest — stood among a pack of friends, gawking; Sadie, who, by some mischief of genetics, looked more like Mama than did Frieda herself: that same blade of mouth, those scoffing eyes.

Sadie turned her smug, awful gaze now on Frieda, and Frieda felt it strip away her jaunty, borrowed hat, her fake mole, her happy-squaw smile, to lay bare her old West End self.

"C'mon," Tip said. "There's folks waiting on us."

Dimly, Frieda sensed the crowd's agitation, but she was stuck staring at her cousin. Would Sadie, having spied her, rush off and snitch to Mama? Of course not, that would give *herself* away. But rather than relieving Frieda, the realization crushed her: nobody from the neighborhood would learn that she'd been here; nobody would think of her at all. Less and less would they remember her until she truly would be dead—like Papa, for whose loss they'd always blamed her.

"C'mon," Tip urged, his voice quietly brutal.

If Frieda budged, she thought she might be sick.

She *hadn't* killed Papa. They were wrong! He'd stayed late one Friday at Slotnik's Kosher Meats, trimming a roast he'd promised to their neighbor. But with sunset washing fast across the sky, Mama came and ordered him to stop. "Izzy! Izzy Mintz. It's almost *Shabbos!*" At the scare of her voice he jerked, and the knife caught his knuckle—an inch-long slice that should have bled but didn't. She rushed him straight home and into his Shabbos suit; in the rush, he neglected to clean the wound. Within a week, a devil-colored line spread up his arm. Less than four days later, his heart quit.

It was Mama! Mama, who knew which *b'racha* to chant when you swallowed a grain of barley—and which when it passed into the toilet—but who wouldn't know the Lord our God, King of the universe, if He swooped down and seized her by the throat. Yet Frieda was the one held culpable—as if her love of Jack were the knife that had sliced Papa. At the shivah, Mama had pointed at her. "What *she* did, that's what killed him!" And no one had said *That's crazy talk* or tried to hush her up—not the rabbi or the chazan; not Hannah, who, having long blamed Frieda for being their father's favorite, had no trouble endorsing this new indictment; and certainly not Sadie, who had sat carrying on by Mama's side as if *she* were the second daughter—weeping less from grief (Frieda, seeing her now, guessed) than from fear her own misdeeds might be exposed.

Sadie now looked poised to say something, her mouth puckering into the shape of condemnation, but with a final snubbing turn she walked away.

Frieda, woozy with a sense of being jettisoned, realized that Tip had dropped her arm.

"You said sheeny girls was fast," he griped to Frankie, who stood three steps above, cuddling Lou.

"What can I tell ya, Tipper? When *I'm* with one, they are."

"If you've had such good luck, then let's trade."

Firmly, condescendingly, Frankie shook his head, like a bookie saying *Sorry, all bets closed.*

"C'mon, Frankie. What'm I gonna do with one like her?"

Four

———★———

MAMA FAULTED FRIEDA for the scandal with Jack, for Papa, but for something else, too, Frieda sensed, something older; had Mama ever *not* held a grudge?

What are you *smiling about?* That was her first memory of Mama, of Mama speaking and expecting a response. Frieda sat in an oblong of twilight below a window, grinning at the wink from a wrinkle in the glass — at nothing, really; at absolutely everything. Then came Mama's shadow as she stepped before the pane, and her question: "What are *you* smiling about?" — asked, it struck Frieda as she thought back through the years, not in anger or amusement so much as plain bewildered envy.

Other girls grew up wanting to be just like their mothers; if Frieda never got to feel that hopeful veneration it was because, for as far back as she could remember, it seemed that even Mama didn't want to be herself. There was nothing about Mama physically that should have kept her from being lovely. She had moody eyes that shifted hue according to sun or storm but that always gave off glints of self-possession; her face was built of sharp, assertive bones. It was the way Mama handled herself—or failed to; her repudiation of anything like charm. How often Frieda had watched her nag the iceman for a discount or scold the *downstairsikehs* for noise: her every body part, from balled fists to jutted jaw, ready to defend against attack—even though the aggressor had been she.

And too, working against Mama's should-have-been beauty was her voice: her graceless, throttled English. In Russian or in Yiddish, her chatting might be fluid, but the syllables of English clogged her throat. So she stumped through the streets of the West End with tightened lips, looking full of things she hoped to say but couldn't.

Why couldn't she tell Frieda that she loved her? Was it a failure of ability, or of feeling?

She never acted as hostilely toward Hannah, but did this prove Frieda's sister to be more loved, or just less noticed? Their mother sometimes didn't even remark on Hannah's presence, but if Frieda so much as blinked, Mama would say, "What is it *now*?" From early on, Frieda sensed that she was Mama's passion, and that passion and exasperation were the front and back of one page.

Hannah was punished often enough for *doing* something wrong—spilling wine, moving the candlesticks on Shabbos—but Frieda's crime, it seemed to her, was *being*. She was five or maybe six when Mama left one morning. ("For a minute only, just to go next door. Mrs. Pinsker needs eggs. You'll be all right?") Hannah must have been at school; Frieda was alone. On the table sat a bowl filled with homemade liniment: wintergreen mixed with linseed oil. Mama, who took in sewing to supplement Papa's wages, suffered aches in her knuckles and her wrists. The liniment was her latest attempted balm. Its smell was sharp and clean, like changing weather.

Frieda climbed up onto a bench and then the table, and she dipped a finger into the fragrant oil. She tasted it and spat (pff, so bitter!). But then, when she rubbed the excess oil onto her arm, the feeling was like a million feelings melted into one, creamy-cool-awake and tickle-sharp. Like someone's front teeth nibbling her skin. Now she dunked her whole left hand, now both, into the liniment and raised her skirt to reach her calves and thighs. Ting ting ting, all the way along her legs, a prickle so keen she'd swear it made a sound. She feared that it might fade away as most strong feelings did, so she kept rubbing — arms, neck. More.

She was so slippery that when Mama returned and cuffed her by the wrist, Frieda slithered, giggling, to freedom — slipped away without even trying. Which made her giggle harder, which goaded Mama's wrath. Yiddish curses pounding like a fist. Mama's real fist, too, at the ready.

Lucky that just then Papa came home for lunch. He scooped Frieda up, and again she couldn't help how she squirmed. "My little minnow!" he said, and his hold on her — the relief of his big hands — was almost enough to erase her fear of Mama.

Mama said, "Your daughter. She's revolting."

"Mama, what? Some oil," he said. "Who cares! I'll go buy more."

"It's not the waste, it's — look at her. Just look!"

He hugged Frieda closer and kissed her slick brow. "She looks happy. How any girl should look."

"Happy why? Tell me what's the reason. As if a girl's purpose is to sit and feel so pleased. No! That's not the way life is."

Mama scrubbed her so hard, letting soap run into her eyes, that Frieda felt the sting of it all day. And even now, just breathing the glossy scent of linseed oil (at Jordan's some pine cabinets had recently been refinished, and the store, for a week, was thick with fumes), Frieda always felt a pang of — what? Dislocation? The shame of not having known that she should be ashamed.

Thank God, then, for Papa. Thank God. A great muscle of a man, with hands the size of hatchets, he could well have whacked his way through life; instead, he cupped each moment in his palms and coddled it. At Slotnik's, he was the butcher asked to butterfly the loins: ladies said his touch was the most tender. They were right, Frieda knew, and it wasn't just his touch, but his voice, his gaze, his very soul. And Frieda was his favorite — *she* was, no other — which formed a hard pearl of pride within her.

Beneath his waggish mustache, Papa's mouth was so naturally upturned into a smile that to frown, it seemed to Frieda — to show indifference! — took exertion. ("Izzy," she heard his boss, Sam Slotnik, ask him once, "was your mama's womb a laugh riot or what? 'Cause it looks like you was born with that grin.") His smile could break the fall of Frieda's every disappointment.

He spoke English with a more-than-passing accent, plus Italian enough to rib his greenie neighbors. When he himself had arrived green and avid in this country — the year that both a new century and Frieda had been born — he forbade himself Yiddish and Russian for twelve months (a feat that he recounted to all comers). America was the land where what you sold was who you were; he fixed to learn its language store by store. Each day at his lunch break he visited a new shop and studied the names of all he found. Years later, to Frieda's unending entertainment, he could still tick off the lists he'd memorized: sheathing paper, rubber roofing, asphalt shingle, felt; Rose condensed milk, Crisco, Jiffy-Jell.

In religion, Papa had his own way, too. At shul he was a reverent, ungrudging regular, honored frequently with calls to the Torah, but any given evening he might skip the *ma'ariv* service and steal Frieda away to Castle Island. ("See that sunset? *That's* blessing enough.") He would shrug if, during Nisan, he forgot to count the *omer*, but ever was he mindful of a rainstorm's holiness, of God's mystery in the marrow of a bone. "Feel it?" he would ask Frieda at seemingly random moments. "Oh! Friedaleh, can you feel it?" "Yes," she'd say, not knowing exactly what this "it" might be, except that it was everything she longed for.

Frieda wondered how a man like this could marry Mama. She asked him once, and instead of seeming angry, Papa brightened. "You're asking all backward," he said. "How could I *resist*? The prettiest hills are the hardest ones to climb." He loved Mama — he seemed to — with playful devotion, like a jester trying to keep the queen pleased. Evenings, after supper, he would sometimes pinch her sides, and Mama hardly tried to swat him off. Frieda came to see that there was something between her parents — an "it" — that was not for her to know.

Did Papa still smile when he found Frieda with Jack Galassi? Of course not. What earthly father would?

The son of the greengrocer, three doors down on Chambers Street, Jack moved to the block when Frieda was fifteen. He was nearly thirteen, and his full name was Giacomo, but everyone except his mother called him Jack. He had dark-of-night hair and awestruck, blue-gray eyes. Through a gap in his teeth he whistled homespun opera.

She'd first seen him one Sunday as his family left church: bolting past his parents, tugging at his tie, yowling like a creature uncaged. She couldn't have said why, but she yowled a matching call from the stoop where she'd been basking in the sun. He stopped, gave the air a sniff, turned to her, and pounced. "Taste you!" he said — at least that's what Frieda heard at first; in truth, he had challenged her to race. Ready, set, go, and they flew along the street, heels slapping like an ardent crowd's claps. She led, then he passed her, then eventually they both flagged. Because they had neglected to agree upon a finish, there was no way to determine who had won.

When Frieda started walking home from school some days with Jack, Mama watched with wary disapproval ("A *Talyener goy*, this kid, and we should trust him?"), but Papa was partial to him from the get-go. He gave Jack cold-cut trimmings, and said, "Here, have a picnic." And to Mama: "Just a little *boy* he is!"

Not too little for Frieda's experiments. (Or was littleness — inexperience like her own — just what she sought?) The unconcealed fragility in Jack's face, his romping gait — she sensed that he might not have learned yet to squelch yearning, that he might share her urge for urge itself.

In the years since she'd smeared herself with Mama's oily balm for no purpose but pure joyful feeling, Frieda had taught herself to hide bliss. She minded Mama's warning — "That's not the way life is" — but *her* life was (*couldn't* it be?), every second, every inch: pleasure up for grabs, for no good reason. Her body always so alert, even when she slept; new hairs like a cat's clairvoyant whiskers. Sensation was the kindest sort of bully.

She had tested herself in the hush-hush place she knew she shouldn't touch: a perfect fit, a cradle to rock her finger. Again — soon every evening, and any time she could — she tucked her finger into that tight swaddle. Rock-a-bye, rock-a-bye, sweet dreams.

It was hard to keep a secret so encompassing, so *always*. She longed for a confessor, an accomplice. Did other people feel this hunger too?

The first time, all she said was "Come on," and Jack followed. They'd developed a way not of exploring together so much as always just arriving, a trust that each new *there* would soon be *here*. An abandoned tannery, a cellar full of spools — all manner of hideouts, each found as if by homing, unplanned. (They scarcely spoke. Did wolves speak, or doves? Who needed words?) But the alcove beneath the bridge where the subway crossed the river: *this* place she had scouted on her own, ahead of time, knowing they would need more privacy.

A faintly bloody smell of corroding paint and steel mixed with the subway's fiery odors. Pigeons chuckled sadly in the bridge beams. She told Jack to crouch down before her, and he did, his fraying newsboy's cap turned brim-to-back. A train's approach tied a knot in Frieda's gut, untied it. Rat-a-tat above her and inside.

She wanted to know, for starters, what she looked like down there: how would she have had the slightest chance? (She bathed in a tub behind a sheet hung on a string, and the family saw every movement's shadow; too dark in the dingy toilet stall.) Mama said that some parts should be covered, others bare, but why? Who determined which was which? She wondered how her nose's edge knew when to become nostril, and when exactly lip turned to gum.

She hiked her flowered school dress. Drawers down past her knees. "How does it . . . what's it like?" she asked him.

As though he'd been jolted from bottomless sleep, Jack's eyes went wide and heavy all at once. He made a quibbling sound, or maybe it was the pigeons.

"Tell me," she insisted. "What's it look like?"

Jack, in the sulky voice of someone who's been wronged, said, "Guts, that's what. The parts you throw away."

Frieda didn't let the insult rile her. As the mascot of Slotnik's, she'd grown up with her hands in guts, poking into livers, kidneys, hearts. The insides were where the life dwelled.

She took her time in pulling up her drawers, righting her dress; the air felt so good on her nudeness. All the while, Jack stared, and his eyes looked deep with fear — of what he'd seen? of never seeing it again?

The next day, it was he who said, "Come on."

As if being chased, he scrambled to the alcove, and Frieda could barely keep up. A train, close above them, gunned across the tracks. He shrugged out of his thin leather suspenders.

Jack's father sometimes halved fruits and vegetables and propped them on his store's sills and shelves; it made people more likely to buy, he said. Once, he cut a pepper and showed Frieda: inside, near the stem, was a second, smaller pepper, like the real one but sadly pale, with softer skin. That's what Jack's putz made her think of.

For now, she only looked, but the next time, she touched, and his thing grew to something more convincing. Eventually he touched her, then they both licked his finger: like a mussel, he said, the juice from a raw mussel, didn't she think? Yes, she said, even though she'd never eaten *treyf*—happy to take his word for it, ecstatic at the thought: that she herself, in her most *herself* part, could taste unkosher. It proved the rules —Mama's rules—wrong.

In school and on their block they stopped palling around as much, because normal life now seemed a lie—all those people pretending not to *feel!*—and to watch each other being false was painful. Not that they spoke of this; Frieda read it in his face: the loosening of his muscles when it was just the two of them in the alcove and the truth of their bare skin.

She marveled at his organ's many phases: sometimes curled and fetal-looking, sometimes savage. She, too, changed according to mood and moment. One day all she could bear was the shush of his breath upon her; the next day, his thumb's jabbing was too gentle.

Jack was scared to finish—that was the word he used—because, he said, to waste seed was a sin against God; that's what he had learned in catechism. Frieda thought of Papa, how he found God everywhere, how a sunset could be holier than Hebrew. "Is laughing a sin," she asked Jack, "because it wastes good air? Missing the chance to feel the way God made you—*that's* the waste."

So finally, one afternoon, he let her keep going, her hand up and down as if marking a tune's beat, a hurly-burly tune like wedding music. She started to get frightened by the way his body stiffened—his neck's cords so tight she thought they'd snap—but then his mouth opened and he made a little yowl that told her he was fine, he was perfect.

And on a Friday in December when a snowstorm canceled school, they broke into the North Station rail yard. In a boxcar that smelled of the Christmas trees it had brought, she asked Jack to put himself inside her. Snag of skin, impossible. All her flesh a fist. Then gulpingly past it, unclenched, disbelief. Sharp and dull, a plunge in cold seas.

She told him (as she would every time they did it—each

time less painful, more slippery, more sweet) to pull out and finish in her hands. Girls at school had claimed to know: that way, no baby. Mama had never spoken of such matters.

Frieda wiped her hands on the boxcar's grimy floor, but some of what had spit from Jack was still smeared on her skin; it dried in sticky flakes like old paste. Even if she hadn't had to guard against a child, Frieda would have done things just the same, she decided, in order that she might hold this proof. Proof that she could carry home and wave in Mama's face (though lifeless old Mama wouldn't guess it!): that she and Jack had done this — this wonderful, wasteful thing — for nothing at all, nothing but the want.

It was raining — a wintry, late-March storm — and neither of them wanted to walk as far as their secret alcove.

"Tomorrow instead?" asked Jack, when they met out on the stoop.

"No!" she said with an insistence that took her by surprise, a dogged tone that made her sound like Mama. "No, let's just find someplace closer." (Shivering from the cold and the need to feel his weight, from fear that she relied on this too much.) Slotnik's back doorway should be safe, Frieda guessed: it was Pesach; all Jewish shops were closed. Besides, who else would walk out in the storm?

But there had been burglaries that week. Gangs of Irish thugs, in cahoots with their cop pals, took advantage of the Jewish holiday; the unmanned stores made all-too-easy targets. "Crooks," Papa would explain later. "*Crooks*, I thought they were." He heard some noise and thought he'd catch the robbers. Instead (Frieda pictured it through Papa's anguished eyes) he caught his daughter, hips heaved onto the lip of a trash barrel, head tossed as if gasping at a punch line. And Jack on her, a frantic rawboned blur.

"No," said Papa. "No!" And he kept saying the word, even as Frieda came to him and begged him to be quiet, wiping tears and rain from off his face. "No"—each next time less enjoinder than rejection: No, you got it wrong; no, you're not mine.

They were both soaked through by the time they got home, her hair a mess, her dress a snaggled weight, and Mama demanded to know what had happened. "Crazy?" she said to Frieda after Papa had explained. "Don't you know? Do you want to have a child?"

Frieda said she *did* know, but no thanks to Mama. She knew and she'd made sure to be careful.

"It's harder," Mama said, as if she hadn't listened. Her voice was shocking in its softness. "To love a child is harder than you think."

Less than a week later came the slip of Papa's knife, and his blood turned, and suddenly he was gone.

The day of the funeral was the day that Jack was banished (Mama had told Jack's father, who told the whole world)—sent to Puglia, to his uncle's olive groves. They shipped him across an ocean, to a continent at war, because Frieda posed a more pernicious threat.

Papa had maybe lived by the law's spirit more than its letter, but it turned out he couldn't die that way. It was found that he had lapsed on his burial society payments; he'd also left a bill or two unsettled. The funeral took all the Mintzes had.

Hannah, six months earlier, had married a rabbinical candidate, who'd moved her to Cleveland, where he studied. Impoverished—haughtily so, as a point of pride, it seemed—the couple couldn't offer any help. An hour after the shivah's end, Hannah packed her case and returned on the night train from South Station.

They might have been eligible for the Emigrant's Relief Fund, but Mama was too stubborn to apply, or too dazed. To their neighbor Mrs. Pinsker, who made the suggestion, she said, "Ask? Ask for what? A different life?"

Instead she took in seamstressing, five times her load before.

She banned Frieda from going out and made her quit school. ("What a shame," said Miss Starr, the literature teacher. "I had you pegged for, I don't know, a suffragette, or . . . or a poet. But then, look at me. What was *I* once going to be?")

Frieda's days: sewing, sewing, sewing. She couldn't quite bring herself to care; caring would mean thinking about the future, and the future was another day without Papa, then another. Without his smile, his sturdy arms. Another.

Besides, it was easier not sitting in her old classrooms, where all the other kids still had fathers. Easier not having to walk past Slotnik's, past Jack's. Easier not having to hide her face.

The only place she went — Mama forced her to — was shul. Friday evening, Saturday all day. When Frieda took her seat in the women's balcony, whispers crackled around her like branches set afire. "Sit up straight," Mama would order. "Let them see what shame looks like." But Frieda's shame was less for the thing she'd done with Jack than for letting herself be domineered by Mama. Shame, too, for the memory of Papa's shattered gaze, and for not having managed to explain before he died that she'd only been trying to do like him, to *live*.

Hour after hour trapped in shul (the heat, the crackling), and Frieda could never wait to get home.

Not that home offered much relief. Papa everywhere: rags that had once been his ratty bloodstained aprons, his favorite cup, his stubble on the sink (she'd scrubbed but still, for weeks, found tiny flecks). One day she was sweeping under the kitchen cabinet's edge, and her broom loosed a clump of old sawdust — Papa must have tracked it in from Slotnik's. She bent down and took a pinch, inhaled its sprucy smell. For a second she could almost feel his arms, his hug, the boxcar — but no, that was Jack. That was Jack! Everything was mixed up, appalling, annulled. No one's arms, no one's touch at all.

And Mama, with her glaring, her sitting in the dark. (To save on fuel, their landlord had puttied the gaslight jets so they barely leaked and gave out but a scrimpy, wan glow, but Mama forbade Frieda from lighting candles. Noons and nights were all a sickish gray.) For long hours they sat side by side at their makeshift workbench (a wagon footboard stretched from sink to stove), speaking no words but those needed for the task, and not touching except for the inadvertent brushing of sleeves: the snakelike noise of fabric against fabric.

But there were long hours, too, when Mama did no work, when Frieda couldn't rouse her from the chair where she sat praying; days when Mama kashered and rekashered all their cookware or scrubbed at knives still clean from their last scrubbing. ("You're filthy," Frieda heard her once mutter beneath her breath, and she didn't know if Mama was talking to her or to herself.) Day by day they fell further behind.

To every uppish lady whose dress's yoke needed mending, or who wanted her husband's topcoat taken in, Mama said yes, certainly, she could do it. "By Tuesday, five o'clock? I give my word." But she'd have promised much the same to a dozen other women: a dozen jobs, and sometimes not one started. Come Tuesday, when the customer showed, expecting to collect, Frieda was dispatched to block the view from the front room and to cover with any poor excuse — *Just a last smidgen of hem work, can you wait?* — while Mama, in the back, hectically sewed. Afterward, when Frieda took payment from the ladies, she always made a point of saying thank you; how she hated their tone of beneficent condescension when they answered, "Oh, my dear, you're so welcome," as if *they* were the ones who'd done a service.

At the end of an especially horrid day — two jobs canceled, a third finished but so late that the customer wouldn't pay — Sam Slotnik brought the gift of a London broil. "Any time you need some meat, just tell me," he said. "Izzy was — well, I think you know. I'm sorry." When Sam left, Frieda returned diligently to work, shoring up a dress's fraying selvage. She heard Mama's bustle in the kitchen, a whetted blade. This would be their first good meat in ages.

The clang of dropped metal and a high, uncertain cry sent

Frieda, breathless, to the kitchen. (Mama too? Cut? *Both* her parents?) Mama's best knife lay on the floor. And Mama, with her open palm, pounded at the meat. Blood spattering her skirts, on the wall. But it was dark blood, old blood — the beef's, Frieda saw. Mama wasn't cut. She was fine.

"Mama," she said. "What? Tell me what." Was Mama mortified at having to rely on Sam's handout? Was it the thought of a knife's slip, a twinge of guilt?

Mama held her bloody hands up before her face, hiding herself as she did when she blessed the Shabbos candles. Then she pressed them close against her nose. "Your papa," she said. "The smell. When he'd come home after work. Oh, Frieda" — and the cry again, a rank, distended sound. "His face. I was trying to remember, and I couldn't. Just . . . nothing. I couldn't. I have nothing."

Frieda was shocked, shaken. She started crying, too — for the ache of Papa's absence, but also with a satisfying upsurge of relief, to know that she and Mama shared this sorrow.

She recalled once, long ago, in the haze of early girlhood, seeing Mama peeking at some photos. A small, yellowed bundle tied with string; the private, dreamy look on Mama's face. If Frieda could find those photos now, get them framed, make a display . . . a surprise, a loving sign for Mama: *Not nothing. Still this. And still me.*

The next day, when Mama left to buy fabric, Frieda searched. On the cabinet's top shelf? Beneath the mattress? At last, at the bottom of a drawer of Mama's dresses — small-waisted ones that no longer fit her — Frieda found the photos, tightly cinched. Carefully, she tricked the knot loose.

Here was Papa, smiling, his mustache full and wild, at the edge of some bright body of water; Papa posed formally by an onion-domed building with an infant (if this was Russia, it must be Hannah) in his arms.

But the man in the next photo was different, clean-shaven, a gleam of provocation in his stare. High-hipped, as darkly handsome as a racehorse.

The next photo showed the same man.

And the next: this man, his arm around Mama. (Mama, recognizable as herself, but just barely: her features loosely graceful, full of dash.)

On the back, a Yiddish date: January 6, 1900. (A month, Frieda thought. A month before her family sailed across.) Below the date, some words it wasn't difficult to translate: *Waiting for you, Shayna, if you ever change your mind. Waiting with all my love—Leo.*

Shayna, not Mama. (Papa had always called her Mama.) The same woman, not at all the same.

Frieda was retying the bundle, her mind atilt with questions—waiting for *what,* this Leo? to resume something they'd started? to start something that Mama had resisted?—when Mama returned, and saw her, and snatched the stack of pictures.

"Even this?" said Mama. "Even *this* you take from me?" She raised the bundle like a weapon, but her hand shook, and she dropped it. She turned her back on Frieda and walked out.

As her mother's form receded, Frieda could only gape: at this woman who, all of a sudden, was just fractionally her mother; the rest was someone secret, someone rife with strangled hopes. She felt a swell of sudden kinship, but along with it, horror—horror not that Mama might once have betrayed Papa, but that she might have betrayed her own heart; that America—that Frieda herself!—might have meant for Mama not a prospect gained so much as one abandoned.

It was soon after that Mama one day brought home Pinchas Hirsch. Hirsch, a wool wastes merchant, had been their longtime neighbor, but moved up Beacon Hill when business prospered, and with the latest boom moved again, across to Cambridge. (The Army, in its rush for three million uniforms, was paying well for wool in any form.)

A fleshy, slab-jawed man, Hirsch had a killjoy way of looming in a room; to Frieda he looked like a scavenger. A facial tic

—he was forever scrunching his nose and lips together—made him seem always to be smelling something foul.

But Mama, apparently, smelled something sweeter: opportunity. Hirsch, she told Frieda, had lost his precious wife ("Sarah. With those green eyes, remember?"); she'd been struck by a streetcar the very week that Papa died. Since then, Hirsch was struggling by himself to raise their sons, all the while managing the business, not to mention mourning Sarah.

"Look at him," said Mama, when she ushered Hirsch inside. "See those lines? Poor man isn't sleeping! What you need," she added, pointing at Hirsch with a kindly chiding finger, "is another pair of hands. A girl to work. What you need"—she grabbed Frieda's arm—"is *this*."

In minutes, they concluded an arrangement: Hirsch's driver would pick Frieda up every morning, in time for her to cook breakfast in Cambridge; at night, she'd be deposited back home. "You're a good man, a pious man," Mama said to Hirsch, by way of explaining why she'd entrust her sixteen-year-old to his care (as if the salary he named, three times what they earned from sewing, played no part).

Hirsch's house, months neglected, was an ailing organism, all cloggings and moldering ooze. His boys were hellish, sewer-mouthed brats. ("Farta," they called her: "Farta, hey, you stink.") But no matter that she forfeited her pay envelope to Mama, that her fingertips bled from scouring floors, she was glad for the chance, six days a week, to leave home. Away from Mama's grievances, her gloom.

She came to love her rides with Sy Rosenstern, Hirsch's driver, a grandfatherly fellow with a sunny grin like Papa's. They talked (or not) with the ease of old friends. Sy saw her interest in his feet's busy pumping as his Model T roared down Cambridge Street; he asked one day if she might like to try. He taught her to position the throttle and the spark like clock hands at ten minutes to three, then, when the engine caught, five to two; he taught her to ease off the low-speed pedal. But the rest was up to her, and how she flew!—blood, like a lit wick, firing through her veins. Often, after that, Sy let her practice; he gave her a pair of driving gloves. She felt fast — fast enough that she might vanish.

If Frieda was pleased with her employment, Hirsch was only more so. He praised Frieda's work, grinned fatly in her direction. Gave her bonuses: a nickel, a box of figs. One evening, a couple of months into Frieda's service, he drove her home himself, in his own car. Frieda missed the chance for time with Sy.

"I'll be straight with you," Hirsch said to Mama when they arrived.

Mama, in the murk, flipped *siddur* pages.

"Frieda's a godsend. She's quick. She doesn't carp. And — how shall I put this? — she isn't hard on the eyes." He flashed a grasping glance in her direction. "I'd like to have her with me all the time."

"She'd move in with you?" Mama asked. "A live-in house girl?"

Hirsch's twitchy lips approached his nose. "I'm a businessman. Let me speak in business terms. Having Frieda as my wife would be of great advantage, both personally and for my two young boys. I believe you, too, would find it advantageous. I'm prepared to make good on any debts your husband left, and to offer you, above that, a thousand dollars."

Did he think he could buy Frieda like another bale of wool wastes? Outrageous! She looked across to Mama.

It was Mama's face — an expression of such startled buoyancy, not unlike her look beside Leo in the old photo — that chastened Frieda into saying nothing. She stood there, diminished, a speck.

They negotiated Frieda's future as if she weren't right there before them: the wedding date, how much cash up front. (Had Hirsch, living in Cambridge and attending a different shul, not heard of Frieda's dishonor? Or was her fallen state precisely what he preyed on?) He had brought with him, as a token of his honorable intentions, a stately garnet ring for Frieda's hand. Against her skin, the stone clashed like a scab.

The next morning, Frieda served breakfast to the Hirsches, then promptly, as usual, retreated to the kitchen to eat her own eggs and toast in private. But Pinchas Hirsch summoned her at once. "Sit," he said. "Sit here at the table. You'll be family now. Let's start acting so."

Frieda sat at the table's foot, but she couldn't eat a bite. Hirsch's boys, too, looked disheartened.

When Hirsch said, "Mama, butter," Frieda was confused; the words were like babble, pure noise. Only when he spoke again —"Could you pass the butter, Mama?"— did it dawn on her what Hirsch was saying. Dawn on her what she would be. Whom.

No. Not now. Not on her life.

It was Sy she turned to: the driver who'd spent years employed by Hirsch, but whose true master, she guessed correctly, was dark-horse justice. Sy knew a superintendent at Jordan Marsh and vouched for Frieda; he put in a word at a decent rooming house. On a rainy Monday morning — every drop's cool prick distinct — he brought Frieda and her smuggled valise to Keegan's Pawn Shop. The garnet ring, hocked, brought enough for two weeks' rent, plus a dollar and fifteen cents to get her started.

Five

★

$\mathcal{A}$ WEEK AND A HALF after the Independence Ball-room fiasco, Frieda was ready to try again. Ready, at least, to get Lou off her case.

"I know it stings," Lou had said, as they slunk home from the dance hall. "But hey, those guys were rats. I mean, Tip? The one-eyed wonder?"

A muzzle of chagrin silenced Frieda. Her arm still felt nude where Tip had roundly dumped it. She felt the burn, still, of Sadie's glare.

Lou had drunk only the single cocktail Frankie'd bought her, but she started crooning off-key, overloudly, like a wino: "It's a long way to *Tip*-perary, it's a long way to go. It's a long way to *Tip*-perary, to the dullest guy I know."

The joke finally broke Frieda's spell. "God, did you see the poor guy flailing? Like trying to dance with a soggy union suit."

"So you'll get back in the saddle, toot sweet?" Lou had asked.

And had asked again, every day since.

47

They'd settled on tonight for Frieda's reemergence because it was Patriots' Day, and there'd been a massive Army-Navy parade. From the windows of Jordan Marsh, to which they flocked at every chance, they'd heard the hurrahs all afternoon. Brass bands played Sousa, and bagpipers trilled, music billowing into the spick-and-span sky. It seemed the whole world was uniformed: royal-clad police on their frothing black steeds, naval aviators in stormy greenish gray.

The parade had long ended when Frieda and Lou left work, but Washington Street, outside the store, was still chock-a-block. "You can't swing a dead cat around this town," Lou said, "without smacking right into a soldier. Look sharp, now, it's time to get busy!" She squatted to the curb, where confetti had thickly drifted, and scooped a bunch to fluff all over Frieda.

Frieda flicked the bits away like bugs.

"Don't look at me in that tone of voice," Lou said. Puckishly, she smacked Frieda's shoulder. "Whaddaya say? Gaiety? Bowdoin Square?"

"Where was it that you met that multigraph operator? The one who said he has a younger brother?"

"Bowdoin Square," said Lou, "so Bowdoin Square it is. Let's get home and eat and pretty up."

Lou spun on the needle-pointed toes of her shoes, and Frieda pirouetted to keep pace. But she was blocked by a soldier standing right by Jordan's door—just where, more than a month ago, George Eaton had stood. He was tall and fidget-thin, with forceful features and an agitated poise. The uniform, a quarter-inch short at every cuff, made her think of bursting seams, magic beanstalks.

She moved to step around him, but he moved in the same direction, his body caught in a puppyish wag, and only then did the recognition dawn. The big-grinned laughing soldier. *Her* soldier!

"Pete's sake, took you long enough," he said. "You should unionize, fight for shorter hours. Let's get moving or the game'll be all over."

Through a tightened throat, Frieda managed to ask, "The game?"

"Sox–Yankees. Game two of the doubleheader."

Had they arranged a plan, and she had somehow missed it? Had she missed her whole life until this instant?

"But my friend and I . . ." Frieda turned to introduce Lou, but Lou was already way down the block, having left her there sputtering, excuseless. Frieda fingered air as if to clutch a fleeting thought. Then her hand was in his broad, compelling palm.

"How'd you find me?" she thought to ask as he tugged her.

"'Brunettes and blondes, buy Liberty Bonds,'" he said. "Didn't take a genius. You were marching with Jordan Marsh."

Of course. How perfectly simple. How plain perfect.

"Felix Morse," he said, and pumped her hand in a tighter squeeze.

She squeezed back, almost fiercely, and said, "Frieda."

"Do you have a last name, Miss Lovely Frieda?"

"Mintz," she said, as if to claim a prize.

He didn't seem to shrink, as some men did, at its Jewish sound but repeated it in a promissory voice: "Frieda Mintz. F.M., same as me. You wouldn't have to change your monogram."

What do I have that's monogrammed? she almost said. Instead she blurted the slogan of the clothier across the street, an upscale rival to Jordan Marsh: "Morse is more!"

He lengthened his stride. "Indeed I am!"

Boston was a party, with Felix the honored guest — that's how it seemed as they spurred to Park Street station. It was *hey-pal* this and *you-betcha-buddy* that. The woman in front of them in line to buy tokens might have been Felix's beloved godmother, the way she beamed when he flashed his dimples at her. Did the conductor call him by name as they stepped up? Everyone liked a soldier, sure — especially today, the town chummy with parading. But there were other servicemen in their car (a couple of doughboys and a sailor in dress whites), and none drew the same response as Felix. When he passed, men tipped their caps and called "Attaboy"; women, as if tickled in some private place, flushed.

Frieda started to plan how she'd tell it to Lou on Monday: "You wouldn't've believed! Shaking hands left and right, acting like he owned the whole world." But no, that wasn't quite it — it was like he owned *himself,* like no one else could nab a piece of him. He had a glamour cobbled from unlikely makings: eyes the shade of axle grease, lips set to a smirk. When he doffed his campaign hat to answer a scalp itch, his hair rose in brilliantined tufts, spiky and char-black, like lamp wicks.

Standing in the subway car, they clung to leather straps. Above the clatter, he asked, "Peanuts or pistachios?"

Frieda looked at him blankly. Why did everything he said seem to start in the middle?

"At the ballpark. My treat. Which do you favor?"

Mama, inexplicably, had forbidden her pistachios, as if a Persian nut might be unkosher. (Or maybe it was their appearance: those lewd-looking slits.) Frieda, embarrassed, hesitated.

Felix held a palm up in surrender. "So fine, then, you can't choose? I'll get you both. But you can't keep me in the dark on *everything.* Honest, now: Red Sox or Yankees?"

The Sox were the hometown team, so she picked them.

"Thank goodness. If you'd failed that one, we'd be done for. Now: Ruth on the hill, or Ruth swinging lumber?"

It had the ring of something Frieda should understand — like Mama's midsleep mumblings in Russian — but these words, too, were impenetrable, a riddle.

"Oh, brother," he said. "You don't know baseball? Something simpler, then: spring or fall?"

"Spring! The way everything smells just cracked open."

"How 'bout dancing? Grizzly bear or monkey glide?"

This she could talk about. "Oh gosh, monkey glide," she said, instantly imagining him as her partner. "But the grizzly's colossal, too. Or any kind of trot. I love to dance! Just this week I learned a new one, shaking the shimmy. Have you? With the slow walk and then the . . . ?" She let go of the subway strap to twitch her shoulders.

A turn in the tracks sent her grasping for his arm, which was like a sapling, lean but taut with promise. She blushed, excited partly by his closeness, partly by the way he treated her: not like a working girl, hardly like a girl at all. He wasn't asking the usual warm-up questions: Where are you from? Who are your people? And it was better this way, she decided, without their histories. The key was making *this* moment together, then the next, then a hundred — a hundred thousand — more.

He was older, but she couldn't tell precisely by how much. Twenty-one, she guessed. Twenty-two? His pale skin still had a pampered boyish sheen, but his temples showed early hints of balding. (She liked this small suggestion of a future foreordained, a future that might have her written in it.)

"My turn now," she announced.

Felix nodded for her to give it a whirl.

She wanted to ask him head-on: Was he a scoundrel or a mensch? Did he plan to marry for love or for convenience? But the game wasn't played that way, it seemed. She thought, momentarily, of Mama's kind of question, but she couldn't quite gauge if he was Jewish: he was dark enough, but his name rang slightly wrong. It was thrilling not to know, not to care.

Finally, she asked, "Land or sea?" — and immediately wished she hadn't. Could she ever love a man who wasn't drawn to open waters? Should she risk being disappointed this soon?

Felix emphatically grabbed her pinkie. "Rockport! There's a hidden cove. Do you know it? The tide leaves these pools where the water gets all warm, and you can soak there for hours upon hours."

The back of Frieda's throat went raw and salty.

At Kenmore, they emerged from the subway's stuffy air to the crisp spring bluster of the day. Felix, in his swiftness, created his own breeze; how could she not ride on that tailwind? On Jersey Street, the nut man paced, bragging of his wares

("*Noth*ing fresher, roasted 'em this *morn*ing"). Felix bought two fist-sized brown bags: peanuts *and* pistachios, as promised. A group of collegians stood nearby, peddling cigarettes for fifteen cents a pack — profits to aid soldiers' dependent families. When Felix asked to buy a pack, one of the students told him, "Forget it. You're doing your part already. Here, it's yours." But Felix dropped a quarter in the can.

They entered a dull-brick building (it looked to Frieda like a warehouse), and Felix shook hands with the fellow at the turnstile, a man so stiff and old he might have been part of the structure. The man nodded gravely and, somewhere within the handshake, received the pack of Lucky Strikes from Felix. "Nice looker," he said to Felix, and let them both through. Were tickets part of the deal, or did Felix know the guy? The exchange was so quick, so much like magic, she couldn't tell.

They huffed up a steep, switchbacking ramp through a trapezoid of gritty late-day sunlight. There it was: the green splendor of the place. Glowing, alive with human fervor. It was as unexpected a change from the park's drab exterior as — well, as her own insides were from the cover of clothing. Her insides that now went seltzery and loose.

All she'd seen of baseball was West End alley contests: kids swatting broomsticks at balls of twine and rag. She'd loved watching Jack — his speed, his whiplash wrists — but Jack rarely played, for fear of angering his father, who thought the game promoted idleness and worse. When Jack's nose was cracked by a rival's errant curve ball, he hobbled home for sympathy and ice; what he got was his pop's fistprint on his jaw. But why? What made a sport like this so threatening?

Poised now at the grandstand's top, Frieda thought she knew. This lush, grassy playground in the heart of a paved city, this freely mingled crush of perfect strangers, was the opposite of old-world parents and their *shoulds*. There were walls here, but built just so that they might be surmounted, so thousands could hope and pray that they would be. How could someone fail to dream big here?

They followed an usher down precipitous concrete steps and settled into seats he wiped clean. While Felix gleaned details of the game from the fan beside him ("Shoulda seen the Babe last inning—hit one so high, I swear it come down covered with frost"), Frieda started in on the bag of pistachios, imagining Mama: how she'd plotz!

Frieda munched nut after nut, cracking the next before she'd downed the last, for their flavor and because she hadn't eaten since her gumdrop snack at noon. As she gorged she read the advertisements that covered the park's far wall. Whiskey, razor blades, gasoline. *Every homer wins a Delano hat!* This was clearly a venue in which to persuade men to buy things. A place where men went weak and could be swayed. She was one of just half a dozen girls in the whole section. On all sides, row after row of derby hats, like the keys of a huge Underwood typewriter.

She didn't care about, or fully understand, the game. She cheered when Felix cheered, booed when he booed. But the swagger of it all—she couldn't get enough. The players in their leggings, muddied up and scraped; their private tugs and twitchings all on view. The air was a textured weave of maleness, chivalry cross-stitched with brute force. One batter—McInnis was the name the crowd hurrahed—danced tauntingly away from first. (Felix was teaching her the lingo.) When the pitcher threw at him, he dove back to the bag, then stood again—triumphant, smugly boyish—and unbuckled his belt to shake dirt from his trousers. No one looked away—Frieda the least.

It was whip-cold in the park, gusts of wind upturning men's lapels. Felix should have offered her his coat; it was the proper gentlemanly thing to do. But he didn't—he just leaned, trapping heat and something more personal between them—and she relished his impropriety. He was treating her the way she'd seen boys treat their marbles: most precious when shaken, scuffed, spun.

She paid attention to Ruth because he was the one Felix had

quizzed her about: a pug-faced bruiser with a ravenous smile. He was faltering on the mound ("Cold fingers," someone kibitzed), but next time at bat he launched a ball into the sky that sent the Yankees' fielder toward the bleachers.

"That's our Babe," Felix said. "You can feel it. Can't you just feel it?" The Sox had been world champs in '16, he explained, and also the season before that. "Choked last year, but so far this season, four-and-oh. This year we're going all the way."

"If there *is* an 'all the way,'" the man next to Felix said from around a mangled stub of cigar. "Secretary of war's gonna cut the season short."

"Nah," said Felix. "Give up baseball? Might as well crawl up with a white flag to the kaiser."

"No, but all these fellows chasing around the field, when there's other fellows on, you know, other fields? Surprised it don't irk an enlisted man like you."

"Hell, if I had the chance, I'd sure rather chase grounders."

The man glared disparagingly at Felix. He puffed a burst of bone-colored smoke. "Anyhow, plenty of the players have figured as much for themselves. Duffy Lewis signed up. Herb Pennock. Ernie Shore."

Felix nodded. "Word is, Dutch Leonard's going to work at the shipyard down in Quincy."

"And y'hear about Cappy Jones? The Athletics' backup shortstop? Caught by a shell on the Lorraine front. Both legs gone."

"Hadn't heard," Felix said. "Hadn't heard." He stared toward the vastness of the outfield.

Frieda stared, too, wondering how much her view diverged from his. With all the excitement the war whisked into her life — the parades, the soldier-filled dance halls — it could seem like one big pretext for a party. Last Tuesday, Mary Pickford had spent two hours at Jordan's, signing autographs for Liberty Bond buyers. Frieda knew that if men weren't being shot on distant shores, none of this hoopla would be needed, but the truth was, when it ended, she would miss it.

She inched closer to Felix: her own soldier for safekeeping.

A horsy batter sauntered to the plate. "Sam Agnew," Felix said. "He's a tough one."

Agnew, face impassive, let a couple of pitches by. One nearly clipped his chin; he shook his withers. With the next pitch, he uncoiled a terrifying swing, and the ball ripped a seam in the air straight at them. Frieda dodged, but Felix vaulted up and almost caught it; his strain produced a throaty, bedroom groan.

"By an inch!" he said. "Wow, he really lammed it. C'mon, now, Sammy, straighten it out."

But Agnew, for the life of him, couldn't. He tipped an easy pitch that looped softly toward the backstop; the next dribbled into the Sox dugout. Then he cracked another one right at them. It sizzled a scant yard above Felix's upraised arms, smacked a girder, and ricocheted back; a sailor, three seats to the left, snatched it.

Felix slumped back into his chair. "All these years," he said. "How many games — a hundred? And never. Can you believe it? Not *once.*"

Frieda couldn't understand such a fuss over a ball, especially one missed by pure chance. But she saw how the lack of the fickle prize derailed him. This must stand in, then, for deeper disappointments. Had something else in life passed Felix over? Had someone's love bounced away from him?

The batter finally popped a ball implausibly high, which sent the first baseman toward the fence. "Mine," he yelled, "I've got it," with a frantic corkscrew dance, "I've *got* it," until he finally gloved the ball.

At the inning's end, Frieda excused herself.

"Sweetheart," said Felix. "I'm afraid the ladies' facilities leave a bit to be desired."

But she worked a brash grin and made her way toward the field — to where the batboy, with laden arms, teetered. "Sweetheart," she said, usurping Felix's inflection, and the kid halted dead in his tracks. Despite his grass-stained uniform and his man-in-the-making grimace, he was still clearly a boy and nothing but: hatchling hair and pudgy, cream puff cheeks.

"Tell you a secret," she said, and waved him closer. When he stepped up she hooked him by the wrist and reeled him in, then bussed the crisp cartilage of his ear. She felt the rest of his body, too, crispen in response. "Now tit for tat," she said. "It's only fair."

His cheeks ruddled as he appeared to plan a reciprocal endearment, but she said, "Silly, not that. A *ball*."

"Sorry, miss," he stammered, "but I'm not supposed —"

"Oh, now! You've got a bagful. You can spare one." She aimed her tickling gaze at his ear. (Men could swing bats, she thought, but girls — girls had *this*.)

The kid, quivering, dug out a ball; he looked as if he'd have dug out his heart if Frieda asked.

The ball weighed in her hand, hard and ample. She twirled around and stepped back up the aisle, past the stares (wide with shock? with desire?) of a hundred strangers, to the bull's-eye, the only man she wanted. "Now you can't say 'never' again," she told him.

She pressed the baseball into Felix's cupped palms, and he turned it, and turned it, gently buffing. He kissed her on the knuckles — her binder's twine-chafed knuckles — as if thanking an heiress for giving alms.

New York scored in the ninth, but it wasn't enough. The Sox had their second victory of the day, their fifth of five chances this year, and Frieda caught herself thinking: we'll always say our first date was a win.

The man beside Felix lit a new cigar. "Hang on to her, soldier," he said. "Good luck charm."

"And sweeter to hold than a rabbit's foot," said Felix. His dimples saved the line from being bawdy.

They were borne from the park on the jubilant tide of fans. Nut shells crunched satisfyingly beneath their heels. Conscious of the force a mob — even a happy one — could wield, Frieda clutched Felix's elbow. Fellows on all sides of her chucked shoulders and patted backs as if they'd each had a hand in the team's triumph. And who was to say they hadn't? Moral support surely counted for something. The girls at Jordan's often talked about this: the edge that would help us whip the Germans. Which is why parades and Thrift Stamps and Smileage books were crucial — and why Frieda, hand locked on this kinetically handsome soldier, shivered with a purposeful jolt of joy. She pictured him on a lonely field in France, lifeblood draining from some gruesome gash. Would he think of her, of today, of her giving him the baseball? Would her image be what gave him the strength to make it through?

"We should celebrate," he called as they turned a tight corner, counterbalancing as they might on a polished dance floor.

The presence of this jocular, perfectly healthy Felix made Frieda ashamed for what she'd just imagined.

"But I'm afraid," he said, "this is no place for a lady."

The doorway of the saloon in front of which they passed was jammed with rowdy Sox fans. As if crazed by the prospect of imminent Prohibition, the men guzzled beers in frenzied gulps. (Three weeks ago, on the night of the legislature's vote, the city's churches had tolled their gloating bells. Immaculate Conception shared the block with Frieda's building; just remembering it, her temples still throbbed.)

"No," she said, "not here," but she leaned to nab a peek. A musky, pent-up light glowed on the boozers.

Dusk had snuck down the sky. The chill, which during the baseball game had livened Frieda, stole feeling now from her fingertips and nose. She wished Felix *would* lend her his coat.

"What would you have done tonight," he asked, "if I hadn't barged along?"

"There's a dance at the Bowdoin Square Ballroom."

"We could still go if you'd like."

They could. And she was pleased that he'd offered. But her

longing for the dance had been a longing to meet some man; now she didn't really want to dance, she wanted *him*. "I'm not dressed," she said, and felt obscurely guilty.

"Well, that's fine. That's fine. I understand."

A street squall roused a cloud of litter that teetered like a drunk in their direction. They held their hats against its gritty sting.

"Chilly," she said, broadly hinting.

"I know," he said. "And practically May!"

"It must be worse at Devens. What do you all do for heat in the barracks?"

"Camp has its own steam plant. Wouldn't be too bad if they didn't make us open the windows every morning. Say it cuts down on spreading germs, but my hunch is, they're building 'character.' Funny—all this concern for our character before they ship us across the pond to get shot."

She was surprised to hear a soldier talk this way, and even more surprised that it didn't detract from his allure.

The mini twister thwacked a piece of trash against his ankles and held it there, a spat made of paper. Frieda bent to grab it, but just as she did, the wind surged and swept the scrap away. Still, she let her pinkie brush his ankle.

"When do you have to go back?" she asked.

"First thing tomorrow."

"Shame," she said.

His Adam's apple bobbed, as if agreeing. He had the baseball in his left hand and was tossing it erratically: one toss would barely leave his fingertips, the next would stray almost out of reach.

"I guess I should be heading home," she said, emphasizing *guess*.

He caught the ball and stared at it like a fortuneteller studying a crystal orb. "There's a place we could, you know, maybe go."

"A place?"

58

"A house. Belongs to a guy in my unit. His parents are out of town — left yesterday on the Clyde Line down to Charleston."

"But we can't just bust in."

"Nah, I've done it a dozen times. I know where they keep the spare key."

Sensing another gust, Frieda reached up and pushed a hatpin until it pricked against her scalp. She knew she was supposed to show resistance. "Are you loony? I don't know you from Adam's cat!"

It was true. He was a soldier, but what else might he be? A uniform hid distinctions, good and bad.

"I don't know *you* from Eve's baboon," he countered.

"But you're a man."

"Guilty as charged. And you're a girl."

They faced each other in an ambiguous standoff. A passerby wouldn't have known if they were lovesick newly-mets or a long-married couple in a tiff.

Felix gazed into the purpling sky as if remembering Sam Agnew's mighty pop-up. When he lowered his eyes again, he trained them straight on Frieda. "Ask me anything. What do you want to know?"

A hundred questions jostled for the chance to be asked, but for now it was enough just to know that he would let her. All she asked was "How much farther to this house?"

They quickstepped up Commonwealth Avenue. The chill hurried her, as did an unspoken fear of losing nerve. Frieda had never seen this part of town, where traffic diminished and the buildings bulked as if healthier from breathing better air. With each block, the sidewalks gleamed cleaner. They passed Temple Israel, which Frieda could recall Mama badmouthing ("A shul, they call it? Try the Taj Mahal!"), and although it was Friday at sundown the place appeared abandoned.

A trolley jangled by, then a sedan whose chauffeur acknowledged them with a slight professional nod. From behind the sedan, swerving, came a sleek gray motorcar, more like a gesture than a steel-and-chrome machine.

"'Cat," Frieda said.

"Pardon me?"

"Darn, didn't you see? A Stutz Bearcat."

In a gesture that could as easily have marked respect as condescension, Felix laughed and took her hand and kissed it. "What's a girl doing, knowing makes of autos?"

"It's the same kind as Pearl White drives, except that hers is yellow. I read an interview with her in *Photoplay*. 'Pearl White: The Peerless, Fearless Girl.'"

"Oh, I see. You want to be in pictures."

"No! I mean, of course, movies're swell. But what I like is automobiles. Driving."

"Riding, you mean? Going for auto rides?"

"Driving. Or better would be racing."

Felix regarded her with what seemed like double delight, as though he'd bitten into a pastry, content to taste sweet dough, and found instead that it was filled with chocolate. "Dare I ask, have you indulged in such a feat?"

"Driving, yes, but not racing." Then, nonchalantly: "Not yet."

In fact, her interest in cars, since her initiation by Sy Rosenstern, had been anything but nonchalant. She scoured *Photoplay* and *Movie Pictorial* for accounts of actresses who drove. Whenever a theater screened a girl-driver film, she skipped meals to afford the entrance fee. Gloria Swanson in *The Danger Girl*, Mabel Normand in *Mabel at the Wheel*. She especially admired Anita King; her film *The Race* was inspiring, but more so was the fact that its story was based on true life: the "Paramount Girl" had driven across America unescorted—the first person, man or woman, who could claim so.

What would Frieda stake as her own claim? Racing would be a thrill, sure, but even as she dreamed of it, she knew it wouldn't be the life for her. (Some dreams were more stirring if they stayed dreams.) For now, it was enough to live out on her own, but she wasn't going to wrap bundles forever. What had

Miss Starr suggested — a suffragette? A poet? No, those weren't right either (Frieda didn't know from sonnets), and if they had been, she might well dispense with them anyway, just because the teacher had proposed them. What she wanted was for no one else ever to define her, not even to define her own self. She wanted to stay free to chase "it" — Papa's "it" — never to settle for something out of fearfulness or duty. That's why she'd run off: not only to get away from Hirsch's awful scowl, but so she wouldn't end up like Mama (or so she guessed): warped by regret.

Frieda sensed that Felix might be able to understand, but she couldn't quite — not quite yet — explain. Instead she focused on something more practical. "I want to drive so I can help out with the war," she told him. "Maybe drive an ambulance, if they let me."

His face tensed with genuine-seeming worry. "Promise me you'll stay away from that! Bad enough that guys like me don't have any choice. Driving's fine, just not at the front lines."

"Well, they need drivers here, too — picking up the wounded at the docks. They say that's what Edith Storey's doing, why she's not in movies now."

"Okay, okay. I see you can't be stopped. But do you mind if I say I wouldn't want to ride in your ambulance? I'm hoping not to have to ride in *any*." He kissed her hand again, as if for luck.

They left the avenue and entered a leafy neighborhood where the twilight, tinged with green, seemed to flutter. At Worthington Road (she turned the name silently in her mouth, and it tasted like a creamy, high-class pudding), Felix placed a hand on Frieda's back. In a husky, furtive voice, he said, "That's it."

She had never seen a private home so large: three stately stories proud with brickwork and carved granite, twice the width of her Harrison Avenue building. It had obviously just been constructed; straw covered the lawn in lieu of grass. But hedges must have been transplanted to guard the flagstone walkway; their trimmed corners looked sharp enough to wound.

61

"Wait here," said Felix as he headed toward the portico, where a kingly new Locomobile was parked. "They're supposed to keep the house key in the car."

"Wow," she said. "A Gunboat Speedster. Wow!" It was the same model that Mary Pickford drove. The auto's license number was 1874, the year of her papa's birth: an omen?

Felix rummaged in the door pocket and came up empty-handed; he uttered an oath under his breath. Then he seemed to remember something, and he squatted beside the wheel well. The key he found caught a streetlamp's glow.

He beckoned her to the mansion's side door, the iron grating of which was forged into an elaborate cursive letter, so fancy that she couldn't quite read it (a *W*?). He worked the lock and took her by the wrist.

"You sure about this?" she said.

"Told you, I've done it a bunch before."

"But won't they notice?"

"Rich people never do. If anything's out of place, they'll just assume that the girl moved things, cleaning."

"My gosh," said Frieda, "the servants!"

"Nah, they're on vacation, too—he told me the house is empty. Trust me." Felix clung more tightly to her wrist.

As Frieda passed through the doorway, her shoulder grazed something. A mezuzah!—the smallest she'd ever seen, of white enamel and thus neatly camouflaged. "They're Jewish?" she said.

"What? What makes you say that?"

"This," she said, pointing. "Jews put them on their doors." (And she thought: So he's not. So there, Mama.) "I'd never have guessed there'd be Jews in a house like this, here."

"Precisely the point of a house like this," he told her. "So you wouldn't think. So you wouldn't ever ask. But they still hedge their bets, right? In case."

Frieda was confused: Was his buddy's family acting *too* Jewish for Felix, or *not enough*? Certainly he could have no doubts by now that *she* was Jewish. Would she herself be too much or too little?

She followed him through a shadowy vestibule, into a kitchen she sensed was bigger than Mama's entire flat (Felix still hadn't turned on any lights); the ceiling seemed alive with hanging pots their steps had jarred. They mazed their way forward in a tentative soft-shoe, and when he paused, Frieda was thoroughly turned around. She smelled the house's new, expectant scent: wallpaper glue and varnish and — could it be possible? — the lingering sweat of the workmen who had built it.

Felix flipped a switch at last, and a single bulb shone in a sconce meant to mimic a leaping flame. This must be the main reception hall, thought Frieda. Before her rose a staircase that could have come from the movies, sweeping up like the very shape of hope. "It's wonderful," she said, and ran her thumb along the lacquered banister.

Felix shrugged. "They only put it here to impress the neighbors. If they thought a pile of crap would work, they'd have sprung for that, too."

He pulled her to the living room and lit another sconce. A marble table, big enough to deserve its own roof, held a crystal vase filled with crystal flowers. On imposing dark wood bookshelves, recessed into the wall, was displayed a family of bone china plates.

Felix brushed past a grand piano, its bare form suggestive in the gloam. He struck a nervy chord and let it sound.

"Do you play?" she asked.

"Banjo's more my game. And I write lyrics."

"Well, then. Will you write about me?"

As if testing a melon for ripeness, he tapped her temple. "Don't be so sure I haven't already!" But instead of offering a tune of his own, he dropped a record on a Victrola. Caruso's plaintive voice crooned "Eyes of Blue."

Frieda was moved by the music — but strangely, in no clear

direction. She stayed by the piano, on top of which sat a glass decanter shaped like a swan. The liquid inside looked smoldering.

Felix must have caught her staring at it. "Help yourself," he said.

"But—"

"I told you. To this kind of folks, it's nothing."

When she lifted the decanter, the sloshing of its contents made shards of shadow break upon the walls—a trick of light, but she felt she'd ruptured something. She gripped a squat, somehow mannish tumbler. The liquor, as she poured it, rose through the swan's neck, then out its mouth like a vital fluid leaking. She swilled half the glass in one gulp. Only a handful of times had she drunk liquor straight; it was sweeter but also sharper than she expected. She finished the remainder and poured more.

Her inexperience conspired with her nearly empty stomach to hasten the alcohol's effect. She stroked her own smooth neck, which felt satiny, impeccable, like something that belonged more inside a self than out. Deliciously she reeled, aware of every blink, as though her body dreamed while her brain stayed wide awake.

Caruso's croon slowed, scratched to silence.

Felix faced her from across the room. He had withdrawn the baseball from his uniform pocket, and he balanced it on the scale of his upturned palm. He tossed the ball higher than what prudence would have called for, then caught it and tossed again, even higher. Pause, then slap of skin; pause, then slap.

Then without a word he hurled it at her.

Quick as a sucker punch. At her chest.

With animal aptitude, she jerked and trapped the ball in a nook between the tumbler and her bosom. A spurt of liquor splashed onto her thumb.

"Fast hands!" he said. "Sox could use you at the hot corner. Replace McInnis."

"You crazy?" She set the glass shakily on the piano. "I could have missed. I should have. Almost did."

His teeth dimly shone. "Throw it back."

She wouldn't. She gripped the ball tight.

He marched to her and yanked it back, then crossed the room again. "Now, *this* time" — but instead of finishing his sentence, he flung the ball harder, at her gut.

That she caught it again was surprising and not surprising: a necessity, a flinch against fate. Her palm went blistery and hot.

When he dared her again to return the throw, she did — tipsily, but right into his hands.

He sent the ball back, swerving wide; she was lucky enough to knock it to the floor. His error had been purposeful, she sensed. He wanted her to stretch for it, to sweat.

She retrieved the ball and begged of him, "Why are you doing this?" But she threw the ball again, couldn't help it.

"Why are *you*?" he said, catching it. "Why are *you*?"

Everything around her was breakable: crystal vase and flowers, see-through swan. The air itself felt fragile, thick with risk.

"Ready?" he asked. "Ready? Do you want it?"

She braced herself, but to guard what? For whom? Who were the owners of this lavishness to her, and who would she ever be to them? A slummy shopgirl, a bundle wrapper.

"You're not impressing me," she called through trembling lips. "Go ahead, wreck this place. I don't care."

Felix cocked his arm but didn't throw the ball. She knew she was being tested — for what, she wasn't sure. She was furious and unaccountably grateful. Her breath came in lopsided gasps.

At last he approached: truce? surrender? He placed the ball in her hand, then covered hers with his own, bore down until the seams stippled her fingers.

The ball dropped, and she grasped for something: Felix.

The thrusting of their bodies up against the piano was what

finally knocked the tumbler to the floor. In the corner of her gaze, she saw it falling. There was no hope of saving it—and her mouth, superbly smothered, couldn't form any word of warning—but she thought: I've *got* it, I've *got* it.

"Yes or no?" he asked.

She knew he meant *Should I finish?* The wise response—the specific one—was no. But his question sounded to Frieda like the game that they had played: *Red Sox or Yankees? Spring or fall?* There was only one true answer. "Yes. Yes."

Afterward there was the odor, which she had assumed particular to Jack Galassi but now realized was inherent to the act: fresh and also sour, like trampled grass.

But other aspects, with a man and not a boy—with *him*—were different. He'd seemed to know, seconds before she herself did, what she wanted. He'd made her feel not creaturely but, more than ever, human.

Sprawled against his form, her head on his long thigh, she drowsed and hoped she'd never have to move.

She awoke to a clock's bell, and from its brevity understood midnight had passed. "Oh!" she called, "oh!" as if she, too, were a clock, a panicky cuckoo bird who cried alarm. "Felix. Wake up. We have to go."

Dreamily he sighed, touched a finger to his lip, then rose from sleep displaying the charismatic grin of a man certain he's gotten away with something.

"Honestly," she said. "It's late. What'll we do?"

"What we'll do," he said, sounding fully awake and efficiently military, "is clean things up quick and get you home."

"But the streetcars don't run this late, do they?"

"Don't be silly. At this hour? I'll drive you."

"You don't have a car."

"The Locomobile, in front."

She almost asked, *The keys?* But of course he would have

them; he seemed to have the key to everything. She stood and said, "Fine, I'll have to trust you."

With an old *Boston Globe,* Felix swept up bits of glass and tossed them into a metal dustbin. He showed Frieda where she could freshen up. In the bathroom she dabbed a dampened washcloth on her brow, then stared into the mirror's silvered shine, where she saw a girl flush with sudden windfall.

While Felix had his turn at tidying, Frieda cased the adjoining rooms. She felt strangely proprietary, as though, by letting herself be taken in this house, she'd earned a kind of claim upon the place. She nosed into a dining room, a study. In the funereal library, on a marble mantelpiece, she encountered a family photograph: magisterial father, plump mother, two sons. Another photo showed a group of young men in straw boaters, holding banjos of varied lengths and girths. A sash with some slogan cut across each fellow's chest; to read the words, Frieda leaned closer. She had made out *Harvard College* when the toilet's sluicing flush, followed by the bathroom door's creak, jarred her into rapid backpedaling. She reached the living room just as Felix, too, returned. She felt nerveless, still a touch drunk.

"Change of plan," he announced. "I don't much feel like driving."

"But we have to. I have work tomorrow." She glanced at the clock. "Today!"

"Nah," he said. "Not in the mood to drive." He approached her, pressed something into her hand. With a bright, baiting smile, he said, "*You.*"

It was a key on a silver loop of chain.

She shouldn't, of course she shouldn't. Automatically, she shaped words to that effect. In her palm, which still smarted from catching his hard throws, the key seemed to pulse like something live.

"Figures," he said.

"What? What do you mean?"

"You expect me to believe all this business about you driving? Why should I? Put your money where your mouth is."

"Ha! Where my mouth is? Where it just *was* isn't enough?" The reckless power of what they'd done together now resurged. Without another word, she shouldered past him. She banged through the hall and the dark, titanic kitchen, through the door with its fancy, wrought-iron emblem. She climbed into the Gunboat Speedster's seat.

"Come on, soldier," she hollered. "On the double. Toot sweet!" — appropriating the last phrase from Lou. But it struck her, as her fingers authoritatively set the throttle, that she didn't have to copy anyone.

She adjusted the control for the ignition timing and then, just as Felix stepped up into the car, pushed the starter button on the dash. Promptly, with the sound of a jolly fat man's chuckling, the engine whooped wondrously to life.

Reversing was such voluptuous peril! She backed out from the portico, barely missing its rear left column. Holding to the steering wheel with clenched judicious fingers, she headed onto Commonwealth Avenue. (The road, at this hour, was all but void of traffic, like a private driveway, rolled out just for them.)

Felix said, "*That's* your best Pearl White? Step it up."

"This beaut's not ours to run aground, remember?"

"So what? The big shot who owns this, he'd probably thank you — a good excuse to buy the newer model."

Pavement cracks made Frieda bounce, and the leather seat sighed, giving off a pampered scent of oil. She pictured someone buffing it, a hireling on all fours. She let a slight downgrade raise their speed.

"Good," said Felix. "Now: accelerator."

The Locomobile's surge sent Frieda falling back. Trying to gain purchase, she pressed her foot down; the car roared flamboyantly faster. It made Hirsch's Model T seem like a pony cart.

Felix kissed her neck. "Now you're talking!"

And she was falling again, as in the living room, impetuous and perfect; the wind in her ears, the engine, made strange, audacious music, like the sound from the piano when they'd thrusted.

At first she let him guide her—"Switch lanes, keep to the right"—but soon she heeded only her own whim, using the foot brake so infrequently that she might as well have forgotten it existed. Like a censuring finger, the speedometer needle shook. She grinned with the pure pleasure of defiance.

As she zoomed along Park Drive (only blocks from Fenway Park), her mind filled up with fantasies: she was Anita King, the Paramount Girl, setting a new speed record; or an ambulance driver in Belgium, with Pershing in the rear, saving the great commander's life. She shifted gears importantly.

"All right," Felix called above the engine. "No more doubting!"

She cut a sharp turn, which sent him heaving against her—just as happiness, all at once as well defined as a ball bearing, caromed pell-mell within her chest. Helplessly, she conjured one more vision: striding through a gauntlet of good wishes and tossed rice, then mounting a motorcar like this; Felix, climbing in with her, her groom.

Lost in her reverie, she nearly missed a curve; finally—too late—she tugged the wheel. Up on two tires, the Locomobile teetered. Hanging, hanging, undone.

At last it fell to earth and hurtled onward.

"Sorry, sorry! Gosh," she said, "I'll cool it."

"Cool it? You're barely getting warm."

"No, but seriously. Imagine if I wrecked?"

Felix let out a devilish cackle. "Told you: Father wouldn't care a rap."

"Father?"

"I meant—"

But his voice gave it away.

She braked so fast they nearly smashed the windshield. The engine, tricked by sudden slowdown, quit.

"You lied."

"I didn't say anything untrue."

"You lied!"

"No. Just not the whole truth."

She held to the wheel as she might a tossed ship's railing. The pinging in her heart was now pain.

The door of the house (*his* house): not a *W*, an *M;* and the small, nearly camouflaged mezuzah. "So," she said. "So, then you're Jewish?"

"Couldn't tell? Father would be delighted."

"But . . . Morse?"

"Psh. Originally Moskowitz."

She didn't know if this information pleased or displeased her, but of all the sudden questions that swirled within her head, these had been the easiest to phrase. She asked, "Does your family go to shul?"

"Temple Israel—passed it walking from the ballpark? Father paid for practically the whole building. Thinks if his synagogue looks kind of like a church, the neighbors won't mind him being here."

Frieda toggled the throttle, the ignition. "Why?" she said. "Why didn't you tell me?"

"What? 'Hi, my name is Felix Morse, and my father wants to be something he's not'?"

"No, that it was *your* house. Who *you* are."

"If I told you, you'd have *thought* you knew: 'the heir to Morse's Menswear.' You'd have gotten stuck on that, I know it."

"You're no better than him, then. Pretending to be different."

"Come on, now, you're twisting it around. It's just that there are more important things to know *first*. More important things than how much money."

Frieda scoffed. "Easy for you to say." But she looked at him: an heir, a man who lived in a mansion. His face was galling, gorgeous. She almost laughed.

"It *is* easier for me than for you," he said. "I know. But that's what I like about you, Frieda — that you came from where you did, by your own bootstraps. You're someone Father wouldn't even talk to."

"So *that's* it, then? You're with me just to get your father's goat?" She stared at the dark, deserted road. "Sick is what that is. Sick and mean." She clambered over him and out the door.

Felix feebly half stood from his seat. "Get back in. That's bullshit, and you know it!"

But she didn't know, she didn't know at all. Nor was she now certain why *she'd* done this. How much of tonight — all the romp and risk of Felix — was just a way to spit in Mama's face? Still, always, after all this time?

"Frieda, honestly," Felix said. "Come back. Talk." He patted the speedster's leather seat.

The auto, such a fluid force beneath her when she'd steered it, now looked like a clumsy cage of steel. Heavy, hard to handle, prone to wrecks. She thought she'd been freeing herself, but if you were always running away from something, wasn't that another kind of bondage?

Wordlessly, she set off down an alley.

"Wait! I want to see you again," he called.

She paused in the passageway (too narrow for the auto; he couldn't follow, even if she wavered).

"I'll find you," he promised. "I did once."

Her flesh, where he'd entered her, felt raw but not wrong: a throb — part twinge, part balm — she couldn't measure.

Six

*S*HE STUMBLES FROM her rooming house, stuporous
with lack of sleep, her thoughts minced, her head full of
ache — but she has to get to work or she'll be late. All night she
stayed up, haunted by Mrs. Sprague's words and by a prickle:
infection? pure shame? How will she face anyone at Jordan's?

Yesterday, after Mrs. Sprague left her there, dazed, none of
the other girls came to Frieda. Had they overheard the accusa-
tions and immediately shunned her? Were they afraid to draw
Mr. Crowley's wrath? Lou tried to catch her when they clocked
out for the day ("Frieda, hey, wait. Wait! What happened?"),
but Frieda was too panicked to respond. She lowered her face
and made a run for home.

How rash she'd been to say yes to Felix. To herself! Rash to
let things go so far and fast. Now they were saying that she'd
given him this curse. Which meant *she* had it, but where had
she acquired it? Hell, for all she knew — she'd been ignoring
the thought for days — for all she knew, now she might be pregnant. All those times with Jack, never once letting him finish,

72

and then with Felix, right away, *yes*. They could arrest her — not now, but the next time, they could. For wanting Felix again. Always wanting. Would they find out she'd lied about Mama?

At home, she didn't bother to ignite the gas lamps but sat in the chill, abasing darkness. The notion came — darting, like the bother of a bee — that she might open the jets and let them leak, unlit. (She'd heard of certain girls who'd been found by their landladies, eyes calm in their glazed farewell glances; it was said the fumes smelled tempting, like bananas.) She imagined Mama filled with grief, with shame — a suicide! — but also secretly contented: that pleasure without purpose had been shown to bring doom, that Frieda had reaped her just deserts.

No. Frieda couldn't; she wouldn't give up yet. Resignation alternated with disbelief: that Felix had freely named her (there must be an explanation) and that she really had what Mrs. Sprague had said.

She lifted her skirt, moved her hand toward the cleft; she could barely bring herself to touch it. There was moisture — too much, too sticky to be normal. In the window's paltry light, she held her finger. Red! She was bleeding. She was sick.

A dreadful cold sweat had erupted along her spine before it occurred to her: her monthlies. She counted the weeks since last time — right on schedule. Relief put a halt to the sweat, but still she couldn't rest; she sat waiting for dawn to come. Waiting.

She slogs now toward work, trying not to think, tamping down her fears of what might happen. The girls heard, she knows it; they'll snub her again today. And Crowley, too — mustn't he have heard? But no, if the floorwalker was going to dress her down, wouldn't he have done so right away? She trudges past the still dim windows of Walton's Lunch, with its half-fallen broadsheets (SPECIAL: LIBERTY CABBAGE, 12¢). She feels separated from everything, as though she herself is but a flimsy, precariously pasted sheet that might fall, any moment, to the ground.

The gibberish of a delivery truck's idling combustion gives

way to a newsboy's hollering, his voice primal, serrated with desperation. "'Steamship *Saint Paul* Overturns, Three Men Lost.' Read all about it in the *Herald*!" The boy's fingers are blackened from handling the inky papers, his nose and chin black, too, from where he must have scratched. Is Frieda's trouble — the spread of it — as plain?

A woman crosses in front of her from a half-hidden alley, heels clacking like a ruler's rap on knuckles. With each stride, the woman's braids swing. Frieda is reinfected with her sleepless night's panic: Can Mrs. Sprague have cornered her so soon? The woman halts to fix her skirt's bustle, and she turns. She's nobody, a stranger.

Frieda walks on, still hazy, weak-kneed, but more alert with every forward pace. She has on the shirtwaist she wore yesterday — she never bothered last night to undress — and she feels the pinned weight of Papa's brooch. (When he gave her the treasure, on the day she turned thirteen, she thought it was a small sculpted snail. "A whelk," he corrected her. "A *special* kind of snail, for Friedaleh, my special, special girl.")

At his customary spot in front of Leavitt's Cigar Shop sits Neville, the imbecilic beggar, with his loose-socketed eyes, his pitted nose. He sings "God Save the Queen," the only tune in his repertoire (even the change to "King," apparently, has stymied him). Normally Frieda disregards his greasy, outstretched palm and merely gives a sympathetic smile. Today, though, some impulse sends her fingers to her pocket and she brings forth a lint-covered penny. She isn't quite sure why she's done it — she can barely manage to keep *herself* afloat — but something (superstition?) guides her hand. She thinks of kind Papa, of his whelk, of watchful spirits. And when Neville interrupts his song to say, "God save *you*, miss," all of her erupting fears subside.

It's as though she's fed a coin into one of the Kinetoscopes at the Revere Beach penny arcade, and a new one-reeler flickers into view. No longer is this the picture where she's doomed and downtrodden, her world a wash of thundercloud gray. In *this* story she's glimmering with luck. She's the girl who, despite her own troubles, helps the beggar, for at least *she* has the comfort of employment. And it's Friday, it occurs to her: payday!

The morning begins anew; Frieda quickens her pace toward Jordan's. Every mindful step is a tightly sewn stitch, hemming her self-assurance where it's frayed. She sees a fresh unfolding of events: She'll arrive a neat minute ahead of schedule at the store, time enough to admire the new display (FLORAL-PRINT FROCKS FOR SUMMER FUN!). Then proudly through the door marked EMPLOYEES ONLY, PLEASE, where Gus, the elevator boy, will give a quick wink. In answer she will turn loose the enigmatic smile that she's perfected in a dozen dance-hall mirrors, her lips set at the balance point between innocence and worldliness.

The smile will hold as she strolls the third floor, through Gloves and Notions to Ladies' Undergarments, where Lou and Grace will be waiting. Frieda will neaten the wrapping counter, stacking tissue, untangling twine, until everything's in apple-pie order. And if some girl approaches to inquire in hushed alarm about "that business yesterday — who was that woman?," Frieda will only pull her smile wider. "Oh, that? Just a silly mix-up."

It *was* just a mix-up, wasn't it? For one thing, her body feels all right. There's a slipperiness, a tepid itchy creep, but that's normal around the time of her monthlies. And just as she mistook that flow last night for some dread symptom, this whole business with Mrs. Sprague is an error. Felix wouldn't have named Frieda — never, she's just sure (which means it's *all* untrue: she's *not* diseased).

When she left Felix in the Locomobile, she let herself feel sour. She doubted every syllable he'd uttered. But when the sun came up and burned away the fog of shock, her doubt and anger, too, dissipated; she focused on the sparkle of his charm. At work, when she breathlessly told Lou the whole tale, Lou called him a cheat, a yellow-belly. "But he didn't really lie," said Frieda, repeating his own contention. "The house *did* belong to 'a guy in his unit': to *him*!"

Lou smirked skeptically, so she continued.

"Don't you see, Lou? He was making sure I wouldn't feel outclassed. It's the same as how he's a private when you know he could have been an officer: he doesn't want to seem 'better' than the others."

"Sure," said Lou, "but don't you wonder what *else* he didn't tell you?"

"That was just at first. Now he knows me."

Which is why she can't believe that he'd betray her. And the thing is, there's no *evidence* it was him: Mrs. Sprague never confirmed a name. But who else? Who would file a false report?

It comes to her: Sadie. Her scheming, spiteful cousin. She must be the one behind all this. It's the first thought that's made good sense all morning.

Her chest swells, and she turns about and heads straight in to work. There's the satisfying *ponk* as she clocks herself in. Then Gus, at the elevator, bats his sweet brown eyes, just as she envisioned that he would. "Miss *Mintz*," he says, as if her name's a code word — a magic spell to make a genie rise. With a coy, bewitching grin, she plays along.

The elevator jerks like a dog in rut, obscene. Obscene but also secretly exalting. It lifts her high above the world of petty retribution, above Sadie and Mrs. Sprague, to her own realm. At floor three she emerges, staring confidently ahead. (Ahead, she thinks, look ahead; don't ever turn around — as though the truth's a demon at her back.) She's comforted by the store's morning hubbub: chamois polishing cloths swish on countertops; girls hail one another on the fly. ("Hey, don't you look sharp!" "Hey, yourself.")

Grace Fitzroy's in Girdles, dusting the upper shelves. Frieda remembers having something to tell her yesterday, before being so rottenly ambushed: there's a new novel on the shelf at the Old Corner Bookstore, by an author she doesn't know, Effie Swan. The clerk said it's nearly as good as a Laura Jean Libbey. *The Shopgirl's Wooing* — set right here in Boston! Maybe she and Grace can split the cost? But she'll save the news for later; they open in five minutes, and she has to get the wrapping counter ready.

"Happy payday," Grace chirps in her bright budgie voice. "Say, Frieda, before the rush," she adds, pointing to some boxes, "could you help? New shipment of brassieres."

"Since you asked so nice," Frieda kids, "I'd be delighted. First let me check my wrapping table."

Her wrapping table. What if she left the workstation a fright? (After Mrs. Sprague, all she remembers is a grayish buzzing.) But no, it's all squared away — boxes, tissue, twine — not a single bit of string awry. Good for me! she thinks, and she looks for Lou to tell her, but Lou apparently isn't here. That's not unusual: she's a slugabed who dashes in last-second. Frieda tells herself she doesn't mind the wait for Lou; it's pleasant to be looking forward to something. (*Look ahead!*)

From Grace's manner, it seems the salesclerks *didn't* overhear, so Frieda will tell everything to Lou. They're not arresting me, she'll emphasize; they can't, it's just a warning. And she'll prove it's no big thing by being flip. *I gave her a wrong address, the dumb cluck.*

Behind her comes the *tap-tap* of expeditious feet, and she turns around on hopeful toes for Lou.

"May we have a word?" asks Mr. Crowley.

"Yes, sir," she says — you always *yes* the floorwalker — "but Grace asked me to help her with some boxes."

"That won't be necessary," he says.

"No, but she asked specific. Just now."

"There won't be need for you at the bundling counter today."

His face is like a fist, all pinched-up boniness, his whiskers spittled more than usual; Frieda thinks of a rat soaked by rain. She wants to reach up, pat him dry.

"Miss Mintz. Do you understand? Miss Mintz?"

Her name — the very words that from Gus made her grin — from Mr. Crowley's mouth sounds like a curse.

"I'm afraid," he says, "we have to let you go."

"But," she bleats. A verbal flinch, an instinct.

"After yesterday, we have no other choice. We wish you all the best in your . . . personal situation, but when the personal intrudes at work, we draw the line."

She stares at the cadence of his pulsing jaw muscle; the hairs below his lip that he missed shaving. (Does he live with a wife, with his mother, anyone — a woman who could tell him he shaved poorly? Only now does it occur to her to wonder.)

The rest of his explanation reaches her in bursts, like mortar blasts punctuating smoke: "Casts doubt . . . irreparable . . . reputation."

"You don't understand," she manages. "It was nothing. It was just—"

Yesterday's gray buzzing is back.

"I'm sure I understand it all too well," says Mr. Crowley. "Do you think I don't know who that woman was, Miss Mintz? Would our customers want clothes wrapped by filthy fingers?"

Frieda cowers. Bees swarm in her skull, sting her brain.

Hiss hiss rushes through her ears. *Miss miss.*

"Miss Mintz, are you listening? I've tried to be discreet. Please don't make me haul you out by force."

The gray fog parts to show Grace and the other clerks. They don't even pretend not to listen. Lou is there, too (when did she arrive?); her head is bowed slightly and her eyes won't meet Frieda's.

Frieda almost calls to her, but what words would she use? (The only word she wants to call is *Papa.*) Besides, she can't expect Lou to challenge Mr. Crowley. She can't expect a thing from anyone.

Mr. Crowley says, "Shall I call for someone to walk you out? Gus? Will someone tell Gus to come at once?"

"No," says Frieda. "No. I'm going now."

She glances one last time at the well-kempt bundling counter, the place where she has learned to hold her own. With dead steps she scuffs past the employees' elevator. She walks out like a common customer.

Seven

WHEN FRIEDA OPENS her door, Lou bounds up, both arms wide, but then stops, just shy of a hug. "Oh, is *that* it? We heard Crowley say 'filthy.' Should've guessed."

Are there lesions on her face? How does Lou know?

"The smell," Lou says, reading her. "The smell."

Frieda thought she'd cleaned herself enough to blunt the odor (like cheese caught and rotting between teeth), but the rags with which she's dabbed herself — she forgot to burn the rags! — are stashed in a heap beside the sink.

"Wait," says Lou. "I'll run home, be right back."

It's two and a half days since the shock of Frieda's firing, a span in which she's spoken to no friend. Mrs. Norcross, the landlady, came knocking once each day — first with the announcement of someone here to see her ("Blond thing, all painted up and powdered"), next to ask if she might need a nurse — and both times Frieda begged her to go away.

Her room — ratty mattress, leaking sink, mingy light (the jets are plugged even more scrimpingly than at Mama's) — is cavelike and punitively close. To keep time, there's the tolling of Immaculate Conception; the graying that brings night, then dawn. But for two tins of sardines, she hasn't eaten; she's too harried even to mind the hunger. Is this how Mama felt when she lost Russia? Toppled into turbulence, not a snitch of air to breathe; every move futile, misdirected.

Frieda's ventured out only to shamble to the toilet. She's dripping all the time, or at least that's how it seems: blood still (a bit of it, the tail end of her flow), and the other stuff, tackier, which stinks. Constantly she feels as though she has to pee or burst, but when she tries, practically nothing will emerge: a trickle that mocks the urgency of her need. She felt it first — this burn inside, this sharp insistent flare — the evening of her exile from the store. Morning found the burning worse; the next night worse still. Her flesh (all she's ever fully trusted) turned against her.

But how could she tell anyone the cause? How could she name the parts aloud, or show them? (And to think she'd been so proud to show Jack.) Which is why, when Mrs. Norcross came knocking again just now — "The blond gal is back, and she won't take no this time" — Frieda finally agreed to see her friend. Lou would have a plan, wouldn't judge her.

When Lou returns, Frieda feels a billow of relief. Just the sound of Lou's breathing (she must have hurried up the stairs) is a comfort: another being, here beside her.

Lou has brought a satchel from which she pulls out vials and pouches. There's an offishness to her movements, a fussiness of the wrists; Frieda's seen it before, when Lou rebuffs a customer who hasn't bought.

"Honestly," Lou says, "didn'tcha take precautions?"

Frieda, stung, merely shrugs one shoulder.

"You gonna tell me safeties ain't kosher?" Lou continues, her voice tight with teacherly disappointment.

Is that all Frieda is to her? An investment of time gone bust? She can't keep the bawl in her swollen throat from leaking.

Lou turns at the sound, and her face, from a new angle,

gains lenience. "Listen, sweetpea, I'm sorry. This happens to the best of us. Hell, I've had the whites. Had 'em twice."

"The whites?"

"You know, the clap. Or something like it." She joins Frieda on the mattress, pats her thigh. "I've got some stuff left over from my last time. It should help. But oh! If I ever get my hands on that scamp!" She reaches out and wrings a phantom neck.

"No, Lou. It's not his fault. It's mine."

"Yours! How could it possibly be yours?"

"I've gone with so many fellows — men I didn't even know."

"But you told me that you only went the limit with just Felix."

"It's true. He's the only one for that. But the others — I let them kiss me and, you know, use their hands."

"You don't get it from doing any of *those* things, Frieda! Christ, you West End girls're sheltered. Trust me, it was him. *He* gave it to you."

"Then why would they make *him* report *me?*"

"Don't you get it? They always blame the girl. But he should know better! And he hasn't lifted his little finger to help you. Has he even answered a single one of your letters?"

Lou thinks Frieda's written him; she promised Lou she would. But she hasn't. So how could he write back?

Maybe Lou is right to urge anger, accusation; but Frieda, through her terror and her crippling abashment, still feels, above all else, grateful. For if Felix has given her this — she can't name it — this affliction, he's also given her affirmation: a sense of herself as worthy of his charms. When she thinks of him, she doesn't think of a soldier reporting her (her illness has made her face the patent truth that it was he), nor of an heir who lied about his life. What she pictures is the man on the crowded subway car who questioned her about her likes and dislikes, who wouldn't rest until he understood her; the man who handed her a key, and said, "*You* should." To write him begging for rescue (which is what it would amount to) would unbuild the buttress he helped her raise.

"This is my problem," she insists to Lou. "Not his."

"Then you goddamn surely make it his," Lou says. On a plate — Frieda's only one, still slick with sardine oil — Lou's laid out a row of sugar cubes. Now she agitates a brown-bottled potion. "Frieda, you just got sacked. You don't have nothing saved. I aim to take up a collection from the girls, but how long will that last, you tell me?"

"I got that job. I'll go and get another."

"And I hope to high heaven that you do. But put your brains together for a sec. He's a Morse, right? One of *the* Morses? Morse's Menswear? And you know where his family lives, yeah?"

"You know I do. I told you the whole story."

"So what you do," Lou says as she uncaps her bottle, the top of which is attached to an eyedropper, "you go to 'em. Tell 'em what their good soldier's been up to, how he ain't been so good after all. Then you ask —"

"Oh, I couldn't. *They* haven't done anything to me."

"That's the worst lot of bilge I ever heard! Ain't they the ones who raised the creep? Besides, think on it. These people're rich! I'll bet they spend more on floor polish every week than you spend on half a year's rent. What's it to them to give you a little help?"

As if to demonstrate how the Morses might part with token sums, Lou droppers a dot of liquid on some sugar. Then more — drop, drop — the tincture slowly seeping until the cube has turned the copper of a coin. Lou is so casual, as if she does this every day. But surely once (how long ago?) she would have found this daunting and, too, would have balked at fleecing strangers. Is this how people change, a slow seep? Frieda tries to gauge if what seems natural to her now would a year ago have struck her as abhorrent. A year from now, will today's unthinkable be the norm?

"If you won't go," says Lou, "hell, maybe I'll go myself," and her mouth forms a sneer of planned reprisal. "But on the subject of handouts, look, like I said, I got this stuff left over from my last time. Don't ask. I know a lady in Jamaica Plain who makes it. This here's sandalwood oil, and you're gonna want, oh, eight or ten drops on a piece of sugar — goes down nice and smooth that way. And you can do that three or four times a day, 'cept there ain't but a day or two's left." Holding out the fish-smelly plate close to Frieda, Lou chortles, and says, "*Corpus Christi.*"

Frieda, not quite getting the joke, stalls.

"Go on, now, it ain't gonna kill you."

In her throat, the cube feels jagged, but all she tastes is sweetness. A strong leafy scent tweaks her nose.

Lou then gives a lesson on the proper care of self for a girl in Frieda's condition. Bed rest and daily bowel cleansing are a must; spicy foods and fat should be avoided. "Skimmed milk's fine. And seltzer, plenty of seltzer, keep things running. Potash water, too. Mix a spoonful of this" — Lou hands her a pouch of powder — "with a tall glass of water from the tap."

Frieda can't bear looking at the grayish, chalky substance. She wonders at Lou's offhand attitude — as if it's common knowledge that being a girl these days takes the knack and the stockpiles of a druggist. Perhaps Lou's nonchalance should allay Frieda's embarrassment, but it only heightens her chagrin: Is everyone more worldly-wise than she? Frieda failed at "good," and now she's bungled being bad.

Tugging tight the drawstring on her satchel, Lou says, "That should ease you, but you really need a doctor."

"A doctor? You know I can't afford that."

"Can't afford *not* is more like it. There's a clinic at the Dispensary — if you're poor, they don't charge."

"What, I'm some kind of hardship case?"

"Better than a *nut* case," Lou says. "The pox does that, you know. Makes you crazy. Like Neville, that beggar on your street, they say he's got it. And *that* ain't gonna cure itself with sandalwood and potash. What if you've got that, too? What then? The only way to know is see a doctor. So you go to the Dispensary, and you walk in the front. There's signs pointing the way with red arrows. Just keep following till you find the right room."

Dispensary. It sounds to Frieda like a place for throwaways. "In front of everyone?" she says. "'Just keep following' so the whole world knows where I'm going? No, Lou, I can't. I just can't." She has to hold her breath to keep from crying.

Lou takes Frieda's chin with two fingers. "Listen, I know you feel like everything's gone wonky. Don't worry. You'll make it through this fine." From her handbag she takes out a curvy blue glass flask. "This helps, too — for pain down here, and here." Lou touches her belly, then her forehead.

Curling at the corners, its print a little smudged, the label reads MRS. WINSLOW'S SOOTHING SYRUP.

"Couple of nips," Lou says. "Three at most." As if to prove it's safe, she takes a pull. She hands the flask encouragingly to Frieda.

Licorice is what it tastes like, undersweetened licorice, trailed by an after-bite of balsam. Shyly, Frieda draws a second sip.

"Better?" asks Lou.

"Maybe. Yes, I think so."

"Good. Now try to get some rest, relax. Tomorrow, you wake up early, and you get the morning paper. Before you can say Jack Robinson, you'll find a new job. And I'll see what the girls can pitch in to help you out."

Wincing, Frieda turns her head away. "They all heard, didn't they? I know there's talk. It's awful."

"Don't be such a silly!" Lou rebukes. "What you need is to mind your own self. Which means the potash and the sandal-wood oil, like I showed you. And the Dispensary. Soon as you can. Promise?"

Frieda pictures the clinic: blood-red arrows aimed at her.

"Promise?" Lou says.

Frieda tries to nod.

"All right, then. You're being a good Injun. We'd both better get some beauty sleep."

Lou hugs her — a snug, somber clinch — and Frieda hugs back, clutching tight. Before, all she wanted (*thought* she wanted) was seclusion. Now she wants Lou to stay forever. To give her secret remedies and gumption.

Lou lets go. Rising from the mattress, she knocks her head. "This room's for midgets," she says. "How do you stand it?"

"Get used to it, I guess," Frieda says.

Lou, shaking her head, says, "I wouldn't."

Does she mean that she herself wouldn't settle for such limits, or is this guidance? *Don't get used to anything.*

With a final blown kiss, Lou walks away.

The door slams. The room shudders as stale air is rearranged. Frieda, too, spooked by the change, shudders.

Alone again.

Reaching for the flask of Mrs. Winslow's Soothing Syrup, Frieda notes her thumb, stained brown with Lou's tincture. Furtively, as though she's being scornfully observed ("Would our customers want clothes wrapped by filthy fingers?"), she wipes it on the underside of the mattress. She downs a throat-tingling draft of syrup. Then one more.

From adjoining rooms, she can hear girls settling in for the night. A muffled cough, the sulky sounds of plumbing. She pictures them brushing hair and teeth. Does any one of them picture *her*?

The need to pass water (the illusion of need?) flares. She could try, but she knows it won't come.

Unsure if the syrup has induced any effect, she thinks about chancing another swallow. From the eaves outside her window comes a pigeon's broody murmur. She moves to the glass but still can't see the bird. "Who who?" she mimics, and it seems to coo in answer. "Better now?" she says. The bird coos yes.

Minutes pass like silk; the air — time itself — seems softened. A milky and expansive smell engulfs her: baking bread?

(Strange, the nearest bakery's blocks away.) Now it smells more like apricots.

Was she considering something? A task? An undertaking?

The syrup. She was going to taste some more. Like steam, though, that want has evanesced. She's syrupy enough herself: she's succulent. There are bubbles in her blood, smooth round *o*'s of relaxation. Suddenly she wants Felix, the soothe of him, the touch. She wants him here, cradling her, nursing her to wellness. Or, no, not here, in *his* house, the mansion. A feather bed. Broth from a silver bowl.

But how could Felix find her, not knowing her address? If he came back to Jordan's, she'd be gone.

The pigeon purrs. Frieda's vision swims.

From the trinket box (a seashell, one of Jack's marbles) that Frieda keeps underneath the bed, she fishes out a stub of sharpened pencil. There's no paper, so the box itself will serve: she tears off a cardboard flap. On one side of the makeshift postcard she writes his name; following that, in parentheses, *Private.* (Let them assume she means his rank.) *Camp Devens,* she pencils. *Ayer, Massachusetts.* Then she flips the card to its blank side. How could she fit the thoughts that glut her mind?

How dare you, Felix?

When will you dare again?

In her hand, like a magic wand, the pencil throbs with portent. She marks down the fact of her address. Isn't that enough for now? Enough for him to find her. Above, she draws a monogram: *FM.* In this, she thinks — in this at least — they're equals.

Eight

★

T HE NEXT MORNING, on waking, she caps Lou's elixir and takes up instead the vial of oil: four drops on a sugar cube, one swallow. She mixes potash powder with a glass of tap water, and her backbone stiffens with resolve.

It's trash day, and Harrison Avenue is bracingly pungent with scraps of rotten vegetables, bones. Yes, she thinks: folks eat, toss things out, they move on. Everyone moves on. So will she. She draws a deep breath of city air.

At a newsstand, she buys the morning *Herald*. She pages past maps of the Flanders front, past "Sports" ("Matty May Quit Reds for War Work"), to the smaller-type "Girls Wanted" section. The American Rubber Company needs upperers and lasters — what does Frieda know of shoemaking? Bookkeepers. Comptometer operators.

A small boxed advertisement steals her eye:

Assistant Head of Stock for Negligee Dept. Apply in person to the Supt., E. T. Slattery Co., Tremont Street.

Slattery's! A pang of guilt pokes her: the store is one of Jordan's fiercest rivals. But no, *she's* not the traitor — it was Crowley who cast her out.

A scant hour later, she's in an overlit office, embellishing her history of employment. (If Lou could do it, with Frankie and Tip, why can't she?) "No, sir, you're right, it wasn't very normal to be moved up to saleslady so soon. But I was the quickest wrapper that they'd seen. Helped with stock, too. Even modeled once or twice. 'Well rounded' was what I was aiming for."

"Indeed," says the superintendent, a genially ample man whose chrome nameplate reads P. J. CADDIGAN. "It's quite striking for a girl of your age." Caddigan's hair is combed back in strands as true as pinstripes, just as in his likeness on a *Dry Goods Reporter* cover, which hangs, framed, behind his desk. "And you say you know Negligees?" he asks.

"Yes, sir. At Jordan's we called it Ladies' Undergarments, but I believe it amounts to the same thing."

"Ah, how very right you are, Miss Mintz. Once the clothes come off, isn't it all the same?"

He laughs a big, bottomless laugh, shaking his pencil so hard that Frieda fears he'll snap it.

The atmosphere of chuckling generosity continues (is she batty to think his overtures flirtatious?), and Frieda shows her best dance-hall grin. Caddigan grins back. Her spirits swell. Then he asks to have a look at her letters of reference, and all at once her optimism fractures. She admits that she has brought none along.

And why, he inquires, did she leave her job at Jordan's?

Because a soldier reported her, and they always blame the girl. Because everyone always blames *her*. She would tell him, she'd defend herself, but why — so he can scoff? He's the superintendent. Who is she?

With a scraping of his chair, Caddigan jumps up, his mouth now skewed into a sneer. "You expected me to hire you on good faith alone? For a position of this level? No, I'm sorry."

· · ·

The whole next day she spends on the tramp. The city is buffeted by a breeze that ruins hairdos. Frieda's skirt gets tangled around her ankles.

A soreness like sunburn gets worse the more she walks. But the slipperiness and the smell aren't as noticeable anymore; her bladder isn't quite so demanding. She cons herself into thinking the Dispensary isn't needed, that she doesn't have to brave those red arrows. But what will happen when Lou's remedies run out?

The New England Confectionery Company wants girls for candy packing (free Necco Sweets as a bonus of employment). At the very stroke of nine, she arrives at the factory and finds thirty other girls in line. The anteroom smells of caramel and underarms. When a hawk-faced boss asks for hands ("Who's packed before?"), ten arms lift; only those ten are taken.

A mail-order house on Broad Street seeks envelope addressers. Perfect, Frieda thinks. She earned good marks for penmanship in school. Yet by the time she ascends to the fusty attic office, the writing test is already in progress. She tries but can't catch up to the girls who started first; she labels twenty envelopes to their fifty.

When Lou comes that night, she bears a gift of two bananas: "From the store cafeteria. Snuck 'em out."

Frieda is so hungry that she grabs the bigger fruit and gobbles almost half in one bite. Before she can swallow, Lou launches an inquisition — Has she been to the Dispensary? *Has* she? — and the mush of fruit sticks in her throat. She gags it down and softly tells Lou no.

"Well, Christ! What in hell're you waiting for?"

"I'm trying, it's just that — it's just hard."

"So what it's hard? Who said it would be easy?" Lou stabs a goading finger at her. "If you don't take care of yourself, nothing is worth shucks. Don't be the dregs they say you are. Here." She brings forth a small waxed-paper bag, which she hands, in a crumpled wad, to Frieda.

Inside, Frieda finds half a dozen gumdrops and two nick-edged fifty-cent coins. She checks the bottom for bills, but comes up empty. "Thanks," she says. "But is that . . . there isn't more?"

Lou looks her bluntly in the eye. "Not *one* of the other girls pitched in. This war's just got people picking sides on everything. It's loyalty or lynching, no between."

The next day, after another grim, cold-shoulder afternoon (Royal Laundry, *no;* Belle Waist Company, *no*), she finds herself splurging on a token for the streetcar, using some of the money Lou gave her. She takes the first car on the Commonwealth Avenue line — outbound, though home's the other way — and even as she walks back and finds a strap to cling to, she's not sure if she'll really raise the nerve to see the Morses, and less sure what she hopes to gain by going. She certainly won't find Felix at the Worthington Road house, and what can she possibly tell his parents? How will she explain why she has come?

If she were Lou she'd make demands, stab threats at them like shivs, but Frieda can't imagine being brutish. Money isn't on her mind, nor vengeance. Maybe she wants to stand again — just stand — where she was treasured.

When she gets off the streetcar she's blasted again by wind, but surrenders, letting its force gird her. There it is: Worthington. She quickly takes the turn, her stomach a slosh of nervousness. She stares at her feet, willing each next step.

She's halfway up the drive before she sees that the Locomobile is joined by a dozen other autos. Men in waistcoats (chauffeurs? footmen?) mill about. The motorcars are waxed to regal shine.

She's back on her heels — it's preposterous to intrude; it's a party, or a funeral (*what if?*) — when a woman appears at the side door. From her chin hangs a ruddy, inelegant dewlap. She brandishes a thick rolling pin. "Well, look what the cat drug in!" she shouts.

Frieda freezes, tight with discomposure.

"C'mon, c'mon. Don't have all day. Get in here."

Such is the authority of the woman's massive presence — menacingly, she lifts her wooden pin — that Frieda is impelled to step closer; it's like sleepwalking while terrifyingly awake. The *M* in the door's finely forged iron grillwork, seen in daylight, is even more haughty.

Then she's in the kitchen, the vast and shining kitchen, conscious of the footprints she might leave. The woman ("Mrs. Reilly, and you can call me Mrs. Reilly") assaults her with rapid-fire aspersions: Hardly any way to start, late on her first day; normally she wouldn't brook such nonsense. But what with all these dignitaries, no time now for fussing, just climb into the uniform and start. "In the closet by the icebox. Last girl was about your same size."

Through the doorway Frieda has a view to the reception hall, crowded with men in crisp suits. At the bottom of the upsweeping daydream of a staircase is a plump woman wearing a fox fur piece. (Mrs. Morse? Yes, the matron from the photo.) The fox's grin — frozen before the creature grasped its fate — eerily matches her expression.

A yard away stands Mr. Morse, glad-handing. He has the very same antsiness as Felix, the same outsized features, mouth and nose — but on him they seem less winsome than imposing. He's meatier, and he throws his weight around. "Senator!" he calls, and claps a tall man's back. "An honor to have your support for this campaign."

"My pleasure to return the favor," the man responds.

Mr. Morse smiles tightly and tilts his head just so, as if posing to have his likeness struck on a coin. "Do you have a drink, Senator? Let's have someone fetch one." He scans the room; his gaze alights on Frieda.

What will she say to such a man? That his son has left her ruined? That he saved her?

"Quit staring! What in heaven's got you, girl?" Mrs. Reilly grabs Frieda from behind, pulls her back. "The agency calls this 'experienced help'? My foot!"

She shoves Frieda past the hulking stove, past the icebox, to the closet where uniforms are kept. But Frieda, shame thickening the walls of her dry throat, stumbles and keeps going to the door.

Riding the inbound car, Frieda gives in to despair (it's a rapid; she's helpless in its spate); by the time she remembers to look up, her stop has passed. Panicking, she bolts up and starts to call the driver, but it strikes her: What does it really matter? Nobody is waiting for her. Nothing. Just her room.

She transfers to the subway and boards the Cambridge line, which will kill the longest stretch of time, she thinks: out and back should take at least an hour. She sits near the door, by a pair of old ladies, each doggedly knitting a soldier's scarf. The regulation wool matches their gray hair. The woman on the left wears a dutiful expression and a button pinned to her lapel: WE CAN CAN VEGETABLES AND THE KAISER TOO. Across from the women is a man reading the paper, engrossed in the stock-market pages. All these people on their way to somewhere.

With a yammer, the train rounds an unforgiving curve, and they burst from the tunnel into daylight. A slight falling mist blurs the view. Frieda feels the prickle that Lou's cures have not quite stopped — the flare of that and something else, deeper. As they rise up the incline of the bridge across the Charles, it occurs to her what they're hurtling over: the alcove; her and Jack's secret.

From below, with Jack, the trains sang a dare: loosen up, set yourself free. Now all she hears is steel on steel. She's free to ride the train all day — no job, no Mama looming — ride and ride to . . . absolutely nowhere. No, she tells the ghost of a girl who sits within the alcove, it's not enough to dream of freedom *from;* you have to learn to dream of freedom *to.* But to what? Who does Frieda yearn to be?

Someone who wants to better the world and begins with her own self; a girl who chooses sky-high over safe. Not like Mama, who thinks everyone, to keep the world in spin, must be dragged down to her level of frustration. No, not a mother at all, if it means losing her self. (Who will Frieda's Leo be? Might it still be Felix? Whoever it is, she'll never give him up.)

But also, Frieda thinks, as they rattle across the bridge — also not an out-of-work wrapper on a train, staring out the window through her tears.

Nine

※

*L*OU'S REMEDIES DWINDLE, then are gone.

Every day Frieda wakes up hoping she'll be well, but every day she still feels . . . something. Not sick, but not entirely herself. The way her palms go moist when she's anxious or ashamed, and stay moist despite how much she wipes them: that's the way it feels now, *inside*.

And what about the illness she can't feel?

She knows she should go to the Dispensary. But she's sickened just to see her own reflection in the window; how could she ever let some doctor peer? She might as well lie naked in the street. (When she thinks *doctor*, she envisions the one who came for Papa: Dr. Herzl with his yellow, wasted eyes. Papa's soiled sheets, the stink of piss.)

The sock beneath her mattress, where she keeps her secret savings, gets heavier — but that's only because the bills have gone to change. She pays the weekly rent all in coins.

She has to look for work again. She must.

On a Tuesday, she dons her soiled waist, ties her hair, and

steps into the shocking urban stream. Pushcart peddlers, mangy dogs, policemen. Her head is light and hollow — all she's had today is water — and she debates spending a nickel on a roll. When a coal truck pulls away from the curb, unblocking the busy streetscape, she's met by the jangled form of Neville. His bugged eyes, his "God Save the Queen." Before she can dodge, he has her fixed in his stare; his smell of gamy desperation surges. Here comes his grubby hand, stretching for her, jerking, so pale in the sun it looks like bone. Frieda reels and staggers straight back home.

Mrs. Norcross, duster in hand, stops her on the landing. "You just missed your visitor by a hair."

Visitor? Not Lou, it couldn't be, she's at work. Frieda asks the landlady to describe whoever came.

"Older woman, and pardon me, but not much to look at. Something sour about her in the eyes."

Frieda sees the face of Mrs. Sprague. "What did she want?"

"To know if you were here, where you'd gone."

Can they arrest her now? For giving a false address? "And *did* you?" Frieda asks. "Did you tell her?"

"Couldn't tell what I didn't know, could I?" Mrs. Norcross flaunts a cursory smile. "But listen, Frieda. I can't spend my days directing traffic." Fussily, she dusts the banister. "That's what I says to the man she was with, I says, 'What do you think I'm running here, a depot?'"

"She was with a man?"

"Big fellow. Kept scrunching up his nose like he didn't like the way my place smells. Well, fine. He doesn't have to come back!"

Hirsch. Hirsch and Mama. They tracked Frieda down. She feels as though her flesh is wrung of blood.

Late that night, Lou visits for the first time in a week, her rouge badly blurred, skirt atwist. Warily, Frieda asks where she's been.

Lou reveals a jumpy smile, stays mum.

"Where?" Frieda asks again. "Dancing?"

"Bravo, Sherlock Holmes. That a crime?"

Envious, and embarrassed for being so, Frieda flushes. "You could've . . . could've asked me to come along."

"Come along?!" Lou says, slurring. "You're not fit for being seen. Couldn't look worse if you'd been buried and dug up."

Frieda recoils from the insult, from its truth. "I thought," she says. "I thought you understood."

"Oh, I do. You think you're worst off in the world."

Frieda stares darkly at her own lap. Lou's never badgered her like this.

"Know what you really are?" Lou says. "You're a pitiful little girl."

"Are you drunk? You're drunk! Lou, what are you doing?"

Lou snaps to straight-backed attention. "Doing? I already *done* what I can for you, Frieda — more than anyone ever done for me. But you sit there, squanderin' yourself away."

"Squandering? What do I have to squander?"

"You've got yourself, what you *make* of yourself," Lou says. She crosses to the door, tottery but decisive. "Hear me? You gotta make *yourself.*"

"Lou, don't go. Please. Let's just talk." She wants to ask if Lou has more oil, more Mrs. Winslow's. She wants to ask: How long till I get better?

"No, you're right. I'm tipsy, I'm tired. I'm going home. But here." From her purse, Lou unveils a bar of chocolate. "My date bought me this on the way home from dancing. Looks like you need it more than me." She tosses Frieda the candy, and she goes.

A couple of days later, next week's rent is almost due; Frieda's scrounge for coins yields precious little: a penny on the sill, her empty sock. What will she eat when the last of the sardines and soup is gone? She gives up, hardly bothers leaving bed. But no matter how many hours she sleeps, she isn't rested; it's like trying to fill a tub without a plug.

Is she sleeping or awake when she feels Papa, wrapping around her shoulders in a hug? She knows she's at home, but she smells Castle Island. His muscled butcher's arm, the salt air. Deep in dream, she doesn't hear the door.

It's Mrs. Norcross, barging in, demanding is she deaf?

Panicking that Mama's back — she and scowling Hirsch — Frieda blurts, "I'm not here. Say I'm not!"

The landlady inquires if she's gone loony.

"Just this once, please? Just tell them I'm not here. And I promise, I'll get them to stop coming."

Mrs. Norcross smirks, chuckles softly. "If you're not here, I guess you can't take *this*?" She holds out a package wrapped in sheets of newspaper. "The postman dropped it off for you just now."

In her fright, Frieda didn't note the package. She takes it now and marvels at the franking mark: Camp Devens. "Oh, thank you, thank you! How can I ever thank you?"

"By paying your rent on time," she says. "Tomorrow." She's smiling as she leaves, just enough to show she means it.

Frieda, feeling whiplashed from torment to delight, jounces around the room in her bare feet. Then she settles down to take a look. The newsprint has been folded, and her address kept to the side, so a sports-page squib can be made out:

> "It's so far away," complained Babe Ruth as he went back to the bench after his first-ever stint playing outfield. There is a world of speculation as to what regular playing will do to the $150,000 Babe Ruth arm. Hurling them in from the outfield is not conducive to helping a flinging wing. And, as Babe lamented, "Gee, it's lonesome out there."

Lonesome is underlined, and there's a message scrawled beneath: *How can my wing fling from so far?*

She tears apart the paper (taking care to save his writing) and discovers a Columbia phonograph record: Billy Watkins, a singer she's not heard of. "Who Paid the Rent for Mrs. Rip Van Winkle?"

It's too strange to be anything but magic.

"Dear FM," begins the letter that falls from the record sleeve (was he hiding it from military censors?), "and I hope that doesn't stand for Fickle Maiden! I worried as much when you ran off without giving me your address (I deserved it; I'd made a donkey of myself), and my state of mind went straight to the bow-wows." His handwriting is adamant, all forward-tilted strokes, like a hurdler dashing for the tape. As breathless as a sprinter herself, Frieda reads on:

What joy, then, to get your coquettish — or merely concise? — card. If I may, though, can I ask: Why cardboard? No matter, you could write me on moldy bread, and I'd be marvy.

Speaking of marvy, it's how I rate the enclosed. I heard it played during a "hang-out" at the Hostess House at Camp, and it put me immediately in mind of you. Not in voice (you're not a tenor!), but in spunk. Can't recall if you have a machine to play it on, but knowing you, you'll improvise a way. (Just promise me that the song on the back side isn't true, or I'll turn every jealous shade of green.)

She flips the record over — "Everybody Loves My Girl" — and for the first time in what seems a month she laughs.

As for my own songwriting, I'm afraid I've no romantic ditty for you just yet because my services have been enlisted for the Boston's Own Band. I've rhymed Devens with "heavens" and Ayer with "Over There" (no one here picks up the sarcasm). My banjo strumming, too, is highly in demand. Perhaps this is due to the dearth of, shall we say, "less wholesome" entertainments.

The closest thing to dancing here in the cantonment itself is our daily round of what we call "Kelly's Thenics" (doesn't that sound more appealing than the proper word?). As for the outside world, they've recently shut the dance halls in Ayer, and now we've no alternative but the War Camp Community Service balls. To make things "socially hygienic," they keep the lights full-on and enforce countless rules about

99

positions. No ragtimes. Never any "fancy" dancing. And the girls! The girls, who've apparently been rounded up from women's clubs in these enervating environs, are nothing but a horde of blinkety-blank debutantes who can't conceive of any subjects beyond bodices and basket weaving.

Oh, how it would chirk me to see you come bunny-hugging across the floor. Better yet: behind the wheel of a Stutz Bearcat. "Peerless Fearless" Frieda, first-class feisty. See what you do to me? I'm a panting doggerel; you're my master.

But honestly, FM, you've got something none of the girls here can match — something priceless, something genuine and true. You're the only girl I've met who throws the ball back hard enough.

Which is why I can be straight with you — at least here's hoping. It'd be easier to talk about this in person, but I'm not sure when we'll get the blessed chance. We get checked here periodically at what they call the "propho station." Checked for things one couldn't term polite. ("Short arm" inspection. Get the drift?) Well, wouldn't you know (and God help Father if he ever finds it out; prodigal sons make such bad press), the other day I came up positive. Which makes me fear I might possibly have exposed you. I cringe and shrink and sicken with the thought.

They asked whom I'd seen recently, and before I realized what they wanted, your name came out. Luckily, I didn't (couldn't!) tell them your address. I guess you were smart to keep it from me.

But I wanted you at least to know that maybe you should be checked. If you need help, I'll do everything I can.

Can I possibly now end on a brighter note? I'd hoped to do so by citing the primacy of our Sox, but yesterday — gad! — they slipped to second place. Are you not praying enough? Have you not dyed your hair red and donned Hub Hose? We're counting on you, Frieda, to lend a hand.

While we're on the subject of handy, though, my own skills as a "pill server" are proving patriotic: it seems that fastballs are good training for grenades. If I make believe

that the Fritzies in their trenches are damn Yankees, I'll nail
'em the way the Babe blanks New York batters. From games-
man to grenadier in a jiff!

But still, I'd rather go to bat for you.

Eagerly, endlessly,
FM

She reads it straight through again, two and three times
more, blood churning wilder with each perusal. She wants to
hug him, to hug the whole world.

A few words and phrases she can't quite understand (doggerel? enervating environs?), but she relishes his lack of explanation. He tenders no apologies, asks for none — except, of
course, in the one place where he should: *If you need help, I'll
do everything I can.* Which makes even the unfamiliar words
reassuring — a strange, lovely poem of his ardor.

Ten

*F*ELIX? SURE I KNOW HIM, *everyone* knows Felix." The
redheaded soldier winks impishly at Frieda—or is the
gesture intended for his pals?

The quartet of doughboys, when Frieda came upon them
on this B&M train bound for Ayer, was deep in a contentious
game of stud; she hesitated to interrupt their fun. But the red-
head, Flynn—the big smoke of the bunch—told her no, delighted, have a seat.

The soldiers face one another in pairs across a table. The
train hasn't yet left North Station.

"But you're sure," she asks, still standing, "he's the same?"

"Yeah, Felix: dapper guy, sort of"—Flynn looks to his chums,
who stare back, pokerfaced—"sort of stocky?"

"No, he's tall, like a beanpole. Felix Morse."

"*Morse*, you say? The tall one? Tall and skinny?"

Frieda nods. "Writes songs. Plays with the band?"

"Sure, sure. The song guy. Great set of pipes. Him and me

102

was on fatigue duty not ten days ago, building a road out past the snipers' range."

Frieda swoops into the slippery leather seat. "Oh you *do*, you really know him, then? Thank God."

Flynn inches closer to his seatmate, Komanetsky, but with three on the bench, it's still tight.

"See, I need him," Frieda says, "need to find him. But I don't know the first thing about how. Take this train, but after that I'm hopeless."

With a flicking of nimble fingers, Flynn deals a round. "Lucky for you," he says. "Stick with us."

The soldiers bet and bluff, the brakeman hollers, "All aboard!," and Frieda feels fortunate indeed. Felix's letter is tucked into her brassiere.

It took her not an hour after opening his package to recognize the proper course of action. The stumbling block, as usual, was money. She didn't have enough even to buy herself a meal, let alone a ticket to Camp Devens. All she owned of worth was Papa's brooch.

And she knew at once what she was meant to do.

Hadn't Papa visited her that very afternoon? She didn't need his jewelry to keep him close to her heart; he'd be there every time she shut her eyes.

At Keegan's — the same pawnshop where she'd traded Hirsch's ring — she got half of what she'd hoped, but more than plenty. After a late chophouse lunch of T-bone steak and bliss potatoes, she marched herself down to Filene's (good riddance to Jordan Marsh and all its finks). First she bought perfume — an emerald bottle called Zephyr — and ducked into the ladies' room to dab her neck and crotch. (She couldn't smell infection any longer on herself — when she wiped, the paper came up mostly clean — but maybe by now she was only accustomed to it. What if a salesgirl — what if Felix — could smell?)

She set about buying a whole new outfit. The boots were Russian calfskin with striking gray vamps, the hat trimmed with plumes of burnt goose. And the dress — "the very latest," said the chesty, milk-skinned salesgirl — was so chic that it had a name: Bubbles. ("See how the pattern looks like bubbles on blue sky? And the crêpe veiling — I think it's just colossal!")

On the train now, in her new clothes, Frieda feels even bolder than she hoped for yesterday when she bought them. All she carries is a bag with some waists and spare stockings, her toiletries, the Billy Watkins record. Her perfume smells extravagant and clean (so clean that she herself is almost fooled). And if the way these soldiers are reacting is a measure, she's certain to please Felix when he sees her.

Flynn says, "Mmm, ain't she fussed up somethin' fierce?"

Komanetsky, weak-chinned but with a certain skittish charm, sucks in his breath admiringly. The two across — Cooper and Tucci — raise their thumbs.

"But listen, doll. Tell me your name again?"

"Frieda."

"Right, Frieda. You sure you know what you're getting into?" Flynn's voice is a ringmaster's, all sovereignty and sway, but he corks it up to a confidential whisper. "Pretty girl like you, especially in them knockout clothes — the inspectors'll be on you like ants on applesauce."

Frieda's neck crawls. "What inspectors?"

"Jesus! You weren't kidding. You don't know nothing! The vice squad, O'Halloran and his boys. Plus all those social work ladies, from the committee on diddly-do. You gotta keep your eyes peeled. These trains are swarming with 'em."

"And once you get to Ayer, too," Komanetsky chimes in, "they're everywhere. Got every entrance covered."

"Some pose as jitney drivers," Tucci adds. "They'll nab you when you try to hire a ride."

"For what? I haven't done a thing."

Flynn takes her wrist and administers a gentle shake, like a father trying to wake his napping child. "Course you have. Weren't you born a girl? Plus that dress, that perfume — seems like you *might* do more."

She pulls her hand away. "But how do *they* know?"

"What, you think you're the very first? Think there ain't a hundred a day who just *need* to see their soldier?"

"It's no accident they put posters on *this* train," says Cooper, the fourth soldier, with an underbitten pout. He points a grimy finger up above.

One poster shows a mother in a spotless white apron, adding fruit to a freshly baked confection. "Remember the Folks at Home," reads the caption. "Go back to them physically fit and morally clean. Don't allow a whore to smirch your record." In the next one, a cherubic toddler spoons herself porridge. "Remember Your Future Children. Give 'em a chance. Don't start 'em out with a mortgage on body or mind."

How small she feels, how suddenly shrunken. She's seen — she *must* have seen — placards like this before, on subway cars, in movie hall lobbies, but she never bothered to pay them any mind. Now it's *she* they're referring to. Is it obvious to the soldiers? Even with the perfume? Even now.

Then she sees Cooper aping the toddler's blank expression. And Tucci, eyebrows bunched to a single hairy squiggle, wails in a mock ghostly voice, "Re-mem-ber!"

They think it's *mishegoss;* they're on her side! She grins at them and basks in their guffaws.

"Settled, then," says Flynn. "You're with us."

"But why risk it? You don't even know me."

"Nah, but we got imaginations, right? We can see ourselves as that lucky feller waitin' back at camp. We know what *we'd* want guys like us to do."

"And you think you can get me past the" — she can't quite say *vice squad* — "you know, keep me safe, at the station?"

"Trust me. Done it a dozen times."

There's his wink again — is it aimed at her or not? — like the punch line of a joke she didn't hear.

"New friends," Flynn toasts from a flask he unpockets. He checks for snoops, tosses back a gulp, and hands it over.

The flask has a silver-dollar shine. Warm from Flynn's body

heat, the whiskey goes down soft. Frieda wipes her bottom lip. "New friends."

The train is in full trundle now, wheels singing on the tracks; the seat emits a furtive, quick vibration. A good half of the passengers are soldiers in their khakis, but plenty of civilians also ride. An avuncular man with a nicotine-stained beard plays pony with the small girl on his knee. Two spinsters write messages on postcards. Experimenting with expressions — not too smiley, not too stern — Frieda tries her best to blend in.

In deference to their guest, the soldiers quit poker, but the one-upping continues as they vie for Frieda's esteem. Tucci boasts of mounting his Kerensky gun in record time and beating his instructor in a race. Then he and Cooper argue about who "killed" the most "heinies" in a sham bayonet battle last week, and this feud leads, not quite logically, to Komanetsky's long account of sneaking back from weekend leave one Sunday in the middle of a rollicking rainstorm. ("Cats and dogs? Hell — pitchforks and hammer handles!")

At intervals, Frieda nods and murmurs her endorsement, but she's not paying much attention. She stares out at passing hedgerows and rolling fields. From the bank of open windows comes a rush of rural smells — apple blossoms, clover, upturned soil — the striving, athletic scents of spring. The carriage bumps, lurches from side to side.

She thinks then of Felix, of their ride to the Red Sox game, when the subway turned and tossed her up against him. His taut, lanky strength, his gutsy laugh. She imagines how she'll fall against him soon — this time on purpose — when he sees her and opens up his arms. ("There, there, darling, now I'm here.")

No, that's wrong, it won't be all that quaggy; he'll start in midstream, as if they never parted. (He's better than any dime-romance figment, for he's *real*.) "Ready?" he'll say, and without asking *For what?* — without caring — she'll nod, lock her arm in his, and follow. And because it was he who gave Frieda the disease, there won't be shame in saying why they can't do more than kiss. There won't be shame in letting Felix save her.

"Now, see," says Flynn, "you gone and bored her, Komanetsky. She ain't listened to a rap of what you said."

"No, I have," she says, "it's . . ." But she can't admit what.

"Bosh is what it is," says sneering Flynn. "Machine guns and bayonets and mud!"

Flynn hands her the flask again and watches as she sips, his cheeks flush with obvious satisfaction. With his firestorm hair and his lips that don't quite meet around the jut of his overcrowded teeth, Flynn is no Fairbanks, that's for sure. But there's something about him that's deviously appealing—the swagger of a truant on the hook from school.

"For a *girl*," he says, "a story's got to have some kind of moral. Girls want the good guys to win."

"Stuff a rag in it," says Tucci. "Quit trying to honey her."

But she's charmed enough to toss Flynn a bone. "No, you've got a point—which I guess is why girls don't like war stories. In wars, it seems like everyone's a bad guy."

"How do you mean?" says Cooper, bristling.

"Well, they're all trying to *kill* someone else."

"So girls're good," Flynn says, "and we're all beasts?"

"Is that what I said? I think *you* said it."

One side of his mouth curls cannily. He wipes his wet teeth on his sleeve. "Spry one, ain't she, boys? A real corker. But seems to me she can't think too lowly of *all* soldiers. Otherwise, why's she on this train?"

Admiring his quickness, Frieda concedes the point.

"See," he says to his mates, "it ain't a matter of changing a girl's mind. More like reminding her of what she thinks already. Reminding her that *we're* the good guys. So you tell her, say, 'bout that invitation from Mrs. What's-her-name."

"Mrs. Asquith?" says Cooper. "Down in Cambridge?"

"Exactly. Mrs. Asquith, the very one. So you tell her 'bout the 'bring a soldier home for dinner' business, where civilians take us in, give us a break from Army chow. Normally just one soldier, maybe two at a time. But Mrs. Asquith, don't she got a name to keep up high, wants the world to know how big she is."

"As if the world can't *see*," says Komanetsky. He gestures indelicately at his rear.

"So," Flynn says, "the old lady telephones to Devens, says she wants to have some soldiers over. Major Stebbins asks how many. 'Forty,' she says. He says, 'Forty?!' 'No, you're right, that's not enough. Fifty.' She tells Stebbins she'll be utterly delighted and blah blah blah . . . as long as none of them are 'of Irish or Hebrew extraction.' 'Cause there's limits to everyone's charity, right, Frieda? Which means you and me — I'm guessing that you're Jewish? I knew it! Jewish hair is so pretty! — it means you and me'd be out of luck."

He chucks her on the chin, a kidding blow.

Jittering, the train slows for Lexington.

"'Wouldn't dream of it, Mrs. Asquith,'" Flynn says in the major's voice. "But what Stebbins don't tell her is, there's no Jews or Irish 'cause he's sending her fifty *colored* boys! A gang of 'em, up from Florida!"

"Niggers!" says Cooper, bright with mirth.

"What I wouldn'ta paid," Flynn says, "to see that old bag's face when fifty dinges stroll right up her — wait. Hold on. Everybody quit." His voice constricts again to hush-hush tones. "D'ya hear that? Listen up. Listen!"

With reluctant pings and hisses and a hot grind of steel, the train halts at the Lexington platform.

"What?" says Tucci. "What's the big to-do?"

"Shh," says Flynn. "O'Halloran. Heard him talking."

"Hell," says Komanetsky. "Here? You sure?"

Flynn's mouth puckers in disgust. "His weasely little voice, or I'll miss a bet. All right, doll, better come with me." He pushes Frieda roughly from the seat.

The men conduct a frantic, tight-lipped negotiation: Komanetsky is deputized to lead in Flynn's absence; Flynn will steal

Frieda away to the toilet compartment's safety, and when all is clear Komanetsky will knock in code.

But wouldn't Frieda be safer — less suspect — going alone? Why does Flynn insist on coming with her? She's about to voice her doubts when Flynn cuffs her wrist and hurries her down the narrow aisle. Why so wild? Won't they draw attention? Yet Flynn's momentum can't be argued with. Rattled by the forcefulness of his double-time alarm — this cocked-up soldier scrabbling in fear — Frieda, too, succumbs to flaring panic.

She's shoved into the toilet room, Flynn at full tilt behind her. So close, she thinks. So very close to Felix, and now *this*.

Flynn shuts and locks the door and keeps the light off. The stall is dark and rankly ominous. Frieda hears an endless swirling hiss. A leak in the toilet? It sounds like threat itself: swift, infinite.

She listens above the noise for angry voices, clomping boots; she hears only the pulse of her compunction. On her neck, Flynn's breath is hot and smells of whiskey. His hand grips her wrist with sweaty force. And now she thinks she knows why he insisted on coming with her.

In the gloom, Frieda starts to lose track of up and down. Her mind swirls and hisses like the toilet.

"Okay?" whispers Flynn, looming closer.

Her throat crackles. She can't honestly say.

"Wait," he says.

She hears the word as *weight*. The darkness; his panting, sweaty bulk.

With a lurch, then another that jostles Flynn against her, the train resumes its journey down the tracks. The whistle's wail sounds thin and incomplete.

Would telling him she's infected keep Flynn from going further? I'm catching, she could say. ("Remember Your Future Children.") Just as she is gathering the courage to speak up, there's a knock — *the* knock — on the door. One long, three short, another long.

"Clear," says Komanetsky from outside.

Back in the main carriage, in the streaming springtime air, Frieda swoons with fluttering relief.

The men laud one another for teamwork in tight straits, and Frieda imagines how they'll tell the story—each time a little bit more epic. She pictures Flynn's false modesty when Felix sings his praises and insists on buying everyone a drink ("No really, Flynn, I owe you—all of you"). Later, alone with Felix, she'll admit she doubted Flynn: his too big smile, the way he tugged her wrist. "But sometimes," she'll say, "you just have to go on instinct. Trust in goodness, it'll come your way."

"Hold on—you think it's all that simple?"

And she'll say, "Worked that way when I met *you*."

"Goodness? But Frieda, I gave you this—this thing."

"Sure, but now you'll see to it I'm cured."

If there existed muggy misgivings before, now the atmosphere is crisp with goodwill. They ask Frieda's age, and she reports it as "Eighteen . . . well almost, to be honest, just about," which causes an uproar of amusement. They sing "Good Morning, Mr. Zip-Zip-Zip" and "Oh! How I Hate to Get Up in the Morning." Then they teach her a brand-new soldier song:

> *We don't want the bacon, we don't want the bacon,*
> *What we want is a piece of the Rhine.*
> *We'll feed "Bill the Kaiser" with our Allied appetizer.*
> *We'll have a wonderful time.*

On the second pass, they bawdily improvise—"We don't want the ham, we don't want the ham, what we want is a peek at girly gams. We'll feed Sue and Liza with our doughboy appetizer. We'll have a wonderful time"—and they can barely complete the chorus for their chortling. Skirls of laughter spew from Frieda, too. At last she feels let in on the joke.

Stops are called for Concord, South Acton. Every mile is a mile closer to Felix.

. . .

At Ayer, Flynn acts as the battle-wise commander. "Hat off. Keep your face down. Don't smile." Frieda, only slightly more afraid than excited, is the eagerly obedient draftee.

Flynn hails a jitney driver he knows to be legit, who'll rush them out of view as fast as possible. Meantime, the other three will hike straight to camp, to inform Felix of where Frieda waits. "Remember," Tucci says, "you might be sitting for a while. Sundown, prob'ly. Daylight's just too chancy."

"So long," says Komanetsky. Cooper mumbles a quick "Good luck." Frieda allows herself an instant's grave smile.

"Off with you," Flynn calls grandly, and flashes his trademark wink.

This time it isn't caddish, Frieda thinks. It's a sign of faith. She winks at the soldiers, too.

The jitney is a jury-rigged Buick motor truck with a canvas roof over benches in the back. "Face down," Flynn reminds her. "Keep it down."

She stares at her hands, at the Billy Watkins record, until finally Flynn taps her knee.

"All clear."

The driver hightails over washboard-rutted lanes, looking back occasionally with a chapped, persistent smirk. Frieda can't discern from his puffy, half-closed eyes if he's bored or tantalized by some dark thought. She'd be scared of him, of his creepiness, but Flynn is here beside her, and she tells herself again: trust in goodness.

They stop before a tumbledown farmstead. The air hangs heavily with a steamy brown smell—manure, she thinks, but sharper than what horses drop in Boston, wilder, as if only half-digested.

"Ready?" Flynn says. "Here we go."

They strike off through the farmer's unmown field. A barefoot little girl, in overalls with no shirt, peeks from the forebay of the barn. Is she wondering how it feels to be a lady in a dress, walking with a strong redheaded soldier?

At the field's edge, their path is blocked by a rusty barbed-wire fence, and Frieda's almost pierced before Flynn comes to her rescue, prying wider the top and bottom strands to let her through. The woods are sparse at first — supple, upstart shrubs — then dense, with full-grown trees whose dark leaves block the sun. (Papa used to tell her tales of the forest back in Russia, fairy tales in which magic lurked within the lush old growth. Only having walked among the woods of Boston Common, Frieda never understood the mystery. Now she does.)

"Trees, trees, trees," she says.

Flynn shrugs. "Ask me, it's sort of nice."

"But how do you keep your way? I'm all turned 'round."

"I guess men have a better sense of direction." He snaps a hanging branch to clear the trail. "From when we had to hunt and make it back."

Frieda lets forth a slack laugh. "That's plain silly. *You* never had to do all that."

"Some things," he says, "you're born knowing."

They tromp deeper, bushwhacking, and despite the leafy shade, Frieda works up a pleasant sweat. Has she ever been this far from crowds and pavement? So much ground to cover, but at the end of it: Felix! She gives in to ecstatic disorientation.

The wind picks up. Her skin feels fresh and porous.

On the far side of a rise, they come upon a shack, with a single glassless window, an unhinged door. Walls of skewed clapboard prop a corrugated roof, the edge of which shows a rusty, skull-sized dent.

"This is where I'm meeting him?" she asks.

Flynn points with his chin. "Go on in."

"Maybe I'll just sit and wait outside." She scans the ground for a suitable stump or rock.

"Go on in," he urges her again.

Because he's gotten her safely all this way, she complies. The shack is not quite tall enough for her to stand upright; she stoops and feels her back muscles knot. The odor of urine-soaked wood overwhelms her — and another smell, too, at once dirty and clarified, like a stain that's been worried through with bleach.

"Not exactly the Copley Plaza, is it."

Flynn doesn't laugh. He says, "Get on the floor."

Her eyes have adjusted to the scanty, brindled light. Animal droppings are scattered all about. "The floor? Don't be silly. It's pure filth."

"I said get on the floor!" He knocks her down.

She lands on one knee. Gropes the air to save herself. Her bag drops and the Billy Watkins record. "I'll ruin my dress." Her voice is naked, flayed.

Now Flynn laughs, a quick disdainful "ha!" — the audible equivalent of his wink. "Is that all you've got left to ruin?"

"I don't understand," she says, but with a terrible tough finality, she does: She's a girl alone in the woods with a total stranger.

The bottle of Zephyr must have spilled when her bag dropped; the smell — too much at once — makes her gag.

He's on her now, a hand vising each shoulder, thumbs dug in. "You never thought I knew this Felix, did you really, doll? Not out of forty thousand men!"

Frieda's thoughts are choppy. Her breathing. "But you said. And the others. Komanetsky?"

"If I'm nice, next time I'll let *him* take the girl."

With a pinch to her neck he shoves her closer to the floor, on her hands and knees now, and he's behind her. Her hat falls off, her face is pressed to wood. Flynn yanks her dress up until the fabric rips. The sound must madden him: he rips more. A finger, maybe two, worms inside.

When Frieda gasps and tries to scream, his hand slams her mouth. Her gums sting with the tinny taste of blood.

"You're not gonna scream, no you're *not*." So close that his spit sprays her ear. "First off, nobody's gonna hear you if you do. Plus, I don't think you'd want 'em to. Who do you think's around here but inspectors?"

His thumb, his breath, press against her.

"So I don't have to hold your mouth now, do I, honey? I can let go and you'll keep the damn thing shut?"

In the instant he lets go, she bucks with all her might. Her skull clocks his jaw. He jolts back.

Scrambling, she turns herself, stands, blindly stomps. The heel of her new boot spikes his gut.

She doesn't scream — she can't — her throat is terror-choked, so it's Flynn's "fucking cunt" that she hears as she takes flight, plus the crack of Felix's record beneath his writhing.

Frieda's not aware of having found her way back, but here she is, after running for what seemed a full hour, pushing through the farmer's barbed-wire fence. Her dress hem catches on a barb and snags.

It's sundown (or is the dimming in her head?), and the grass sags with chill, viscous dew. From the barn comes the slop and hiss and moan of milking time. The farm girl sees her, stops, baldly gapes.

On the road now. Hampered by her straggling, torn dress. By the buzz in her ears: a sickly yellow seethe. (Not loud enough to quash the memory of Flynn's final shout: "You want this story's moral, doll? Here goes. If it walks like a whore and quacks like a whore, guess what?")

She doesn't see the inspector until he grabs her by the arm. "I said, miss," he snaps, "you'll have to come with me."

Eleven

★

WHEN THE GUARD PUSHES Frieda through the heavy oak door, another girl tries to squeeze out, through the gap, but the guard shoves her back and throws the bolt. "Didn't *do* nothing," says the girl. "Let me go!" She raps on the small round window in the door. "Jesus Christ, come on. Let me go."

Getting no response, the girl approaches Frieda and shoots out a glamorous arm. "Flossie Collins." She shakes hands firmly, like a man. "All you need to know about me now is that I'm peeved. I'm peeved and I'm getting us out of here." When she turns about, her hair — a bouncy flapper's bob — sparkles with a quick audacious shimmer. She resumes her exasperated rapping.

Frieda wishes she'd stop. The sound's too loud, too near. Everything around her closes in.

The room is in the basement of the Ayer Town Hall, and must normally be a secretarial office: there's a multigraph machine, an unplugged percolator. Filing cabinets have been uprooted and pushed against a wall and now support piles of cotton facecloths. By another wall are four canvas cots. Thumbtacked to a corkboard are outdated notices — Easter hours, last year's hunting regulations — and a poster promoting income-tax compliance: GOVERNMENT CAN ONLY BE AS WEALTHY AS YOU ARE: OF THE PEOPLE, BY THE PEOPLE, FOR THE PEOPLE.

Flossie bangs again now on the glass, three brutish times. "Come on! For Christ's sake, open up."

The guard appears at the window with mirthless, yellowed eyes. "That's enough, now. Quit your racketing."

Leaning fiercely forward so her nose bumps the pane, Flossie says, "You can't lock me in here."

"Can and did, so shut your saucy mouth."

"I got rights!"

"And we got responsibilities. Section Thirteen of the Draft Act says no prostituting within five miles of a military —"

"Don't give me 'Section Thirteen'! I wasn't prostituting, and you know it. How could I be prostituting all alone?"

The guard's eyes narrow in sallow exasperation. "Fine, then. Suspicious conduct. Vagrancy. The charge don't matter. Didn't you read your circular?"

"Aw, *hang* your damn circular." Flossie gropes behind her for a multigraphed directive, which she crumples and hurls at the window. "Hang it, and go hang *yourself*, too."

"You little chit, don't you talk to me that way. Now you can stew till the protective officer comes." His fleshy face disappears from view.

Flossie inflicts a last ineffectual blow on the door, then turns, eyes alight with accusation. "What's a matter with you, girl? Not helping me out a whit."

Frieda says nothing. It hurts to breathe — not physically (her ribs are hardly bruised), but in an unappeasable, existential way. Each breath means that she's alive and has to face what happened, has to face whatever happens next.

Flossie flicks a wrist in her direction. "You obviously didn't come in without putting up a fight. Why ain'tcha fighting anymore?"

Is that what everybody will assume — that Frieda's dress was torn, her face muddied and scraped, in a tussle with the arresting officer? She's enraged — and consoled — that no one might know the truth.

"Where'd they nab you, anyhow?"

"Don't know," Frieda manages to say. "Some road."

"With a feller?"

Frieda shakes her head.

"Good, they got nothing on you neither. We'll both be out of here in no time." From her handbag, Flossie takes a gaudy pink beret and settles it atop her blond bob, as if readying for imminent release. "Trust me. I've been in the life a while now, and I've had my run-ins with the law. No john means no witness, no conviction."

Wouldn't Frieda *want* a witness, to attest to Flynn's cruelty? How could they jail *her* for what he did? She's not a hooker! But the guard said the charge doesn't matter. Frieda points to the circular, crumpled on the floor. "What about —?" she starts to ask, but Flossie interrupts her.

"What's it with that shittin' piece of paper? You'd think it was the Holy Writ or something."

When Frieda asks if she's read it, Flossie turns aside; she rakes her beret to a stiff, defensive angle. "I guess I . . . I've never been much for reading."

Frieda retrieves the notice and carefully unfolds it. It's printed on a quarter page of thin, off-white paper, as if the girls aren't worth a whole sheet. "'ATTENTION WOMEN,'" she reads aloud. "'You are in quarantine and cannot be released on bail. You will be sent to the detention home and examined by a medical doctor. If you are found ill with a venereal disease you will stay until such time as the doctor deems you negative. All criminal proceedings against you will be deferred until this notice of cure has been received, at which point any possible conviction, and related sentencing, will be addressed. No lawyer can obtain your release.'"

"Quarantine! What're we, lepers?" Flossie crosses to the door, whams her fist. "I'll be goddamned if I—let me *out* of here!" She paces, a caged cat, all hiss and hackles. Then she stops short with the dawning of a notion. "'No lawyer,' huh? How 'bout a *judge*? Gent I know in Boston, we went together some. One night he snuck me with him into the courthouse, and we did it right there, on the bench. Bet he might not want *that* spread around. You're good with words, sister? Could you help me write a letter?"

But Frieda, dumb with fear, thinks, No use, it's too late. The doctor will know everything. He'll know. She flinches—as if already she can feel the doctor's fingers, probing in the place that aches from Flynn.

Flossie claps her hands in Frieda's face. "What're you, a hophead? Aw, forget it." She flings herself down onto a cot.

Frieda lies down also, her limbs fetally bunched, wishing she could go to sleep forever. Secretly reaching into the cup of her brassiere, she searches for the only comfort left: Felix's words. All she finds is fabric, dirty flesh. The letter must have fallen as she ran.

They're sitting on their cots eating dinner—burnt pea soup—when the guard lets in a tall, big-boned woman. She enters in a fluster of exerted reassurance, eyes wide, her spine mainstay-stiff.

"All yours," the guard mutters to the woman, and takes his leave.

"Call me Alice," the woman says. "I'm the protective officer . . . but don't worry about the 'officer' part." Glancing at both girls, she presents a lax smile—or maybe it's just her overbite.

Protective sounds good to Frieda—Alice's voice is like tapioca—but Flossie wants nothing to do with her.

"I know your type. You're one of them awful creepin' Jesus

ladies, come to rescue all the friendless girls. Well, no thanks!"
She heaves about to face the wall.

Alice's cheeks quiver with visible affront, but she tightens
her smile and coughs decisively. "I'm afraid to say, Miss Collins, that creeping's not my style. But with that attitude I can
see why *you'd* be friendless." Looking pleased with her rejoinder, she sends a wink to Frieda. Her eyes are the blue of a Mrs.
Winslow's bottle.

They move away from Flossie, to some functionary's desk.
Alice urges Frieda to take the rightful seat, while she pulls up
another, lower chair. For a long minute she lets them sit in silence. Can she tell that talking might crack Frieda in two?

Finally Alice says, "You sure look down on your uppers."

With her jutting teeth, Alice isn't overly pretty, but has a
purposeful, built-to-last face: high cheekbones and a plain,
straight-edged nose. Frieda guesses her age just shy of thirty.

"My father," Alice says, "calls it 'a case of the mulligrubs.' But
I guess you've got reason to be blue." She asks if Frieda has ever
been arrested before, if her family will be worried by her absence. Is there anyone they should reach by telephone?

No, Frieda tells her. There's nobody.

With a stung look, Alice shakes her head. "I can gather, then,
why you'd feel desperate, Frieda, but desperate measures only
make things worse. When you break laws, you can get yourself sent away for years. In places far rougher than this. Do you
want that?"

Frieda looks away. She mumbles no.

"Of course not. And nor do we. But we also don't want girls
writing their own ends when they should just be barely starting
out! You need to be kept from the soldiers, and they from you."

Frieda tugs the knob of a warped drawer that sticks. "You
don't even know me. I'm not like that."

"Oh, but I *do*. I know your type up and down, Frieda. You're
no hardened case like some others that I've met." Here she
points bluntly back to Flossie. "You're not really a bad girl at all
— or maybe one who's been told she's bad, so acts it. You've just

119

come to flirt a bit with soldiers. But you've got to understand, Frieda, that being a U.S. soldier doesn't make a man into a saint. He's still the same creature that he was before induction. What's needed of you now is self-control."

Across the room, Flossie sniggers. "And *them*? They go scot-free?"

"The Army" — Alice's voice turns flat, domesticated — "is holding soldiers to a new standard, too. And to prove to the higher-ups that this is the right course, *we* have to help as best we can." She takes Frieda's hand, firmly squeezes. "Can you tell me about the soldier you were caught with?"

"Wasn't caught with anyone," Frieda says.

"The one you 'visited with,' then. Will that do?"

Felix — how she wanted to fall and let him hold her up. She says, "I never saw who I wanted to visit with."

If only she could say what really happened. There would be questions, though; her answers would be wrong. *Did this Flynn force you into the jitney?* No. *Force you to the shack?* No.

How, then, can she say she didn't want it?

"... a bit more cooperation," Alice is saying. "I've heard enough tall tales to reach the moon. Now, nineteen? Is that correct? I see that's what you told the inspector."

For some reason — exhaustion? Alice's calming gaze? — Frieda is inspired to tell the truth. In a spent voice, she offers, "Seventeen."

"You're still your parents' child then, legally. When was the last time that you saw them?"

"Dead," Frieda says.

"I'm terribly sorry. Both?"

Again the truth trickles out of her. "My father. Guess my mother's still alive."

"But you've quarreled. She's locked you out. The ties are cut."

Frieda nods. The account is near enough.

Alice scoots closer, and the difference in their chairs is emphasized; it's as though she wants Frieda to feel taller. "Look at you," she says, her voice lowered. "All tatters and scratches and down-in-the-mouth, sure, but even so, your innocence pokes through. You don't have to come to this. You don't." Because Frieda isn't yet of age, Alice explains, they might possibly circumvent the rules. If she agrees to reconcile with her mother and go home, if she proves herself capable of control . . .

"But the circular—"

"Let *me* worry about that." Alice stands; she towers over Frieda. "Think about it tonight—about how much freedom means. When morning comes, maybe you'll be wiser."

All night, Frieda is kinked with sleeplessness, two strands of fear raveling within her (seeing Mama again; never seeing her). She pulls one strand loose, the other tightens.

Flossie is awake, too, and churlishly tossing. "'I can see why you'd be friendless'? What a load! You think *she* has friends? You just *think?*"

Yes, Frieda guesses, Alice does. But she keeps the thought prudently unspoken. And doubles up again with indecision.

When a clock somewhere strikes two, she thinks, *Felix! Oh God, Felix!* All these hours, waiting in the woods. But no, it hits her: no. The whole thing was a trick. Felix doesn't know she tried to come.

Between her legs she feels raw, as though the skin has been pared. Like a catch in the throat before a cough. It's from Flynn, or from Felix, or maybe she has to pee. Could that be all it is? She calls the guard.

"No funny business," he says. "I'll be right outside the door."

In the bare, airless bathroom she thinks of Flynn, the train's toilet. She knew she shouldn't follow him—would have known, if she wanted to. But she wanted more to trust him, to trust them all, find Felix. (Were the other soldiers against her, too? Is everyone?) When will she learn to stop letting *want to be* trump *is?*

Now the need to pee is overpowering. She squats and she clutches at her hitched-up, ruined dress. ("Ruined?" Mama would say. "Hardly! Let me have a go." And she'd find a clever way to mend it.)

Maybe if Alice helps. If she keeps Hirsch away. If Alice talks with Mama first, maybe.

Frieda pushes and pushes, but barely a dribble comes. Still, she thinks. Whatever else, still sick.

In the morning, Alice brings company: Mrs. Sprague.

Mrs. Sprague, with her strange girlish braids and cleanly smile, her voice like someone urging a dog to stay. (Of course. She said she visits just-caught girls.)

"This?" she says, wheeling on Alice. "*This* is the girl we should be soft with?"

"Her name," Alice says, "is Frieda Mintz."

"Oh, I know. I met her back in Boston. I tried to find her, but she gave a false address."

Alice stares at Frieda: accusing? apologizing? To Mrs. Sprague, she says, "She's young. She could still change. Remand her to her mother, where she belongs."

"Oh, really? *Which* mother—the one she swore was *dead*? Now, Alice, we can't always get so sentimental and risk being constantly made fools of." She fusses around the room, running her thumb for dust, as if this were the parlor of her home.

Frieda can't tell how much of the bluster comes from anger and how much masks embarrassment for having been too trusting. (They share at least this one thing, then, this failing.) Mrs. Sprague has a jilted look—her eyes darting sadly—that makes Frieda want to say she's sorry.

But then the woman cuts a glance at Flossie, who's lain all this time on her cot, feigning sleep, pink beret pulled to shade her eyes. "If I'm right," says Mrs. Sprague, "I think I've met her, too. Or maybe they all start to look the same."

Frieda clamps her jaw. "I'm not like her."

"Oh, really?" says Mrs. Sprague. "Well, how strange then that you're both here."

"But I'm *not* a hooker. I've never sold myself."

This gets the woman's veins bulging. "Is *that* what you think this is about—money?" She punctuates the last word with a gray, jabbing finger. "Does debasing yourself for free make it somehow patriotic? Tommyrot! It makes no kind of difference."

Alice steps between them. "But it does. It makes a difference. That's the point of intervening now. Keep in mind whom we're trying to protect."

"'Never sold myself,'" mocks Mrs. Sprague. "What she apparently fails to grasp is that charity girls like her are just as bad—no, worse than prostitutes. With a prostitute, at least the soldier knows he's courting trouble. She . . . she's like a spy is what she is."

Frieda says, "You act like I've gone and slaughtered someone. Why do you care so much? I'm just one girl."

Mrs. Sprague looks apt to throw a fist. "Just one girl, yes. But the soldier you infect—that any one girl does—will be sidelined for three weeks at the least. How many more lives will it cost, Miss Mintz—tell me!—when this soldier, lying sick in some hospital ward, can't make the charge beside his mates?"

I didn't infect, Frieda might say, *I was infected*. But she's stymied by Mrs. Sprague's outburst. Suddenly Frieda wonders: Has a son of hers been lost? Is that what gives her eyes their mournful look?

Alice, face cast down as though it's she who's been steamrolled, lifts an interceding hand, then drops it. Across the room, Flossie slowly rises from her cot, looking flummoxed in the morning light, diminished.

Mrs. Sprague faces Alice, hugging her own chest in a posture of private agony. The bluster and the jabbing imputation have dissolved, replaced by what seems genuine dejection. Frieda can now see her as a mother: a woman who at one time must have held a newborn child, nursed it, powdered its soft skin, only to suffer the inevitable treason of its growing up.

"Oh, Alice," says Mrs. Sprague. "Is our work entirely wasted? Do they even understand the harm they cause?"

Twelve

★

THEY'RE DRIVEN TO FITCHBURG in the constable's
Dodge, which smells of cigarettes and what Frieda imagines as the sweat of nervous crooks. In place of Bubbles, the
tatters of which no longer kept her decent, she wears a different dress that Alice found her. (Two sizes big, badly jaundiced
beneath the arms, it's as elegant as an old burlap sack.) Alice
hoped to chaperon them, to help them make the switch, but
Mrs. Sprague argued against the plan: there were more girls,
she said, still at large, to be corralled.

They skirt the town proper, then curve through a dogleg,
past a sprawling, down-at-heel roadhouse, after which the way
turns rumbly with potholes. They pass an auction barn, a cem-
etery, a rendering plant.

Flossie asks, "What're they . . . turning us into, *glue*?"

The Dodge stops at a high board fence surmounted by
barbed wire, and the constable sounds a croupy horn. A section of the fence swings open to admit them, and they're met

by a watchman in dungarees and a chambray shirt. "Guess I'll take 'em," he says, as if doing a favor.

Escorting them across a yard of bare, hen-pecked dirt, the watchman stays close by their sides. His brimmed sentry's cap is pulled down to his ears. With his eyes hidden, his age is hard to tell: twenty, or maybe twice that old. A dimple flickers petulantly in one cheek. "Home sweet detention home," he says.

At first glance, the building could be a respectable manor: a well-timbered outline with gingerbread trim, a weathervane in the shape of a strutting rooster. Looking closer, though, Frieda notes the motley paint job: patches over patches over patches. A swing on the porch dangles cockeyed, one chain missing. To each window, an iron grating has been bolted.

"Thank you, Albert," says a woman who appears on the porch, her head canted to the angle of the defunct swing, as though bent on bringing a skewed world to plumb. "You've been acquainted, girls, with Mr. Burnham, the day watchman? If you were the sort to run — of course I'm *sure* you're not — he would be the one to rope you in."

"Yes, ma'am," he says through a coy and avid smile.

"Thank you, Albert, you may go back to your post."

With bowlegged showiness, he bulls away.

"I'm Mrs. Digges, the matron. And you are?"

Frieda and Flossie both mumble their names.

"And don't you look just as sad as funerals! Let's not see this as an ending — it's a *start*." She's a butter tub of a woman in a dress that calls to mind a tea cozy. Her dark eyes, too small for the bulk of her pink face, resemble cloves in a glistening ham. "The patients," she says, "are at lunch. Have you eaten? Follow me."

In the dining room, where bars of shade from grated windows fall, a mealy potato smell dulls the air. Some twenty residents hunch at long tables.

"Girls?" says Mrs. Digges. "Two new arrivals. I'm sure you'll give them all the help you can."

Each patient wears an identical uniform: a denim frock the color of rinse water. Some of them look up; some don't bother. A spidery girl, with dark hair like a cloud before rain, smiles without showing any teeth. At the next table, two colored girls, one hefty and one thin, snicker at a joke that might be Frieda.

More unnerving is the presence, among this female pack, of a single, scrawny young boy. He stands facing the corner, nose almost against the wall. Ticklike scabs cling to his shaved scalp.

The meal is a watery mash of sausage and potatoes. Frieda, who couldn't stomach breakfast back in Ayer, is desperate now to fill her hollowness. She takes the chair beside the spidery girl.

"No," shouts Mrs. Digges.

Frieda freezes.

"Not there! For goodness sake, not there."

As if caught stealing, Frieda drops the chair.

Mrs. Digges budges through the overcrowded room; her stomping makes a loosened floorboard squeal. "Now, Frieda, I know that you haven't yet been tested. We'll get to that tomorrow, first thing. But, please! You must *act* like you're infectious. The patients here are making such progress toward their cures. You wouldn't want to mar that progress, would you?"

Lou said you could catch it only by going the limit with men. Was she wrong, or is this woman? What else might Frieda misbelieve?

The matron takes her shoulder. "Now, would you?"

Frieda, her jaw burning, says, "No, ma'am."

"Good, then we'll count on your compliance. New patients are given separate tables, rooms, and toilets. The two of you can sit there, in the corner." She points to a table near the frail standing boy, who still hasn't turned, or moved a muscle. "At the Home," she continues, "we live by certain guidelines. Learn them and obey them, you'll be fine." Her lips form a tight, priggish bud. "For example, at the Home we don't wear hats." She whisks the pink beret from Flossie's head.

"Hey! Hey, give it here," says Flossie.

"I'll do no such thing."

"But it's mine."

"Yours?" Mrs. Digges hoarsely laughs. She stumps across the room to a glowing coal stove; she lifts the lid and shoves the hat within.

Silently, abjectly, Frieda claims her seat, with red-faced Flossie close beside her. She feels the other girls' appraising glares. Are they angry with her and Flossie for violating the rules? Or do they scorn her for submitting so quickly?

A wide-boned brunette serves their meal. The sausage goes down well enough, but something—the crockery?—is slippery with the perilous taste of bleach.

Mrs. Digges hails the standing boy. "Enough. Your cornering's done. You can join us."

When he turns, Frieda sees that he is not in fact a he, but a girl, with muddy freckles like mistakes. She has a newborn's startled, startling eyes.

"Next time," says the matron, "I venture you'll think twice. You won't skip breakfast soon again now, Jo?"

The girl picks a scab. "Told you, ma'am," she says. Her voice is slight, the echo of a wingbeat. "My stomach . . . my stomach wasn't right."

"Bosh! Right as rain, I'd have to bet. What isn't right is you and all your shirking. You see," she says to Frieda, "at the Home we live together: we eat and we work as a group. Not make-work, mind you. Worthwhile tasks. As soon as you begin to feel a part of something worthy, you can't help but become worthy yourself." Prayerfully, she joins her pudgy hands. "Now, can I count on someone to show these girls their home?"

"Yes, ma'am" comes a sudden sheeplike bleating.

The matron, in a round pink flash, is gone.

When lunch is through, most of the girls decamp; a handful stay. The slimmer of the colored girls approaches.

Black, Frieda thinks, doesn't quite do her justice; her skin's darker than black, but also bluer: the color of a hammer-hit thumbnail. A patch on her left eye — a fist-sized round of fabric — appears somehow more fashionable than tragic.

"By rights," she says, "I guess I should show you gals the ropes. I been here the longest — me and Melba." She gestures to her sidekick, two times her weight at least, with ale-brown skin and breasts like cannonballs. "I'm Hattie," she continues. "Hattie Walker. Y'all need anything, you come to me first." Given the narrowing of her good eye as she says this, it's hard to tell thoughtfulness from threat.

The girl with the storm-cloud hair pokes at Frieda. *"Tshepe zikh op fun ir. Zi iz gornisht vert."*

The fraught, familiar sound of Yiddish jolts Frieda. She feels as if she's been caught at something, red-handed, by Mama, caught in the act of — what? Being herself.

"Yetta, shush!" says Hattie. "No one wants to hear your Jewish."

But Yetta mulishly goes on: *"Mir darfn haltn zikh ineynem, vayl mir zaynen mir un zey zaynen zey."*

Does Yetta know that Frieda's Jewish — could the matron have announced it? — or is this just a lucky, clannish hunch? People always seem to think they know who Frieda is: a Jew, a reckless girl, a slut. If the first label's right, how long can she keep resisting the conclusion that the other charges, too, hit the mark?

Flossie leans to Frieda. *"What's* she saying?"

"I'm saying," Yetta butts in, "stick with *me* if you've got sense. If you let me organize, we'll be much stronger."

Yetta has stripped the bigotry and the scorn from her translation, but Frieda's scared to call her on the difference.

If Frieda had her druthers, she'd stick with Jo, the bald girl, who stands quietly, scratching at her scalp. She's drawn to something mild and yet firm in Jo's demeanor, a forcefulness that comes from lack of force. (She knows that Jo, at lunch, stood cornered as retribution, but her apartness looked inspiringly like defiance.) "Can't we just," says Frieda, "go together?"

Silence. Has she made another blunder?

"Sounds like she suckin' up to the matron," Melba says, but she smiles and chucks Frieda on the shoulder.

It's agreed: they troop off in a bunch.

First stop is a parlor of dark wood veneer, with two sofas and a velveteen love seat. Brocaded drapes fall across the tall windows. A Victrola dominates the far corner. On the ceiling, a multitude of tiny plaster cupids, a hundred of them, aim tiny arrows.

"Careful," Hattie says. "Might get lovestruck." She lets out a watery, thin laugh.

Frieda's stunned; it's plusher here than anywhere she's lived. But too, there's a sodden, squandered aura. The cupids' paint is chipped; they're missing limbs.

"Why'd they take the pictures down?" asks Flossie.

Some patches of veneer are less faded than the rest — rectangles and squares, the size of artwork.

Yetta scoffs and says, "Unsanitary."

"What?" says Flossie weakly. (Without her beret, she seems sapped.) "What kind of picture makes you sick?"

"Just telling you what the doctor and Mrs. Digges told us. They run this place on lies and worse. Paranoia. You'll catch on."

Frieda considers her blunder at lunch, the separate tables. If it's all lies, why do they go along?

The tour continues: bathroom here, linen closet there, the door to the matron's office (PRIVATE). From the hallway, Hattie indicates another set of doors. "There, at the end, that's where we do the sewing, and closer, this side here: the treatment room. Y'all will get to know that place *plenty*."

The door is padlocked (to keep girls out, or keep something in?); Frieda both wants and doesn't want to have a look inside. She imagines sharp tools to match the sharpness of her pain — the flare (like a match being struck within her tissues) plus new aches: in her temples, her lower back. Swellings at the places where her legs join her trunk, small throbbing nodes, as hard as marbles.

"Now, now," says Hattie. "Don't you go and faint on us! The doc's no fun, but it ain't like he'll *kill* you. Let's head on up to the living quarters."

They enter a wide foyer, and Hattie ascends the staircase, caressing its varnished newel as she passes. The post's tip is carved into a plump, suggestive shape. (It can't be *that*, thinks Frieda. It just can't.) Surely it must represent some unoffending object — a pinecone, perhaps, or a mushroom. But Flossie, too, looks rapt with titillation.

"Yes," Hattie offers, from above them on the stairs. "The answer to your wondering is yes."

"You've gotta be fooling," says Flossie.

"No, ma'am."

With casual expertise, Flossie strokes the newel. "Okay, then, explain me this," she says. "If they're so bent on turning us all Sunday school and sweet, why'd they make this place look like a whorehouse?"

"Didn't make it *look* like one," Hattie says, and laughs. "Till a month and some weeks ago, it *was* one."

"Don't pull my leg."

"Ain't pulling nothing. This place was a sporting house — a booming one, I hear. Then the Feds bought it, turned it into this."

"It's what they're doing," adds Yetta, "near all the Army camps. Come in and shut all the red-light places down, then change the houses over into jails."

"How do you all know so much about it?" Frieda asks. How does everyone always know more than she?

Hattie strikes a teacherly pose. "Me and Melba, we lived down in Storyville — in New Orleans? — till they came and they wiped that place clean. Headed off to Georgia, to Camp Wheeler: twenty thousand lonesome soldiers, mmm! But the agents nabbed us, hauled us to a home down there in Macon

— like this one, used to be a whorehouse. After we got out, decided to come up north, 'cause we heard them Boston boys, they like chocolate." She smirks just enough to show a ritzy, gold-capped tooth. Seductively, she readjusts her eye patch. "We hadn't been a week up here, and they caught us, drug us in. Like I said, me and Melba was the first. I swear you could still smell the spunk!"

Frieda blushes. She can't look at Hattie.

"You telling me," says Flossie, "they locked you up so fast that they didn't even bother to remodel?"

"Mrs. Digges?" says Melba. "She a little dim sometimes. Claims she was married once, and widowed young, you know? But she don't quite seem to know what we *got* here." She fondles the newel post obscenely.

The girls share a chuckle at Mrs. Digges's expense. Frieda grins, going through the motions, but her chest is so flimsy with doubt and dislocation that no sound actually emerges. Maybe the patients' merriment and ease should assure her: they're fine, they still laugh, they're surviving. But she doesn't want to laugh. She wants to sob.

Upstairs, Hattie indicates the main bathroom, then the smaller, separate one for newcomers. The walls here are also stripped of pictures. At the hallway's far end, she announces, "This room's y'alls'. Girls, let's go. Let 'em settle in."

At once, Frieda and Flossie are alone.

The atmosphere feels tacky and congealed. There's no rug, no dresser to keep clothes (just bare shelves), no curtains to hide the window grating: iron tines as thick as rifle barrels.

Flossie thrusts her chin at the hospital-cornered beds, four of which are jammed side by side. "Well?" she says. "Want to have first pick?"

Frieda stands benumbed, as blank as the room's walls. "No," she says. "No, I don't care."

After supper, the patients gather in the parlor for "coffee hour." The matron, before retiring to her quarters for the evening

— her nightly hour with her dime novels is apparently inviola-
ble — explains to Frieda and Flossie that real coffee is forbidden. ("Each vice conquered makes the others weaker.") Instead,
under the watch of the ceiling's chipped cupids, the girls drink
from mugs of Beech-Nut Jaffee, a gritty substitute that smells
of toes.

The Victrola plays a wobbly, dated song. *You've got some
smile, you're pretty too, and I've a million dollars that I'll
spend on you.* Flossie, who has made herself the center of attention, nearly drowns the music with her bragging: a tally of
the bigwigs who have hired her. "Honey Fitz" Fitzgerald, the
Boston Pops conductor, most of the current Red Sox team.
"Babe Ruth?" she says. "Had him just last month." Holding up
her hands, palms facing, a foot apart, she might be boasting of
a prizewinning trout.

Knowing giggles ripple through the group.

"How 'bout Everett Scott?" asks the girl named Angelina, a
Portuguese with provocative lips.

"A sweetheart, that one," Flossie tells her. "But shortstop
don't mean just his position!"

This time the laughter comes full-force. Melba looks liable
to expire.

Flossie says, "Hold on, though. Hold on! It ain't how large
his barge, it's the motion of his ocean. And Everett? Ooh, can
that man make waves!"

From the room's edge, where she hunches at a creaky roll-
top desk, Frieda fails again to laugh along; she's lost in the letter she's composing. Writing Felix is the only thing she's been
able to think about — writing him, reaching him, how soon
he'll get her out. False starts line the bottom of a waste bin.
"This won't be Harvard quality," began her first attempt; then
she considered Felix's own footloose style and how little mind
he paid to such credentials. Her new draft starts plainly: "How
I miss you."

She writes to him of Flynn (though just spelling that name

pains her), of Alice and the holding pen at Ayer. While the other girls joke, she writes and writes. "The patients," she tells him,

— that's what they're called here — what I'm called — are just that, they're *patient*. Can you tell me how that's so? (All but Yetta, the one I mentioned, with the hair.) They're laughing now, telling tales. Laughing! And me just here shaking, sick to death. Please come soon.

I guess they'd maybe say it's not so awful. I'm sitting in a nicer room than any I could rent, my stomach's full of food I didn't buy. And the work they made us do this afternoon was scarcely that, sewing hospital gowns and washing our own laundry. Is that what these girls think — a free ride? I swear, I'd rather starve. Live in a cave, if it was *mine*. I'm dead tireder tonight than I ever was from working — being nothing takes more strength than you could guess.

It wears me out that no one knows the truth of why I'm here, but part of me never wants to tell. To tell or not's the last thing I've got charge of. I don't really blame you any more than I blame myself. A lot, some days. Some days not at all.

Haven't seen the doctor yet — tomorrow morning, I guess. How am I supposed to sleep at all tonight? I know I've got the one bug, or had it back in Boston — seems like it's starting to clear up — but the other, the one that you can't see or feel for certain, the one that comes back later, makes you crazy? God, what if I — what if we — have *that*?

Just writing that — that *we* — almost helped. Oh please come soon.

She's struggling for the words in which to phrase a pressing fear — "Do they tell you when you might get shipped to France?" — when a burst of shouting comes across the room. Flossie's showboating has given way to a new scheme: to move aside the furniture and dance.

The girls yell their bids for first song. "'Wedding Bells, Will

You Ever Ring for Me?'" says Angelina. "'Pack Up Your Troubles,'" counters Melba. Even Yetta lobbies for her favorites. But Hattie, having commandeered the Victrola, calls the shots; it's she who sets the first disc to spinning.

Meet me tonight in Bubble Land, so far away from Trouble Land, where there is lots of joy that is waiting for each girl and boy.

The girls twirl across the makeshift dance floor. In a corner, by herself, Jo slowly swivels, her face pale and lunar and uncanny.

Flossie shouts, "Hey, Frieda! Come and dance!"

"Don't think so, thanks. Sort of busy." All that she has left is a paragraph of closing, but she wants to get it perfectly poetic. How can she make poetry from fear?

"Forget it," Flossie says. "You can finish up later. Dance! It's good medicine, come on."

Hattie, too, stops gamboling to scold her. "What all're you writing, anyways?"

Shyly, unable to keep the passion from her voice, Frieda says, "Letter to my sweetheart."

"A letter? Ha!" Hattie rears back and laughs. "Didn't no one tell you 'bout the rule?"

So many rules. Which does Hattie mean?

"No mail in," she says, "no mail out."

"Which really means," adds Melba with a lewd roll of her hips, "no *male* in, no *male* out."

The dancing party lapses because none of the girls can budge, so doubled-up is everyone with mirth. Egging them on, Melba thrusts again.

Limp with sudden languishment, Frieda drops her pencil; her fingers hold the thin shape of its absence.

From the Victrola, a lifeless voice sings: *Hearts break like bubbles in the air, but there we'll never know a care. Let all our troubles fade like bubbles — meet me in Bubble Land.*

Thirteen

★

M RS. DIGGES INSTRUCTED Frieda not to "void" herself, since doing so might thwart the doctor's findings. The holding of her water all these hours since waking up, joined with fear, has turned her bladder into a bomb.

She sits in a chair outside the treatment room door, waiting for Flossie to come out. A shelf holds teetering stacks of leaflets: "The Soldier, Uncle Sam, and You"; "The Nation's Call to Young Girls." Queasy, she picks up a leaflet and reads. The need to pee goads her thumping heart.

DO YOUR BIT TO KEEP HIM FIT

Women have believed that:
- They should know little of sex matters — and never discuss them.
- A young man's "wild oats" should be forgiven; a woman's, never.

Women know today that:
- There is danger to themselves and to their children in

irregular sexual relations because of the probability
of venereal infection.
- They are responsible for their acts not only to themselves,
but to their community, their country, and their future;
and that "desire" is a fatal excuse.
- Social and industrial inefficiency result from the selfish
indulgence of an appetite. We scorn the glutton; we are
beginning to exercise social control over the alcoholic;
we must now control venereal diseases.

Women's duty is to:
- Refuse to be ignorant and to raise their moral standards.
- Believe that men and boys with whom they associate can
and will lead clean lives.
- Help their communities to close evil resorts and to
organize in stamping out disease and delinquency,
thereby aiding the government in saving our country
from the gravest menace.

Scanning through the words leaves Frieda feeling scummy.
The leaflet sounds like Mama (if Mama could speak good English): *desire kills, appetite is evil.* Mrs. Sprague, too, thinks
Frieda, and now Mrs. Digges . . . all these people, cinched up
tight, terrified of wanting. Were they born that way, or have
all of them sustained some awful blow that changed them
into quavering prigs? (*Waiting for you, Shaynah, if you ever
change your mind. Waiting with all my love — Leo.*) What if
the Home — being here — is the blow that will change Frieda?
Get me out, oh get me out, she prays.

Flossie scuffs from the treatment room: pale, her sass
drained.

"Next," comes a voice from inside.

"How . . . ?" Frieda starts to ask, but Flossie bows her head.

Frieda weakly rises, feels faint, sits back down. Her throat
balks at a rising up of acid.

"Next!"

She tries again and this time stands.

"Come in," says a man in a shabby white smock, the cuffs of

which appear freshly spattered. Greeting her, he doesn't bother looking at her face — just her trunk, as if assessing livestock. "This shouldn't take long. I'm Dr. Slocum."

The bags beneath his eyes are the color of liverwurst. Big ears, a bald pate that scatters light. Frieda suffers another surge of acid.

"Boldt's table, as usual. Dorsal position."

He addresses a man Frieda didn't note until now, standing, like a butler, to the side.

"Stirrups?"

The doctor nods. "Yes, of course. I'll be right back." At the door he adds, "Oh — and this is Miller. Medical student from the Boston University. His practicum."

Frieda and the student are left alone.

The room is too cold. Her fingers shake.

Backed against the wall, as if facing a firing squad, Miller says, "Could you please loosen your clothing? Corset, waistband — anything constrictive."

It sounds as if he's reading from a textbook. Can't he see she wears nothing but her denim frock? She stands there. She can't calm her fingers.

"On the table, then?" He points to a white contraption with metal bracing and a smudgy glass top. "You . . . you don't have to remove . . . we'll make arrangements."

The suggestion of apology allows her to obey. Tremulous, she scoots onto the table.

Miller's left eye wavers on the verge of being crossed, which gives him an air of inquisitive concentration. He reminds her of someone — his strickenness, his absorption — but she can't put her thumb on just whom.

"Lie back, that's right. Knees up high." He covers her with a flimsy cotton sheet. "And the frock." He pushes the fabric above her waist.

Glass against bare skin, shocking chill. She fears she'll stick to the sting of it, as to ice.

Miller guides her left heel, then her right, into the stirrups, and turns a crank to force her feet apart. She's open. She's a hole. A running sore.

With a squeaky snap of rubber, Dr. Slocum walks back in, pulling two gray gloves onto his hands. (The rubber's smell: powdery, neutered.) He peers between her legs, and says, "Wider."

Fumbling, the medical student readjusts the stirrups. He, too, snaps on a pair of gloves.

"Typically," says the doctor, looking absently at Miller, "you'd obtain a patient history before beginning. But the girls here tend to be unforthcoming."

Above her knees, Frieda catches a glimpse of the doctor's nose: bulbous, riddled with burst vessels.

"And," he adds, "we can fairly well surmise the story, can't we? Especially with a girl of this one's race."

Miller's left eye quivers. He says, "Sir?"

"She's a Jewess, if I'm not mistaken, no?"

"Yes, sir. I believe so, sir. She is."

"Well, it's the Jew traders — the Jews and Italians — who run the rings. And the girls they traffic are most often their own."

Miller mumbles, "I . . . Do you know I'm Jewish, too?"

"That so? Name like Miller? Wouldn't have thought." In his voice, not a note of discomposure. "Didn't you tell me you were from the Middle West?"

"Yes, sir. Not far from Kansas City."

"Kansas? Didn't know they had Jews there. Well, be that as it may, let's get to business. Visual exam, smears, draw blood for the Wassermann. If you will now, Miller, aim that light."

Frieda flinches, tries to shut her legs; the cold stirrups clamp her heels in place. What will the doctor see? What will Miller? ("Guts, that's what. The parts you throw away.") She stares up at the ceiling, its pattern of pressed tin: a jumble of infinitely joined vines.

"Note all this clitoral irritation," says the doctor. "Habitual self-abuse, it seems clear. We see evidence of delinquency here . . . and also here. The hymen is predictably destroyed. By this

138

trauma — see it? — we can estimate the latest indiscretion. Less than forty-eight hours ago, I'd venture."

The vines could be ivy, maybe grape. Each curling stem joins with another, with another . . . impossibly, as plants might grow in heaven. She smells the lush green blast of such a place.

". . . the difference from a common leukorrhea?"

"Difficult, yes, admittedly," says the doctor. "The inflammation is strong presumptive evidence. More so if the canal is patulous."

"And could this chancre here have been syphilitic?"

"We'll see when the Wassermann is done. Feel the glands here at the groin — see how hard? I'm guessing yes."

Glove against her ankle. Whisk of skin.

Clamminess: Did they wet her? Did she leak?

". . . and swab up some of this gleety discharge," Dr. Slocum is saying. "So if you'll label those glass slides. Numbers one and two, 'vulva'; three and four, 'urethra'; five and six, 'glands of Skene' —"

A telephone bell overpowers his voice.

"Oh, of all times! Could you answer that, Miller? I'll get the alcohol flame lit."

Frieda's muscles clench. She shuts her eyes.

She listens to the hurry of Miller's footsteps in the hall, an overeager greeting, a brief pause. "I'm sorry, no, he's with a patient now. . . . Oh, yes, ma'am. Right away, Mrs. Slocum."

Then it's the doctor's departing footsteps, and his voice, airy and stiff, like beaten egg whites: "It's wartime, darling. These things are hard to come by. . . . You really can't make do with molasses? . . . Oh, don't fret me to death! I'll try my best to find some."

Frieda opens her eyes to see Miller, standing tall, but peeking down between her knees with a look of squeamish thrill. She remembers now the boy he makes her think of — in shul, when she was twelve, Morris Berman. The morning of Morris's bar mitzvah. A wispy kid, not more than four feet ten and ninety pounds, his arms shook when he went to lift the Torah.

Raising it, he saw her, and she held his gaze and smiled, and suddenly his forearms turned to steel. *As I hold this, now,* he seemed to say, *I could hold you. We'd grow old together, hand in hand.* She lifted her arms, too, as if to hug him across space, hugging the future that lay before them both.

"I do, too, darling," comes Dr. Slocum's voice. "All right, then. Soon as I can. So long."

Who would want to grow old with Frieda anymore? Not Morris Berman. Not Miller — who looks up now and sees that Frieda's caught him. He inhales with inscrutable vehemence: ashamed of himself, or of her, maybe both. "I beg," he starts to say just as the doctor strides back in, laughing about his wife's endearing spoiledness.

"Won't settle for less than perfect, that one. Which I guess must speak fairly well of me!" Dr. Slocum chortles overloudly. "Now, where were we? Ah, yes, the smears. Miller, take one of those applicators and sterilize it in the flame. Ten, fifteen seconds does the trick. Good, then the cotton. And in we go . . ."

The steel swab penetrates. Frieda stares up: vines upon vines, an endless knot.

She finds the girls working hard at hospital gowns again, the cloth cut from pigeon blue bolts. The clatter of stitching needles sounds like rodents running wild. Bobbins whiz, treadles clack and hum.

The workshop must have been the bordello's poshest suite. The wallpaper — repeated images of mating birds and bees — is yellow with smoke stains toward the ceiling. On a chandelier, glitz competes with dust. Frieda takes the Singer next to Yetta's.

"Hope it wasn't *too* bad?" Yetta offers.

Frieda can't quite find the voice to answer.

"Gets easier," Yetta says. "First time's worst."

The other patients gabble as they pin and hem and stitch, like gossips at a country quilting bee. Melba, with her booming voice, thick-lipped Angelina — each of them has lain on that glass table. How do they still smile and not scream?

Yesterday, during Frieda's initial session in the shop, it was Yetta who approached and sat with her. Before Frieda could start on the hospital gowns, said Yetta, first she had to sew her uniforms (one to wear, a spare for being laundered). Yetta found the right-sized pattern, helped her mark the denim, then hovered like a jumpy mother hen.

"Okay," Frieda said to her cumbersome instructions. "All right, yes. I think I understand." She could stitch a dress like this with shut eyes.

Meantime, Yetta unspooled her life's story (thank God she spoke to Frieda now in English). Raised in Manhattan, just east of Union Square; fled north at eighteen (six years ago). Father was a pettifogging shoe-factory boss. Or had been. Could be dead, for all she knew.

Frieda, during the monologue, stitched a flawless seam. Yetta finally saw, stopped her story. "Look at you! You don't need sewing tips."

Frieda shrugged. "The work I did, back home."

"In Boston? Were you Local 253?"

"What?"

"Come on! Garment workers' union."

"No. It was just me and my mother."

Yetta's face sharpened up with angles. She had quarrelsome features; a man's wide, blunt nose. "And that's the problem," she said, as if resuming an old argument. "All these girls working on their own, for less than peanuts, 'cause they need *this* dollar, *this* one, the next. And they can't stop to think a minute forward. You try to organize, but so many of the girls" — her gaze swept around the sewing shop — "so many just can't seem to be bothered."

"Unionize prostitutes?" said Frieda.

"Is that what — you think *that's* what I am?"

"You're here. Here with all the other girls."

Through clenched teeth, Yetta asked was *she* a whore?

"No," said Frieda. "Told them ten times: no."

"All right, then," she said. "Exactly. So."

Yetta, brushing strands of wild hair behind her ears, told her tale of landing at the Home: how she'd worked as a captain in the WTUL, urging wage hikes for switchboard operators; how she'd been arrested once for what the cops called "agitating" and was sure she got put on someone's list. They'd caught her out at night. She'd been framed. "Still not sure exactly how they gave me it," she confessed. "Towels? Infected towels, that's my guess."

Framed? Frieda deemed the girl a phony. A phony, or just mad with man-hatred.

But now, still atremble from the doctor's rubber touch, from the daze-inducing shame of being probed, Frieda is more credulous, forgiving. Her own story, to a stranger, must sound equally farfetched; who'd believe that what got her here — her legs cranked wide, exposed — that what got her to this heinous place was love?

If Felix knew, if he saw her in those stirrups — a running sore — would he ever want Frieda's love again?

"You said it gets easier?" she says to Yetta lowly.

"Sure," Yetta says. "A bit each time."

"I don't want it to. I don't *ever* want to think this isn't awful."

Yetta nods. "Good girl. That's the way to think. Remember, though, you're probably going to be here quite a while. So you can't spend every second fighting. You've got to pick your moments, then let loose."

Frieda asks how long. How long can they detain her?

"Depends. Whenever the doc says you're cured. For the syph, if you've got it, it's whenever the blood test's negative. For the clap, four clear slides, a week apart."

"A *month*? They'll hold me here a month?"

"Four weeks from when they *start* checking, which could be

two months, or three. That's what I meant — you've got to pick your moments."

Frieda looks around again at the patients, who still gossip ("Kissed her *where*?" "You heard me, girl, you heard"), like the Home is fine enough a place to be. Like life hasn't stopped. Like this *is* life.

Only skittish Jo sits quietly on her own, working at a sleeve, removing pins. Forgoing the tomato-shaped pincushion on her table, she stores each needle in her palm: the bulge of pale meat below her thumb.

"That Jo!" says Yetta, who must have followed Frieda's stare. "Just won't stop hurting herself."

From the looks of her, though, Jo's jabbing doesn't hurt: each prick evokes the small twitch of a grin. Maybe, Frieda thinks (with a kindred sort of longing), such localized pain is a relief. She asks Yetta, "Why's her head like that?"

"Uch! When they brought her in, the lice were so bad, all that they could do for her was shave it. Still scratches, though — scratches like the itch is in her brain."

"What happened, do you know?" Frieda asks.

Yetta pauses, wraps a piece of string around her thumb. Above the string, the skin goes puffy, red. "Jo won't talk. She never talks about it. But the word is, she was drugged — in her drink — at a dance hall, and captured by, you know, a white slaver."

Frieda's heard stories, seen films of such things. But she's never met an actual white slave. "Jo?" she says. "Jo was . . . was forced?"

"Woke up in a brothel, where they raped her, made her work. I don't even know how she got out. When the committee found her, she was living on the street."

"God," Frieda says. "How horrible." So far, Jo's the patient that Frieda's felt most drawn to; she's sensed that they are somehow most alike. Now she sees that maybe what attracts her isn't kinship, but contrast: Jo's much worse off than she.

(Frieda *chose* her path. Chose Felix.) "And at *her* age?" she adds. "So horrible."

Yetta smiles a skintight, toothless smile. "How old do you think she is, Frieda?"

Jo's waifish form. Her baby face. "Couldn't be more than fourteen? Fifteen?"

"Nineteen, Frieda. *You're* the youngest here."

"Which we hope gives you the greatest chance of saving!" It's the matron, who's snuck up on them, eavesdropping. "And I know you're both game to get acquainted," she goes on, "but there's time for yabbering and time for work."

"We've *been* working," Yetta insists, "all along."

Mrs. Digges rolls her beady eyes. "Oh, Yetta — always such a crank! I wish you might just sweeten up your temper."

Yetta falls silent as she starts to wind her bobbin. Her whole body seems to form a fist.

Is that how Frieda looks, too, the next afternoon, when Mrs. Digges pulls her aside and gives the news? "Wanted to tell you right away," the matron says gently. "Your Wassermann test's back. It's positive."

Fourteen

✦

*W*ILL I GO MAD? she asks the doctor (picturing Neville, the loose-eyed beggar). *Will I ever be able to . . .
to be with men?* And although Yetta told her she'd be stuck at
least three months: *When can I get out? When? How soon?*

The doctor says she's lucky: they've caught the syphilis
early, just the chancre and some swelling of the glands. A few
weeks more — a month — she'd have seen the rash of pimples,
the scales on her scalp, loss of hair. Was she thinking of these,
he asks, when she opened her legs for men? Or of later: being
paralyzed and utterly blind, with her nose's bridge caved in to
nothing? No? Maybe next time she will.

With the regimen offered here, he says, if she follows the
treatment fully, the syphilis should eventually be made inac-
tive. The gonorrhea, too, should respond to what he'll give her;
it appears as though no permanent damage has occurred, the
inflammation localized, not chronic. So yes, in due time, she
might lead a normal life. She might, if she's lucky, still bear
children.

But *would* that be luck, she thinks, or would it be a curse? A normal life is the last thing she's dreamed of. She stares at the play of light on Dr. Slocum's baldness, the way it seems to erase his head by half.

"In terms of timing," the doctor says, "the name of the game is patience. Some more of that, and you wouldn't be in this mess — am I right? It would be criminal — hear me, now, a sin against life — if you married a man, or, God forbid, attempted to have a child, before the illness is *permanently* resolved. A year with no symptoms? Maybe two. It's bad enough contending with the results of your own folly, but to add *innocent* victims? A sin!"

But what if the man she marries isn't innocent in that way? What if he knows; what if he has it too? This is Frieda's secret from the doctor, her salvation: that she has a man already to go back to. She and Felix won't have to wait those long years; they won't have children — fine — but there's nothing to stop their coupling, nothing to keep the two of them apart.

"When?" she asks the doctor again. "How soon will you let me out?" She'll make it through, she'll do whatever it takes, because there's Felix.

"I told you, young lady! The point is not to rush. The point is sitting tight until you're healthy."

"July?"

He sniffs. "July! Far too soon."

"August?"

"Well. Well, perhaps."

August, she thinks (and knows, even as she anoints the thought as truth, that's she doing it again: *want* over *is*). But the doctor told me so, she thinks. *August.*

Flossie's tests, too, come back positive on both counts. "But I don't care," she tells Frieda that night as they lie in bed. "I'm getting out anyway. Break out, if I have to, or . . . well, or something, I swear."

"But aren't you afraid of — you know, being sick?" For the

first time in her life, Frieda's scared in her own skin; her body's what she wants to break out of. But without her body — the heat of it, the million avid nerves — without that, who then would she be?

Flossie says, "Sick shmick. Had it before, I'll have it again — hazards of my line of work, right? But could you imagine just sitting here forever? Some of the girls — Hattie and Melba? — it's like they *like* being here, big fish in a small pond. Or I don't know, maybe their kind are just meant to live chained. But I hate to watch 'em. Christ, I hate this place!"

No, Frieda thinks. Nobody is meant to live chained. And she falls asleep imagining herself a fish within a pond, the water draining, bleeding away to mud.

She wakes to noise: the thud of something stubbed, a sharp breath. Shocked alert, she lifts her hands, defending. "Flossie! Wake up. Someone's here."

Flossie is a calm voice in the darkness. "Only me. Don't worry. Back to sleep."

Frieda hears her tiptoe to the door, baby it shut, hears the footsteps waning down the hall.

She assumes Flossie's gone to the bathroom, that's all, but when ten minutes pass — then twenty, half an hour — it dawns on her what Flossie must be doing. Breaking out already, running free. Is she strong enough to dig beneath the fence?

Envy and chagrin keep Frieda wide awake. She should have guessed that Flossie would act upon her threat — should have guessed and should have taken advantage. Her letter to Felix is hidden beneath the mattress; Flossie could have taken it, delivered it to him. If he knew, he could find her. If he knew.

And Lou! She could have written Lou, explaining, with a plan, and Flossie could have brought it to the store.

Frieda has to find a way, any way to reach them. Reach across the fence to her old life.

It must be past midnight (the moon's arced into view) when the door, with a tiny whinge, opens. *Fff, fff* — the sound of Flossie's socks as she clearly tries her best to stay quiet.

Frieda coughs to let her know: don't bother.

"Oops. Sorry." Flossie giggles.

Frieda giggles, too, with rejuvenating cheer. Here's a second chance, and she won't blow it. "It's okay," she says. "I've been up. I was worried I'd maybe seen the last of you."

"Why would you ever think a thing like that?"

Flossie's voice is fine-spun with a canny, furtive tone. Tonight, she must only have been scouting ways out; tomorrow night, or the next, she will run. Frieda could ask—should she?—to join the getaway, but as frightened as she is of languishing at the Home, she's more scared, for the moment, of never getting cured.

August, she thinks. She'll need a new job, a place to stay. If she tells Lou she's sorry, that she'll stand up for herself, Lou will help her out again, won't she? Or maybe, with Felix by Frieda's side, she won't need help.

"Flossie," she says, reaching toward the edge of her mattress. She imagines she can feel her letter to Felix tucked beneath, folded to a hard lump of hope. "I was wondering if... well, whatever you do is fine by me, you know." She tries to match Flossie's covert tone. "But how are you going to make sure that Rattigan doesn't catch you?"

Rattigan—Donald Rattigan—is the leering night watchman, who takes over from Burnham after supper. He sits, mutely menacing, in the guardhouse every night.

Flossie crawls beneath her sheets, silent in the moonlight.

"If he catches you," adds Frieda, "then he's sure to tell Digges. And if he tells her ..." The thought's too dire to finish.

Flossie now props herself up on one elbow; for a long, laden moment she gives stare. From the tricky half smile that sneaks onto her face, all at once Frieda understands: far from obstructing Flossie's early-hours ambitions, Donald Rattigan *is* her ambition.

Frieda feels simultaneously let down and lifted; the weight of this place is both heavier and more movable than she guessed.

Flossie, in a whisper, says, "He traded me tobacco. If you promise not to snitch on me, we'll share. Got a feeling" — she winks cleverly — "there'll be more."

There is more.

The next night, again, she steals quietly out, then comes back with precious contraband. A couple of nights later, the same. With denim scraps pilfered from the sewing room's bolts, she rolls cigars — pudgily immoderate creations — and smokes them down to nothing by the window.

Frieda never joins her (the smoke stings her throat), but when she catches Rattigan and Flossie trading looks — at "light's out," passing in the hallway — she breathes something every bit as potent. A whiff of danger, secrecy. Of freedom?

By week's end she's learned the house rules. No coffee, no mail, no meals or work missed. No telephone. No guests but family. Sundays are the Sabbath, and a minister comes to preach; she and Yetta are the only girls exempted.

Burnham brings newspapers, but erratically, sometimes late, as if to break the patients' grasp on time. Frieda fights to keep her sense of urgency alive — she tries to add a paragraph, in secret, every night, to the letter she still hopes to send somehow — but the days run together, the same food, the same chores, and all her thoughts, too, seem the same. The matron touts the threat of some government agent's visit. *When Miss Longley comes,* she cautions. *Miss Longley* — but the agent, often warned of, doesn't show. Decoration Day passes unobserved.

Two days a week, the doctor calls. She expected to see Miller, low rung on the medical ladder (she could tolerate him and his brainy, almost contrite air), but never again does he appear. Only Dr. Slocum, with his gin-blossomed nose, his callously bumptious bedside manner. His pale, droopy eyes always verge on falling shut, as if doctoring is a tonic he takes for sleep. Or maybe it's the booze that makes him sleepy; she smells it on his breath when he walks in. Is that why he's assigned to them, this band of disgraced girls — stuck, just as they themselves are stuck — instead of off in France, saving soldiers?

Aside from the frugal monotone of his instructions ("Open, please"; "Steady now, quit flinching"), the doctor never says much to Frieda, nor Frieda to him. They've reached a truce. For as humbling and as vulgar as she finds the whole business, she's desperate for the throbbing to end: the throbbing of her glands, of her fear.

Still, the cure rivals the disease. The swabbings, the blue pills to swallow with each meal, the injections of urine-colored liquid. And worst of all, worst of all, the tampons (a word she'd never heard before he used it). Dr. Slocum makes her stand with one foot on a chair, her denim frock hitched above her hips. Then he wets a swab at the end of a steel probe, inserts it and toggles it around, as though baiting a mouse to come out of its hole. (The first time, when she saw the vial in which he soaked his probe, she was staggered: nitrate of silver. Had Mrs. Digges, in her zealously alchemical crusade, instructed him to fill her up with bullion?) When the swabbing is completed, Dr. Slocum takes a tampon — a thumb-sized plug of rolled gauze — and soaks it in some of his other vials (Ichthyol and Argyrol, they're labeled, like the names of crazed fairy-tale villains), then stuffs the sopping wad into Frieda.

Every time he does it, she thinks of the hermit crabs that Papa showed her once on Singing Beach. She was nine and begged him constantly to take her to the shore. "See their funny shells?" he said. "It's not the shell they're born with. When they grow too big, they move into another." Exactly like Papa, she thought, who'd moved from Smother Russia. Like herself, too — the self that she dreamed of someday being — who would crawl out from the confines of the life that she'd been born to (from Mama, from *You can't, you're just a girl*) and claim a new, spacious sanctuary. Curiously, while Papa went wading in the surf, she pried one of the crabs from its shell (helping it, speeding its transition). She yanked out a second crab, a third.

The crabs squirmed in sunlight, piteous and pink. In minutes, they dried and stank of death.

It's not the gauze tampons that remind her of the crabs —though their stink, when she extracts them, and their size are similar. It's herself, her own stripped-bare self.

As the days warm, they spend more time outdoors. Mornings now begin with alfresco calisthenics: knee bends, stretching arm lifts. A leather-cracked medicine ball gets tossed. ("Kelly's Thenics," thinks Frieda, guessing—hoping—that Felix, at this hour, is making similar exertions. Does he picture her, too? No. No, of course he can't. He can't until she finds a way to reach him.) Afterward, the girls hoe and cultivate the rows in the sandy quarter acre they call "the garden."

There's a chicken coop, too, filled with temperamental hens, but Jo, showing an overwrought affinity for the birds, insists on taking care of them by herself. Frieda watches her holding the hens, talking in baby talk. Does Jo like being able to control them, is that it? To control *something* after what she went through? When Frieda thinks of Jo's ordeal—sees what Jo's become—she redoubles her resolve to get out. Maybe Jo's been beaten, but not her.

One muggy afternoon, as the girls spade manure (donated by the rendering plant next door), Flossie quits. She won't work, she says, until the matron tells her *why*. What good will it do to fling this shit?

The swear word has Mrs. Digges lifting her shovel, but she seems to close some valve inside herself that lets out anger. She lowers the shovel and turns to Flossie, smiling. "Do you think folks are meant to live in cities, all cramped up? Of course not. It's our modern aberration. Girls need a taste of what's *normal*. So we take a girl like you, who's known nothing but the streets, a girl who's never even seen a sunset—"

"A sunset?" Flossie says. "Seen a million."

"A country one, no city smoke to block it. So we bring you here, miles from all those buildings. You work the land and learn about patience — nature's time — and the tool you've all lacked: self-control. Just smell it," she urges everyone as she kicks her spade deeper, her face pale in the washy June sun. "Isn't it just scrumptious? All this air!"

Frieda smells only the dung under her nails and the rendering plant's stench of singed hair. She gags on it, hungry for the harbor scent of Boston, for how the city, on those days when a northeast breeze purled in, smelled like distant swells, sunken treasure.

What would she be doing now at home? One o'clock: half an hour left of her lunch break. She'd be walking out of the sweet-shop, maybe, savoring her gumdrops. Or browsing through the penny rack at the Old Corner Bookstore for classics like *The Wide, Wide World*. Flirting with the boy at the Bijou Dream's window, angling for a free movie ticket. Any given day's destination didn't matter; what mattered was that nobody but she could decide. Sometimes just taking a turn — from State Street, say, to Broad — was enough to make her neck hairs go electric. *Nobody who knows me,* she would think, *knows I turned. Nobody knows where I'll turn next.*

Stabbing at a tough clump of dung with her spade, she wonders if she'll ever feel that latitude again. Maybe once she's back in her routine — the work, the breaks — maybe then . . . and finally it hits her (how skilled she is at burying hard truths): she has no routine to go back to. No job at Jordan's, so no lunch breaks. Even her dreams of freedom now are false.

Later that day, as if her sermon got her thinking, the matron announces an inspection. Because she begins in Flossie and Frieda's room — "Last girls in, first girls searched," she tells them — they've no time to better hide their secrets. In a minute, Mrs. Digges unearths Frieda's letter, and then, moments later, Flossie's stash.

"Aha!" she says. "And what have we here?" She seems at once cheered by her doubt's vindication and heartbroken not to be proved wrong.

"From the garden," Flossie blurts out in ludicrous dissemblance. "Flowers. To make a potpourri."

The matron affects a supercilious smile. "Well, isn't that the height of enterprise. I'm eager to learn more about your . . . floral experiments, but if you'd please leave, I'll speak with Frieda first."

"Yes, ma'am," says Flossie. "Thank you, ma'am." On her way out, she pauses behind Mrs. Digges's back and locks her lips with a make-believe key. Glaringly, she gulps it and slinks out.

The matron sits on Frieda's bunk, perusing the letter, and Frieda, sick with embarrassment (only Felix was meant to see it! her fears, her silly babbling endearments), wants to grab the pages, tear them up. Embarrassment yields to panic: What did she write of Mrs. Digges? Did she call her a mean old butter tub? The matron will surely corner her — or worse.

Mrs. Digges folds the letter closed, then folds again, and weighs the square thoughtfully in her palm. "Frieda," she says. "Frieda, Frieda, Frieda."

She's too calm, thinks Frieda, a cat about to pounce; her double chin quivers with something: rage?

The matron puts a hand on Frieda's knee and gently pats. "I can see you're a romantic. Me, too. We both believe in the hope that the hero will do right and the girl will live happily ever after."

Except for the glistening in Mrs. Digges's eyes, Frieda might think she's being mocked. She still wants to grab the letter, hide it.

"Are you by chance," the matron asks, "a Laura Jean Libbey fan?"

Yes, Frieda says, she's read them all.

"Thought so! *I've* read them all *twice*." The matron gives a girlish little laugh. "And do you know how many Laura Jean Libbeys have bad endings — endings where the girl is left unhappy?"

"None that I ever read," says Frieda.

"There was one. Just one. She got reams of protest letters

—the maddest of which was written by yours truly. And she's never made *that* mistake again. Now, why do you think so many of us complained?"

Frieda shrugs. "People don't like to read bad endings?"

"No! It's not that people don't *like* unhappy endings. It's that no ending *has* to be unhappy. There's just no reason that it has to be so! In this world of ours, any girl's story can turn out well—so, given the choice, why not choose happy?" The matron's voice dips down and swells like a song, a tune so sweet you hum it without bothering to learn the words. "I can see from this letter, which we'll both try to forget"—Mrs. Digges stuffs the pages in her pocket—"I can see that you've made some poor choices. Well, who hasn't? But now you have the chance to stop and make some better choices. A chance to choose your own happy ending."

Frieda asks her how, by doing what?

"How about we make a start with *this*?" The matron lifts Flossie's sack of tobacco. "Would you like to tell me where this might have come from?"

The music of the matron's words suddenly is gone; the sound that fills Frieda's head is *snitch*. She stares into her lap. She stays mute.

"Oh, let's dispense with the fooling, shall we, Frieda? We've been seeing each other eye to eye so well! I know that this tobacco is Flossie's, not yours. Say so, and you'll be in the clear."

Between them falls a harrowing silence. *Flossie*, she could say. Two syllables, so simple, the truth that Mrs. Digges already knows. But would a Laura Jean Libbey heroine betray her friend's trust? A friend by happenstance, but still a friend.

"If I can't confirm whom it belongs to," says the matron, "I'll have to assume both—and both of you will pay." Her face has reddened past its normal steamed-ham color, her cheeks like a bottom that's been spanked.

Frieda counts the whorls on her fingertips, clamps her teeth.

"Well, then," says Mrs. Digges. "That's your choice. This will hardly reflect well on you in Miss Longley's assessment."

Frieda braves a chilly, anxious shake. "Miss Longley," it turns out, is not an idle threat; the date of the agent's visit has been named. The Home has lately crackled with rumors of her power, of how much rides on her evaluation. ("These nut pickers," Yetta said, "they can call you 'feeble-minded.' Lock you in the loony bin forever.")

She's on the verge of yielding when she sees a bit of paper peeking from the matron's dress pocket. Her letter, her hope, her plan for reaching Felix — stolen, just like every other thing. The matron said that girls must learn patience, self-control? Fine, thinks Frieda. Here's your self-control.

After breakfast on the morning when Miss Longley is expected, the girls make their way out to the garden. All but Jo, who skipped the meal — her third time in a week — because she said her stomach was upset. To punish her, since cornering has proven ineffective, Mrs. Digges makes her bleach the bathrooms. No feeding her precious chickens until she's done.

(Frieda and Flossie bore their punishment already: two suppers without meat, only beans; plus a full day barred from conversation. "Being sent to Coventry," the matron called it. "You didn't *want* to talk. Now you *can't*.")

In the garden, they harvest the season's last asparagus, kneeling in the cool, clumpy soil. It's the final week of June, but it feels like April. From his guardhouse by the fence, Burnham keeps watch, his arms crossed in virile nonchalance. The matron, awaiting their guest, has stayed inside.

The sky looks somehow seedy, blue dulled by gray, like veins beneath a sickly old man's skin. A fickle breeze swirls with the rendering plant's stink, then shifts and brings a waft of apple blossoms. There's the ominous, ammonia smell of hens.

I'm sorry, Frieda practices, preparing for Miss Longley. *I know I've fallen short of expectations.* Would a feeble-minded girl say "fallen short"?

If the other girls are worried, no one shows it.

"Hey, Floozy," Hattie calls. "How's the shirking?"

"Too good for farm work?" Yetta goads.

Flossie has been crouching, feigning to be busy, but not a single stalk is in her basket. They're peeved at her already for not sharing her tobacco, and, worse, for having gotten caught. Now they'll all be scrutinized more closely.

Flossie lifts her hands, turns them front to back, as if displaying sparkly diamond rings. "I gotta baby these — my best assets. Fellers die for fingers soft as these."

"Fingers?" Hattie says. "Honey, if men're only dying for your fingers, ask me, you're doing something wrong."

Flossie snaps a stalk and jabs it at Hattie. "You don't know where to *put* 'em like I do."

Other girls have stopped their work to watch the two spar; they pipe in now with "ooh"s and "got you good"s.

"Know what I bet?" drawls Hattie, her accent twice as cottony as normal. "Bet she just scared to find one of them small white ones — you know, that ain't seen the sun?" She toes through mulch and unearths such a shoot: freakish and pathetic, an albino.

"Why'd the girl be 'shamed by a stalk like that?" asks Melba. Her smile betrays that she must already have guessed the answer.

"S'pose it reminds her of her mick sweethearts' privates. You know what they say: Irish curse."

Flossie balls her fists. "Shut your mouth, you one-eyed coon. I'll show you *curse.* I'll show you —" and she lunges.

They fall to the ground in a welter of flung limbs, flattening asparagus as they tumble. Dust snarls in the air. Bodies blur.

"Stop it," Frieda shouts. "Stop right now!" The slapping makes her think of Flynn's hands. She wants to jump between them, but what if Burnham sees and thinks *she* was the one who started fighting? What if she's reported to Miss Longley?

The adversaries kick and swat and roll.

She's about to dive in anyway to separate the girls — not for their sake, for her own — when a high, unholy keening splits the air.

Everybody freezes. They all listen.

Again it sounds: a hideous wail. Less than human, more than animal.

Hattie and Flossie both drop their fists. They pant and stare, repentant, at the ground.

Frieda scans the yard, half expecting to see a dybbuk, until suddenly she finds the cry's source. It's Jo, hunkered in the chicken coop's entrance. When did she join them in the yard? She rakes her scalp and rocks, soaked in blood.

Rushing to her, Frieda and the girls shout, "Jo, what happened?" "Show us where you're bleeding." "Are you hurt?"

Jo continues rocking, unresponsive. Cradling a package — no, something living, barely. One of her cherished birds, awash in gore.

Now Frieda sees the scrambled feathers: shredded tufts strewn all around. A fox must have raided in the night or early morning. Where could it have breached the fence? How?

"Oh," she says. "Jo. I'm so sorry."

Jo gapes, her eyes unfocused, empty. Her hair has lately grown back to a tender flaxen stubble, but patches of baldness glare through.

"It's alive," says Angelina. "See it moving?"

"Help it," someone calls.

"It's still breathing!"

Yetta barges in. "It's okay. We're all here now. Everything's okay. We'll save it, Jo."

But she does nothing. Nor do all the rest. Hattie, Flossie, Melba, all just stand there.

Quailing, breathing faintly, the chicken tries to flap, but only one wing's upper half responds. Its neck, stripped of feathers, shines too pale.

The ground is amuck with spills of blood and sawdust, like the floor of Slotnik's Kosher Meats. Frieda kneels and touches Jo's neck. Doesn't rub, just touches with two fingers. "Give the bird?" she says, not an order, but a question. "I can take care of this. Okay?" (She's seen Sam Slotnik do it, seen Papa.) She studies Jo to know she comprehends. "It's all right," she says. "Hand it over."

In a sudden crumple, Jo's shoulders loosen. Her grip on the chicken loosens, too. It makes a noise like knuckles cracked in water.

Frieda strokes the chicken's neck, the spots of bare skin. She hums and strokes and tells the hen to shush. Tenderly, with skill, she wrings its neck.

The hen's broken wing flinches, spattering dark blood. Frieda's frock gets doused in thick blots. One more twinge, and then the hen goes limp. Jo looks glazy, vacantly delivered.

"Of all the — what on *earth* is going on?"

They turn to face the matron, her mouth cinched into a shape of squeamish rage.

"When you *knew* that Miss Longley would be coming!"

Beside her, tall and unflappable, stands Alice, in the same dress she wore back in Ayer. Alice! Her affirming, glass blue gaze.

"Jo Humber!" says Mrs. Digges. "Are you a glutton for punishment? And Frieda — again, a disappointing choice."

Yetta steps before the fuming matron. "It wasn't Jo's fault, really. Or really Frieda's, either. Something got the hens, and she was helping."

"By covering herself in filth? On the day of her evaluation? Have you no respect — none — for Miss Longley?"

Frieda looks to Alice, with her durable twill dress, her expression of vehement calm.

"Couldn't be helped," says Alice. "What a shame."

Fifteen

---★---

WOULD YOU LIKE to change your dress before we start?" Alice asks.

They sit facing each other in the chilly treatment room, where Alice will conduct her assessments (Frieda's now, Flossie's after lunch). The calcimined walls are the green shade of nausea. Steel probes in rows of glass jars shine.

Frieda shakes her head. She'll stay as is.

"You're sure?"

Her lap is sopping, stained. Impossibly, there seems to be even more blood now — as if the stains bespeak not the hen's mortal wound but a deep-seated hemorrhage of her own. Chin tight to her chest, she says, "No."

"'No' not sure, or 'no' don't want to change?" Alice's mouth stays firm, but the rest of her face smiles. She reaches for the attaché case resting by her ankles, lifts it to her thighs, and flips the latch, keeping her gaze all the while on Frieda, who doesn't answer. "Fine, then," Alice says. "Why don't you tell me what happened."

"The bird was going to die, but no one did a thing. So I put it out of its misery, like you should."

"Like you should?"

"Yeah. Anyone knows that."

A twinge of something — horror? respect? — scores Alice's brow. "Remarkable," she says. "Was it hard?"

Frieda still thrums — galvanized, alert — all the more alive for having held death in her hands. She shakes her head. "My father was a butcher."

"Still, isn't it such a dreadful shame?"

Shame isn't what she feels — more like a blister-popping alleviation. And, too, the relief of seeing Alice, when the "Miss Longley" she imagined was an ogre. "I wasn't expecting you," she says.

"Mrs. Digges didn't say that I'd be coming?"

"She did. I didn't know that you'd be *you*."

Alice flashes her half smile again. "Despite all my efforts to the contrary," she says, "I have difficulty being anybody *but*."

Frieda looks more deeply into Alice's eyes and sees in them a roiling undertow: color at once vibrant and poignantly depleted, like light through an empty wine bottle. Her blond hair is veined with early gray. "Do you mind," Frieda says, "if I ask what you are?"

"What *am* I?" Alice laughs expansively. "Friend or foe? Animal, vegetable, mineral?"

"No, what are you? Some kind of psychiatrist?"

"Oh, I see. How disappointingly mundane. I'm trained as a medical social worker."

Alice seems so different from the matron or Mrs. Sprague, so much easier and less accusing. Frieda feels assuaged (no, more than that, electric), as she did when she spent the day with Felix and he treated her equally: an accomplice. But she's *not* Alice's equal, she's her *work*. "So how come," Frieda asks, "you're here now?"

Alice extracts a notebook and a fountain pen from her case. "Am I crazy, Frieda, to have thought *I* was the one who'd ask the questions? That our task is determining why *you're* here? Oh, but I *am* crazy. I remember how you spoke to Mrs. Sprague!"

"What I meant," Frieda starts. Her throat catches. She stares at the green wall. "What I meant is, how come you were in Ayer, but now you're here. And there's Mrs. Sprague, too. And the vice squad. No one wants to be stuck with us, I guess?"

"No, it's more like everyone wants a piece. Some people, like Mrs. Sprague, are working for the state, others for the town of Ayer. I'm with the War Department, Commission on Training Camp Activities, Law Enforcement."

"So you're not a social worker. You're a cop."

Alice stiffens and tucks a strand of hair behind her ear. With the tip of her bite-marked pen, she taps her teeth. "I'm very sorry," she says, "for what happened out at Ayer. For filling you up with false hope. I didn't know you'd had a previous run-in with Mrs. Sprague. Once you're on her bad side, it's no use. But I haven't forgotten you, Frieda. Far from it." Alice scoots her chair a foot closer, then another, so Frieda can smell her coffee-tinged breath. "Dear, tell me. How are you holding up?"

Maybe it's the tantalizing, sharp whiff of coffee — a small reminder, but all the more forceful for being so, that even her tiniest freedoms are curtailed. Or maybe it's the softheartedness of Alice's voice, how she takes Frieda's hand and gently cups it. Frieda's eyes fatten with hot tears. "Awful," she says. "Alice, it's so awful."

"Are they mistreating you? Is the food inadequate?" With her free hand, Alice digs through her attaché case and comes up with a pad of yellow paper. She lifts her pen as if to write a grievance. "Tell me," she demands. "What's the problem?"

Frieda wipes her eyes, and the room returns to focus: the hostile glare of steel and glass, the probes, the potions with their spooky, spiteful names. She could tell about the doctor and the things he shoves inside. The matron and her cornering. Barred windows. But all these things, it hits her, she can bear, has been bearing; these things every patient here must

161

bear. And *that's* what's so awful: that they take it, that they can, that it's so easy to lose the fighting edge. (She almost snitched on Flossie — next time, she might.) What's worse is seeing, here, that she might be like the rest — not special, as Papa told her, not singularly favored, but just another foolish girl who dreamed she deserved more and whose dreams, like her blunders, were routine. That she might be who Mama always said.

"It's not *them* so much," Frieda manages, "it's me. I feel so . . . I just feel so dumb."

"Dumb? You seem anything but that. You're going to have to tell me what you mean."

Frieda isn't certain how honest she can be. "Dumb for not knowing about all of the diseases. For thinking that I wouldn't end up here."

For believing that passion's not the problem but the cure. For still now believing so — still.

Alice grips her hand more tightly, so tight that it stings. "Frieda, you wouldn't be here if it weren't for someone else. You trusted someone? Someone who betrayed you."

Her own self: that's who she trusted, who betrayed her. Or is that what they're wanting her to think? She's losing track of the sound of her own thoughts. "The soldier," she says (and for an instant isn't sure which she means). "The one who did it. I didn't even know him."

"Tell me how it happened," Alice says.

The story lurches out: the train, the hissing toilet; the jitney and the hike into the woods. She's flimsy-feeling, rippable, it hurts to say the words, but Alice, with her stalwart grip, gives Frieda the strength to talk. The shack, Flynn's hard hands, what he did.

This is the outward crime, the blow she can explain. But the worst part she still keeps to herself: that Flynn, like Mama — like the world, it often seemed — told her she deserved it, she was nothing.

All her hurts fuse: Flynn's attack, Mama's scorn, the pain

of Slocum poking at her glands. And the ache of missing Felix (the only one who thought her worthy), of clutching still so tightly to that hope.

"Please understand," says Alice. "I have to ask this once. But then I'll never, ever ask again: Is everything you're telling me the truth?"

Frieda's tears have stopped now, but her eyes feel pulverized. Yes, she tells Alice. Everything.

"Thugs," says Alice. "*Thugs* is what they are. You don't know him? Could you at least identify him?"

Perhaps. But to see Flynn again? She blanches. "I just want to stop thinking about it."

"Oh, my dear. My sweet girl, I'm so sorry."

Alice pulls her into a hug — awkwardly, since they're sitting — and Frieda lets herself sink into it. When was she last held by strength so soft? For a full minute they cling together, joined in tandem breathing. She nuzzles into the smells of coffee, sweat.

When Alice pulls away, her eyes are red. "Earlier, when you called me a cop? How could you have known? But you put your thumb smack dab in the pudding. I never thought I'd . . . oh, it really gets me! What I want . . . what I'm trained for . . . is to help girls like you. It's just, I guess, how my heart is built. After Wellesley I moved into a settlement house — one of my professors was the founder — and chose to make social work my life. So I went to New York. Maude Miner, know that name?"

No, Frieda says. She's never been to New York.

"Waverly House. We rescued prostitutes. You could see the girls changing, lifting up. We helped girls to testify against the men who sold them, then cared for them and kept them safely hid. Then the war came, and they asked Maude to head the Committee on Protective Work for Girls. Our same work, but on a national scale, with the government's full backing. What a chance! So we went. And saved some girls."

A flush comes to her face, and she juts her chin, heroic. Her features have the smooth sheen of marble.

163

"But now it's clear the Army doesn't give a rap for girls. Protective? Is *this* protection, locking you in with barbed wire while the soldiers who infected you run free? Now they're even calling us the Law Enforcement Division. That's when Maude resigned, when they changed the name last month. It's sickening is what it is. Sickening!"

Alice has worked herself into what seems a near euphoria of outrage. Frieda finds the fervency contagious. The thrill of blame being cast, for once, away from her.

Outside the treatment room: the sounds of squabbling girls. Their yard work must be done; it must be lunchtime. Frieda doesn't want to end the meeting.

"Oh, dear, why am I spilling all this?" says Alice. "I shouldn't, it's the height of indiscretion. But I see you there"—auspiciously, she touches Frieda's shoulder—"and I can't go on pretending this is right. Believe me, I thought hard of leaving when Maude did. Even typed a resignation letter. But if we *all* left, who would look out for girls like you? So I'm trying to make some headway from within. Nothing grand, just local casework. It's better that way, right? That's how I'm here now. How we met."

How we met. Like they're friends. Like that's what they will be. Frieda feels herself begin to quaver.

"Poor thing," says Alice. "You're still so shaken up. Come here, let me hold you steady."

They hug again, a buttressing embrace.

When Frieda pulls away this time, she sees something she missed: bloodstains have blotted from her dress onto Alice's. "Oh, no! Oh, Alice, I'm so sorry."

When Alice follows the line of Frieda's pointing, she too startles.

"I'll pay!" Frieda blurts. "For a new one." Even as the words come out she hears their witlessness: in her palmiest days a dress like this would have cost beyond her budget, and now she hasn't got a red cent.

Alice stands and flaps the botched fabric. "Silly! You will not. It's just a dress."

"I'll give you mine," she says. "I've got a spare."

"And you'd stay in *that* frightful thing? No."

She's only being polite, Frieda thinks. She's scared of illness. And Frieda's indignity is doubled. I swear I'm not infectious anymore, she wants to say. I haven't spotted pus in two weeks.

"Besides, Frieda, think of it. I'm half a head taller. I couldn't very well expose my knees!" Alice playfully hoists her skirt to mid-thigh and executes a sassy fox trot.

Frieda's too stunned to smile. "You're not mad?"

"These days there's plenty that calls for madness, don't you think? Why waste my anger on a dress?"

"But how will you explain—"

"What? That I was holding a frightened girl? Frieda, don't you see? That's my job."

What they'll do, Alice says, is wash both of their dresses. There's a sink here and liquid soap: perfect. While the dresses dry, they'll keep each other charmed.

Is it a trap, Frieda wonders—trying to get her to undress? To prove how easily that she will? Mrs. Digges might knock on the door at any moment—*time is up, lunch is on the table* —and what if Frieda's standing here, unclothed?

But Alice, in a flash, has already stripped, and the sight of her, so earnest in her gauzy underthings, makes Frieda bury all her doubts. Alice's body boasts a slender, muscular austereness, her high pragmatic hips like fine woodwork. Her breasts, in their brassiere, are quite small.

"Don't just stand there," Alice says. "Let's start."

Frieda, too, steps out of her frock. It's nothing like disrobing for the doctor.

"Well, now," Alice says. "Won't this be fun?" She pours a jigger of soap into the sink. "Takes me back to college days, the dormitory."

"Really?" Frieda says. Her skin, where it's freed, goes all tingly. "I always guessed college girls were odd, but not *that* odd. Scrubbing bloody dresses just for fun?"

Alice lets out a burst of laughter. "Oh, that's good. Oh, you're really just too-too." She ribs Frieda with the angle of her elbow. "I guess I just meant two friends alone, and something secret. Wellesley girls are great hands for mischief." Her smirk, in its apparent strain at devilish suggestion, makes her look all the more guileless.

There's not really room enough for four arms in the basin, but they both dunk their hands at the same time. It's blameless, wet fun, thinks Frieda, like bobbing for apples — which gets her humming a song from last year. "You know it?" she asks. "About Eve and the apples?"

"Eve and apples? I can't imagine. Sing it."

"Me? I can scarcely hold a tune." It's a lie, but Frieda tells it hoping that Alice might implore her. She wants the feeling of having something someone wants.

"Please?" says Alice. "You certainly can't sing worse than I — the only girl in the history of Emmanuel Church to be barred from the choir by force."

"Promise not to make fun?" asks Frieda.

"Promise," Alice says. "Hope to die." She proffers an orb of suds to seal the oath.

Frieda takes the slippery warm foam and starts to croon: "'Eve wasn't modest till she ate that apple; that old apple is to blame. The minute that she ate it, she felt humiliated, and hid behind the apple tree till darkness came.'" As she sings, something unbuckles deep inside her. Her hips swivel, her feet whimsically tap.

Alice just adores the tune, she says, and begs to learn it, so Frieda teaches one line at a time. Alice didn't fib: her voice is woeful.

"Now can you understand why they kicked me out?" she says. "Even though my father is the rector?"

"Lucky they didn't kick *him* out," says Frieda.

When Alice finally thinks she has it down, they sing together, Alice droning, Frieda right on key.

> *Once they only wore a leaf—*
> *clothes are getting just as brief.*
> *If every mother's daughter wears dresses any shorter,*
> *we'll have to pass the apples again.*

In time to the melody, they scrub their dirty dresses with frolicsome strokes, in unison. Their knuckles knock, but it tickles, sending them into fits. Their merriment is sharp, invigorating.

The matron's voice, outside the door, sends Frieda to a corner, covering herself with dripping hands.

"Miss Longley? Are you through? Lunch is served."

Alice turns toward the door but doesn't open it. She stands as tall and placid as a statue. "Thank you, Mrs. Digges. We've some business yet to finish. We'll eat on our own, when the evaluation's done."

No, Frieda wants to say. We can't. No meals missed. It's one of Mrs. Digges's cardinal rules.

But the matron says, "Fine. Take all the time you need." And her footsteps fade down the hall.

Alice orders Frieda to join her at the sink. Together, laughing, they plunge in.

As the dresses dry, Alice quizzes Frieda about her home life. Why was she so desperate to escape?

Frieda tells of Papa's death — of the way that she was blamed — and all the other horrid things that followed: being forced to quit school and to sew her fingers raw, the prison Mama made of their apartment. Hirsch — the jowly loom of him, his bratty little sons; the thought of wasting all her life with them.

"Awful," Alice says, in exactly the same tone that Frieda used when talking of the Home. "Frieda, I'm . . . honestly, I'm appalled."

Frieda smears a drop of soapy water on the floor. "But even if she hadn't sold me off to Hirsch?" she says. "Even if it was still just me and her? I had to get out. I felt sick."

"Sick how?"

"In the head. Or, I don't know, the heart? Just for trying, for *wanting* to be happy. That's how Mama meant for me to feel."

Alice stares, squinting, turning by small degrees, as if checking a glass for her reflection. Her eyes look like tiny polished shadows.

"I know she's not evil," Frieda goes on. "Just unhappy. And I know she gave up a lot for me." Russia, she thinks. Leo, with his dashing gleam, his love. "But since she did, you'd think she'd maybe want me to be happy — to prove, you know, that everything was worth it? But it's almost like the only thing that makes her less unhappy is to know that I might be unhappy too."

"*She's* the sick one." Alice's words have a steely, tensile ring. "A mother who wishes sadness on her daughter? I know because — well, because I had a mother quite like that. One who thought it was up to her to choose what I should want. Who chose wrong and couldn't stand it when I said so."

Alice reaches out toward the shelf of medications — she seems to want to grab at something, smash it. But all she does is neaten up a row of Argyrol, turning all the bottles label-out.

"And that's why I do what I do," Alice says. "Don't you see? So girls will have someone on their side. Someone to help them make *themselves* happy." With her forefinger, she taps Frieda strongly on the knee. "What would make *you* happy, Frieda? What do you want to be?"

"To be? Like a salesclerk or a stenographer — like that?"

Alice nods. "Would you want to go back to school? Be a teacher?"

"A teacher? I don't think I could ever manage that."

"Of course you could, if you set your mind to it. You just taught me — tuneless me! — that song."

"Well, sure then. Or maybe a band leader!" Frieda laughs.

"But to be honest I — just anything, really. I hope that doesn't make me seem spineless." She looks at the bottles Alice ordered on the shelf, one after the next, all in line. "I know this will probably sound silly. But what I want is . . . is when people see me, for them to think, *Wow*. Not 'There goes a shopgirl' or 'a girl from the West End' or 'There goes a' fill in the blank. Not 'a' something. Just something. Really something."

When finally it's time to go (their clothes damp but wearable), they help each other pull on the dresses. Alice drops her pen and pad into her case and shuts it. She straightens her dress and says, "Then we're set?"

"But what about . . . isn't there some kind of evaluation?"

"Frieda, what do you think we've been doing?" Alice smiles, then flips open her case's latch again and takes out a multigraphed form.

Clinically oversexed has a blank square beside it.

Feeble-minded.

Defectively delinquent.

Estimated equivalent mental age.

In swift, decisive script, Alice writes Frieda's name, but she skips all the boxes, leaves them blank. At the bottom she writes, "Patient's mental capacity appears normal." "There," she says. "Now don't let's keep worrying about all that."

Sixteen

---★---

*N*ow frieda has something to look forward to
— and not just the bleary dream of getting out, to
Felix, but something clearer, closer: Alice's return. Alice, who
might make that dream real. If you want to sail away, thinks
Frieda, you can't just pray for breeze; first you have to find
yourself a boat.

She almost wonders if she made the whole thing up — Alice's fond candor, her forgiveness. She asks Flossie (who
loathed Alice initially, back in Ayer) how her evaluation went;
this time, was Alice any different? "Yeah," Flossie admits. "She's
all right. Even promised to get me some new shoes 'cause mine
are shot."

Sure, Frieda thinks, but did she fox-trot before you? Did she
offer you a warm orb of foam? Whenever Frieda dons the frock
that Alice helped her wash (the worst of the blood is gone, but
a faint stain persists), she brims with a sweet secret pride. Is
Alice — wherever she is, at the brig in Ayer, in Boston — wearing her own dress, with matching stain?

Frieda asks the matron when "Miss Longley" will be back, trying not to sound overeager. When the day comes at last (there's a new government study, and Alice is due to interview some girls), Frieda tries to plot out what she'll say. She won't tell Alice about Felix — not yet, not given Alice's fury at the soldiers. But Flynn — Flynn's a soldier they can both agree to hate. Flynn might be (how strange!) her best hope. I've been thinking, she might say, maybe I *could* identify him. Stop him before he hurts another girl. If I saw him again, yes, I'm sure I could.

Would Alice then arrange a special furlough to Camp Devens? A visit to the place where Felix waits?

Alice arrives after lunch and immediately goes to work before Frieda has the chance to see her; she's cloistered in the treatment room for hours. Angelina, Hattie, and Jo go in and out — and upon leaving, each girl holds a token Alice gave her: lavender soap, a length of grosgrain ribbon. Why isn't Frieda on the list? Is she too sick for the study? Not sick enough? Maybe she should fabricate some crisis to get in. As if just being here's not bad enough!

Finally, at six o'clock, Alice emerges. The word spreads: she's joining them for supper. Frieda importantly saves a place beside herself (for a week, she and Flossie have been sanctioned to eat anywhere, the doctor having deemed them noncontagious), but Alice sits at Mrs. Digges's table — the two of them, alone, with no patients. Intently, the women tuck in.

Frieda is despairing. She *did* make it up; Alice's seeming kinship was a fluke. (And why do I insist, she thinks, on pinning all my hopes on anyone who treats me better than Mama?) Then Alice, in a moment of the matron's avid chewing, looks around, finds Frieda's gaze, and rolls her eyes, as if to say *Rescue me, please!*

Frieda feels a wash of cool relief. You and me both, she thinks, and she sends a knowing grin. Alice's grin back looks like a promise.

. . .

Mrs. Digges announces a surprise after supper: Alice has brought a film, just for them.

A movie! In the flush of it, in the bustle of preparations, Frieda sets aside her need to ask for Alice's help. What could help her mood more than a movie?

There have been previous evening programs. Two weeks ago, a Salvation Army band performed (anemic marches and a final, shrill waltz) while a man called Pastor Paul gave out a pamphlet: "V.D. — U-boat No. 13!" Then came a Miss Fisk from the Watch and Ward Society; in a series of muzzy stereo-motorgraph slides, she depicted her topic: "How Life Begins." ("If it was *that* boring," Flossie stage-whispered in the darkness, "life would *end*. There'd never be another baby.") But a movie! Right here! Starring Fairbanks? Maybe Chaplin? Alice knew just what they've been missing.

All the girls help to get things ready. The dining room is made into a provisional theater: tables cleared, a sheet hung on the wall, a projector wrangled into place. (Burnham, they learn, picked it up this afternoon, on his way to get Alice at the station; the machine sparkles like money, newly minted.) The dinner crew is drafted to cook pots of popcorn, and the odor — nutty, with luring hints of burn — sensually fattens through the room.

When everything is set, the girls cram onto benches. Alice stands waiting for the crowd to settle down, but the patients chatter as if at a premiere. Has Flossie perked her cheeks with homemade rouge? Even Yetta looks zippy, animated. Hattie presides over the backmost row, like a balcony where she might hide misbehavior.

Frieda slips onto a bench near the middle, next to Jo, who stares down, elbows on her knees — the only girl who doesn't seem excited. Ever since the fox attack, Jo's been almost shell-shocked — flinching at the smallest sounds, at silence — and Frieda wants to help her back to normal. Also, though, she wants to hear what happened today with Alice. *What did Alice want? What did she pledge?* Jo's the girl whom Frieda can

172

ask without feeling awkward, Jo with her own awkwardness so blatant. (Does Frieda hope that Alice protects everyone equally or hope to learn that Alice likes *her* best?)

Frieda pats Jo's knee and is set to ask her questions when the matron demands immediate silence.

"Girls, enough," she says. "Give Miss Longley your attention. Girls!" She claps her hands twice.

"Thank you, but it's quite all right," says Alice. "The quickest way to quiet is through quiet." She offers this observation at a confidential volume, and, sure enough, the room falls to a hush; the girls cock their ears for something missed. "There. That's more like it," Alice tells them.

Her dress's high collar, Frieda thinks, seems too snug. It looks as though the lacing might soon burst. Alice has a body that repudiates containment — that's why Frieda knows she can trust her. That's why Frieda's sure she'll lend a hand.

"I know you're all itching to see this picture," Alice says. "And with good reason — it's been made just for you. The name of it is *The End of the Road*. Girls in your position all across the whole country will be watching it in the coming weeks and months, the hope being —"

"Our position?" mimics Yetta, eyes narrowed. "Locked up with no rights? Not even hearings?"

"Yetta!" says Mrs. Digges, and warns her to mind herself, or this privilege will be rescinded for them all.

"Hear that?" Melba seconds. "Shut your trap."

Further calls are made to "quit your yapping." Yetta shoots them icy glares but quiets.

Alice uncrosses her arms and gathers breath with what appears to be incipient acrimony, but when she speaks she sounds curiously chastened. "As I was saying, our hope — the government's hope — is that you girls might find this motion picture useful. A lesson to help you, once this all has passed." She dips her head in a dutiful sort of nod, and then, before Yetta or anyone else can speak, signals for the lights to be dimmed. She retreats to the back of the room.

With the urgent *fup-fup-fup* of a mallard taking wing, the projector reel spins into action. Light, like something breathing, ebbs and swells. "Two Roads There Are in Life," the first frame reads. "One reaches upward toward the Land of Perfect Love. The other reaches down into the Dark Valley of Despair where the sun never shines."

The heat of bodies pressed up tight in lulling, comfy shadows. Popcorn's salted, smooth, addictive tang. Frieda can almost think that she's sitting in the Bijou, watching the new Anita King adventure.

The film follows two girls, Mary Lee and Vera Wagner, who flee home for the twinkle of New York. Mary's fair, Vera swarthy; they're seventeen.

"So young!" Flossie says. "Wike widdle Fwieda."

The girls twitter, until a *shh* from Mrs. Digges.

In the city, resolved to do her part to win the war, Mary enrolls in nursing school. Vera finds work in a sleek department store, where men ogle her across the glass-topped counter.

The depiction of the store, Frieda thinks, is quite good: wares arranged dynamically, as they always were at Jordan's, and a floorwalker resembling Mr. Crowley — the same mousy, slightly wet mustache. Suddenly, stabbingly, she longs for her old life — even for Mr. Crowley, even him! (If Frieda had the chance again, she'd never disregard him; she'd show him due respect for all his rules.) And Lou. She's so lost without Lou. When she and Lou would catch matinees on their day off, it thrilled her to sit beside her pal in silent union and to know precisely what Lou felt and thought. After, they'd confirm their identical reactions. ("And that part —?" "When she grabbed the steering wheel —" "Fantastic!") What shows does Lou watch these days, and with whom? Does she ever wonder where Frieda's gone?

The projector tuts scoldingly as the first reel runs out. Frieda turns and watches Alice change it. Surely Alice didn't mean to stir such painful thoughts. Or did she? — to inspire Frieda, to remind her what awaits, if only she can get out of this place. (The very day she's freed from this prison, Frieda vows, she'll treat herself to the newest picture show. With Lou — or no, with Felix! Beside him in the dark. She's never even seen a movie with him!) Alice sees Frieda watching, and she pauses to gaze back. There's her private grin again: her promise.

In the second reel, Vera meets a cad and carries on, staying out all night, playing loose; Mary, in the meantime, keeps at bay *her* beau, an AEF soldier bound for France. Though the soldier begs for a memory that he "can never lose," Mary demurs and sends him packing. "I know how hard it is to think of consequences," she says. "Unless we do, we shan't find happiness at the end of the road."

"We *shan't*," comes a broad, mocking voice from the back row, and a salvo of popcorn flies forward. "We *shan't* find happiness with scoundrels!" Two kernels hit the sheet on which the film is cast, and everything is suddenly in ripples: Mary and Vera viewed through troubled waters.

The matron says, "Hattie! Put the kibosh on it. This instant!"

One more floaty white grenade is lobbed, followed by a smattering of snickers.

Frieda doesn't join in all the horseplay. She's rattled, off-balance, pondering the roles: it's obvious that she's supposed to think herself like Vera, but Felix isn't anything like Vera's heedless cad, even less like Mary's nagging soldier (better than both, handsomer, more true). How, then, will her future be: like Vera's? like Mary's? like something else entirely her own?

Mary becomes a nurse and assists a famous surgeon, Dr. Bell, as he operates on patients: women with disease-ruined wombs. "This is the operation," the film explains, "which every year, hundreds of thousands of women must undergo because of some man's criminal folly."

Vera, in the next scene, has contracted syphilis and slinks to a dispensary for treatment, her face a contortion of dishonor.

Close-up photos flash upon the screen: a lesion leaking pus; a twisted arm; discolored skin; a woman with her nose flesh eroded.

Frieda pictures the dump heap in the alley next to Slotnik's: carrion gone to gray, then maggot-pale. Lately, her own body has seemed practically fine — the syphilitic chancre shrunken to a pip, no more sense of never-ending leak — but now she feels a momentary relapse, all her flesh putrid, full of burn.

Gasps fill the room, a bedlam of revulsion. Jo holds her stomach with one hand, her mouth the other, and Frieda hears the labor of her gulping. "Okay?" asks Frieda. Jo stares weakly.

Leaving private practice, Dr. Bell sets off for France — accompanied by Mary, his best nurse. They brave shells and shrapnel, they bandage soldiers' wounds. Soberly, they trade their wedding vows: Mary is now Mrs. Richard Bell.

A hiss, a click, and then the screen goes blank. The film spins wildly on one reel. It sounds as though a child is being spanked.

"Lights," says Mrs. Digges. "The lights."

A flip is switched. The room burns with a stark, reproachful glare.

The projector stands abandoned. Where is Alice? Did she leave to miss the film's grotesque end?

"Somebody," says the matron, "shut that off."

Warily, Flossie sidles up to the machine. She studies it, fiddles with one knob and then another. At last she turns the right one. All goes silent.

Mrs. Digges hurries to the front of the dining room. "As you can see, Miss Longley must . . . must have stepped out for a moment. Perhaps she had to visit the facilities." She shifts from foot to foot, clears her throat.

How will she find words, Frieda thinks, for all those photos?

Next to Frieda, Jo looks as pale as dead skin. The pressure of held breaths is stifling.

"Well, shall we discuss the film without her?" says the matron. "I'm sure you were all as . . . engaged by it as I was." Her voice bucks, but she reins it in, goes on. "The lesson," she says flatly. "The lesson, as I see it, is that every action has its consequence. Did the end come as a surprise? Of *course* not. Each girl got her just deserts."

Frieda studies the matron, trying to gauge her true feelings — she who insists on happy endings. Is that what this ending was meant to be? Happy? Frieda tries to imagine Dr. Slocum — or Miller — asking for her hand as he probes. *Wider, please, and will you be my wife?*

". . . is what separates the child," the matron is saying, "from the adult. We've all seen a bleeding toddler fight the doctor's needle, even though the stitches might well save him. That's *instinct*. It fights against pain. But the adult has *intellect* to overcome his instincts; he knows the pain will help him, so he bears it. Or to think of it another way: Intellect is riding instinct's horse. If the rider can't control it, the animal is a danger — not just to herself, to everyone. With sex-crazed girls, like Vera, that's the problem. They fail to restrain their appetites."

"Why not *men*? Why not *their* appetites?" It's Yetta, in her terrier-tough voice.

Mrs. Digges takes a step back. "Well, you see, we're not . . . just now, we're not talking about men. After all, this is a room full of—"

"But we *never* talk of men. We never do. It's always 'sex-crazed girls,' evil whores. How many whores would there be without the *men* who hired them?"

"Yetta. So smart! Should know better." The matron speaks in niggardly, clipped fragments, her bosom a jut of sanctimony. "Men are . . . they have *needs* we don't. It's instinct."

"Oh, that's right: 'Instinct is a horse . . .' So men just get to gallop all around? Girls are being jailed left and right for no good reason, but soldiers — is a single one detained? It's like mopping a flooded room, and mopping it and mopping, and never thinking to shut the faucet off."

Yes, thinks Frieda, *yes*, and she turns to look for Alice — Alice, who argued the same case. She's still not to be found at her post by the projector, but Frieda well imagines her return: how she'll burst into the room, her voice surging in alliance. (*"Thugs* is what they are! It's sickening!"*)

"What we *all* need's the same," Yetta says. "A living wage. A girl can earn five times as much by picking up men as by slaving in some wretched factory. Tell me why the *girl's* the one to blame."

"What I'll tell you," the matron says. "What I'll tell you is, you're making no sense, Yetta. You're mixing up — just mixing it all up. Men have," and she falters, holding her sides, as though against a flare of indigestion. "Men have certain organs. Organs that need . . . exercise, like muscles."

"Please! What a stinking heap of shit!"

The sound of sudden breaths suggests that something has been punctured. No one speaks to Mrs. Digges this way! Beside her, Frieda feels Jo cowering.

Mrs. Digges demands, "What did you say?"

Yetta sits tall, a shrewish angle to her shoulders. "I said," she starts, then seems to reconsider. Or maybe she's just marshaling her anger.

Again, Frieda wonders: *Where's Alice?* No one else but Alice has the starch to bolster Yetta — not Hattie, who sits docile, her blue-black skin gone ashen; not censured Flossie; not herself. Impatiently, she cranes her neck to peer behind the crowd, and there, like an answered prayer, stands Alice: in the doorway, twisting pale and flighty hands. She sends Alice a grin of confederacy — *their* grin — but if Alice receives the message, she doesn't show it. Stony-faced, she crosses silently to the projector and busies herself packing up the reels.

"I'm waiting," says the matron. "Did I hear you incorrectly? Yetta? Have you anything to say?"

Yetta blinks. She tips her chin back.

"No. I didn't think I was mistaken." Mrs. Digges speaks surely now, her confidence regained, standing on the firm ground of scolding. "In that case, I don't want to see your nasty face. Go up to your room and don't you leave!"

Alice, at the back, seems painfully quiet, her face cast down in effortful disinterest.

Defeated, shaking, Yetta stands and scuffs away.

"Wait," calls Frieda, blazing to her feet. She wants to follow Yetta, pull her back.

"Will *you* make trouble, too?" asks the matron.

"No, but," Frieda says, and scans the patients for support. Flossie stares straight down. So does Jo.

Mrs. Digges threatens, "Want to join her?"

At last, Frieda finds a kindly presence: Alice, who is vehemently shaking her head no, making gestures of containment with her hands.

From the hall, Yetta's footsteps peter out.

"No, ma'am," Frieda murmurs. She sits down.

"Thank God for small favors," says the matron. She turns with a conniving pout toward Alice. "Apologies on the girls' behalf for this bother, Miss Longley. The film struck too close to home, I think."

"No, please," Alice says, "*I'm* sorry. I didn't mean to take so long in the bathroom."

"In your absence, I tried to get them talking about the picture. But maybe you'd like to add your own thoughts?"

Alice's posture seems an arrangement of concerted decorum, her hands by her sides, her shoulders squared. "I'm afraid that I missed," she says, "most of your discussion. But you did, I think, compare a man's . . . his intimate equipment with muscles in need of exercise?"

Mrs. Digges gives a grandiose nod.

"It's not an apt analogy," says Alice.

And the matron's head freezes in mid-assent.

"If *those* organs were like muscles," Alice says, smirking, "then the miserable twelve-year-old boy who flogs them daily would be the greatest Don Juan on the planet. Girls, do you know any boys like that?"

This last line Alice hams up with a comic mug, and the patients come gibbering back to life.

"A better comparison," she goes on, "is the tear glands. Even if a man hasn't shed a tear in ages, he can always, when the need arises, cry. It's the same with . . . with those other, lower glands."

The phrase sparks a laugh that inflames the whole room. Flossie grunts, jiggles her fist obscenely.

"Necessity," Alice concludes, "is a myth!"

The girls, amid their mirth, trade apprehensive looks. Expectantly, all turn to Mrs. Digges.

"Well, I don't know such a lot about the science," says the matron. "I'm not so up-and-doing as you professional ladies." Her face rucks up with constipated pride. "All that I can say about men is what I learned by myself, in my years of being married."

She pronounces *married* showily, a verbal trump card. Does she cut a glance at Alice's ringless fingers?

The air constricts with awkward, standoff silence.

Faintly, through the ceiling: Yetta's stomping.

"The film," says Alice weakly, "isn't really about restraint. It's about girls — girls making their own futures. You, too. You can choose your own road."

But not a single patient meets her eye.

"Now, girls," says the matron, as though Alice has just vanished, "we need to move the tables back to normal. And the floor is all popcorn — just appalling. I want this room clean, and in a jiff!"

A dozen girls get down on their knees.

"You just stood there! Why didn't you say something?"

"I'm sorry, Frieda. Keep your voice down."

"Sorry? What will 'sorry' do for Yetta?" Or for *me*, Frieda thinks, losing faith in her scheme: using Alice to get to Camp Devens.

Fierily they face off in the Home's moonlit yard, where

Frieda has caught up to Alice. Frieda's agile fib — "Miss Longley dropped her pen" — convinced Mrs. Digges to let her follow.

Before them, Donald Rattigan, the loutish night watchman, grapples with the hefty film projector, heaving it into the back of the Home's Ton Truck. The accident-salvaged Ford has been parked in the yard for weeks. Frieda thought its engine was kaput, but it worked fine this afternoon, apparently, for Burnham; now Rattigan's counting on its use.

Frieda toes a divot in the driveway's hard mud. A fug of burnt horseflesh sours the air. "Don't you understand," she says, "how bad she might be punished? But no, you let the matron have her way."

Stepping closer, Alice grits her teeth. "Honestly, now, *think*. Don't be dim. Ever since Maude resigned, they're keeping closer watch. I've got to learn to pick my battles wisely."

"Oh, so saving Yetta isn't wise?"

A low groan from Rattigan steals their attention, and they turn to see him struggling, bent-kneed. The projector slips three inches; he regrips. "I'm fine," he says. "I've got it. Little bastard."

Alice, in the washy light, looks distant, obscured. "Yetta," she says, "is difficult. She's coarse. Nobody is ever going to like her."

"No, she's just —"

"You're different, Frieda. You'll rise above the rest. You're the one who has a better chance."

Hazy with a sudden mix of flattery and outrage, Frieda wonders why Alice would tell her such a thing. What could Alice ever gain by flattering a girl like her? She has to seek to gain *something*, right? But no, Frieda thinks (she wants so badly to be stroked), perhaps it's her own doubt that should be doubted. Alice wants what's best for all the girls.

Softly, Frieda asks, "A better chance?"

"Listen" — Alice leans in, checks that Rattigan's out of earshot — "has Mrs. Digges talked about the Fourth?"

Frieda shakes her head. "The fourth what?"

"*July* Fourth, at the end of this week. A delegation's coming to see the troops at Camp Devens. Senator Weeks, up from Washington. And from Boston, Mr. Storrow, the head of the Committee on Public Safety. A few assorted other dignitaries. They're stopping here first, on their way. To see how their money's being spent."

Frieda bristles. "Will Mrs. Sprague be there?"

"Don't worry about her. She's the lowest on the pole. These *men* are the big guns. Here's your chance."

"For what? What would I ever say to them?"

"Your story. How you were treated by one of their 'brave boys.' How *he* should be the one detained, not you."

"A senator? I can't talk to those people."

"Can, too — all that anger I heard just now, but aimed at *them*."

Alice puts both hands on Frieda's shoulders, leans in close. Frieda smells her warm, bewitching breath. She tries to imagine her anger shooting forth; for so long, it's been a mine submerged.

"Frieda, *you* can tell them," Alice says, "what *I* can't. That you're locked up for a germ, not a crime. That they're taking away the freedom of our own girls, like you, in the name of bringing freedom to the Belgians. Ask how that makes any kind of sense!"

"Excuse me, ma'am," calls Rattigan. "You ready?" He poses with one foot on the Ton Truck's running board. "Don't get going now, you'll miss your train."

"Yes," says Alice. "Yes, I'm coming. Thank you." Then to Frieda, in a rousing voice: "You *can*. I'll see you in a few days. On the Fourth." She climbs into the truck and shuts the door.

Rattigan's third try at the starter fires the engine. In a dusty cloud, the Ton Truck jerks away. Its rumble stirs a wave in Frieda's gut, a surge of power (like swerving in the Morses' Gunboat Speedster), but soon the noise dissipates and dies.

Seventeen

*A*T DAWN ON THE DAY before the dignitaries' visit, Frieda wakes with a fusillade of blisters behind her knees, blisters at her wrists, on her shins. Her body feels like one enormous welt.

Immediately she thinks of how she burned during the movie, when she saw all those horrifying photos. She dismissed that sting as a flare-up of emotion, but what if it truly heralded a relapse? It can't be that, no! All the swabbings, the tampons — she's done exactly what the doctor ordered.

The day before yesterday — the first of July — she allowed herself the private celebration of a milestone, a pre-anniversary of sorts: a month more, she told herself; a month, you can make it. Dr. Slocum had said August — hadn't he? If she tells him now of this setback, he'll surely keep her longer. She won't tell him, she can't. But the itch!

How can she face a senator when she's drowning in this rash? How can she possibly do what Alice wants? Desperate

— hobbling, holding her arms aloft — she gets herself down-stairs, to the matron.

Mrs. Digges, at this hour, seems milder, softer-shelled. When she answers Frieda's knock she is tucked in bed reading, giggling over *Mischievous Maid Faynie*. She invites Frieda to lie down beside her on the bed, pets and pets her hair until she calms. "My dear," she says, "you've got poison ivy."

"Poison!" Did she swallow the wrong pill, too *many* pills? Did she catch something from one of the other patients?

The matron laughs. "You're such a city girl!"

She leads Frieda outside in the grainy morning air — both of them barefoot, like children — to some oily-leafed shrubs along the fence. "See? You must have rubbed them during yard work."

Back inside, Mrs. Digges formulates a salve, a mixture of kitchen soap and soda. Frieda should apply it five times a day, she says. It's nothing much to worry about. It's nothing.

That afternoon, the Home is in a tizzy. In the shop, bolts of bunting — red, white, and blue — are stitched into pleated semi-circles. Every surface in the dining room is bleached. Outside, Angelina weeds the knee-high corn, while Hattie whitewashes the porch railing. Even a sullen Burnham is conscripted to the cause, waxing the Ton Truck's dented hull. The Ford, since its recent trip, has lapsed to relic status and sits like statuary in the yard.

The matron saved the worst for Jo and Frieda: mucking out the fetid chicken coop. ("Who better than our resident bird lovers?") Jo, Frieda senses, wouldn't want a different assign-ment, but still, the task feels like comeuppance. The matron's mildness rarely lasts past noon.

The day has grown hot, the hottest of the year. Within the coop, the swelter's twice as bad. Old blood and rancid yolks reek. The birds cluck and gather into small, balky clusters, glaring with what looks like prissy outrage.

"God," Frieda says, scraping goo with a putty knife and flinging it into her tin bucket. "How can they even stand to live in here?"

"It's what they know," Jo says. "Home sweet home." She nudges a hen gently from its nest and adds fresh straw. The hen, pecked by rivals, shows bare skin on its back; a bent feather drags through sludgy droppings. "Isn't that right, sweetie? Home sweet home?" She hums to the hen, tickles its pink comb.

Jo, for the first time since the fox attack, seems calm. Last night, Rattigan spied a creature by the fence, shot at it, and claimed a solid hit; Jo visibly loosened with the news. Her face appears healthier now, too: cheeks flushed, hollows partly filled. It's been a week since she has gotten sick.

Frieda wishes that she could match Jo's apparent peace. But the heat fouls her mood. The reek, this awful job. And the constant hounding sting of poison ivy. The itching and the burning bother her less now, but the soda salve makes her fingers ache. When she bends, there's a nagging pressure all along her skin, a sense that something crucial might be torn.

Or maybe what really nags is the pressure of tomorrow, the dread she has of disappointing Alice. Dread of not saying the right thing. (Dread and, when she lets herself perceive it, some resentment: that her future might depend on currying Alice's favor, that everything might ride on her performance.)

At first, after their talk, Frieda swelled with hopes. She imagined herself upbraiding the heartless functionaries ("How dare you say *our* freedom doesn't count?"), imagined how her throat would flex with fury. And Alice's face, watching — her pride, her confirmation as she resolved to get Frieda out soon. Frieda even allowed herself to concoct a courtroom scene in which she named Flynn and saw him hauled away.

But Yetta soon deflated her ambitions. The next day was Sunday, and the pastor came for church. Frieda, as always, was exempted from the service; when all the other patients were stuck saying prayers, she padded upstairs to Yetta's room. (Yetta was still confined: matron's orders.) Frieda brought a

Saturday Evening Post to hearten Yetta, and half a sweet roll saved from breakfast.

When Yetta opened the door she looked sleepless, her hair unsprung. But she brightened. "*Oy, vee shayn!* What a beautiful girl you are. To think of me and bring me all these goodies. Won't Mrs. Digges have your skin for this?"

"She's in church. They all are. It's just us."

Yetta chuckled. "You know us Yids — always conspiring." She bit a hunk of roll, chewed it down. "And what of your little Ladies' Aid pal?"

"Who do you mean?" Frieda asked. "Miss Longley?"

"Yeah, her. She and her helping hands still here?"

"No, she left last night. I don't see why you have to sound so nasty."

"Course you don't." Yetta swiped crumbs from her chin. "Why *would* you, when she treats you sweet and nice? It wasn't *you* she left there — just left to be shot down."

Frieda, recalling Alice's defense, offers her own version: "It's easy to be angry at her, sure. I was too. But *she's* not where we need to aim our anger. It's all the *men* who set the rules for her."

Yetta raised her fist like a grenade. "Believe me, I've got anger to go around. I can aim at her and still have plenty left."

Frieda could have explained about Alice's tight bind, her need to be *cautiously* subversive, but she shouldn't betray Alice's trust. Shouldn't and didn't want to, for she liked their special bond, liked being Alice's secret ally. "Can't you see she's on our side?" she said to Yetta vaguely. "Actually, she's risked a lot for us."

"Risked? Come on, Frieda. These mink brigade ladies're all the same. They flit around, yapping about 'bettering' us poor souls and how much they've 'given up' for us. What they don't see is how much they've still got! Talk about 'man control' or a 'single moral standard' and, sure, then they're right by your side. But talk about *money* — about real revolution — and oops!, not so friendly anymore." With both hands, Yetta grasped at

186

the empty space between them. "You really think Miss Long-ley, or any of those ladies, would fight to change the world so the wealth gets spread around? No! They want to keep things exactly just like now, with them feeling good for giving tiny bits of help and us never earning enough to stop having to take it."

From downstairs they heard the other girls joined in song, the hymn that always signaled church's end ("'. . . Praise Him, all creatures here below . . .'") and, loudest, the matron's devout soprano.

Frieda hurried back to her room, stung by Yetta's words — by the nascent hunch that they might hold some truth. What had Alice offered her so far but praise and comfort? What did praise and comfort *cost* Alice? But they were more than any-one else was giving Frieda now; she clung to the notion that Alice understood her: the singular true Frieda who might soar. To soar, though, wouldn't she need more than understanding? What exactly should she ask of Alice?

All of her intentions, which had seemed so clear, went muddy. Trying again to imagine herself accosting Senator Weeks, she faltered: she could hear Alice's voice, but not her own. And so, as the Fourth approached, Frieda grew more miffed: at Alice, for expecting her to defy the politicians; at the politicians, for coming in the first place; at herself, for not knowing what to do.

"It's crazy — so much fuss," she complains now to Jo, breath-ing through her mouth against the smell. She knifes loose an eggy gnarl of straw. "Just because the Great Man is com-ing." Gingerly, crouching, she waddles two feet forward, us-ing her tin bucket as a crutch. Not gingerly enough: the poi-son ivy chafes. The rash makes all this prettifying irk her even more — just when her own body falls to pieces! But maybe the poison ivy will give her an excuse to lie low when the senator arrives. Alice couldn't fault her for that, could she? "All this sweat and toil," she says, and jabs her knife again. "Like the bigwigs are gonna crawl around in here!"

Jo, scratching her scalp (her hair has grown back and looks

now like a doughboy's bristly cut), says, "The coop needed cleaning anyway."

"All right, fine. But whitewashing the porch?"

"Maybe Mrs. Digges was ordered to."

"No, she really *wants* to. You can tell." Frieda mops her steaming, sweaty brow. "It's like she's getting dolled up for a date. Like the senator is next on her dance card."

Jo, bending to scrape away some muck, doesn't answer. Her eyes hold something distant and dyspeptic, which Frieda takes as silent validation.

"But maybe we can earn some points with Mrs. Digges, you know? Style her hair, so the senator's impressed?" Only as she blasts the matron more for all her fawning does Frieda start to sense her anger's root: it's her *own* likely fawning she objects to. She sits back on her haunches. Blisters pop. "Or a headdress," she continues, and scoops a clump of fluff (bits of feather glued by old egg). "A feather headdress to wear for the Great Man!"

Jo bends over, chortling, her hands pressed to her gut — the first time, Frieda thinks, she's seen her laugh.

"Makeup!" she continues, milking Jo's reaction. She gathers up a blob of chalky dung on her knife's edge and threatens to smear it on her cheek. "Wouldn't *this* make her face nice and pale?"

Jo's still doubled over — is the joke *that* funny, really? — and Frieda reaches gaily for her shoulder. At once she understands her mistake. Jo's not laughing, she's retching. Brown heaves.

"Jo!" she says, and grips her shoulder tighter.

The smell now: sour and obscene.

Again Jo heaves. Her eyes are walled, too much of the whites showing. All that comes is air, a string of spit.

"Honey," Frieda asks, "are you all right?"

Jo's face is wrung with discomfort.

Frieda says, "It's awful in here. Anyone would be sick." She herself is close to throwing up. The stench of Jo's vomit and its look: a fecal froth. The heat, like a steady crushing hand.

"Damn," Jo says, and slumps, as though boneless, to the floor. "Damn?" More a question than a curse.

"It's okay," says Frieda. "You're okay."

"No." Jo stares at the vomit.

"I'll clean it. We're cleaning anyway, right?"

But Jo lashes out with jabbing elbows. "No! No, you don't understand."

"What? What don't I understand?"

"I thought—" Jo's voice comes out cracked. "I thought I was finished being sick. Three months. I was sure that part was over."

"Three months?"

Jo's head tips down. "I'm pregnant."

Why did it never cross Frieda's mind? This waif, this tiny scrap of a girl, pregnant? She'd sooner have believed Mrs. Digges with child. "Do you know?" she asks. "Do you know . . . well, whose?"

Jo doubles over again, her jaw widened, waiting. She gags, but nothing rises. She sits back.

Of course she doesn't know, Frieda thinks. It could be anyone's! White-slave girls rarely even *see* the men who rape them. They're blindfolded, tied to brothel beds. (Frieda learned the details from *Traffic in Souls*, a movie she and Lou saw at the Bijou.) "But no," she says, "*that's* not most important, that's not it. What I meant to ask was . . ." She isn't sure what: If Jo thinks she'll always bear a grudge against the baby? If Jo thinks that every mother must?

"Not important. Ha." Jo's eyes turn cold with shine.

"*You* know what I mean. The thing is that it's . . . just that it's here."

The skin around Jo's eyes shows tiny hairline creases, which look jarring on her smooth baby face. They tauten now like threads being jerked. "I'm pretty sure," she says, "it's my husband's."

"Husband! But, Jo, I thought—" Do white slaves have husbands? "Jo, I didn't think—are you married?"

Jo wipes some vomit from her lip. She barely nods.

Frieda stiffens, utterly bewildered. If Jo is married, why would she be *here* — and why so wretched? (If Felix were Frieda's husband, *he'd* never let her sit and rot.) "Does anybody know?" she asks. "The doctor? Mrs. Digges?"

"No," Jo says. "The doctor? You know the way he is. Always half-drunk, barely checks. We make him sick."

"They don't know about the baby *or* the husband?"

Jo shrugs. "I guess I didn't tell the whole truth when I was caught."

Frieda starts to give shape to her shock at Jo's dissemblance when it strikes her that her own lies weren't so different.

They sit there in the silence, in the stink.

The chickens, at first scared away by the human noise, near again with hesitant high steps. The plumpest one pecks curiously at the vomit.

Frieda says, "I don't quite understand. What's the problem? I mean, aren't you happy? If you're married?"

Jo picks up the chicken and cradles it in her lap. "That's what everyone thinks. What I thought." She rubs the hen's beak, keeps rubbing until it's lulled. She, too, looks hypnotized, gone. "At first I was happy. Never *been* so happy. Just the way he looked at me, you know? Or touched my wrist."

Once Jo begins, her story freely tumbles. She tells of how she met him — Walter is his name — one day as she sat by herself watching a movie; how he claimed the seat next to her and took her hand in his, just as though they'd always been best friends. The next day they met again at the same movie theater, and he bought tickets to see the same show, but they didn't watch a minute of the film.

A month was only bliss: more movies, sunset strolls, liaisons in his various buddies' rooms. Walter was twenty-six, and everyone seemed to like him — that was all Jo knew, all she needed. The problem was her parents; when she asked to bring him home, they told her if she did she'd be disowned.

"Why?" Frieda asks. "What was wrong?"

"Walter was — well, he *is*. You see, my parents are quite religious." Jo strokes the hen, which makes a low, baffled cluck. She looks in Frieda's eyes, looks away. "The problem was that Walter is Jewish. They said they'd never speak to me again."

Perfect, Walter told her: now they could elope. He convinced Jo to come with him right away to Newport, where his family owned an old summer mansion. They'd have it to themselves, since it was March. A honeymoon, he said, by the sea. They were married by a justice of the peace.

"What did he do for work?" Frieda asks.

"Not anything, really, which should have been my warning. But I thought he was — well, you know. A mansion in Newport? I thought he could afford to do nothing."

Immediately in Rhode Island, everything seemed strange. The house was cold and dark, but he wouldn't turn on the lights; he kept all the window shades drawn. The neighbors were busybodies, Walter claimed. But there *were* no neighbors. The summer homes were vacant.

Then he brought a friend over, a fellow who smelled of coal. And Walter forced Jo to have relations with the man. Said he'd shoot her if she didn't, showed the gun. The next night, another friend. And the night after that. He was charging each one of them a dollar.

"Oh my God," says Frieda. "How *could* he? How could anyone?"

"Usually just one 'friend,'" Jo says in a threadbare voice. "Sometimes two or three in one night. It wasn't his house at all, just a place he'd broken into. He did it every year when the owners went away. That's how all the men knew where to find him."

"But you were *married*."

"That's what Walter said — that it was different with me and him. That he'd never done *that* with another girl. And these other guys were just to make a living."

If his arguments didn't persuade her, his gun did.

He made Jo use protection with the others, but not with

191

him. And then, after one time — a week later — she just *knew* (a pinchy feeling, low within her gut). She got queasy, missed her monthlies. So she told him.

"At first he was furious. How would we get money? No one wants to fuck a girl who's pregnant. But then he started saying no, that this was what we needed. This was what would make things right between us. Everything would be good from now on. But the funny thing . . . the funny thing was that *that* was worst of all: the thought of any 'from now on' with him. That's when I *had* to try and run away."

How is it that the rest feels predictable to Frieda? When did pain start seeming so routine?

Jo hitched a ride to Boston, but her parents wouldn't see her, so she ended up sleeping on the Common. She found an old blanket that almost kept her warm — a blanket, it turned out, full of lice. A relief, then, in truth, when they cuffed her. The meeting with Mrs. Sprague. The drive to Fitchburg.

"A bed again, and meals. And the girls leave me be. And Walter," she says, "he can't get me here."

But, Jo, Frieda wants to say. You're carrying his baby. What are you going to do about the baby? But Jo looks too shattered to answer anymore, so Frieda only pulls her close and hugs her. The hen between them, quivering, a heart.

Where their arms meet, Frieda feels an itchy, raw abrasion, and it strikes her that she forgot — for the minutes of Jo's story — all about her rash, about everything. Strange, she thinks, how someone else's pain can cancel yours. Strange and, she admits it, almost sweet.

"Oh, poor thing," she says to Jo. "Let me hold you steady." But those words are Alice's, just a copy, not her own. She has to (she will!) find her own. *Tomorrow,* she thinks — and suddenly it doesn't seem so dreadful.

"Brave girl," she says. "So brave. You'll be fine. I'll make sure you're going to be just fine."

Eighteen

⭐

THE BASEBALL, in Frieda's hand, feels promising and full. With a flick, it could sail up, away.

"G'head," taunts Rattigan. "Toss the pill. I'll even give you a freebie. No swing." With a chivalrous sweep of his arm, he liberates the strike zone, courting a pitch straight to home plate (a folded feed sack, tamped into the ground).

Frieda's never seen the night watchman during the day; in the glare he looks startled, indiscreet, with bright fidgety eyes, as blue as match flames. He spent a good hour last night digging out the pit for the roasting of their holiday pig, and he's stayed to enjoy his labor's fruits. From the pit, a thick autumnal smoke now rises, plus the primal scent of overcooked meat.

Behind the plate, his cohort, Burnham, squats on springy knees, doubling as catcher and umpire. He's the one who brought the ball and bat, laid out the diamond ("What's the Fourth without the national game?"). "C'mon," he calls. "Freebie — can't beat that."

"As if it'll make a difference," Rattigan scoffs.

From the depths of center field (the parked Ton Truck marks the boundary) comes the brass of Flossie's sisterly voice: "Show 'im now, Frieda. Mow 'im down."

Aside from Yetta, preemptively grounded by the matron, and watching from behind a barred window, none of the other girls appears to care. Melba and Hattie, assigned to first and second, stand between the bases, trading gossip. At third, Jo looks petrified, forsaken; Frieda can't help guessing that she must have looked the same as she lay beneath a stranger's weight in Newport, with her husband — where? just outside the door? Frieda can't abide the thought of wholehearted romance turning into wreckage, into *this*. She has to fight for a better end. They all do.

Earlier, when Burnham asked if anyone could pitch, Frieda, without thinking, blurted "Me." She'd never held a ball besides the one she threw with Felix, but she took this one as if it were her birthright. (Was this how Felix felt, this entitlement and need — why missing the foul ball had so derailed him?) Now she kicks and rears back as far as her frock allows. The skin all along her arm tightens, seethes with sting as the crust of her poison ivy cracks.

Rattigan hits the dirt. Burnham lunges.

The ball flies wild and head-high to the fence.

"Jesus Christ," says Rattigan. "She'll *kill* me." Shakily he stands up, dusting off his trousers, while Burnham chases down the errant throw.

Frieda should be mortified, but slinging the ball felt dandy: the torque, her arm elastic and adroit. Just to stand outside is good, to move. Late last night a storm crashed through, banishing the mugginess and leaving in its wake a spunky breeze. The sky gleams, expansive, the same spotless blue as on the day of the Liberty Loan parade.

The visitors are late, but that's fine: more time to learn how to play, to hone her aim. (Time, too, to hone the words she'll hurl at the senator; if only Alice were here to buck her up). It's the matron who seems undone by the delay. She paces about the yard, spouting worries: the breeze will rip the bunting loose, will rouse the pit fire's sparks. What if an ember sets the Home ablaze? She frets and finicks endlessly with details. Twice she's restrung the WELCOME, SENATOR WEEKS sign.

Fumbling along behind her, in a bid at pacification, is her nephew, Harold, the sole on-time guest. "D-d-don't worry, Aunt Margaret. I'm sure there's a good r-reason. Maybe the senator had a cr-cr . . . an important vote."

"*Ten o'clock,* they said. It's nearly noon! And what? They haven't heard of telephones?"

"Probably don't want to stop, 'cause then they'll be l-l-later."

Hearing this, Frieda cringes — what a pitiful excuse! — but, amazingly, Mrs. Digges seems to accept it. A moment's calm settles on her face.

Frieda is still floored by Harold's presence, by his references to the matron as "Aunt Margaret." It upends Frieda's whole view of the woman: the pinkness of her face no longer overwrought but jolly, her fleshy arms the better for embracing.

Harold is a bony-limbed boy in his midteens with reddish, slipshod hair and vibrant pimples. He stumbles as he heels behind his aunt. But the matron won't acknowledge his impairments. "Darling Harold," she calls him, and agrees to all he asks. ("Fireworks? If you're careful, darling, yes, of *course* you can. When the visitors leave, send them off with a bang!")

Burnham lobs the ball toward Frieda, letting it drop and dribble. *Harder,* she wants to tell him. *I can catch.*

"All right, now," he urges. "Fling it in."

"*In,*" Rattigan hollers. "Not behind me." His bat ("bludgeon," he calls it) wags with threat.

Frieda clutches the baseball and thumbs its fraying seam. *How can my wing fling from so far?* She dips back, hurtles forward, fires.

"Strike!" calls Burnham. "Attagirl. Right in there."

Rattigan kicks dirt. "A mile away."

"Caught the outside corner. Perfect throw."

"What, you got a thing for her? She don't got *enough* pals? You should see how that Miss Longley dotes on her."

Did he notice? In the yard, the other night?

"But I," he adds, "won't be doing her no favors."

Burnham shrugs, returns the ball, this time on the fly. She nabs it with a nimble backhand motion.

"Attagirl," he calls again. "Another!" He slugs the muddy target of his mitt.

Frieda brings the ball up to her mouth and faintly whispers; tells it that Rattigan will not intimidate her, that a strike means she'll beat them all, this place. Then the wind-up — scabs burning — and the release.

Rattigan jerks his fists and whips the bat.

The sound is like a gunshot and the agony of wounding: the ball in Burnham's mitt; Rattigan's groan.

"Two!" shouts Burnham, holding high a V.

Rattigan mutters "Shit," or maybe "Bitch." Sheepishly, he untangles from the aftermath of his swing and rushes to resume his batting stance, as if to convince them all he never moved — a boy caught picking his nose in public.

Burnham won't let him off so easy. "Been fanned by a girl before?" he asks.

"No. And don't plan to start now."

"Yeah, but who knows what *she's* planning! Good, huh? Sox could use her — replace that pansy Ruth."

Rattigan scowls. "What do you mean, 'pansy'?"

"Didn't you hear? All over the front page. Ruth had a spat with Barrow when the club was down in Philly. Quit and joined the Chester Shipyard."

"Don't sound pansy to me. The players was ordered to 'work or fight.' He's just working."

"Work, my ass!" Burnham slaps the ball into his glove. "How many warships you think the Babe is gonna build? Nah, he's gonna play for the shipyard *ball* team. Spoiled brat! Can't hack it on the Sox, he should join the Big Show."

Their squabbling reminds Frieda of Felix back at Fenway ("Give up baseball? Might as well crawl up with a white flag to the kaiser"). All these men — boys, really — debating their pet games. Do they truly think of war as just a "show"?

Today, though, she understands the impulse; all morning, as she's quavered with the ebb and flow of courage, it's helped to consider her task a game — less, perhaps, like baseball than like chess. (Papa, who coached her on sleepy Shabbos evenings, would say, "Don't move for now, but for later. Always you should think three moves ahead.") Standing up to the senator is a gambit, just a start. Standing up to him, she thinks, will seal the bond with Alice, so that Alice, in turn, will go further. (Sneak a letter to Felix? Help Frieda care for Jo?) Why should Frieda always be the pawn?

"You're bickering like old birds," she tells Burnham. "Toss the ball."

Rattigan says, "I'll show her 'old bird.'"

Burnham throws the ball, just a shade too fast. Frieda pretends her catch doesn't sting.

In the background, Mrs. Digges: "... too late, by that time ..."

"Hey, batter, batter," warbles Flossie.

Behind the men, bright against the Home's paint-chipped clapboards, pleated bunting riffles in the wind, the flourish of a bullfighter's cape.

"R-relax, Aunt Margaret," Harold says. "Everything looks just fine. You can only be what you are, so just r-relax."

Frieda appropriates the boy's instructions. She has to trust the world, its secret marvels: the same woman can be both "Mrs. Digges" and "Aunt Margaret"; a tongue-tied boy can sound wise; and a girl whom the world has written off as sick and shameful can rise up and prove herself true.

She arcs her arm: half physics, half prayer. The ball twirls past her fingertips. It soars.

Pock. Rattigan's swing connects, and Frieda's hopes skid —

until she tracks the ball, a futile pop, the travesty of a hit. It drifts meekly down the first-base line.

"Get it!" Flossie shouts. "Hattie. *Yours.*"

But Hattie, engrossed in Melba's scuttlebutt, can't be bothered. She waves away the sound of Flossie's order.

"Hattie! Move your black behind. Get it!"

The ball drops and dents the ground, foul.

Hattie says, "Teach you once to shut your smart mick mouth." She crooks her arms akimbo, bony bulwarks.

"Lucky," says Burnham to his colleague. "Still alive."

"*I'm* lucky? *Her!* Inch lower and I'd've killed it. Come on, girlie, get the ball and pitch."

But Frieda, when she turns to hunt it down, is stopped short: Flossie's charging in from center, crazed.

"Called me what?" she rages. "Called me *what?*"

"Mick," says Hattie. "Keep the hell away!"

Flossie barrels straight for her and swings.

Rattigan, bat fisted like a giant billy club, takes one step, then stops, looking vexed. Girls rush in, but no one intervenes.

After their first fight, in the garden, Yetta chided: "Girls like us, doesn't matter if you're black or white or striped, the only shade the world'll see is scarlet. Smarten up and learn to stick together!" But both the antagonists then turned on *her* for scolding. Hattie said, "Spare us the sermons, please."

Frieda now looks on, scared to speak.

The brawlers have each other straight-armed, each choking a neck.

Both go down. A yelp. Something rips.

"Don't!" comes an operatic shout from Mrs. Digges. "Stop it. Stop right where you are." It's not the girls she's yelling at but Harold, who has suddenly leapt into the fray. "Don't!" she shouts again. "Darling, don't."

But Harold dives between them, screaming "Not today" and "Stop," his words clear and adamant, unstuttered.

Flossie is still swinging wildly, arms like mower blades. Hattie feints and lashes out, all fists.

"Not—" says Harold, panting hard, "the Fourth—of July. Stop it—you'll ruin—everything."

Flossie glares at Harold, jabs her elbow.

"Owww!" Then, at the same harrowing pitch, but half as loud: "My nose. M-m-my nose? I think she b-broke it."

At once, the girls stop and split apart. Still, they hold their fists tightly cocked.

Darling Harold sits between them, hands cupped to his face, trembling, his forearms streaked with blood.

Hattie is bloody, too: a cut above her eye patch. "Easy, now," she says. "Let's have a look."

Just when she has gently pried open his twiggy wrists, Mrs. Digges pushes her aside. "Careful! Don't let your blood mix. Do you want to catch all the things *she's* got?" Heavily, as though unwinched, the matron falls to kneeling.

"Is it broken? Aunt Margaret, is it b-broken?"

"All right, darling. Hush. Don't you worry." She holds his head until the shaking stops.

Hattie licks her thumbs, wipes clean her cut brow, while Frieda and the others watch and wait. Rattigan and Burnham look forgotten.

"I wanted my sweet nephew just to share this special day. But you spoiled it, you filthy—you all spoiled it."

"*Her*," says Hattie. "Not me. She *hit* him."

Flossie's jaw drops with indignation. "Bull! It was an accident. You know it."

It wasn't. Frieda saw her take aim.

Mrs. Digges says, "Flossie, is it true?"

"No, ma'am. Why would I ever hit him?"

"Why would you do *anything* you do?" The matron has the look she always gets before exploding, her neck as pink and inflamed as a fat lip. "Flossie," she says. "Who else! I should have guessed."

Frieda, stepping up, says, "I saw it, Mrs. Digges."

"And? And so, what did you see?"

Flossie was a brute; there's no reason to defend her. But

199

Frieda looks at Harold—all cosseted, secure—and jealousy jerks a knot within her. "It wasn't her," she says. "It was the ground."

"The ground? The *ground* punched his nose?"

"No, ma'am, but he fell. That's what happened."

A horn sounds—not the jolly, clownish toot of a jalopy, but an impatient, bureaucratic bleat.

"Goodness, no," says Mrs. Digges. "Not *now*."

There it is again, beyond the fence.

The matron lets go of Harold, struggles to her feet. "Albert. Donald. Somebody let them in."

Both men jolt and scurry to obey.

Mrs. Digges assigns a girl named Blanche to care for Harold ("But don't touch him directly. Wash your hands!") and then, with a grimace of improvised repose, turns toward the opening gate.

The automobiles are matching Hudson Super-Six town cars, shining despite the grit of a long drive. The chauffeurs could be brothers: trim, whey-faced boys in stubby caps and flapping mohair dusters. From the first car emerges a stiff-limbed Mrs. Sprague, wincing at the sudden punch of light; she looks as though a pill's stuck in her craw. Frieda wants to hide herself within a caul of shadows, but the noonday sun doesn't offer any.

Thankfully, a mere second later, Alice follows, sensible in a pale blue dress. (Sensible, thinks Frieda. A woman with good sense. A woman with sense enough to save her.) Alice lifts one eyebrow—a question mark's curve—and Frieda gives a quick emphatic nod, the motion of which restores some of her confidence.

The final rider, a turnip-shaped newsman, tumbles out, his camera, on a neck strap, flying wild. "Oop," he says, "oop, watch it!" with winning clumsiness. "Phew. Almost bought the farm that time." He rights himself and marches to the matron. "Queen bee, I presume? The one in charge?"

Mrs. Digges, still looking discomposed from Harold's mishap, says, "Margaret Digges. Pleased to have you with us."

The man's face is dominated by a pale, doughy nose. "Wonderful," he says. "I'm Cushing. Ted Cushing. With the *Globe*. Won't mind if I make a few pictures?" Without waiting for an answer, he says "Wonderful" again and scoots his way around the crowded yard, peering about, crouching to scout angles.

How did Alice bear the drive from Boston, Frieda wonders, stuck between this loon and Mrs. Sprague? She'd ask, but Mrs. Sprague has roughly pulled Alice aside. Is she dressing her down again for aiding Frieda?

As Cushing readies his camera, some patients bow their heads; Jo squats and covers up her face. But Mrs. Digges fixes her coiffure like some fresh starlet, sets her shoulders back to flaunt her bust.

"Hold it!" Cushing bellows. "Stop right there."

Frieda sees he's shouting at the second automobile, the door of which the chauffeur has just opened.

"Like to get a shot," he says, "of the big guns stepping out, being greeted by—remind me, darling?—Mrs. Digges. Better maybe if *she* opens the door?" He strides up to the car and slams it shut. "All right, now, here we go again."

That their entrance should be directed like a stage show seems just right, for that's how Frieda thinks of it: A drama. A morality play, the fight of good and evil. (She's eager to see the men—to match faces to her fears—but clings to this last moment of abstract hatred.) Possibly, these other players think in the same terms, but if they do, they get the roles wrong: How could *she* be evil for following her heart? How could Jo, whose only fault was trusting? *They're* the evil ones, she thinks, the ones who strangle hope. That's the true debasement of what's good.

"Who's first?" asks Cushing. "Mr. Storrow?"

Out steps the head of the Committee on Public Safety. (*Tat*, goes the camera, like a gun. *Tat tat.*) He's a wiry man, with the slightest little pittance of a mustache over a smile that seems to Frieda unattached to any pleasure, an impervious smile of long training. "Sorry we're late," he offers, and his smile stays just the same.

"Quite all right," says the matron, who grins and nearly curtsies. "We're just awfully glad that you could make it."

Mr. Storrow turns to face the girls. "On behalf of Governor McCall, I want to wish you all our warmest —"

"Oop. Excuse me," Cushing interrupts. "Hold the speeches for a minute, if you will? Let's get everyone out of the car first."

Storrow freezes — not bitterly, thinks Frieda, but like a hound called off from the hunt. Laughably, an unbidden image comes to mind: Storrow poised in bed, hearing *Not now* from his wife, and halting just like this before rolling, compliantly, to sleep. Maybe, Frieda thinks, I can do this.

But then comes Senator Weeks; she knows it must be he. She must have seen his likeness in the papers many times. Or maybe he was one of the men standing at the State House when she passed in the Liberty Loan parade.

"Greetings, everyone! Mrs. Digges" — did he know her name already, or just catch it? — "it's delightful, at long last, to meet you. I've heard only the best about your efforts." He's a mast of a man, a head and more taller than Mr. Storrow, with a face that looks catalogue-ordered: clever eyes; a steep, persuasive jaw. He steps forth from the auto. *Tat tat.*

The solemn, awed watchmen look moved to salute but make do with shaking the man's hand. Flossie gets her dainty fingers kissed. Beneath her hat, its star-spangled ribbons all aflutter, Mrs. Sprague appears to be blushing. Even Alice wears a deferential smile.

Him? thinks Frieda. *Him, I have to cross?*

Then she looks to Jo — sweet, trampled Jo — still just standing, staring at her hands. Is she thinking of what a man's charm can hide? Frieda remembers Jo using her palm as a pincushion, stabbing her hand to give her pain form, and she wishes she herself had a thousand pins now; she'd cast them at the senator's foolproof face.

A third man descends from the Hudson's wide door and takes his place among the visitors. Opulently smiling, he shakes out his limbs, then poses with a loose, meaty boldness.

". . . behind schedule, unfortunately," the senator is saying, "and we have to get to Devens, see the boys. But my pal here, Mr. Storrow, insisted that we stop, to see what group of beauties we've collected."

No one laughs. Storrow's grin looks painful.

"No, but seriously, folks, *I* insisted we stop, to share with you this wonderful occasion! On this anniversary of the proclamation that 'all men are created equal,' we stand face to face with a challenge to our freedom, unlike any that . . ."

If the third dignitary was identified, Frieda missed it in the pomp of the senator's oratory. But he, too, strikes her as familiar. Does every politician shed this aura?

". . . two million Americans, the greatest army ever gathered, have donned the uniform on our behalf . . ."

It's not clear if the senator quite remembers where he is (the crowd numbers barely thirty people); maybe he's rehearsing for Camp Devens. The girls' eyes, Frieda sees, have already glazed over. The watchmen, too, look bored, and even Mr. Storrow, who detaches and reattaches a gold cuff link. Only Mrs. Sprague remains rapt at the speechifying, her eyes wide and watery, lovestruck.

As one after the next of the listeners goggle skyward, Senator Weeks directs his speech at Cushing, who scribbles in a thin, narrow notebook. He holds forth on military appropriations policy, frequently inserting contemptuous mentions of "my opponent in this election, Mr. Walsh."

Discreetly, with a hip-height signal, Alice beckons Frieda. "The election? Good God, it's barely summer."

Frieda tries to soak up all of Alice's aggression. She'll need it, every bit that she can muster. Now that there's a real face attached to Frieda's hatred, it's harder to imagine what to say. *We're dying here. You're ruining us. Help!* But how much is Senator Weeks himself the true culprit — this one man with his fatuous charisma? And what could he, alone, do for Frieda?

"Has he noticed," adds Alice, "that even *if* we liked him, nobody here could cast a vote? Has he even said a *word* about suffrage?"

"Rattigan," says Frieda. "And Burnham. There's two votes."

But Alice clearly doesn't want to joke. "There's not going to be much time. They almost wouldn't stop here. I just barely convinced them. Are you ready?"

Is she? Will she ever be more so?

"I can start things," Alice says. "Introduce you."

The wind gusts, then bluffs, then surges forth again with a heavy dose of smoke from the pit fire. The ashy smell of something burned too long.

"No," says Frieda. "I'll do this on my own."

"All right, then," says Alice. "Just be . . . try to be personal. He only thinks of girls as statistics."

Frieda turns back to watch the senator's performance. His foxy voice. His autocratic jaw. Now she sees — what? a speck of something — on that jaw. Yellowish. A smear of egg from breakfast? Is this how life goes when you rise to certain heights: that nobody will say — has the guts to say — the truth? *Excuse me, sir, there's something on your face.* How freeing. How utterly mortifying.

When the senator pauses for a just-too-long breath, Cushing cuts in with a question. "Why here, sir? Can you tell us why you're visiting this Home today?"

"Yes, of course. But really, I've been stealing all the light. Why don't we hear some from my colleagues." Stepping aside, he calls for Mr. Storrow.

"With pleasure," Storrow joylessly begins. He cites the mothers who have "lent us all their sons in freedom's fight," the duty to protect those sons from vice. He checks his cuff link, sees that it's still fastened. "We want the world to know," he says, "in no uncertain terms, that liberty and libertinism do *not* go hand in hand."

"And you, sir?" asks Cushing, indicating the third man. "As treasurer, how would you approach this program?" The newsman lifts his pencil. "Any comment?"

"Oh, forgive me!" says Senator Weeks, horning back in. "I haven't introduced our other guest. And I have a hunch these ladies will be tickled — their fathers have all shopped at his fine store. Folks, he's served admirably on Mr. Storrow's committee, and just now, today, he's announcing his candidacy for treasurer of our fair commonwealth. I surely hope he'll have your firm support. My very good friend, Meyer Morse."

Worthington Road. Of course. *That*'s where Frieda saw him. Him and the senator, too.

How could she have stood all this time, so close to him, and not known his shrewd, magnetic smile? The man who gave life to her Felix!

Frieda staggers. Steps a foot closer.

"Thank you, Senator. I'm not sure I can *tickle* all these ladies, but I'll try to address the man's question." Mr. Morse sets a well-oiled speech in motion. His work on the white-slave traffic commission in '14, his philosophy of "moral accounting" . . .

There's something of the barnstormer, thinks Frieda, in his bluster, but also in his expert use of silence: broad pregnant gaps, full of meaning. Then, when he speaks again — at last, his voice low — the sense is one of intimate rapport. She feels — everyone must — that she knows him, that he holds the key to a lock she must open. And no wonder, it occurs to her, that Felix and he clash: they're opposites whose ways are just the same.

"The facts," he says, "are what matters here. Results. Tally the costs of running a home: physical plant, medicine, never to forget the fine staff!" Mr. Morse winks at the matron. "Divide by the number of encounters we avert by keeping girls like these off the streets, and we find that the cost per prevented exposure is eleven cents. Repeat: eleven cents. As opposed to the seven *dollars* it costs to treat *each* soldier when that soldier is infected with disease. So you see that detention is not only our moral duty, it's darned smart business practice, too!"

Frieda hears the sure-footed romp of Morse's spiel (its *sound* more than the facts that he asserts), and she's drawn to — admit it! — the *Felixness* he exudes. Drawn to him. Scared of being drawn.

"Well done, my friend. Hope the newsman got that down!" Senator Weeks claps him on the back. "Can't you see, folks, what a fine treasurer he'll make? And the first of his faith, I might add."

"In that vein," says Cushing. "If I may, Mr. Morse? Your faith, sir, do you think that it might hinder —"

"*Such* a shame our time is cut short!" The senator speaks over Cushing's voice. "But we promised to be at Devens by one o'clock. It was such a pleasure to meet you all. Mrs. Digges, our thanks. And to you girls, a happy Indepen——"

"Oh, but, Senator! You can't," cries the matron. "We've a pig roasting. You *must* stay for lunch."

"Ma'am, that's awfully generous of you, truly. I'm afraid, though —"

He talks to a turned back. Mrs. Digges has found Rattigan and is fervently instructing him to fix a quick plate for each man: "Cut some from the loin, where it's not burnt."

"Honestly!" says Mr. Storrow, his tiny mustache twitching. From his fob he pulls out a gold watch. "Will we get there by one o'clock in the *morning*?"

Alice looks equally perturbed — but hardly in agreement; she must fear that the men are off the hook.

But the senator, shrugging, says, "Might as well enjoy!"

No one else dares to contradict him.

And Frieda, for the moment, isn't angry or resentful, but bursting with grateful expectation. *Now,* she thinks. Do it. Seize the moment.

The patriotic bunting, loose on its strings, chatters. Beyond the fence, a motorcar speeds by.

"Here's your chance," says Alice, and she nudges Frieda. "Go."

Across the yard, Mrs. Digges admonishes Rattigan: "More than that! Don't skimp on the meat."

Frieda nods and squares her shoulders. Steps. Steps again — now she's almost close enough to touch him.

"Hello!" he says jovially. "Meyer Morse."

"Frieda, sir." She stares at one of his buttonholes. "Frieda Mintz."

"Delighted. Are you having a fine Fourth?"

She sees Alice point to the senator, mouthing something: *wrong one,* or maybe *run! run!*

"Fine enough, sir. Glad for the chance to meet you."

"And I, you. A perfect day, no? You've made this place positively sparkle."

"Yes, sir," she says. "Thank you, sir." A stutter of politeness, worse than Harold's.

"I've hardly ever seen this countryside," he says, "but now I think I'll have to make an effort. Have *you* had much chance to — well, no, I suppose not. Maybe you will after you're released?"

Alice, still looking aghast, glares. How will Frieda explain why she walked right past the senator, why she isn't making the case against detention? Will Alice understand? Has *she* ever been waylaid by romance?

Frieda starts to sweat — at her neck, down her spine — a slow tacky leaching of resolve. But even as she knows that her approach might well backfire, she thinks: What have I been left to lose? (Mr. Morse could report her to the matron, or to Alice, and then what? She's already here, imprisoned and alone.) This is a man who *could* do something, personally, for Frieda; not a man with one vote out of ninety-six, like the senator (charming, but with schmutz on his face), but a father, *Felix's* father. A father who might give his son a message.

"The farms," Mr. Morse goes on. "The fields. The open space."

"Mr. Morse," she says. "I know your son."

"That so? Small world!" he says, as if, from long habit, he thinks he's at a cocktail-hour affair. "I expect to see him shortly, of course, when we get out to the camp. I'll be sure to"—but a tightness takes his face. "I'm sorry. I thought you said my *son*."

"Yes," she says. "Your son," she says. "Felix."

"Felix." Like a dread disease, confirmed.

Alice points again, with great urgency, toward the senator, who chats with a giddy Mrs. Sprague. Frieda turns, evicting them from view.

"We're friends," she says. "And I miss him so much."

"Friends! Ha! Where on *earth* would you have met? Was he volunteering at the Home for Little Wanderers?" He lets forth a spurious chuckle.

"Actually, on the street. At the Liberty Loan parade. He saw me and came and tracked me down."

"Well, of all the—that's preposterous!" He starts to step away.

Frieda steps, too, blocks his path. (Where did she find the gumption? She's someone new, or finally herself.) "I was hoping you might help me, sir," she says.

Would Mr. Morse be able to get Felix through these gates? Is he powerful enough? Or a letter—that, at least?

"Help you?" he says. "I don't have any reason to *believe* you. And even if I *did* believe—"

"The decanter. The swan-shaped decanter."

"I haven't the foggiest notion what you're saying."

"In your living room. It sits on the piano."

Mr. Morse just stares, his pupils like the heads of driven nails.

"I've been there, sir. He took me to your house."

Just as Mr. Morse appears ready to erupt—his neck bloated against his stiff collar—Mrs. Digges approaches, plate in hand. A gob of mashed potatoes, a hunk of dry bread, and grease-oozing shreds of roasted pork.

"The bread is rye," she says. "We observe the wheatless rules.

But the meat is our holiday splurge. We have to allow *some* indulgence, don't we?" She thrusts the full plate at Mr. Morse.

"Thank you, no," he tells her and raises both his hands, as if the plate she's thrusting is a pistol. "You're thoughtful, but I don't . . . it's that I'm . . . feeling indisposed." Given the poached, quivery look that comes into his eyes, the statement has the ring of honesty.

"Bosh!" says Mrs. Digges. "No need to stand on manners. It's lunchtime. I'm sure you must be famished." She deposits the plate into his hands.

He's caught, lifting it up an inch and then unsurely down, balancing against some unseen scale. He cranes, then, to look beyond Mrs. Digges's shoulder, and Frieda tracks his apprehensive gaze. Senator Weeks and Storrow intently chew their meat. Next to them, training a pointed stare at Mr. Morse, Cushing holds his notebook and his pencil.

"It's pork, is it?" asks Mr. Morse.

"Yes," says the matron. "Fresh as can be. Butchered just yesterday noon."

His forehead nears the shade of the plate's heaping meat: sickish and glisteningly pink. Is it possible? wonders Frieda. Does Mr. Morse keep kosher?

"The thing is, you see, I'm just generally not in the habit—" but he stops, and he seems to swallow hard.

Yes, she thinks, it's true: Mr. Morse keeps kosher! This striving modern baron, still bound by superstition! A thrill of leverage buzzes through her fingers.

"Please," says Mrs. Digges. "Enjoy yourself."

"Well, yes. Yes, all right. You're too kind." Mr. Morse spears a scrap of meat with his fork, then tugs to disconnect it from the whole. He bites, chews it quickly twice, and gulps. "Delicious!" he announces, aiming his voice at Cushing. "Now please, if you'll excuse us, ma'am, I was chatting with this . . . young lady. Might we ask a moment's privacy?"

Frieda notes the matron's hands clenching and unclenching.

"Certainly," says Mrs. Digges. "By all means." She walks away with stiff, jilted strides.

Mr. Morse leads Frieda away from the crowd, toward the spot that, earlier, marked first base. "I'm not sure," he says, "where you got this information—this supposed information about my home." He closes to within inches of her face. "But you'd better wise up a little, miss. Do you know whom you're dealing with? Do you?"

Frieda shrinks from his spite, from the hot force of his words; she's almost ready to turn around and run. But the pork smell on his breath tells her: *stay;* stay, hold firm. He's not as invincible as he seems. "I don't want to 'deal,' sir. I just want to see Felix. I just want to know how he is."

"How he is is none of your damn business. I *won't* stand here listening to you claim that my son has—that he'd *ever* consort with the likes of you."

His too strong rejoinder fills Frieda with misgivings: Has he defended Felix from similar charges before? Has Felix left heaps of wrecked girls? She thinks of his letter, his offer of assistance. No, she thinks: the wrecker is his father. "Sir, Felix would want to know that I . . . that I'm in trouble." She lets her voice deepen with suggestion. "He already knows that I might be."

Mr. Morse bends down to ditch his plate of lunch. Rising, he looks primed to grab something. He takes his lapels in tight fists. "Miss, I understand that you're upset to be detained. You're desperate. You'd do anything to get out. But there's nothing I—nor anyone—can do."

"Mr. Morse, we're not even allowed to send mail. If I wrote Felix a letter, would you take it?"

He stomps, just missing the plate's edge. "Not for anyone. Least of all, my son."

Frieda's shocked by how easily her response comes to mind. Is it borrowed from a movie, from a dime novel she read—or just her own chess-playing savvy? "I'd hate to have to ask a total stranger." Her eyebrows tugging together in affected consternation, she sweeps her gaze searchingly about, until she obviously lets it land on Cushing. She waves, and Cushing answers, clearly piqued.

"Really, now, I *must* insist," comes Mr. Storrow's voice, loud enough to stop all conversation. "We can't expect the troops to wait all day."

"It's not as if they're standing at attention," says the senator. A slosh of laughter pours from his big mouth. "But all right, Jim, yes, you'll get your way—even if it means leaving these fine ladies."

Mrs. Digges makes an absurd, spoony sound.

Cushing can be heard bidding for one final photo, a farewell shot: the senator with some girls?

"Enough of *me*," says Senator Weeks with foppish largesse. "Make one of Morse, he needs attention. This election is going to be a squeaker."

Mr. Morse and Frieda catch each other's startled eyes. For once, she thinks, they're on the same side—linked by not wanting to be linked. But here comes Cushing, asking them to step a bit this way, pivot slightly, no, to the right . . .

Frieda trips on something, turns her ankle. The baseball. Left where Rattigan's pop-up fell.

She stoops, ankle smarting, and picks up the ball. It's warm: a sphere of concentrated sun.

"Oop, no," says Cushing, "we want you standing straight. That's right. Upsy-daisy. Can you face me?"

"Please," says Frieda, whispering, ignoring the reporter. "When you see him, will you give him this from me? Just give it to him. Please. He'll understand." She presses the ball into Mr. Morse's palm.

He spins the ball slowly at the tips of his fine fingers. He looks stricken with something like concern. "Felix is in no shape for sentimental games. If you really must know, he's been injured."

"Mr. Morse. Miss. May I have your attention?" Peevishly, Cushing snaps his fingers.

"Injured? But I thought you said Felix was still here. I don't understand. Is he all right?"

"He'll be better if he never hears from *you*."

Frieda's mind fills with the image she once conjured of Felix on a battlefield, bleeding. This time, she's not there to save him.

"Here. It's no use to me. Take it." Mr. Morse pushes the ball back.

Already the ball's scuffed leather has grown cooler; she's aware of it as the skin of something dead.

"All right, let's get on with this," Mr. Morse demands. "Capture your picture, man, and let's be done."

"We are, sir," says Cushing, and pats his camera proudly. "Got the perfect shot while you were chatting. Ready when you are to march on."

She drops the ball and kicks it to the fence.

Suddenly they're leaving, and Frieda looks on at the pageant of make-believe affections: mannered smiles, overblown handshakes.

Soon again, certainly, a pleasure.

Keep up the good work.

Best of luck.

As the pale, twinlike chauffeurs mount their driver's seats and engage the Hudsons' snippety engines, Alice approaches Frieda in a frenzy. "We're going," she says, as if that's not apparent. "That's *it*. Do you think they'll come again?"

Frieda shakes her empty-feeling head.

"I just can't imagine why you squandered your time with *him*." Tactlessly, she points toward Mr. Morse. "Do you have some explanation? Can you tell me?"

"Come on, now, Miss Longley. Step aboard," says Mrs. Sprague from the open door of the town car she's climbed into.

Alice clasps Frieda by the elbow, whispers, "I'll —" A syllable of promise, or of warning.

"Time is up!" hollers Mr. Storrow.

Alice, without finishing her thought, goes.

Through a complicated dance — one advancing, then the other — the drivers manage to turn the cars around. "So long," calls Senator Weeks. "So long, everyone."

The girls and Mrs. Digges call back, "So long."

"Happy Fourth of July."

"Safe trip. So long!"

They motor out, and Burnham shuts the gate.

Mrs. Digges has the dazzled look of a birthday cake recipient who fills and fills her lungs to douse the candles, then finds the task required but little breath. The patients, too, wear frowns of anticlimax. Flossie and Hattie, their fistfight blown over, stand side by side, trading shrugs. The watchmen go to tend the dying fire. Behind them — paled by the sun, disruptively beautiful — Jo ambles toward the chicken coop. (All Jo's work, cleaning, and no one paid attention. No one paid attention to Jo. Did Frieda?)

A nasal complaint breaks the silence. "G-gone? But I didn't even m-meet them!" Harold appears, pinching at the bridge of his thin nose. The nose seems unbroken, hardly bruised.

"Sorry, darling," says Mrs. Digges. "They're busy, busy men. They came and went before we even knew it."

"And what about the sp-sp . . . the fireworks?" He holds up a handful of sparklers and something that resembles a small bomb. "You said that I should light them as they left."

"But see, darling? See? They left already."

"But you *said*!" Harold rattles his munitions, at once babyish and ominously manly. Then he squints. "Aunt Margaret, what's that on your dress?"

"What?" she says.

"That spot. Are you bleeding?"

She tucks her fat chin to peer down. "Oh," she cries. "No! All this time? No one told me." She glares, for some reason, straight at Frieda.

Not *this* stain, thinks Frieda. This one's not my fault. But it feels as though it is. Might as well be.

"It was me," Harold says. "My st-stupid nose. I'm sorry, Aunt

Margaret. Let me help." He paws at the red mark on her bosom. He looks like an infant scared of weaning.

"Stop," she says, and swats at him. "You're just — you're in the way. Just go on now, light your fireworks."

"Really? Aunt Margaret, really, may I?"

"Get Albert and Donald to help you out. Now, go!" She gives him a shove toward the fire.

"Thank you," he says, and "Sorry again," and bolts across the yard, his fireworks brimming in his hands.

Nineteen

★

WHEN MRS. DIGGES APPEARS the next day in Frieda's bedroom, the air in the room changes, bunching tight. "This," says the matron, holding a yellow note, "was delivered just now to my attention."

It's the middle of a breezy afternoon. Frieda — on her knees as she scrubs the bedroom floor — has been floating, her mind awash with dreams, finally having dodged (or momentarily suppressed) the unease that jabbed at her this morning: a malaise of unfinished business. (She didn't speak to the senator, got no promises from Morse, didn't do a thing to help Jo.) She's been floating, yes, relishing the afternoon's reprieve, but she founders now on the matron's sharp voice.

"Addressed to me," says Mrs. Digges, who shakes the yellow page. "But you'll see that it's really aimed at you."

At me, thinks Frieda. Of course. This morning was just the feint. Here comes the combination punch.

• • •

Though she'd tippled no more yesterday than a glass of tepid milk to wash down some burnt ends of pork, Frieda awoke with what Lou used to call a "hangover." She plodded down to breakfast as if through catacombs, as if forced beneath unlucky ladders. Three strikes, she kept thinking: Weeks, Morse, Jo. Plus Felix, injured — how? how badly? (If Frieda had talked to Weeks — if she *hadn't* talked to Morse — would Felix somehow have been spared? Impossible, but still she blamed herself.)

The other girls, too, seemed to be ducking something. Fate? Yesterday, for an hour after the motorcade's departure, they had whirled about in dithering excitement. They'd met a man who knew the president! *Did you see how tall?* one girl exclaimed, and another cried, *His hands!* A third chimed in, *The one I liked was Storrow. Something about that itty-bitty mustache.* Then Mrs. Digges had ordered them to take down the banner (which Melba ripped by mistake, so it said WELCOME, SENATOR WEE), and to untie the wind-tattered bunting. In minutes, the decorations had all been dismantled, and thrill waned to sluggishness, then standstill.

Which remained the girls' controlling state at breakfast. The oatmeal that they spooned was like torpor turned to food. Chewing seemed the most that they could manage. A draft carried the residue of yesterday's pit fire, the dark smell of recently snuffed flames.

Yetta, who had watched everything from her window yesterday and mocked Frieda last night before bed ("That big shot took a shine to you, huh? You'll be rescued soon, right? Your new best friend?"), sat beside her now in boastful silence. Frieda hadn't bothered to explain the situation; Yetta, she decided, was too bent on vindication to offer her reliable advice.

Across from them sat Jo, scarcely eating — just enough to keep from being punished. Now that Frieda was privy to the secret of Jo's condition, she could see nothing *but* the pregnancy. Jo's breasts, her cheeks, even her eyes, looked swollen with a terrifying, bloated sort of beauty.

Leaning across the table, Frieda whispered, "Are you okay?," but at once she heard the question's senselessness. What would she do if Jo responded "no"? What could she ever truly do for Jo?

All Jo did in answer was to shrug.

This was Frieda's own response, not half an hour later, when Dr. Slocum posed the same question. A date with him was plenty, by itself, to make her ill: the treatment room, its calcimined gloom; the ceiling's tangled vines; his sweaty pate. First he checked the progress of her poison ivy rash. Scabs that had broken when she stretched to hurl the baseball were driving her to madness now with itch. The doctor said good, that meant that they were healing. Another while of soap-and-soda balm, and she'd be fine. Then he nodded grimly, told her, "Lift."

She hiked her denim frock, set one foot on a chair, a cow habituated to the stanchion. Despite the heat, her body tensed with chill.

Today, the doctor told her, they were going to draw some blood for a new Wassermann and make some slides, too. "See how soon we can get rid of you" was how he put it.

"But I thought —" she said. "Didn't you say August?"

"Actually, I believe I said *perhaps*." But the Fourth, he said, had triggered a spate of "moral zone" infractions; a large influx of patients would be coming. To avoid overcrowding, some old cases would be quickened. He must now determine who was ready.

Me, she thought. I'm ready. *How* I'm ready. Maybe she wouldn't need Mr. Morse or even Alice. Maybe she would get out on her own.

He asked if she'd been taking all her pills.

Yes, she said. The blue ones. Every meal. They tasted like tea from a rusted kettle.

The pills, the insertion of the medicated tampons . . . she tried to consider it all as just another chore, like hauling trash or scouring the toilet. But when those chores were done she could retreat to her room, relax. Her body — her sullied flesh — could not be quit.

Dr. Slocum scanned her chart, then sat down on a stool, which he lowered by means of a small crank. "Last time," he said, as he donned a pair of gloves, "I noted some clitoral enlargement. If it's no better now" — his hands moved to her thighs — "I'll have to ask if you've been inappro——" And there he stopped; his lips pulled pale and tight. "Oh, come on. Really. Of all things." He stared at her, his eyes small and dark with detestation, then held up his blood-shiny fingers. "You couldn't have had the courtesy to tell me?"

"I didn't know. It must have just started." Now this morning's unease made more sense.

The doctor stood up, stripping off his gloves. "Well, with all this blood, it's no good, we can't make slides. I'll have to try again after your monthlies." He shoved at her one of his gauze tampons (unsoaked), and left her to clean her own mess.

She emerged minutes later, feeling junky, dispossessed (the doctor was an Indian giver of hope!), and was drawn by the noise of some furor. In the parlor, by the sounds of it. Shrieks of disbelief. Yetta's shrill voice: "How typical!"

When she stepped into the room, all the girls turned to face her. They jeered at her and pointed. (Was she dripping? Had Slocum told them?) It was all she could do not to flee.

She stood there, wobbled by a teetery, tightrope feeling — just how she feels now, as Mrs. Digges approaches, holding out the yellow sheet of paper — but when she saw the patients' grins, at once she understood: the girls weren't *jeering* her but *cheering*.

"There she is!" said Flossie.

"Make room," Melba barked.

Yetta, rolling her eyes, said, "Forgot the red carpet." But her coolness seemed to come at some effort. Even she looked flush with inspiration.

From Frieda? From something *she* had done?

She caught sight of Mrs. Digges, over by the lowboy, her mouth taut with a runner-up's forced smile.

"Look," said Flossie, pointing. "Look what Burnham brought."

Frieda followed her pointing and walked up to the lowboy, on which was laid a copy of today's *Globe.*

"You're famous. The whole world'll see," said Melba.

The world? Don't be silly, Frieda thought. Most readers would focus on the double-banner headline:

AMERICANS AND ALLIES WIN BATTLES
ON ALL FRONTS TO CELEBRATE FOURTH

Others, more attentive to battles on the ball field, would delight in a bulletin from Philly: "Babe Ruth Rejoins Sox in Quakertown. Signalizes Return by Making Hit and Fanning Twice."

But for readers who could make it past the war news and the sports, past word of striking weavers up in Lawrence, there it was, below "Mutt and Jeff," on page eight: a photograph of Meyer Morse and Frieda. At first glance it looked as though the two were shaking hands. Close study showed a baseball being passed.

"Doesn't it look just *like* you?" Melba gushed.

"It *is* her," Yetta said.

"Oh, but you know!"

"There's an article, too," said Flossie. "What's it say?"

Frieda saw the byline, Theodore Cushing, but couldn't bring herself to read further. She felt fractured: part herself, part the girl in Cushing's photo. Standing here, but trapped in yesterday.

"If you'd like to read it aloud, go ahead," said Mrs. Digges. "Read it out once, and we'll be done." She made a gesture like shooing a wet dog.

The patients' expectation pressed in from all sides. Frieda drew a breath and she began.

Meyer Morse, proprietor of the noted company that bears his name, manufacturers and dealers in men's clothing, has declared his candidacy for Treasurer of the Commonwealth.

He made the declaration public yesterday while accompanying one of his chief backers, Senator John Wingate Weeks, on Independence Day visits to Camp Devens and to a War Department girls' detention home. The man who would be Treasurer chose the latter setting to underscore a view he called "moral accounting," asserting that the quarantine of delinquent girls — whose diseases, if spread to soldiers, incur costs both in medicine and lost service — is "not only our moral duty, it's darned smart business."

A Republican, who moved recently from Boston to the Cottage Farm section of Brookline, Mr. Morse has been active in civic life, serving on the Board of Commissioners of Sinking Funds for the City of Boston, and, most recently, as assistant executive manager for the Massachusetts Committee on Public Safety.

Mr. Morse is the nephew of Leopold Morse, who served as United States Representative for Massachusetts from 1877 to 1883. If elected, he will be the first Jew to hold statewide office in the Commonwealth. . . .

She recited the remainder in a mumbly, slapdash voice — Morse's growing wealth, his love of golf — and omitted altogether the last line, which noted his charming wife and his two sons, "the older of whom, Felix, a soldier in the 301st, he visited with yesterday at Camp Devens." Was it trepidation that kept Frieda from uttering Felix's name — as Mama would not speak the name of God — or selfishness: she didn't want to share him?

"That's *it*?" Melba griped. "Don't it say nothing 'bout *you*?"

"No," said Frieda, and scanned through the article once

more. "Not unless you count the photo caption. 'Candidate Morse bestows gift on unidentified inmate during visit to girls' detention home in Fitchburg.'"

"That's it?" Melba said again. "You're kidding me, that's it? They don't even call you out by name?"

"Ha!" cried Yetta. "Like I said: typical. He just *used* us. We were barely props."

Flossie asked what kind of gift Mr. Morse had given her.

Frieda dropped the *Globe*. She said, "Nothing."

After lunch, Mrs. Digges announced new room assignments to make space for the forthcoming patients. Flossie and Frieda would move down the hall, joining Yetta, Jo, and three others. Frieda was instructed to clean her old room: "And I mean clean. Like no one's ever lived there."

As she stripped bare her mattress, then swept beneath the bunk, removing all traces of herself, Frieda thought again about the caption — the fraud of it, the way it made the photo tell a lie. Morse hadn't given her a thing! With evidence that a "fact" could be so far from factual — evidence typeset in black and white — it struck her that she was freer than ever to trust her own truths: the truth that Felix waited — would keep waiting — for her (would he see her in the *Globe* and come find her?); the truth of her body and its longings. If the world should believe that Mr. Morse "bestowed a gift," why shouldn't she — why *couldn't* she — believe?

She heard the rough-and-tumble of a motor truck's engine but didn't stop to think much about it. Probably it was the grocer or the coal man. With a fanciful, unbound feeling (her monthlies hardly hurt), she knelt to wash the grubby spruce floor. She pictured herself swabbing the deck of a clipper ship as it sluiced through the horse latitudes. (Where these were, exactly, she couldn't quite recall, but she'd always liked the music of the name.) Swashing her rag in circles she hummed an old tune, which Jack, playing pirates, used to sing: "*something something* sun, a drink of rum . . .*"

That's when Mrs. Digges appeared, and the bedroom's air seized. That's when she produced the yellow note.

She hands it now to Frieda. "Telegram," she says. "You'll see why I'm waiving the no-mail rule."

Frieda holds the page but doesn't look.

"Go ahead. Don't worry, no one died."

FOR THEM HOLDING FRIEDA MINTZ. SAW PHOTO. AM MOTHER. "UNIDENTIFIED" NO MORE. STILL A CHILD. STILL WITH ME SHOULD LIVE.

It ends with the promise — the threat — of further contact. There's a telephone number she recognizes as Slotnik's.

She doesn't know she's shaking until the matron holds her shoulder and tells her to settle down, she'll be fine. But the pound of Mama's voice, even on the page — the beat of her twisted Yiddish syntax — rattles Frieda, knocks within her skull.

Now, when she's released, there will be no release. She'll go from one prison to the next. Mama — and Hirsch — will be waiting to chain her up. How much more severe will they be now? Will Frieda have to try to run away again? *Could* she? Running requires strength of leg but also of ideals. The latter may have atrophied too much.

". . . with Miss Longley, of course," Mrs. Digges is suggesting, "when she comes with the new girls, tomorrow. We'll let her weigh in on what to do."

Frieda should be bolstered by the thought of Alice coming, but all that she can think of now is Mama. She pictures Mama finding the photo. Or did someone bring it to her — Mrs. Pinsker? a friend of hers from shul? How sick, how mortified she must have been! Mama, then, clomping to the Western Union office, having to ask a total stranger's help.

Frieda, on her knees from scrubbing, slumps down even farther, into a puddle of gray soapy water.

"Really, now," says Mrs. Digges. "Pull yourself together. For both our sakes, Frieda, please get up."

The wetness — wicking up her frock, along her legs — is for Frieda the very feel of shame.

"You thought you could run from her forever?" asks the matron. She pinches at the meat of Frieda's neck.

Frieda scarcely notes the matron's fingers. She's a girl again, sprawled across Mama's kitchen table: limbs drenched and slithery with wintergreen and linseed, and Mama's hand hard upon her wrist. "*Farshtunken* girl! Look at you. Revolting." The wrench of Mama scrubbing her, chafing at her skin. The sting of soap running in her eyes.

Which sting now, too, as she sits slumped on the floor, with tears she can't hide from the matron.

"But I didn't cry," she explains to Jo, that evening after dinner, "from thinking about how rough Mama'd been. Or not even, really, from worrying what'll happen — if she'll make me get married to that man. She *will*, I know she will. What can I do?"

Around them, in the parlor, girls are playing Twenty Questions. (Yetta asks Hattie, "Is this man dead or living?" "Alive, sorry to say. Live and kicking.") Frieda and Jo stand together in the corner, defectors from the other girls' amusement. Jo is the only one she's told of Mama's message — Jo, who entrusted Frieda first with *her* confession, who knows what a parent's scorn is like.

"What did it," Frieda says. "What *really* did it?" Her voice tightens, reedy with dejection. "It's not as if I haven't thought about that stuff before — the way Mama treated me back then. And I've always been so sure that she was cruel. But this time — this time I almost wondered who was right. What if *she* was, Jo? What then?"

Jo looks depleted, her eyes pale and drained. Lowly, she says, "Why do they even have us?"

"What?" says Frieda.

"Our mothers and fathers. Why? If all we ever do is cause them trouble. And why . . . why didn't we listen?"

Frieda sees how thoughtless she has been — wondering, ask-

223

ing if she should have heeded Mama, when for Jo the answer couldn't be more clear.

Across the room, someone accuses Hattie of deceit. (The girls have spent all of their twenty allotted questions, and still they haven't guessed the secret name.) "Don't blame *me*," Hattie says, "if y'all's too dumb."

Jo plucks at a tuft of her scraggly, half-grown hair, as if weeding a thought her head has sprouted. "I always wanted to raise a kid — dreamt of it all the time. I'd show my parents: *See? This* is how. But now." Her mouth hangs empty. "Now."

Mrs. Digges arrives to say five minutes to lights out. Everyone out of the parlor. On the double.

The game ends abruptly in a cantankerous standoff when Hattie tells the name she had in mind. "No fair," Yetta grouses. "You said he was alive. Uncle Sam isn't . . . he isn't even *real*!" They snipe at each other all the way upstairs.

Frieda, in the new bedroom, settles close to Jo (she chose the bunk beside hers, almost touching) and asks her what she plans to do. Surely she can't hide the truth much longer?

Jo says she's frightened — not of having the baby, but of after. "What if," she whispers. "What if . . . I hate it?"

"You won't," Frieda insists. "You'll love it, 'cause it's yours."

Jo shakes her head. "It's *his*."

Twenty

★

HE NEXT DAY, feeding bed sheets into the Home's laundry mangle — watching steel rollers wring the cloth — Frieda, for a crazy instant, pictures shoving something (Mama's hand? her own?) between the wheels. She succumbs to the certainty of its crush. But as soon as she's outside, snapping sheets into the wind and pinning them up onto the clothesline, she thinks, No; *this* is what I need — to be untangled. From Mama's grasp and Hirsch's, but also from herself, from the snag of her unrelenting hopes. Isn't that what gets her into trouble all the time? If only she could learn to hope for less.

The morning's hot and waspish, but the wet sheets keep her cool as a rising breeze ripples them around her. Her mood, too, billows as she readies to see Alice. Alice will know how to fend off Mama and her threat. Maybe there's some social-work maneuver she can pull — a document to sign, keeping Frieda away from harm (like the evaluation she so handily dispatched). Or, at the very least, Alice could talk to Mama; Alice is so good at talking, soothing. Frieda turns her name into a psalm: *Alice, Alice, all is well.*

But when Burnham lets a truck into the yard and then it parks, and Frieda, from behind the sheets, spots Alice — Alice with her eyes all puffy, sweat beneath her arms; Alice floundering down from the high cab — Frieda's expectations sag. (She's done it again. She got herself tangled up in hope — even as she promised herself not to.)

From the driver's side, a man descends to chat with Alice briefly, and Frieda recognizes the constable — the same one who delivered her and Flossie. Then, he drove a Dodge; today, this gnarring truck that looks built for hauling cattle, maybe mules. A fence of steel stakes and wooden slats around its bed. Peering through the slats: eight pairs of eyes.

A hand emerges, and a voice that seems attached to the hand moans. "Put it out, it's burning. Help, it hurts!"

Alice, without turning from the constable, shouts back, "Enough now, Bess. Keep it to yourself."

"But it burns."

"Yes," says Alice, "sure it does. It's your body getting rid of the addiction."

The girl's cries simmer to a fitful nickering. Her hand grabs a stake and weakly rattles.

Frieda thinks, Did *I* seem that sordid when I came? A moment's satisfaction (surely she was not so bad) is followed by an anxious sort of envy: Will this pitiful girl distract Alice? All these new girls might, or have already. Holding back, hidden by the swells of flapping laundry, Frieda pins another dripping sheet.

Mrs. Digges has now come out to greet the new arrivals, an acquisitive gleam in her eyes.

"Help!" comes another cry from Bess. "Make it stop."

A different girl says, "Cat's sake, shut her up."

The matron ignores both girls' appeals. To Alice, she says, "Looks like quite a handful."

"*A* handful? Your hands must be bigger than mine, I guess. I haven't slept a wink in two days."

The constable, a thickset man in dun, misfitting clothes, nods with practiced-seeming exasperation. "Truth is, we're not equipped to handle these big numbers. You've seen town hall —busting at the seams. We need a holding pen for the holding pen."

"Honestly!" says Mrs. Digges, in a tone of sociable commiseration. "You'd think they'd see their chums locked away and be deterred—but there's no end of foolishness, I guess."

The constable says, "Heard that Wilson's signing a bill this week? Hundred grand to fund detention centers."

"That so?"

"What the paper said, I think."

Mrs. Digges gives a busybody's cluck.

And did you see where the price of milk is up almost a nickel?

Mosquitoes'll be fierce this year, they say.

The wind slaps a sheet at Frieda's face.

"Hey!" calls one of the girls from the truck's bed. "Hot in here."

Again, the truck's metal fencing shakes.

"Are you ready for the transfer?" asks Alice.

The matron enacts a smile. "We'll do our best."

"That's not what I asked, exactly, is it?"

Alice plucks at the sweat-darkened underarms of her dress, an undainty move that heartens Frieda: she's worn down, but her haggardness is an alley cat's, feisty. Maybe she'll be all the more protective. Frieda pictures Alice pouncing at Mama, claws bared, venting a haughty threat: *Keep away!*

The constable unlocks the truck and helps the girls down, his demeanor incongruously chivalrous. "All right, darling. Easy does it. There!" He could be a carnival hand, squiring ladies from a hayride.

Alice commands the patients more firmly. "Ethel, over here,

can't you see your boot's unbuttoned? Introduce yourself to the matron, Olivia." Her hat's trimming—fake cherries and grapes, made of wax—looks as though it's melting in the sun. She does, too. She mops sweat from her brow.

The girl that must be Bess (sickly thin, a limp frown) totters in a jelly-eyed stupor.

"Bess," chides Alice. "Pull yourself together."

"Has a habit?" the matron says. "We'll see to that."

Bess, as if unaware they're talking about her, unaware of much beyond her pain, breaks toward the fence, the open gate. (Why has no one noticed it ajar? All this time, someone could have run.) But her legs are no match for her intention. She trips on nothing, wobbles, crumples down.

The constable hoists her up and smacks her on the cheek. "You stay put!" He slaps her, hard, again.

Where, Frieda thinks, did his chivalry run off to? Are all men triggers waiting to be tripped?

Alice hurries out to Bess and bodily shields her.

"He *hit* me," Bess says.

"I know, dear. I'm sorry." To the constable, then: "You'll *not* mistreat the girls!"

Frieda, too, has rushed out, not conscious until she's almost clear across the yard that she hasn't burst forth in solidarity with Bess, but to pry herself between the girl and Alice. She stands there, blinking, breathing hard. "Help?" she asks, edging close to Alice.

Alice casts a dark, cutting glance. "Do I *need* help? Yes. Can *you* give it? I don't think so." She leads the group of greenhorns to the Home.

There follows a great flurry of logistics. Girls being shown their rooms, squabbling over beds. Dresses stripped and traded for plain frocks. (In preparation for the influx, spares were sewn.) Baths, followed by delousing ointment.

Alice has decamped somewhere behind closed doors with Bess, and Frieda is consumed with watchfulness. Can she hear a cry of woe? A soothing coo? Is Alice telling Bess, as she told Frieda, that she's "different"?

Mrs. Digges puts everyone to work. A trio of newcomers — "Too cocked up," the matron judges — are banished to the yard in Melba's charge; a defunct outhouse needs dismantling. The rest are herded into the sewing shop.

The order to stitch hospital gowns has been supplanted by the job of rolling gauze bandages for soldiers. As the girls measure the gauze, they take the measure of one another. The snipping of cloth makes a steady hiss.

Yetta nudges next to one girl, starts her union shtick, the folly of not rising up together — same as she did, weeks ago, with Frieda. The new girl keeps quietly to work.

Gnashing of the scissor blades. *Shh, shh.*

The one called Lisbeth — black hair bobbed, eyes still stained with kohl — pipes up in a melted-taffy voice. "Wha? Ya tellin' me they don' take *these* away?" She holds high a glinting pair of scissors. "In the slammer down in Queens, ya *bet* they did."

"Prison?" asks Hattie. "What for?"

Lisbeth sucks her teeth and says, "Which time?"

Out comes a tale of apprehension and escape, double crosses dodged, dirty finks — a tale that could be straight out of the movies, and likely is. But no one questions Lisbeth; no one seems to want to. They all appreciate the entertainment.

Hattie shares her own adventures — why hasn't she before? — with a banjo-playing crook in Baton Rouge.

Gauze remains unrolled. Scissors quit.

Soon the talk turns to how they ended up in here. "A rinky-dink clink," Lisbeth says, "if I ever saw one." In quick succession, Angelina, Hattie, and Flossie speak, each girl's story higher on a ladder of bravado. (Frieda recalls Flossie in the brig as not quite dauntless, but she doesn't say a word to contradict her.) Yetta recites the charge that she was framed.

Jo sits with a pair of scissors balanced in her palm. What if one of the new girls asks her story? Last night, when Frieda and Jo whispered about the baby, Frieda said that Jo should tell *someone*. Mrs. Digges, or one of the more experienced girls, at least? To help her choose: keep the child or let someone adopt it. Jo said no, she *wouldn't* tell, made Frieda promise silence. All Jo wants is to get out of this place with no one knowing (if the doctor clears her soon enough, before she's really showing, if her test results this week come back clean), then go off by herself — no parents, no Walter — maybe head up north, to Montreal? Somewhere she can make her choice alone.

Frieda couldn't bear to watch if the girls ask Jo to talk, and she doesn't want to tell her own story — not about Felix (would they mock her wide-eyed romance?) or Flynn (the details are too gruesome). "Toilet break," she says, and steps out.

She stands in the hallway, listening for Alice. She strains but she doesn't hear a thing.

When she comes back, the new girls are recounting their misfortune. There's Olivia, and Ethel, and Fleur. Until two days ago, none of them had met.

"Party," says Olivia, the one with the hard jaw. "Went with a guy I met the night before — a shavetail, getting ready to ship out. Fourth of July, he says. Support the soldiers! Beer and hamburg, sparklers — the works."

"And the sparklers clinched it, right?" suggests Flossie.

Olivia laughs. "Honest, just a party."

"Plain old summer fun," Fleur agrees. She has big teeth, a look of thwarted ardor. Her sun-bleached hair is all afrizz. "The other day I'd met a buck private up in Lowell. He asked if I liked parties. Sure, I said."

The gathering took place at the home of a shady doctor, who'd been bootlegging to soldiers — booze and worse. His scam involved prescribing morphine to long-dead patients, collecting the dope, then selling it to doughboys. The girls didn't know this. Nor did their dates, it seemed. No one did until the vice squad came.

The doctor gave up easily, boasting of his lawyer's prowess.

Ordered to get lost, the soldiers did. The girls were hauled to the makeshift brig in Ayer.

"Said we're all coozies," Fleur complains. "I told 'em we're not either. Least *I'm* not." She flashes a half-second glare at Lisbeth.

Lisbeth says, "That Bess didn' do us no favors. They found her in the basement of the doctor's house, doped up — squalled like a baby when they cuffed her."

"Thank God," Fleur says, "for that social worker lady. Would've been ten times worse without her."

Frieda twists a length of gauze around and around her wrist, wondering what Alice did for them. Did she sit beside them, all night long, assuring? If only Frieda herself could start fresh with Alice (or make her first impression last forever). This time she'd keep all her promises. *The senator? And who else? I'll talk to anyone you want.* This time she'd make Alice proud.

The patients who've been here awhile want news from the outside. Not battlefronts — they get that in the paper — but the flux of daily goings-on, of *life*. How are the season's dresses? Have hems gone even higher? Fatty Arbuckle's latest — have they seen it?

The talk turns to what they miss most.

Angelina says the Public Garden. "The Swan Boats, and people dressed so nice."

"Kidding?" Hattie says. "I'll spell you what *I* miss. Starts with *m* and ends with *e-n*."

What Flossie really craves, she says, is dancing. "I wouldn't even know the new steps."

"Nah," says Lisbeth. "You'd do fine. Nothin' much has changed. They shut some ballrooms down, but others opened."

"The Independence? They didn't close *that*, did they?" At the sound of her own voice, Frieda starts. All at once she's stricken with an image of the ballroom, chandeliers gone dim, mirrors cracked.

"Independence? Not far's I know," says Lisbeth. "But the

Scollay . . ." And she's off on a new jag: a fight outside the dance hall, when a drunk stole some cop's horse . . .

"Wait! I know *you*. You're that girl!" It's Ethel, who until now has scarcely said a word.

Frieda bristles, bracing for indictment.

"That girl from the Independence — sure! Always there with the other one. With Lou."

"You know Lou?" says Frieda.

"Who doesn't?"

A bubble of promise grows in Frieda's chest. "How's she doing? Tell me. Have you seen her?"

Ethel is a plump girl with thick, brambled hair. Her modest face shines with perspiration, as white and weepy as an apple cut open. "Not for a month," she says. "Maybe more? Thing is, I had a steady, so I didn't go out lately. Only reason I came here for the party was, we split. In the market for a new beau, right? Tough luck."

Frieda isn't interested in Ethel's tale of woe; she wants to hear of her own life — her *real* life. "But you knew her?" she persists. "Knew *us*?"

"Knew *of*, I guess is more like." Ethel lifts her face as if to catch a ballroom's glow, or maybe it's the glow of memory. "The first time's the one I won't forget. I'd just moved from Hingham to the city. Five times I must've circled round and round the block, trying to get the nerve to go in. Then I saw you and Lou — I didn't know your names — flouncing to the entrance like you owned it. She was in a pink number, falling off her shoulders. And you — you had a heart, I think, embroidered on your gown."

Frieda recalls the dress — borrowed from Lou at the last minute — tight across the chest, at the neck. The embroidery wasn't a heart, it was a rose.

"She said something, and you threw your chin back and laughed and laughed." Ethel pantomimes what she's described. "I went home and practiced all that next week in the mirror.

232

If only I could make myself like *her*!" Her eyes have a hazy, dream-bound look.

"Well," says Frieda, shrugging. "Here you are." It comes out more sourly than intended. *Make yourself like me?* is what she means. *What did I know? I was nothing but a silly, hopeful fool.* "That was all forever ago," she tells her.

Alice, in the fading afternoon, looks even worse — dumpy, slackened with exhaustion. She's found Frieda working with the crew out in the yard, finishing the outhouse demolition. The whine of nails pulled from wood resounds.

She clasps Frieda's arm. "Take a walk?"

The long hours deprived (was Alice with Bess all that time?) have filled Frieda with feline chariness. "What," she says, "from here to the fence and back?"

"Good gosh, no. Away from here. Outside."

"But," says Frieda, scanning for the matron.

Alice says don't worry, Mrs. Digges gave permission. "I told her that I needed to have a few tough words with you, and that we needed a bit of privacy. The treatment room's in use. This place is packed."

Was Alice's reason true, Frieda wonders, or a ploy? From Alice's drab tone, she can't tell.

Frieda will have to stay within her sights, Alice says, and they'll have to return before nightfall. "An hour or so, but still a break. We could both use that. Come on."

Frieda's shocked by how easily — how offhandedly — Alice arranged it (when she herself could beg and beg for weeks, to no avail), but the dangled lure of freedom — of a furlough just for her — distracts her from the rising of resentment. An hour away, outside. Outside!

Burnham looks cheated as he opens up the gate: the keys are in his hand, but he must stay. Frieda feels the pressure of the patients' jealous glares. She lifts her chin and marches past the fence.

She wants there to be some immediate difference: a shift in the world's taste and texture; she wants to feel a falling away of chains. She breathes, but her lungs remain tight, the air familiar. The only appreciable change is a thickening of insects, the air busy with gnats and deerflies.

Alice doesn't seem to mind the bugs. Along she plods with shoulders hunched in a drudgery of silence, as if wholly unaware of Frieda. Maybe *because* of Frieda: chiding silence.

"Must be dog-tired," Frieda says to break the ice, sympathy a hedge against rebuke. "All those new patients, all at once!"

Alice gives a tight, shopworn chuckle. "It's not the quantity, it's the quality. Or lack thereof."

"That one girl — Bess? She'll be all right?"

Alice nods. "Weak. But she knows it. She'll recover. The trouble are the ones who *think* they're strong." She focuses a wearied stare on Frieda.

Around a bend, and they're struck by a hard, gamy smell: the rendering plant, with its maze of rusty fencing filled with stock, and, beyond it, the brick fist of a building. By the entrance, a truck disgorges horses.

"Mind if we walk a different way?" asks Frieda.

Alice lets a long ten seconds pass without responding. Then: "Mind telling me what happened the other day?"

The anxious chuff of animals milling in the yard competes with the plant's metallic clamor. At intervals, a sharp but deadened *pock*.

"The senator," Alice says. "You were going to talk to him."

"Came and went so quick. There wasn't time."

"But you found time to talk with the other man."

"The other man," Frieda says with no inflection. This is hardly the fresh start she envisioned with Alice. Why is she so scared of being honest? Does she sense that the truth may anger Alice more than any small fib or omission?

On either side of the road, barbed wire hems them in; they're forced within a yard of the parked truck. A gelding, its eyes the blue-gray of cataracts, clops after a sun-withered farmer. The horse wears a bridle, but the farmer doesn't hold it; the beast follows of its own old accord.

"Morse," says Alice. "Why'd you talk to him?"

Frieda skirts a pile of fresh manure and trudges on, avoiding the sight of Alice, or the gelding. In the dust of the road ahead are two faint pairs of shoe prints, one square, the other pointed: male and female. She could do what Bess tried. Make a break for it. Sprint. Escape the Home, and Alice's disappointment.

A whinny jags across the stockyard. *Pock.*

Alice would be on the hook for letting her run off. Could they fire her then? Wreck her reputation?

"I'm sorry," Frieda says at last. "I should have explained."

Seeing the hint of smile that breaks on Alice's lips, Frieda brims with sudden certainty: she doesn't want to run, not at all. To be free, yes, but not to take flight. What she wants is to *not* get away with anything — to be held to account by someone who respects her. "I know Morse's son," she says. "Knew him."

"Back in Boston?"

"It's complicated," she says. Immediately she wonders: is it really? Maybe it's the simplest of all stories. A girl with a crush. A girl crushed.

Slowly, deliberately, she bares the whole saga, from the Liberty Loan parade onward. Felix's finding her at the store, the baseball game. Afterward, his house, his father's car. She doesn't hide her thrill in recounting certain details ("...*fast* — I mean, he didn't hold back ..."), but neither does she hide her disillusion. When she learned of her infection, she says, she tried to despise him. Maybe she should have tried harder.

"When those men came, and I found out that one was his father, I just — I just had to talk to him. I thought he could help, maybe. Get me out of here? And then I could help the other girls?" Hopefully, she lets her voice rise on the final words. A whiff of something rank and horsy passes. "Okay, no. That's not true. Just partly. To be honest, I . . . he looked so much like Felix."

235

Alice stops and turns to her, her face parched-looking, tough. "You *swore*. You said you didn't know him."

"I didn't. Never met him till that day."

"Not the father, Frieda. The son."

A deerfly burrs by Frieda's ear. She flinches. "How could I swear *that*? I never mentioned Felix!" She didn't. She consciously refrained.

"Our first interview. You said the soldier was a stranger."

"You mean the one who? — *he* was. I didn't know *him*. I was trying to *get* to Felix when that happened."

"So," says Alice. "So. You kept this from me."

"No. I just—"

The deerfly's buzzing loudens, and she ducks, but it stays close. She feels its hissing wingbeats on her neck.

Flynn she could explain: a monster and his prey. Or, rather, didn't have to explain; what Flynn did was nothing she had asked for. But Felix she had chosen — she'd let herself be chosen — so the consequences seemed at once more dear and worth the price. How can she tell Alice that given the choice again, she might choose all the same mistakes?

"Even when his father came," says Alice, "you said nothing? When you *knew* he would be coming. Not a thing?" With unrelenting strides, she stalks away.

But Frieda *didn't* know, did she? Or is she fibbing to her own self, misremembering to shield herself from blame? She follows Alice, whirring with doubt, slapping at the fly. Slaps and slaps, but all she gets is skin.

"I thought we agreed on a plan," Alice says. "A plan, I might add, to help *you*. I went to great lengths to keep the senator to his promise. To bring him here. To give you your one chance."

"The senator, you said. Storrow, you said. 'Dignitaries.' That's all. You never mentioned Mr. Morse. Never."

Alice stops, an engine whose gears have been stripped. She studies Frieda — is it anger or apology in her eyes? — then lifts one pale blade of palm and swats. The deerfly is smashed on Frieda's neck.

"I owe you an apology. I stand corrected."

With tender efficiency, she cleans Frieda's neck, then resumes a compatible, even gait. Gone is the scowl and the snappish fatigue. The flush of antagonism fades. The turnabout is startling in its swiftness, as though Alice goaded Frieda into this dispute only so they could then make up. Frieda is left lightheaded, but not unpleasantly so. When did someone last apologize to *her*?

Now, finally, the air does seem changed. There's a whipped-cream smoothness to each breath. Frieda wants to stare up at the sky — at everything — but finds herself overwhelmed by just the road, by the chuckholes and the litter lodged within them. A crushed sack of Bull Durham, leaking brownish grit; a Wrigley's gum wrapper, wadded up — the sordid, splendid leavings of indulgence. Someone chewed that gum, she thinks. Someone *chose* to chew it. Someone smoked, then tossed that sack away. The full gamut of trivial, commonplace choices that, added all up, mean everything.

This, she'd say. This choosing is what she misses.

Alice leads them left onto a smaller country lane that runs between tumbledown stone walls. The canopy of maples, chinked with bits of sky, turns the world a watery blue-green. They pass a brook, a lightning-struck stump.

"Here," says Alice, opening a gate.

The graveyard is small — a score of stones at most, all with the name Higgins or Thayer — and carpeted with thick furls of moss. A hedge of hawthorn screens it from the road.

Alice sits and leans against the largest of the stones (EZRA HIGGINS, FAITHFUL HUSBAND, FRIEND), her legs splayed with a schoolgirl's insouciance. "Ah," she says. "Nice and peaceful . . . at least for the still-living. Knock on wood." She raps the looming headstone. "Well, on marble!"

Frieda stands in the aisle between graves.

"Don't be spooked! All these folks've long since gone to dust."

But no, in the corner of the plot, behind Alice, is a grave so fresh it's bare of grass. At its head, a wee stone. BABY THAYER. "Isn't this sacrilegious?" Frieda asks.

"Fff. Don't be silly, now. It's earth!" She pats the ground like a loyal mutt's rump. "My father — the Very, *Very* Reverend — always took us picnicking in graveyards. 'Makes the food taste heavenly,' he'd say." She laughs and tugs Frieda by the wrist.

Frieda sits experimentally on the moist, cloud-soft moss — close to Alice, facing, leg by leg. She leans against a smooth expanse of slate.

"See?" says Alice. "Father knows best. Relax."

Any spook she felt is scattered now by her friend's nearness. The air smells elemental, full of rock. She studies all the skulls and the weeping trees of life etched on the small, faded stones. WIFE OF THE LATE; TWO SONS MOURN HIS LOSS. Carved into a tall, tilted marker: PEACE BE WITH THEE OUR FATHER IN THE SPIRIT LAND. VAINLY WE LOOK FOR ANOTHER IN THY PLACE TO STAND.

In a panic of forgetting, her heartbeat clogs her throat. What did they have carved on Papa's stone? She tries to picture the plot in East Boston.

She remembers, then: she never saw the marker. She fled before the Yahrzeit, the unveiling.

"Is he still alive?" she asks Alice. "Your father?"

"Oh, ho, I should say! Alive enough to row his scull every day at dawn — all year until there's ice, including Sundays. I should think he'll live to a hundred and fifteen." She rolls her eyes with tender exasperation. "*His* father — my *grand*father's going strong. Eighty-three the first of last month. Captain in the Civil War, Grandpa Longley was, and oh!, you should hear him on the secretary of war. 'Newton Baker — a pacifist — to lead us into battle? What we need's a butcher, not a baker.'"

Alice, in bombastic impersonation of her grandfather, has hoarsened her voice to mannish depths. It's meant to be funny, but Frieda, for some reason, finds it sad.

"Grandpa always asks how I can work for the secretary —

as if Baker's my own supervisor, you know? Then again, he'd rather I not work for *anyone*. 'Now, why can't you just settle down?'" Alice steeples her fingers, then closes them to fists. "Father has the good grace not to ask. Not, anyhow, since Mother died. He remembers how she and I would fight."

Frieda feels the stone's corrective pressure against her back. *Mama.* She almost managed to forget.

"I got tired of explaining myself," says Alice. "So I started just to answer her with coyness. 'I'm married already,' I'd say, 'to the hope of being happy. If we split, Mother, you'll be first to know.' Oh! Did that get her ears smoking!" Alice makes a devilish face. "But maybe," she says, darkening, "Mother got the last laugh. Turns out that happiness cheats as much as any husband."

Overhead, branches blow and scratch; the wind warbles. Frieda reads the inscription for "Baby Thayer":

SHE WAS BUT AS A SMILE
WHICH GLISTENS IN A TEAR
SEEN BUT A LITTLE WHILE
BUT OH! HOW LOVED, HOW DEAR!

"Mama," she says. "My mother. She tracked me down."

"Yes," says Alice softly. "Yes, I know."

"You know?"

"Yes, dear. Mrs. Digges told me." She brushes Frieda's shin, a benefaction. Quickly she pulls her hand back to her lap. "It's why I wanted to see you. Part of why. We have to think how best to handle this."

We. It salves the sting in Frieda's bones.

But still: All this time, Alice knew? What else does she know and not tell? Frieda pictures Alice and Mrs. Digges conspiring, deciding on Frieda's fate without her. Is that why the matron granted her this furlough?

"Best? There *is* no best," says Frieda. "Not with Mama. I told you. Didn't I tell you? She makes me feel *sick*. Like it's my job to stay miserable just for her." She scalps a patch of moss from a stone. "But maybe you want to send me back and see me married off. Would that look good on your charts — like you rescued another girl? Isn't that what you wanted all along?"

"Now, Frieda. Now listen. Let's stay calm."

"Calm? Calm like *you* were just before? When you gave me the third degree on Mr. Morse?"

"The reason I was cross — not cross, *concerned* — is that everything is teetering on the edge. Your position. And my own. This whole mess."

She manages somehow to move closer to Frieda while making it seem as if she's inched away. Her jittering reminds Frieda of someone.

"I want to help you, Frieda, don't you see? But if I can't trust you . . . trust you to stay true . . ." Alice makes stymied, futile movements with her hands. "Tell me why, when someone is right *here*, giving help, you'd run toward the source of all your problems."

"Mr. Morse isn't the source of —"

"His *son*."

"Sure, but —"

"Frieda, please! You just told me the story. *He* was the one who made you truly sick." Her knee knocks insistently into Frieda's, stiff and skull-like. Frieda is cornered between her and the gravestone. "You blame yourself, Frieda. Blame your mother. Maybe me. Everyone but the man who got you here!"

She says this with a faith, a ministerial conviction, that makes Frieda picture her in girlhood, rapt at her father's Sunday sermons. The tenets of Alice's faith may now differ from her father's, but she does, it strikes Frieda — evangelically, she does — believe. (In a divinity of sisterhood, of female self-reliance?) Maybe, Frieda thinks, that's why Alice seems so threatened, as believers are always threatened by apostates: Does she view Frieda's dogged passion for Felix as backsliding?

"Have you stopped to think," says Alice, "that since you've been detained, *I* might well have contacted your mother?"

No. The thought never crossed her mind. Now it drives a seething down the buttons of her spine.

"But I didn't. I knew you didn't want it. And given the law, I knew that you'd be stuck here for a while. Wait, I thought. See how she progresses." Her knee again, its bony round assertion. "Frieda, you're out and away the most promising girl here. You're just the sort of girl I dream of helping. So I shielded you, I didn't find your mother. Some might charge me with dereliction, but so be it."

"But she found *me*," Frieda says.

"She did."

"And now she can make me marry Hirsch, I know she can. What if she does? What if I spend my whole life stuck with him, and end up some old, bitter woman?"

Alice traces a stranger's birth date with her finger. "Which would be worse: going back or staying?"

"Staying? What do you mean, staying?"

"You see, I thought of something. An idea." Alice explains that Frieda, under law, is still a child, and still, therefore, in her mother's charge — *unless* the state can show compelling cause. Which is why, for the time being, they can keep her at the Home: the government's interests trump her mother's. "Do you see?" Alice asks. "See where I'm headed?"

No, not quite. She stares at Alice blankly.

"Okay. We keep you girls here until you're well, until the doctor says that you can go. But if he doesn't say so — if you *fail* the test — you're safe. As long as you're with us, she can't touch you. Then soon you'll turn eighteen, and that's that." Alice gleams: a eureka of a grin.

Frieda, in a hush, says, "Three more months?"

"Is it that long? More like two, I thought."

"Almost three."

"It's not ideal," Alice admits. "I know." She tinkers with the brim of her wilted straw hat; a cluster of fake cherries flops. "But to keep your mother at bay, you know. To stall."

"You think it's so easy here? 'Stalling'?"

241

"Well, Frieda, I must say, you don't seem to have a plan — so maybe some extra time's not so bad. Have you considered what will happen when you're freed?"

Considered it? She's dreamed of it for months, every day, dreamed of hearing the doctor say she's clean. If only her monthlies would quit, he could test her. "Of course," she says. "It's practically all I think of."

"Tell me, then. What have you got planned? Do you even know where you'll spend the first night?"

Frieda's been so bent on the dream of soaring free that she hasn't wanted to weight it with logistics. Maybe she'll look for Lou and ask to sleep at her place. (Her bed's too small; maybe on the floor? And what if Lou has moved — what then?) She'll hunt for a new job, but how will she be able to explain where she's spent these past months? What if she is asked to show a reference?

Frieda draws a breath that feels precariously thin, and she finds herself, suddenly, with Alice looking on, unable to gather any words. She picks up a tiny wishbone-shaped twig of hemlock. Abstractedly, she aims it at her boot's metal eyelet, poking the hole over and again — a small goal, easily attained.

"A teacher of mine," says Alice. "Miss Nichols, my very favorite. Whenever I was stuck, she would walk up to my desk, and she'd whisper, 'Alice, what *tense* are you in?' That was all. 'What tense?' Then she'd go." Alice takes Frieda's twig away. "What she meant was: Stop slogging in the rut of *was* or *am*. Set your mind on *might be*. Think: I *will*. That's how people change. How they rise."

Alice removes her hat, sets it down. Bareheaded, she looks susceptible, sincere. "I wasn't going to bring this up," she says into her lap. "If I can't . . . I'm not sure yet if I can. What I'm hoping? In the time between your clearance and your birthday? I could arrange a sort of . . . a sort of house arrest. Make a finding that you need to be kept for observation — detained, still, but not at the Home, see? In my custody. Help you start your new life." With one thumb she dabs at the pinkness of her brow, as if to erase her blotchy fluster.

"I'd live with you?" asks Frieda, incredulous. "In your house?" Why would Alice do this—*risk* this—for her? And why has the offering of it flustered her so badly? Who does her jittering make Frieda think of?

"I've got an extra bedroom in the back," Alice says. "Small, but there are windows on two sides." Apology and promise co-exist in her soft gaze.

"And me? What would I have to do?"

"Do? Why—why absolutely nothing."

But no, Frieda thinks. There's always, always something: every gift exacts a certain cost. At long last, she's come to understand this.

Then, almost as if she has heard Frieda's doubts, Alice adds, "Well, no specific thing. If you're ready to let go of this nonsense with the Morses, if you're ready to give a go at being good— the point is, you can do anything. *Be* anything."

Wind dips through the trees; it takes up Alice's words and whirls them. Frieda's suddenly conscious of the world as something spun, of the evening's inevitable encroachment. Have they stayed out beyond the time allowed? She's at the mercy of Alice, of her vouching.

At first Frieda thinks it's a trick of slipping dusk—a ghost of shadow thrown between the gravestones—but it stops and turns to her: a thin red fox.

She knows foxes are meant to be unscrupulous and cruel (the bloodied, battered chicken is still vivid in her mind), but this animal looks anything but mean. There's gallantry in its delicate attention. She sees that Alice sees it, too. They watch.

It's smaller than she would have guessed, all wisp and elegance, its legs no more than brushstrokes in the grass. Its fur holds the full range of shades linked with smolder, from charcoal to ember to ash.

"Beautiful," Alice whispers. "Should we take it as a sign?"

The fox lifts its head in a seeming affirmation. It darts and disappears into the woods.

Alice presses her leg closer. Shin tight to thigh. She leans forward, squares her gaze at Frieda. Her jittering from earlier has returned.

Jack, thinks Frieda. Jack! That's who Alice makes her think of: the fidgeting, the gulpy halting speech.

But Alice couldn't (could she?) want Frieda in that way. A woman? Another woman? It's too strange. (Look at what this awful place has done now to Frieda: doubting, always doubting; doubting just when she should most give thanks.)

Alice puts her hands on Frieda's neck, bends it down, and she kisses the crown of Frieda's head. The kiss is firm, and also, in its firmness, uncertain — something hard encased in something soft.

Frieda should say something — ask *why?* or *what next?* — but she's bound up in the memory of her first week at Jordan's, the day that George Eaton walked in. Lou saw, and came to her, tapped her wrist: *watch out.* As clear as day, Lou's signal, but only if you knew it. Only if you knew what to look for.

In the grove behind the graveyard, something skitters, then goes still. The fox? Something bigger? She can't tell.

Twenty-one

★

W HEN BREAKFAST'S DONE, Mrs. Digges throws wide one of the windows, and she booms out, "Let there be light!" She laughs as if to puncture her own bombast.

No one seems quite sure whether to laugh along with her. Least of all, the new girls, hunched at their own table, stiff and looking scared of what's to come.

"Cheer up," orders the matron. "Such long faces. Sad as funerals!" She tickles the air in the direction of Fleur and Ethel. "The Home isn't your *doom*. It's a *start*."

Frieda recognizes a version of the pep talk that she and Flossie got when they were new. Bunk, she considered it then — the worst sort of smarm — but now she believes she hears the faint ting of truth. Too, she considers the unwonted proposition that the matron, in her heart, means them well.

How can you know, she wonders, what's lodged in someone's heart — what she truly means when she says something? How can you know, and does it really matter? These were thoughts that chased their tails all night as she lay sleepless, evaluating what Alice had offered.

Last evening, when Frieda had rejoined them all for supper, the girls begged to know what had happened. (All but Yetta, who snooted her — "No one likes a stooge" — and moved away in a privacy of scorn.) Frieda said that Alice had just walked with her awhile. They pushed for more, so she told them, "A graveyard."

"A graveyard?" asked Flossie. "Why on earth?"

Frieda shrugged. How could she explain it? Such a lot seemed inexplicable all at once.

For instance, what had it meant when Alice kissed her head? Papa had always kissed her just like that, every Shabbos, when he held her head and made the benediction. *The Lord make his face to shine upon thee, and be gracious unto thee.* A blessing! Why couldn't she just take it as a blessing? Alice would give her a home, a sanctified new start, and Frieda only had to — what? Be thankful?

But was Alice truly helping, or just helping herself to Frieda? Was her giving just another way to take?

All through night's darkness and the murky hints of dawn, Frieda's faith tussled with suspicion.

Then the sun displaced the murk with an orderly sky, a snug blue sheet tucked at the horizon. Frieda saw that it didn't matter *why* Alice wanted to help; it mattered just that she did, that she would. If Alice indeed had some peculiar motivation (it was possible; Lou had told Frieda once about such women — women who sought comfort in one another), then fine: all the more help to Frieda. For all these trying months, she'd felt beggarly and void, stripped of any value to the world. Now she understood her very lack — her neediness — to be a thing that Alice must need. Why not turn her weakness into a strength?

Propped up on her cot, staring through the fly-stained window, Frieda let her tilted vision sprawl. *Out and away,* she thought, recalling what Alice told her: "You're out and away the most promising girl here."

The girl who promises the most.

Who makes the most promises.

She would promise until she got just what she wanted.

The matron, now throwing open another of the windows, proclaims that the day will have a theme: "In a word, girls: decontamination." Judging from her countenance of clean satisfaction, you'd think the word alone abolished scum.

"*Did* that," comes an immediate protest from Lisbeth. "Yesterday. The delousing. All the rest."

"I'm not just talking about you new girls," says the matron. "Everyone. The whole Home needs attention." She explains that, in view of the current overcrowding, precautionary measures must be taken. Reports have arrived from detention homes down south of grippe running rampant through the patients. At the Florence Crittenton Home in Chattanooga, half the girls caught a stomach bug. Air is the cure. Daylight. Wide-open windows. Mattresses hauled into the yard. Then sulfur and soap and elbow grease.

"I thought we were sent here to get *well*," complains Fleur. "Not to catch some other new disease."

"You were," says the matron, "and you won't. So long as you all follow my instructions."

It's not lost on Frieda that the ones objecting most are those for whom confinement's wound is fresh. Where is Flossie's voice? Where is Yetta's? Are they cowed now, or just cannier, picking and choosing fights?

Cannier like Frieda herself, finally.

She told Alice yesterday she'd have to think things over, that she'd answer at week's end, when Alice comes again. (Meanwhile, Alice will work to stall things with Mama: to keep her from coming to the Home, if she threatens; to placate her with the promise of a phone call. Could Frieda, Alice asked, at least *talk* to her mother? A few minutes through the telephone wires?) But if Alice were here now, Frieda wouldn't dawdle. Yes, she'd say, to staying at the Home a bit longer (she could bear it, considering the other option). Yes to letting Alice take her in.

Alice proposed that Frieda, if she lived in the spare room, could use the time to finish up her schooling; she might even set her sights on college, and Alice could recommend her case to Wellesley. Yes, thinks Frieda, schooling would be grand, a dream — college! — but not Wellesley, no. Not there. Frieda wouldn't want to go to school to be like Alice — or not *exactly* like her, not quite. She likes the thought of aiding girls (a teacher? a campaigner?), but not by reaching down from on high and lifting up. She wants to stand beside the girls and push. Girls whom she would always tell where she herself had come from.

Mrs. Digges says, "Hop to it now," and claps her hands. "Scrub this place up fast, and we can all have some free time."

Out into the sunny yard Frieda drags her bedding. Everything looks shifted by a shade: the garden a crisper green (the very color of profusion), the Ton Truck's dented hood like burnished stone.

The other girls tread grudgingly from house to yard, heads bent, blind to all the shine. Jo, especially, looks heavy with displeasure; morning's still her toughest time of day.

"C'mon," Frieda calls to her. "Fresh air's good for you." She'd add "and for the baby," but she can't. She tries to convey the message with her eyes.

Despite her lack of sleep, Frieda teems with alertness, livened by the sun: a second wind. She heads back inside, to the dim and dusty parlor. The sofas, too, the matron said, need airing.

On the parlor floor sits Bess, surrounded by spilled bedding. "Tired," she says. "I'm so tired. I can't."

She might mean this small task, Frieda thinks, or everything. (*This* girl? This girl seemed a threat?) "Sure you can," she tells Bess, and takes her damp hand. "As soon as you get well, of course you can." This is how she'll act someday if she becomes a teacher, or a counselor, or whatever she might be: firmly optimistic and always lending strength, even — especially — to the girls who seem most hopeless. "For now, though, Bess, what you need is some rest. Sit tight. I'll take care of your bedding."

Bess offers a laggard smile of thanks.

Frieda collects the mattress and the pillows and the sheets, and lugs them all together from the Home. Funny, how the sweat that she works up isn't nasty, but something to be proud of, to be savored.

She's heard of how tornadoes will sometimes raze a house but capriciously leave its contents safe. That's what the yard resembles when they're done: sofas and beds carefully arranged on a carpet that happens to be grass. A set for some out-of-doors theatrical.

"Do come in," she says in a trumped-up high-class accent, speaking to imaginary guests. "It's a pleasure to welcome you to my *boudoir*."

That rich word, from Frieda's lips, alone would be a gas. Applied to the furnished yard it causes fits: the girls guffaw and prance and shout "boo-dwawr." She can't tell if they're sharing in her mirth or poking fun. Either way, she's rescued them: she's snapped the holds of gloom.

Promising, she thinks. *I'm promising.*

Soon, as if depleted by their hard-won cheerfulness, the girls subside and settle on their beds — their beds whose canopy is the sky. Reclining, they remind Frieda of diners at a Seder, play-acting the postures of liberation. They laze about and wait for naps to come. Even Mrs. Digges falls eventually to dozing, her snores like a puzzled sort of laughter.

Later, when the rain wakes them — a sudden, beating downpour (how could sun so quickly turn to storm?) — the girls panic, running for cover, and so does Mrs. Digges, who wildly tries to gather up some pillows. "Goodness, no. No! It's all soaked!" Only Frieda stays just where she is, sitting still. If this had happened yesterday — a week ago, a month — she too would have cursed the slashing rain. But here she stands, rain on her scalp, rain on her upturned hands, loving every blissful, blessed drop.

It's like the storm that doused her on the day she fled from Hirsch, when she left the pawnshop, money in her fist. The shop door shut behind her with a tiny tin bell's chime — the sound of someone calling for a toast — and she strode into Boston's misty rush. Terrified, she should have been, and *was* — of course she was — but mostly how she felt was wide awake. She imagined Mama's standard nag — "Your death, you'll catch! Come in!" — but Mama couldn't rule her any longer.

Not her death. Her *life*. That's what she caught.

Flossie slips her the letter two days later, just past dawn, when the rest of their roommates are still sleeping.

Frieda knows the handwriting at once. "How?" she whispers.

"Rattigan. Showed me it last night. Wanted me to tell you to go find him."

Frieda can remember cautious footsteps in the dark: a new girl on a toilet run, she reckoned. Now she understands that it must have been Flossie, answering her own pressing needs.

Flossie says, "I figured that I owed you for the Fourth, the way you covered for me with the matron. And before that, too — the tobacco. So I gave Rattigan . . . let's just say fair trade, and he let me have it. But if you tell —"

"No," says Frieda. "Never."

Flossie scans their resting roommates' faces. "Good, 'cause he could break us both in two."

Saying this, she smiles, as if enthralled by the violent thought, and Frieda, too, is transfixed: by the risk, by the letter in her hands. "Thanks," she says. "Oh, Flossie, thank you, thank you!"

Sweet FM,

How I hope you get this letter. I'm handing it to a guy who knows a guy who claims he knows . . . well, let's just say it's not the U.S. Mail. But then, I'd never count on standard channels to contact you; you've shown yourself the furthest thing from standard.

This morning, when Sgt. Dale bounded in with the newspaper, he aimed to cheer, and thought he knew just how. (I'll tell you later why I'm needing cheer.) "Look," he said. "Your father. Ain't that swell?" Which shows how much Sarge understands me. But I looked, and am I ever glad I did.

How chirked I was to see your face — so sparkly, so sharp!, even in that tiny smudge of newsprint. (If Sarge thought I was grinning for Father, fine.) But then I read the caption. I just died. Oh, Frieda, I'm so awfully, awfully sorry. What Father asked me makes much more sense now.

He explains how his father came to Devens in a snit — "considerably more noxious than normal" — and grilled him about some "scummy girl" named Frieda. His father wouldn't tell Felix how he had met her but demanded to know if what she'd said was true.

Felix says he should have told him, *My friends aren't your business*, but he was so excited just to hear news of Frieda that he said *of course* he knew her, and in *no way* was she 'scummy.' His father, with the senator and everyone else gathered, couldn't pitch the fit he might have yearned to.

Felix says he'd almost given up on finding Frieda; he guessed that *she* had given up on *him*. But now he understands why she hasn't been in touch, and he's sick — just ashamed! — to think of her locked up. Ashamed because he gave her what she has.

It's not Felix's shame that makes Frieda happy, but his nakedness, his sweet, unhusked emotion.

He'd help her, he goes on to say — and will, somehow, he will — but now he's in "a bit of a scrape" himself. No, not in the same way as she (the docs fixed that), but an injury from bayonet training.

251

We fight dummy Huns — really, straw stuffed into sacks, so the jury's out on who're the true dummies. A week back, we're in the trench, waiting for the signal. This kid beside me, Evers — no bigger than a pint of peanuts, but jumpy, always has to push ahead — hauls himself up before it's time. Sarge grabs ahold of him and yanks him back down, and where does he land? You guessed it: yours truly. As this was a mock battle, I was counting on a mock wound (and it's certainly one worthy of being mocked), but alas it's all too real: a broken shin. I'm S.O.L.: *"swear-word* out of luck."

Or maybe I've got nothing *but* luck. The rest of my division ships out for France this week, and I'll stay back, safe (if not sound).

Father's worried that people might think it was on purpose — that I'm "malingering," and it will "sully his good name." (He knows how I loathe all his pretensions.) I'd happily take him down a notch — this campaign of his is bunk — but he forgets that his good name is also mine. Wrong place, wrong time, is all it was.

So here I lie confined — though not half so bad as you. If you want nothing to do with me, I fully understand. If I were you, I don't believe I would. But I got you into this pickle, and I want to get you out. Get you out so I can stand beside you! ("Stand," I wrote, but truly I want to lie in bed beside you — smelling your neck, the skin behind your ear.)

I know that it's unseemly to speak of things financial, but I want to let you know a thought I had: At the end of this year, I'll be turning twenty-one, and the trust that's being held for me is mine. I hope you'll let me share some of it — and share much more — with you.

We'll talk about this further when we see each other (*we will!*). For now, please know I'm beaming dreams your way. They've got us behind in the count, but we haven't struck out yet. We'll foul them off till we get our pitch to hit.

Hopefully, loyally,
FM

She's reading it through again, imagining his voice, when the ruckus of a new day intrudes: Mrs. Digges hollering up the stairs ("Rise and shine!") and Bess (it must be, in the last of her withdrawal) screaming from her room down the hall. It sounds as though she's gargling barbed wire.

"Jesus Christ, what's she now, a rooster?" Yetta gripes. She wipes a paste of sleep off her lips.

"Someone, please," says Flossie. "Put the girl out of her misery."

"Put us *all* out of misery," Yetta adds.

Jo wakes and turns to Frieda and starts to ask something (something about the letter that she's holding?), but Frieda doesn't hear exactly what; her mind is still ringing with Felix's words and now with the phrase Yetta used. *Out of misery* — as though misery is a place that can be left, a pit that one eventually climbs out of.

Eventually is *now* — Frieda's climbing, being boosted; Felix will be there to lend his hand. Frieda would tell Jo, but she doesn't want to gloat (or doesn't want Jo to think she is): that *she* still has a sweetheart and that hers has proven true, that *her* impulsive passion will survive.

She folds up the letter until it fits within her fist, then hides it in the heel of her left shoe. With every step she takes, she'll feel him there.

Only late that evening, as she's readying for bed, does she look again and find the letter's postscript. On the back of the last page, a song Felix wrote:

> (*Sung to the tune of "Over There"*)
> *Frieda Mintz, Frieda Mintz,*
> *lift your chin, try to grin,*
> *Frieda Mintz.*
> *For the foolish Private*
> *with ghoulish privates*

has rued his boo-boo ever since.
So don't wince,
Frieda Mintz,
lift your chin
for this fellow's no chintz.
He will help you, he's vowed to help you,
and he won't give up till he's freed you, Frieda Mintz.

Twenty-two

---★---

W HEN DR. SLOCUM comes with the results, Hattie
goes first to see him.

The anxious gang awaits her on the parlor's too plump
couches (the pillows dry at last from their dousing in the yard,
but seeping an incipient moldy smell). Flicks of daylight tease
in through moth holes in the drapes. The cupids on the ceiling
stretch their bows.

"Grits," says Melba. "Grits with cheese and salt."

Someone else says, "T-bone steak, still mooing."

A bowl of kale soup will be Angelina's treat — like her mother's, "with linguiça wall-to-wall."

How will Frieda celebrate *her* freedom? She keeps it to herself — only Lou might understand — but the meal she can't stop
dreaming of: three gumdrops. With a sad sort of affection she
recalls that long-gone Frieda, who thought each penny saved
ensured salvation.

"Food?" says Flossie. "*Food* is what you think of?" When *she*
gets out, she'll feed a different hunger. "Sully's, d'you know it?

Down by the docks in Charlestown? They've got a deck out back, and the ships can sail right up, tie on so the boys can . . . tie one on." She makes a stormy movement with her hips. "Look for me right there: the deck at Sully's."

Yetta scoffs. "What, so you can catch the clap again?"

"Catch something," Flossie says. "Been way too long." Rattigan, apparently, doesn't count.

Yetta stands and faces the couch, like a lawyer before a jury, with a lawyer's impatient passion in her glare. "Don't you even understand?" she says. "Not *one* of you? It's not peaches and cream from here on out."

"Peaches!" says Melba. "Cobbler à la mode!"

Yetta's face stays serious and sharp. "Getting out of this dump doesn't mean we're in the clear. What's to keep them from rounding us up again?"

"Again?" asks Jo, her first word of the day. "Isn't that against . . . well, the rules?"

"*What* rules? There are no more rules," Yetta says. "They're holding us all here without a single formal charge. What reason would they need to bring us back?"

"They can't just lock us up for nothing," says Flossie. "Even those bastards can't, can they?"

"Not if we're — if, you know, if we're clean," Frieda says.

Yetta shakes her head. "Define 'clean.'"

Hattie returns from the treatment room with conspicuous, heavy steps. Flossie offers a seat, but she refuses. She stands there, shoulders wilted, chest heaving.

"Damn," says Melba. "Girl, what happened? Tell us."

Hattie takes a weak and ragged breath. "I'm sad, is all," she says, "just so sad." Her voice breaks to a thinner, higher pitch. "Sad 'cause I won't see y'all any longer." Now the pitch is revealed as that of laughter; she flashes them a gloating, gold-capped smile. "Good as new, doc said. Can't keep me here!"

She's bouncing on her toes, and the girls jump up to join her. They pummel her with fierce congratulations.

"When?" asks Angelina.

"Few days more. Week at the most. Paperwork is all. Just paperwork."

Melba, bosom jiggling, is the picture of jubilation. Flossie calls for cheers: *hip, hip, hurrah!* Even Yetta mutters, "Mazel tov."

Frieda joins the fray and worms her way close to its center — arms and legs all sweatily entangled — wanting Hattie's luck to rub off. It's like the celebration at the Red Sox game's end, when Felix and the fans touched one another: a pat on the back, a shoulder chucked, a handshake. There was chumminess but also superstition in their contact: the fear of disconnection, broken flow.

"You deserve it," Frieda gushes when she's finally next to Hattie. By which she really means: don't we all?

Melba goes next, and the wait this time seems shorter, with Hattie here regaling them with plans: how she's headed for Chicago, 'cause these East Coast folk are prudes, and she heard the Polacks tip for special favors. Or maybe East St. Louis; she's got kin. Her voice takes on an airy, vital tone.

When Melba strolls back in, she seems to want to play it cool, but her cheeks, in the obvious effort to keep from grinning, look like some sweet baked good, overfilled.

"You, too?" Hattie asks.

Melba giggles. She laughs until her face shines with tears.

Flossie leaves for her exam with fingers on both hands crossed. "Wish me luck," she says, and they all do.

After her will come Frieda's turn, then Jo's. Then someone else's — Angelina's?

"Nervous?" Hattie asks.

"A bit," Frieda says. It's easier, she thinks, than explaining. She hasn't told a soul that Alice might rig her results. Besides, today she isn't going to learn of any outcome, but only have the swabs and blood taken — the tests that her monthly flow delayed.

By now, Melba's merriment has drawn some new girls down

from the sewing room, where they were rolling gauze. Ethel, in the doorway, looks benighted by envy; behind her, Lisbeth works at nonchalance. Mrs. Digges, too, stands at the door, her mouth tight — on the verge either of laughing or lamenting. Frieda recalls a boy she saw along the Charlesbank once, who'd launched an ornate painted model boat; his face, as the boat sailed off, looked pinched with forlorn pride, mournful that he'd built the craft so well.

But no one can stay unsmiling when Flossie pushes through, hurls her arms high, and shouts, "Ta-*dah!*" — simultaneously the magician and the trick. She prances around the room, bussing cheeks with wet smacks. She even plants a kiss on Mrs. Digges.

Hattie's results and Melba's didn't much surprise Frieda: those two have been here the longest. But Flossie arrived with her — the very day! — and now *she's* cleared. Is the doctor, to combat overcrowding, bending standards? Or are all the old gang healthy — have they been so for weeks? — and the doctor never bothered to retest them?

Frieda's budding skepticism is nipped by the exuberance of everyone rallying around Flossie — and by the dawning of the belief that she herself must now be clean.

"Leaving," Flossie sings, "I'm believing that I'm leaving," a ditty no less perfect for having no clear tune, and soon it's echoed by the other patients: silliness and adamancy in chorus.

Fortified by the levity, Frieda leaves the room and makes her way down to see the doctor. He greets her with a grimace, but scarcely does she see him, scarcely does she notice the routine. She's standing, then she's lying; one leg's stirruped, then the next; but now she feels immune to the enchainment. With eyes shut, she untethers nimbly from discomfort, floats to somewhere measureless and bright. Her future — is that what she is seeing? Not the *what* but the *how* of coming days.

She's been here before, this vast realm within her mind: with Jack, that very first time, in the boxcar that smelled of spruce; with Felix, too, taking air from his mouth into hers, every breath a tiny reinvention. She conjures Felix crooning to her, as playful as a flame: *Lift your chin, try to grin, Frieda Mintz.*

She's been conjuring him — trying to — ever since his letter: the steel-sheen of his hair, his skillful hands. But sometimes when attempting to envision further moments, she's shocked to find nothing but a blank. They've been so long separated, she muses, that's why. But what if, by this point, all they share is separation?

A tapping on her knee brings her back into the room, a tapping and a tune sung in time. She looks up to the big-eared grinning doctor. She must have been humming out loud as she thought of Felix, for the tune the doctor sings is "Over There." He sings in a private, barely audible voice, the voice you might use to lull a weary lover to sleep: ". . . the drums rum-tumming everywhere . . ."

He has a wife, she remembers: the woman who telephoned when Frieda was first examined, to whom he promised sugar, because molasses wouldn't do. Does he serenade his wife with this voice? Perhaps, she thinks, he's not devoid of sympathy or grace, but applies these virtues somewhere other than his job. And why not — should she really expect different from a doctor, just because his job is doctoring?

He unstraps the stirrups — has he finished the tests so soon? — and gently guides her knees down to the table, all the while continuing to sing.

". . . We'll be over, we're coming over, and we won't come back till it's over, over there!"

Frieda is buoyed by her new view of the doctor. (If *she* can be lifted by this tide of graciousness, others might be, too, and might come to see *her* newly.) She dresses herself, tightens her boot laces.

The doctor says he'll have her results a few days hence, and, judging by the other girls' results, he's optimistic. He makes a face of contingent congratulation.

He must not understand that Frieda's counting on failure. She has to tell Alice to instruct him.

In the parlor now, it's just the old patients and the matron. (The new girls mustn't have felt festive, and who can blame them?) The girls dance as they did on Frieda's first night here — the sofas and love seat pushed back against the walls, the rug rolled to bare the oak floor. The Victrola's in full spin with some feather-brained song about a "simple Swedish girl was Hilda." Everyone tries to keep up with the chorus:

> *Holy Yumpin Yiminy, how my Yonny can love.*
> *When he kisses me, oh what yoy,*
> *Makes me feel so oh! by Yiminy! . . .*

The dance is not specific — not the turkey trot or the grizzly — but something free and artfully impromptu, a collective fortitude uncaged. Hattie twirls with Melba, their elbows firmly locked. With obstinate abandon, Flossie spins. (Her happiness has pared her to a perfect girlish essence; she might be dancing around a ribboned Maypole.) The air, stirred by all the fuss, feels as ticklish as champagne.

No one questions Frieda when she joins the raucous dance, and she feels not the slightest need to talk; every swishing step and glide tells plenty. And if, for an instant, she forgets what forced them here, she can think: What luck to know this group of girls! Her throat swells with preemptive nostalgia. She won't miss this place, but she'll miss *them*.

She'll miss Hattie and Melba (each alone but most together), their tongue-in-cheek conspiracy of two. And Flossie, with her aggressive, ungovernable yearnings. She'll miss Yetta's opinionated eyes. *Holy Yumpin Yiminy,* and they flit across the floor — these girls, each one clad in a homely, hand-sewn frock but carrying herself as if it were a ball gown; these girls who share nothing much in common but their sex, and thus who share almost everything.

Mrs. Digges, who's been watching from the celebration's fringe, is suddenly tugged into the fray. Flossie grabs her wrists and orders, "Dance!" Stumbling, she rights herself with balky, awkward wiggles, and Melba tells her, "*That's* it, there you go."

The matron's shoulders loosen, and she takes a little step, then a gamely self-deprecating hop.

Her too! Frieda will even miss the matron!

And Jo — she can't forget Jo, whose vulnerability somehow makes her feel more tenacious. She looks around the parlor — a blur of limbs and undone hair, the flaunty pink of open-mouthed grins — scanning for Jo, hoping to partner up. ("You're Some Pretty Doll" is now the song.) Frieda's never seen Jo dance but guesses she has a style whose hallmark is the shunning of all style.

She remembers: Jo was scheduled for the exam after hers. Still, though, by now she should be done.

Frieda breaks free from the maelstrom of dancers — past Hattie, past the queerly hopping matron — and turns left, toward the treatment room. She walks so fast she nearly trips on Jo, who's hunkered on the floor just a yard beyond the parlor, her scruffy head buried between her knees.

Frieda crouches. "Oh, poor Jo. Oh. You worried me."

Jo's neck stays bent. Her shoulders twitch.

"Well, so what?" says Frieda. "So you stay a few weeks longer? I haven't told anyone, but I'm probably staying, too. Who cares if our tests are positive?"

Jo makes a sound like the opposite of sighing. "Mine's not," she says. She lifts her face to Frieda. "He knows. Dr. Slocum knows. He found it."

Twenty-three

━━━★━━━

*F*RIEDA STANDS in the guardhouse, long past lights out, the darkness like a tart aftertaste. Tartness, too, in Rattigan's liquor breath. The watchman crowds beside her, asks if she can see. She can't — not much — but hopes it doesn't matter. Hopes they'll get this over with fast.

She wanted Flossie to do it — gave her the letter to give Rattigan — but the message came back: *he wants you.* So here Frieda stands: bleary, breathed upon. (The only other way to get the letter sent to Felix was through Alice; she supposed she shouldn't ask.)

The letter's just one page but took an hour to compose. All that came at first was *miss you so* and *get well soon.* She aimed to match Felix's easy, flippant tone, but she read his letter again, and it irked her. *You* grin, she might tell him, lift *your* chin. Sure, he can joke about it. Sure, he can sing. Felix isn't a girl, isn't *here.*

She tried writing of Alice and her offer of assistance, telling him she didn't need his money. (She wants him to rescue her, to buy her way to freedom, but also proudly wants not to want this.) *All I need,* she wrote, but couldn't finish. She crumpled up the page and found a fresh one.

You're the only one, she began this new attempt.

. . . who can help me — no.

. . . I care for — no.

What?

At last it was her inability to pick one clear tack that gave her the answer she required — for Felix, all along, had been less a clear answer than a baffling, exhilarating question; less a coast to reach than a wave to ride. Papa used to say: Some love the land, and some set sail. Better to risk shipwreck than to rust away on shore.

I don't want promises, she wrote, *or silly songs. I just want to look you in the eye.* This time, when she told him *miss you so* and *get well soon,* she meant it, and she added *heaps of love.*

She hands Rattigan the letter but lets go before he's ready; it falls between them, sounding more substantial than a page.

"Fuck," he says.

She feels it on her neck.

"Fuck," he says again, a fumy slur.

The space is too small for graceful bending. Awkwardly stooping and groping for the letter, Rattigan brushes up beside her — the slightest touch, dry against her knee. He rises, and the letter crinkles loudly when he stuffs it — where? in the trap of his pants pocket?

"You want that he should get this?"

"Quickly. If you can."

"Your boyfriend?"

"A friend. A good friend."

He laughs up a belching, boozy stink. "A 'friend'? Damn, I need a friend like that."

Did he read Felix's letter to her? He must have.

The low, choked-off sound of more laughter. The midnight wind, banging at the door. She can't see him nearing but thinks she maybe feels it: a turbulence, a tamping of the darkness.

She feared this — knew, and tried not to know, it might happen — but still agreed to come out to the guardhouse. Rattigan wouldn't dare, she thought. If so, she'd threaten screams; if so, she'd . . . she might do anything.

Maybe all he'll want will be a touch and nothing more. A touch or a kiss as compensation. Lou always said you had to give a guy *something:* "You gotta be a good Injun."

Fingers. Callused pads along her arm.

"Stop," she says. No, not even this, she just can't. If she keeps giving herself away, soon she'll have nothing. What would Felix think if he found out?

"Oh, come on." Rattigan's clearly straining to sound playful. "I just — I barely even *touched* you."

"Stop!" she says again and kicks his shin.

"Ow," he says. "You bitch. You little fuckin' bitch. I ought to —"

She elbows her way past him.

The next morning at breakfast, when Mrs. Digges summons her ("My office — nine o'clock sharp!"), Frieda wonders how the matron knows. Did someone overhear her sneaking out last night and snitch? Did Rattigan, in rage, turn her in? No, she decides, it couldn't be the watchman: How would he explain what *he* was doing?

She arrives at the office some minutes shy of nine, sapped by unease, lack of sleep. The door is shut, but a clamor of confrontation sounds through. Maybe, she thinks, Rattigan is getting it good, too. Maybe he will even be fired. Edgily she waits, debating how much to say (she could tell Mrs. Digges of his dalliance with Flossie, but Flossie then, too, might be punished), when the door opens, and out shambles Jo.

She looks worse than Frieda's ever seen: bloodless skin and dark, sunken eyes. "Jo?" she says. "Jo, what's going on?"

Jo shies as if against a blast and says, "He's coming."

"Who?"

"Walter. Coming here to get me."

"When?"

"Day after tomorrow. First thing."

Haltingly, Jo explains what happened. Yesterday, when the matron got the news from Dr. Slocum, she called Jo in and started to berate her. How could Jo have dared to keep this secret? *The stupidest thing a girl could do, just reckless.* Now Jo would require all manner of special measures, would be moved to a home for unwed mothers.

"*Unwed* this and *unwed* that—she wouldn't stop saying it—and I don't know, it just sort of slipped, I said I wasn't. Then she *really* flew off the handle. Said I was a liar and ungrateful to boot. 'A husband,' she said. 'A husband and a baby! Plenty of other girls would be *happy*.'"

"Did you tell her? Did you tell the whole story?"

From the office comes Mrs. Digges's irritable voice: "Frieda, I can hear you're there. Come on!"

"Yes, ma'am. Be there in a second." To Jo, then, in an urgent whisper, "*Did* you?"

Jo says she didn't tell her, didn't think she had to. But the matron made some calls, and she tracked Walter down. The marriage was on the books, it was public. "That's what she was telling me just now: that she found him. And how he said he misses me, he's been out of his mind with worry. How he can't wait to have me *and* the baby."

"She *believes* him?" says Frieda. "That he's some kind of hero? What does she think this is, one of her novels?"

"'He's your husband,' she kept saying. 'Your husband. Whatever your problems are, you'll work them out.' Wouldn't let me get a word in edgewise."

"But, Jo, you've got to tell her."

Jo shrugs. "Doesn't matter. Too late—now he knows where I am."

"Frieda," calls the matron. "Frieda, *now*! It's past nine."

Frieda has no choice but to leave Jo in the hall, to step into Mrs. Digges's office.

"Ma'am," she says. "About Jo? The thing is, well, you see—"

Mrs. Digges cuts her off and tells her to be seated. "Frieda, I know that you're concerned about your friend, but for now you'd do much better to be concerned with your own self. Really!" She makes a denigrating tut.

The well of Frieda's protectiveness drains. "Yes, ma'am," she says, and she sinks into a chair, fearful of the discipline she'll face. Has the incident with Rattigan jeopardized everything — her freedom, her pending deal with Alice?

The matron's office is narrow, with a single porthole window. (What was its use when the building was a brothel? Frieda pictures gun-wielding goons on lookout duty.) Documents and files, in stacks upon the desk, are collated with geometric rigor. Except for a faded, framed swatch of needlepoint (red letters on a blue background: HOME), the walls are all dourly unadorned. A jar of potpourri smells like mold.

"As you know from receiving her telegram," says the matron, "your mother's very eager to reclaim you. Miss Longley . . . Miss Longley and I decided, for a start, that a telephone call would be in order."

Frieda spies the heavy black phone. "That's why . . . is *that* why I'm here?"

"Your mother's due" — Mrs. Digges consults a brass clock — "*was* due to call my office on the hour."

Frieda's relief is immediately dispelled by apprehension. Mama. Too soon. She's not ready.

"I can see you're anxious, Frieda. Don't be. It's a talk." Flightily, the matron mimes something with her hands — *anxious*, perhaps, or maybe *talk*. "She's your mother, the only one you're ever going to have. And all this is is just one conversation."

Alice must have told her, Frieda thinks, about the plan, and that's why Mrs. Digges is so assuring. All Frieda has to do is talk — appease Mama — stalling until Alice fixes things. Still, she can't manage to elude the apprehension, an unseen closing in, like last night's.

The matron notes the clock again. "It's nearly ten past. Is your mother generally prompt?"

266

"No," says Frieda. "She's never been on time."

"Well, for goodness — what example does that set?" Mrs. Digges opens a desk drawer and shuts it, then another, and a third in quick succession, as if searching for a place to store annoyance.

Frieda and the matron sit in awkward expectation, like strangers in a doctor's waiting room. The telephone's earpiece and body coolly gleam with the absolute blackness of a hearse.

Maybe Mama was hit by a streetcar, Frieda thinks. More likely, she's caught up in some trifling affair — a boot lace's price, a missing button — and has no idea that she's late. It's a contradiction that's always floored Frieda: how Mama can be so concerned with her daughter's every move but also be so negligently selfish.

"She's an immigrant, I gather?" asks the matron.

Yes, Frieda tells her. From Russia.

"But she speaks English? Does she have an accent?"

Just the thought of Mama's coagulated voice makes Frieda's gut roil and churn. "*You* would know. You're the one who called her."

"It was a man who answered when I called. He said he'd get the message to your mother."

"A man? What man? What was his name?" Irrationally, Frieda pictures Papa.

"A butcher, I think he said he was."

"Sam Slotnik?"

"Slotnik, that sounds right."

Frieda has scarcely even thought of Sam in months, but suddenly her eyes sting with loss. Not the loss of him, so much. Herself. Sam saw her crawl, saw her take her first step, watched her love Papa and then lose him. She longs for Sam — for anyone who knew her old self — to see her now and measure the vast distance she has crossed (a distance that, in the absence of a witness to its width, loses meaning even as it grows).

"Has it been very long?" asks the matron.

Frieda checks the clock. "Sixteen minutes."

"I mean since you've spoken. You and she?"

The better part of a year, Frieda tells her.

The matron's *tsk, tsk* sounds like the clock, or vice versa. "I know things are troublesome between you and your mother. Between all daughters and mothers, I suppose. But what a . . . what a fine trouble to have." She gazes toward the glowing porthole window, which casts a fuzzy halo around her face. "I always hoped, you know, that I'd have a child myself. A girl, I hoped. But then my husband died. And well, now, what is it they say? If hopes were wings, we'd all fly to the moon."

That's why the matron tracked down Walter, Frieda thinks, why she insists that Jo should be happy: she can't see beyond her own hopes. A well-meaning blindness, but still blindness.

The telephone bell sets the desktop papers shaking. Before it rings again, the matron answers. "Home for Girls. Margaret Digges speaking."

As she talks into the mouthpiece, the matron turns all business — no longer the idealistic might-have-been mother but a stickler for the here and now. She speaks about the likelihood and timing of Frieda's discharge, the logistics of having Mama fetch her.

Frieda panics. Alice *hasn't* disclosed her plan of action! What if Mrs. Digges and Mama make arrangements before Alice can pull all her strings?

The matron, tipping back in her chair, gives a laugh — a chummy, insinuating hoot. "My land! I never realized. You're right." She laughs again. "Well, let me put her on."

Frieda, feeling suddenly, shiveringly outgunned, accepts the cumbersome receiver. She waits — breathing, refusing to speak first, clinging to this last bit of *not yet*.

"Frieda? Friedaleh — you there?"

Only now does she realize that never in her life has she spoken on the telephone with Mama. Reduced to a voice, Mama's threat should be lessened. Instead she gains new degrees of menace.

"Frieda. I know you're there. Talk!"

"Mama." Two syllables like nonsense.

"Were you never going to talk with me? Never?"

"No . . . I don't know. I hadn't thought."

"Of course not. You never think on me." Clearly, through the line, comes a steady thud of chopping. She's calling from the telephone at Slotnik's. "Well, think on me now. For a *second*, try to think. Away you go, and what becomes of me?"

With a shock of reprieve, Frieda says, "Becomes of *you*?" She assumed Mama would want to harp on *her:* her shameful state. But Frieda's also shocked to feel guilty: it's true that she's rarely thought of Mama *becoming* anything, has denied the chance that Mama, like she herself, might change.

"Frieda, don't be such a *yutz*," says Mama. "The money!" She explains that Hirsch paid half the marriage fee up front: five hundred dollars, in cash. After Frieda jilted him, he took the money back—or *tried* to. Mama'd spent it all.

"On what, Mama? Five hundred dollars!"

"It don't matter the what, it's the why. Out you've been, doing . . . I don't even want to *think*—and here I'm stuck working to my bones. Every cent I make he takes away."

"And *I* owe *you* because you're such a fool?"

Mama makes a noise like a match flame touched to flesh. "Sss! You *never* talk like that!"

Mama means admonishment—"don't talk to me that way" —but her poor grammar makes a true statement: talking back is something new for Frieda. It fills her with a queasy, omnipotent feeling, as when she snapped the life from Jo's hen.

Mrs. Digges scowls. On her blotter, she writes, "Behave!"

Frieda sits straight, makes her body like a cliff that all of Mama's ire can tumble over.

"My daughter," Mama says. "Don't you see how much you owe me?" *Chop.* Sam is cleaving meat from bone. "*Leave,* you thought? My little daughter? No."

Frieda was expecting this: the told-you-so tone. What she didn't expect was Mama's sob.

"Every day," cries Mama, "every *day* I thought of you." Her

269

words are high and gaunt, starved of air. "Where, I wondered. Where's my little girl?"

When has Mama cried like this before? Only once that Frieda can remember: her primal, lonely wail in the wake of Papa's death, when the smell of beef made her break down.

Mama says, "I'm such a crazy, I thought my daughter would love me? Tell me how it happened I got no one with me now."

Maybe Mama cried at other times, but in private: for her loss of Leo, of her own potential self? Sorrow shakes Frieda —sorrow like disease, like sudden aging. She's saddened for her mother, who at long last sounds sincere; saddened that she herself is past remorse.

Mrs. Digges taps the desk. "So quiet," she mouths. "You done?"

Mama's groping voice in the receiver: "*Say* something, Frieda. You still there?"

Mama's desolation has the ring of honest pain, but she's longing—she must be—for something besides Frieda. Maybe, Frieda thinks, for the daily strife between them that Mama always misconstrued as passion; maybe for the chance (gone now) that they might start anew. Far worse than pining for a loved one long absent: pining for a love that never was.

"Friedaleh. My little girl. Say something!"

Twenty-four

━━★━━

*I*S SHE DREAMING, the next afternoon, when the Locomobile rolls in? Certainly the auto has the shape of something
dreamed, curvy and voluptuous and sleek. Its growl sounds
both forbidding and seductive. Yes, then: a dream. It must be.
Dreams are always filled with contradictions.

She was picturing Felix as she stared past her window,
thinking she had found a win-win plan: let *him* pay off Mama's debt to Hirsch. (Frieda would then be saved without quite
having taken aid; Mama, more than she, would be beholden.)
Mama thought she'd have Frieda back within weeks, as soon
as the doctor gave approval; the matron had said so on the
phone. But no, Frieda would give Mama the gift of her own absence, and a chance to be — if maybe not exactly happy, at least
slightly less unhappy. That's what Frieda owed her, truly: not
a sum of money, but a freeing from the reminder (she herself
was that reminder) of all the mistakes Mama had made. Reminder of all their mutual mistakes.

Felix would make it possible, would make everything possible. That's what his inheritance would buy her, Frieda thought: a wealth, not of possessions, but of *possibility*. Felix! His very name gave her cheer. She envisioned him abstractly (the thrust of his impatience), and then in more intimate specifics (his thin wrists, hard and sharp with bone).

So when Burnham opened the gate and the Locomobile skimmed in, how could she not think that she had called the car forth by the power of her concentrated longing? She'd assumed that Rattigan, enraged by her spurning, had tossed out her letter, maybe burned it. Even if he *had* sent the letter off to Devens, she didn't expect Felix to come this soon — not until his fractured shin had mended.

But here now is the speedster with its thuggish elegance, even its fabric top full of luster. She checks its plate: the year of Papa's birth. Tipsily she rises and stands at the window, practically disabled by desire.

She watches as Burnham swashes out to meet the car and leans toward the driver's side curtain. He beetles his brow, listening. He nods.

It's not fair that *he* gets to greet Felix first! She wants him, undiluted, to herself.

Flossie and Yetta, too, clamber from their bunks and fight for elbow room before the window.

"Who the heck?" asks Yetta.

"Don't know, but I'd sure like to. Rode in a car just like that, once — Mayor Curley's."

The Locomobile glimmers with golden flares of light, like a flipped coin spinning in the sun. Frieda puts her palm up to the pane. Should she tell them? Should she run out to the yard? The matron would have her neck for it; no, she needs a plan. Better to wait, to think what fib to tell.

And here she comes, Mrs. Digges, kicking clouds of dust as she strides out and takes Burnham's spot beside the driver. (God damn the sun and its glare upon the windshield, which keeps hidden Felix's face.) The matron starts a speech that from this height can't be heard, but Frieda well imagines her gist: *I'm afraid not... too disruptive... our policy... never come again.*

As Flossie ogles the auto ("Don't you just want to *lick* it?"), Frieda starts cooking up her story. She'll say that he's a cousin, her father's sister's boy. A cousin who made good but remembers where he's from, and now has come to rescue his relation. (The matron seems to fall for plots like that.) A Harvard man, she'll say — that part's true.

Mrs. Digges appears to be hearing Felix out. A small, flattered smile breaks on her mouth. Is he charming her? Frieda wouldn't doubt it. The matron's smile then sinks to a flat, mistrustful line, and she walks back unsparingly toward the Home. The Locomobile idles in its place.

"Maybe it's her beau," jokes Flossie. "And they're having a lover's spat."

"Beau?" says Yetta. "Who would go for *her*?"

Frieda, keeping quiet, fluffs her hair, smoothes her cheeks. If she waits any longer, she fears that he'll be gone. How will she ever sneak past the matron?

"Frieda! Frieda, come right down." The matron's voice sounds like a stuck drawer being yanked. She's calling from the bottom of the staircase.

"Yes," says Frieda, "coming," in her most kowtowing tone. If Felix can be charming, so can she.

She scurries down the staircase in such an anxious bother that she barely hears the other girls stalk after her. Not just her roommates, but half a dozen more who must have been watching from *their* windows. There's Edith, with her shivery, undue veneration, and Lisbeth, and even sickly Bess. The only one conspicuous by her absence is Jo. The fox killed another hen last night, and maimed a second. The squawking and the flapping woke the girls, but not in time, and now Jo is holed up in the coop. Just as well, thinks Frieda; the last thing Jo needs, with Walter due tomorrow, is to watch her and Felix reuniting. But maybe Felix will have some advice about Jo. Maybe he'll know how to stop Walter, or buy him off. Can a soldier arrest a crook, turn him in?

Mrs. Digges stands before the door, barring passage. "A guest," she says to Frieda, "is most unusual, as you know. A clear violation of the rules."

Girls whisper: "Who is it?" "Why *her?*"

Frieda isn't conscious of her hand rubbing the newel — up and down the unwholesome carving — until Hattie takes hold of her arm. "Easy, girl," she says. "Steady now."

"In this instance, however," says the matron, "I'll allow it. Only because he comes with such impeccable credentials. If Meyer Morse is vouching for him, that's good enough for me. But you'll greet the guest outside, by no means in the building. Twenty minutes for his business. No more."

"Oh, thank you," says Frieda, the words leaping, as does she. In three floaty steps she's through the door.

"Another thing," calls Mrs. Digges. "I don't want you other girls —"

Too late. They've bustled out behind her.

The full-bodied Locomobile exerts a sort of gravity; tittering, the patients moon around it. But Frieda approaches the speedster more slowly, relishing the pull of it, the thrill.

"Girls!" shouts the matron from the porch. "Keep away. Come on, now. Have some decency."

Not one girl scatters, but Frieda doesn't mind. Let them all watch her good fortune!

The matron retreats into the Home. Is she offering Frieda some measure of privacy, or can't she bear to see Frieda's romance reignited?

Worshipfully crouched beside the Locomobile's hull, Burnham runs his hands along the molding. The wheel well, the double spare tires. "Jesus H. Christ. What a gem."

You don't know the half of it, thinks Frieda. She opens the door and hurls herself in.

From the driver's seat, a question: "Miss Mintz?"

She harks back to the first question Felix ever asked ("Do

you have a last name, Miss Lovely Frieda?"), but this man — this oaf — isn't Felix. Not Felix at all. Just a stranger.

"Who are you?" she says.

"Mr. Morse," he responds above the engine's baffling thrum, "sent me here to have a word with you."

"But why did Felix . . . why didn't he come himself?"

"Not Felix. His father. *Mister* Morse."

She swallows the tannic taste of disappointment.

He's Jewish by the looks of him, his hair dark and curled. Fish-pale and belly-proud, less fat than overstuffed, like a skinny man suddenly pumped with air.

"Mr. Morse was very pleased to meet you on the Fourth." The driver's silky voice belies his size. "But he tells me there was some misunderstanding? A case of mistaken identity?"

Frieda glares. "It wasn't a mistake."

The smooth leather seats smell just as she remembers: an unctuous, overindulged scent. The buffed dashboard shows no fingerprints.

"Okay, okay now," he says. "You're clearly ruffled. Which brings me to the point of my coming." He shoots his cuff. A platinum cuff link beams. "Mr. Morse is sorry that he may have left you feeling less than . . . well, fully appreciated. He's prepared to offer you a helping hand."

Mr. Morse? Sorry? It's nothing but preposterous. Unless Felix managed to persuade him. "A helping —" Frieda starts, when a knock interrupts her.

It's Flossie, with a meddlesome, monkeyish expression, peering through the side curtain's pane.

Frieda squints at her and snaps, "Quit."

Flossie pretends she doesn't hear. The other girls, too, have closed in on the auto, hiving about, pruriently abuzz. "Lookit," Edith marvels. "See his cuff links?"

Where is the matron now, this once that Frieda needs her? "Please," she says. "Please, leave us alone."

"Frieda's got a feller," Lisbeth taunts.

"Please." She hides her face within her hands.

The girls must think she's bashful with romancing. Together, they take up Lisbeth's taunt.

"Can't they see," the driver says, "we're talking?"

She might appeal to Burnham, but how could he take charge when he's so busy loving up the car? He fingers the grille, shines it with his sleeve.

The girls pound the hood. ". . . *got a feller!*"

"Christ!" shouts the driver. "That's enough." He jabs the horn button—the patients stagger back—and shoves the gearshift into reverse. He stomps the throttle pedal to the floor.

"You can't!" Frieda says—Mrs. Digges will have a fit—but their rapid backward motion contradicts her.

Burnham, looking dumbfounded by his brush with luxury (or maybe by its sudden revocation), stands there on rigid legs, gaping. Does he realize he left the gate ajar? The girls, too, look stunned, but break into applause. Flossie pumps her fist into the air.

The driver brakes, shifts, performs a tight turn. Frieda now remembers: the teeter and the risk, the Locomobile's prowess as it surges. In one stirring swoop the car escapes.

The engine as it races makes a rising war cry. Frieda has to stifle her own whoop. "I don't believe you just—I can't believe it!"

The driver chuckles. "Well? Start believing." His gut jiggles against the steering wheel.

They drive past the rendering plant, the narrow graveyard lane, turning corners—Frieda loses track. Wind spills through the curtains with an agreeable swish. The air is charged with leafy summer scents.

It's madness: this stranger could make off with her *anywhere*, but she's happier—happy—not to ask which way they're headed. How long since she's had a good surprise? She lets herself forget about the punishment she'll face; the deed is done, might as well enjoy it.

"I knew it," he says.

"Knew what?" Can he read Frieda's thoughts? Can he tell how free, how malleable, she's feeling?

"I knew," he says, "that once you smiled, you'd be even prettier."

If she wasn't smiling before, now she is. Self-consciously, she feels the grin widen.

"Attagirl," he says. "Just like a model."

Will she ever grow immune to the spell of a man's sweet talk? Even a man as glib and slick as this? She'll have to ask Felix if expertise in flirting is a prerequisite for service with the Morses, as it surely is for membership in the clan. "Should've seen," she'll tell him, "this roly-poly man — no one I'd normally look at twice — acting like some raging Casanova. So silly it was almost sort of cute."

The driver turns right, at the next lane right again, then pulls onto a smaller, bumpy track. In the bower of some craggy elms, he parks.

The engine's noise quits and is replaced by forest sounds: leaf-damped breeze, a rhyme of birdsong. He asks if there is anything she wants.

"Anything of what kind of thing?"

He reaches behind the seat and whisks away a blanket, unveiling a small wicker basket. "Chocolate? Don't imagine you get that here."

"No," she says. "But no thank you. Not hungry."

"Hmm. Something stronger, then. Gin?" He shakes the basket. Glass bottles clink.

Again she tells him no thanks, she's fine.

He pokes at her knee with fat fingers. "I *really* can't tempt you? Not at *all*?"

She shoves him off. "What did you mean before: 'A helping hand'?"

"Ah. Business first, pleasure later?"

His breath smells metallic, like old coins. She twists her body closer to the door.

"Okay, okay," he says. "How *much,* you want to know? How does two hundred and fifty dollars sound?"

Frieda looks down so he won't see her shocked expression. It's half a year's salary at Jordan's. Half what Mama owed to Pinchas Hirsch. "Two hundred—"

"And fifty dollars. A lump sum."

What will she have to give—to *do*—as recompense? Something half as bad as marrying Hirsch? Skeptically, she says, "Just like *that?* From the goodness of his heart?"

"He's a goodhearted man," says the driver. He flashes her a tight, evasive grin.

She waits for something more (is it something about Felix? a promise not to go after *his* money?), but the driver only sits there. His grin. He fastens a loose button on his vest.

Two hundred and fifty. She could live out on her own.

Or no, a place big enough to share—a sanctuary. For other girls in trouble. For Jo.

"There are, of course," he says at last, "a couple of conditions."

She knew it, so why does the word still catch her off guard? "Conditions?"

"Only reasonable," he assures her.

One: Mr. Morse keeps his good deed confidential. Two: No further association will be allowed. With Mr. Morse or any of the Morses.

Stop right there, she says. She's not interested.

"But you are. You *are.* Look at you!"

What does he see? Does her neediness blaze? She sets her jaw, trying for dispassion.

"Think about it," he says. "All that dough for doing nothing —actually, for *not* doing something. It's simple: just meet all the terms of the agreement, the money will be yours, end of story."

Maybe she can take the cash and still run off with Felix. Once she has it, what could Morse do? "But how," she asks, "would I get it from you? It's no good to me here. I'd need it on the day they let me out."

"Oh," he says. "No. I guess I didn't mention? The money would be yours in November."

"November? That's almost four months. It's too far—" And she stops as it hits her: the election. "A bribe? To keep quiet! That's outrageous."

"A gift," he says. "A charitable contribution." From his vest he unfurls a monogrammed handkerchief and emits a patronizing sniff. Neatly, he folds the cloth again. "You understand, I'm sure, that political campaigns can get nasty, full of slung mud. Especially when the candidate is . . . well, you know, of our faith."

It's not clear if he means to include Frieda in that *our*. She wants to have no part of it, of them.

"It seems there's a reporter—I believe you met the man —nosing at some spurious story. A story about you and Felix Morse." He pauses, as if expecting the name to hypnotize her. His breath, aimed right at her, is clammy. "We doubt that this reporter will be idiot enough to push any further with his lie. But simply to make sure that his bases are all covered, Mr. Morse has to be prepared. And that's why, Frieda, you're going to sign a statement affirming that you never met Felix."

"I won't. I won't! *That's* the lie."

"Oh, Frieda. Stop a sec. Think about it."

"No," she says. "What makes you think I will?"

The driver reaches deep into his jacket's inside pocket and rustles something papery, like bank notes. "Would five hundred dollars do the trick?"

"I don't need it." She *doesn't*—doesn't need these thugs at all. It's *they* who need *her*, and she'll refuse. She'll make them tremble with fear of what she'll say.

"Don't be dumb, Frieda. You do so need it."

"No, I don't. Not when I have Felix. When he gets *his* money, I'll be fine."

279

The driver laughs a soft, ghostly laugh. His fingers find her knee again, a blade upon a neck. "You think Felix would risk his inheritance for *you*? For a sad case he's never even met?"

"What do you mean? Of course he's met me. Of course he has. You're crazy."

He saws his fingers slowly back and forth. "Funny — that's not what Felix says." Now, from his pocket, he takes the rustling thing — not cash, but a letter, creased square. With the deftness of a schoolboy plucking wings from a live fly, he unfolds the page, crease by crease. "Can you read?" he asks.

She snatches the letter from him.

The driver starts to explain how it's signed and notarized, but Frieda needs no proof that Felix wrote it. Who else but he could have penned these antsy strokes? She feels in them his urgency, his slant.

Father, it begins, and she's heartened by his bluntness (nothing like the "Sweet FM" for her), but that's the only hopeful part about it. She gets stuck at the second paragraph:

> The girl you met is someone who has hounded me of late, because she somehow found out who I am. Or rather, she found out who you are. It's our money she's after, nothing more. Nothing is what she'll get from me.

"That's not him," she says.

"See the notary seal, there?"

"No, but it's — you *made* him. Or someone did. His father." With each word, her confidence tatters. It's Felix, but not Felix, not the one she knows. What if the one she knows is the impostor?

Again she scans the writing, his adamant black marks. She crumples the page and flings it at the driver.

"Hey," he says. "Let's calm ourselves, all right? I hate to see a girl get all worked up." With a chill, meaty hand, he reaches for her wrist, and grips it as, before, he gripped the gearshift. "The statement's in the pocket of the door."

"Ow. Your hand is hurting me. Let go."

He does. But his ease, his bulky calm, is just as bad.

"Sign the thing, Frieda. You'll be happy."

"Don't make me," she says, almost wishing that he could; making the choice herself is much worse.

And that's what hurts the most about Felix: he might have been — probably was — made to write the letter, but what, in the end, does "made to" mean?

Yes, she thinks — she hopes — he was pressured by his father. And maybe all his lying was strategic: deny Frieda now to secure his legacy, and then, his wealth assured, come and find her. But even so — even so, what future could they share? Wouldn't she always worry what the next time would be when he'd deem her trust expendable again?

"Sign it," says the driver. "Or else you've got nothing."

She stares at the smooth lacquered dashboard. Not nothing, she thinks. Her honor. Her self. If she doesn't accept something, it can never be rescinded. Sometimes taking less gives you more.

"I want to go," she says. "Take me back."

"Back?" he says. "Where do you think you *are*?" Chuckling, he points through a gap between the elms: the high wooden fence, the barbed wire.

All this time, parked behind the Home.

Twenty-five

★

*J*O'S BEEN PICKING at her scalp again. Her hair is now full enough to mostly hide the sores, but Frieda, looking close, sees new blood: tiny black clots, like ants in grass. She and Jo sit where the yard verges down and two lengths of fence form a corner. Overnight, hissing gusts of rain fell for hours. This far nook of yard is all mud.

Frieda says, "I found the hole — the holes — where it got in. A dozen or so, all along this section." She noticed the tunnels yesterday as she walked back to the Home, following the outside of the fence. Tidy holes, just big enough for a fox to push through. She connects the holes' tidiness somehow to Felix's statement, to the clean break he made with her, the puncture. Also to the way her own thinking neatened up when she saw what a fool she'd been to trust him.

"Let's patch them," she tells Jo. "Block them up."

Jo remains motionless, staring at the muck. Her very skin looks lax, apathetic.

"Come on," Frieda tries again. "Let's do it. The ground's

so soft, it'll be a cinch." To prove her point, she stabs a patch of bare mud with her pinkie, which disappears up to the last knuckle.

"It's not going to stop him. He'll just dig somewhere else."

"And *not* patching? *That's* going to stop him?"

Why is Frieda being so insistent? Of course the fox isn't what she's talking about, it's Walter. By this hour tomorrow, he'll be here. She's driven to try to stop him — to convince Jo to try — driven to prove that passion doesn't have to end in horror. Trouble, yes — pain — but not horror. Jo can survive. So can she.

All these weeks she looked at Jo and thought how they were different; now she sees only their alikeness.

Yesterday, when Burnham let her in ("Back so soon?"), Frieda had to face the matron, waiting on the porch. Mrs. Digges, fists like pistols ready at her hips, said, "*This* is how you thank me for bending the rules for you? For trusting? For trying to be *nice*?" She grabbed Frieda's shoulders with both hands and shook hard, as if snapping wrinkles from a blouse. "How did I ever think you'd do what's right? You wouldn't know right if it slapped you on the chin." Raising her open palm, she looked ready to test the theory — but held it there, a sinister six inches from Frieda's face.

The patients stood, recoiling, full of turncoat blame, as though Frieda had ruined all their fun. And Frieda — weighted by their sad, accusing glares, by the matron's wrath, by Felix's denial — sat down on the porch steps and cried.

At first Mrs. Digges seemed even further galled ("Get up! Stand up straight when you're addressed!"), but then she must have seen Frieda's tears. "Now, Frieda," she said. "Really, now. Please." The matron, her face clenched with the effort of relenting, pulled Frieda back up to her feet.

"Sorry," Frieda said. She wiped her eyes.

"Go up to your room. Get some rest to calm your nerves. We'll deal with this tomorrow, with Miss Longley."

She invoked Alice's name in a timbre of foreboding, but

Frieda heard it only as a gift. "Tomorrow? Miss Longley will be here?"

"After lunch. To make final the plans for reassignment. And now she'll have another task at hand. If *she* can talk some sense into you, fine. Now go. Go on up to your room and stay there."

In her room, Frieda fell onto her bunk and lay curled, staring at her pillow's bleached-white case. From underneath her mattress she retrieved Felix's letter, and she scanned through its gentlemanly vows: "I got you into this pickle, and I want to get you out. Get you out so I can stand beside you!" Tears came again; one fell onto the page. How pitiful to allow a mere letter to have such power. Stiffly, she turned her face away.

More pitiful! Snubbing a piece of paper!

What surprised her, finally, as she tossed the page away (with an emptiness oddly like repletion), was not the fact that Felix should have come now to betray her, but that she had ever hoped he might not.

This morning, she awoke full of crisp determination. The night's rain had ended and the clouds were slowly ebbing, the horizon a challenging gray. She expected a thorough interrogation from the girls, and now that the story had its end, she'd finally tell it: the silly wide-eyed rube who trips on some man's feet, thinking she has fallen into love. She knew just the self-dismissive tone she would affect, a hardened, morning-after voice like Hattie's. Hardened and, because of that, resilient.

At breakfast, though, the girls kept a skittish sort of distance (not grilling her, not ribbing, scarcely speaking), as if, having witnessed Frieda's breakdown yesterday, they saw her now as something broken — as dead weight that imperiled their precariously rising fortunes and had to be soberly discarded.

I'm not, Frieda wanted to announce; I'm light as air; I've jettisoned my own misfortune, too.

When she went in search of Jo it was to tell her of the fox holes — to urge her to do something, to *act* — but also to share with her this new auspicious outlook. Now that she had finally tossed away the crutch of Felix, she was remembering how fine it felt to walk all on her own.

At first she missed Jo at the back of the chicken coop; that's how tiny Jo had made herself. But after searching the yard and every room inside the Home, she peered within the coop again and saw her: squatting in the farthest corner, hands tucked under toes, eyes the only part of her that moved.

The hole-filling project, Frieda knew, was a fool's errand — no amount of mud would stop a fox — but she needed a ruse to lure Jo from the coop. And Jo, in her distress, was suggestible enough that Frieda didn't have to make much sense. A sturdy voice is sometimes all that matters. "Jo," she told her, "Jo, come out, I need you."

Out Jo crawled, blinking, into the gray morning — the kind of gray that's brighter than clear blue — and right away looked brimful with resentment aimed at Frieda, for having tricked her out of her retreat. (That's all right, thought Frieda, if that's the cost of helping — recalling the way she herself, at first, resented Alice, when Alice tried to yank her toward freedom.) Taking Jo's elbow with forcible assurance, she steered her to the corner of the yard, where Jo, with a caved-in look, sat down — and where, a half-hour later, she still sits: gaping at the waterlogged ground.

Out here in the brightness, Jo looks worse than ever, nicked and broken, bunged up by despair. Her eyes are the shade of old coffee. She reaches up and picks another scab.

"Stop!" Frieda says. "You're going to pick clear through to your brain."

Jo just rolls her shoulders and keeps at it.

"Stop," Frieda says again, and swats her hand away. Maybe that's what Jo needs now: a blow. A shock back to sense, like Frieda's yesterday. Sitting here, she's told Jo the whole Felix saga — up to his last statement, his rejection; told Jo how it's strangely liberating. "Jo," she says, "don't you understand what I've been saying? I don't even think you paid attention."

Jo, her features sharpening, looks up. "Sure I did: you

285

thought you loved some man and he loved you, but it turns out he's a rat, just like Walter."

"No, the point — the point's you have to change the way you think. That's the only thing you've got control of."

"Sure," Jo says. "*Thinking.* That's the perfect cure. Think different, and everything'll change."

Yes, Frieda wants to say. Yes, that's it, exactly. At least that's the sense she has — she *wants* to have — today. Can't Jo feel the upswing of the clouds?

"What the hell will thinking do," Jo says, "about *this*?" She jabs at her belly with a fist.

"Careful," Frieda warns her. "Jo, please." She wonders if the baby in Jo's belly weakens her — this life within a life, staking claim — or if the extra heartbeat keeps her going. If, without it, she might just give up. "You're going to have this baby, Jo, can't do anything about that. But we *can* change how, and what will happen after." Frieda's far from certain if the words she says are true, but saying them feels like a first step. "We can fight to keep you both safe from Walter."

Jo hits her gut again, but weakly. "How? You know he's coming here. Tomorrow."

That's when Frieda tells her about Alice: her secret proposition, her protection. "Tomorrow," she says, "the doctor's going to give me my results. If I'm clean, they can send me back to Mama. I should be terrified, right? But am I? Look! Today I'm going to tell Alice yes to everything. Whatever it takes to avoid Mama, to get out on my own. Whatever Alice wants, I'll agree." Conclusively, she slaps the muddy ground. She doesn't tell Jo of her doubts about Alice, that Alice might well want things that Frieda *won't* give. That's her secret power now: this hunch about Alice. (You have to be aware of what the person giving wants. Aware, she thinks, and prepared to withhold.) "Maybe if I explain things, Alice can help you, too. Jo, I bet she will. I just bet."

"Why? Why would she do something for me?"

She might not, thinks Frieda. *But for* me — *for me, she will.*

To Jo she gives a plainer explanation: that Alice has devoted her entire life to girls, to protecting them from the evils of men. "I guess," she says, remembering what Alice once told her, "I guess it's just the way her heart is built." Did Jo know, she asks, that Alice's first job was at a home for rescued prostitutes? If girls agreed to testify against the men who'd sold them, Alice would keep them hidden until the men were off in jail. "So we'll tell her," Frieda says, "what Walter did to you, and tell her that you'll testify against him. Think of all the others you might save if Walter's stopped!"

As she speaks, a plan begins to form in Frieda's mind. She'll spruce herself up (as much as possible in this place): wash her hair, don a clean frock. She'll ask Alice to take her somewhere private again, just them. The treatment room, or possibly the graveyard. Alice will have questions: *Will you let me make arrangements? Live in my spare room, go to school?* But Frieda, at the start, will defer. "I have something to tell you," she'll say. "I think you'll be proud." (Alice *will* be proud, won't she? Won't she fairly beam when she hears how Frieda turned down Morse's offer? How she faced this final test and stood firm?) Between them will throb the same ladenness as last time: a mystifying pulse of *What next?* But this time Frieda will be ready, in control; this time she'll use it for her gain. "I have something to tell you," she'll begin, almost teasing. "But first . . ." And she'll make the case for Jo.

For Jo's gain. For Jo's *and* her own.

Alice will see how thoughtful, how bighearted, Frieda is: shielding Jo, scheming (just as Alice schemed for her), acting as a kind of social worker. Alice will see how well Frieda's followed her example — that she's worthy of what Alice plans to do for her, and more.

It won't be like with Felix, when she gave too much, too soon. Her gift will be the readiness to receive.

"Trust me," she tells Jo. "You'll be fine. We both will." *Trust me.* Even though Frieda herself trusts no one. Trusts no one to save her but herself.

Jo's right hand rises — poised to scratch her scalp — but she stops; the hand falls, she goes still. "I'm scared," she says, wincing in the sun.

"I know, hon. I know. Course you are."

"What if —" Silence swallows Jo's fear.

"Listen. They haven't locked us up because we're weak. They locked us up because they know we're strong. For once I don't hate saying they were right."

"If *this* is strong," says Jo, and she pinches her own wrist, "then boy, I would sure hate feeling *weak*." It's an inching toward humor, toward healing.

"You know what?" Frieda says. "I think you'll be just fine, just perfectly okay when this all ends. I think you'll be giving *me* a hand."

In a gesture that acknowledges doubt and also overcomes it, Jo does just that: she gives her hand. Frieda takes her fingers, squeezes hard. For long minutes they sit like this — tethered, hand in hand — as the grayness of the clouds lifts around them. Antidote of blue. Salving sun.

By the time Jo suggests that they rise and patch the fence line, Frieda can admit the plan was nonsense: "Mud? What could we do with mud?"

Jo appears to take this as a challenge. She unlaces her fingers from Frieda's tight grip and digs her hand down into the dirt. With the fistful of soil that she excavates and dumps, she gamesomely builds the start of something.

Just a little girl, thinks Frieda. Both of us too young for all this grief.

Jo digs down again and scoops some more and dumps it. "Well?" she says. "Don't just sit there. Dig!" She catapults a dare of dirt at Frieda.

"For what?"

"For whatever we decide. A hiding place? Maybe just a tunnel."

Frieda plunges in with the spades of her flat hands. Her calluses from months ago — from tugging twine around bundles — are lost now in overall toughness, the rugged rough skin she's acquired.

Masterful, swift, they both dig. Between them grows a pile of soil, lightening in shade, as though exposure frees from it some burden.

Frieda finds her fingers building something like a rampart, banking mud around the central pile. "I used to make sandcastles with my father," she tells Jo. "Up at Singing Beach. Ever go there?"

"No. My parents never liked the beach."

"We'd make these big castles with whatever we could find, crab legs for beams, clamshell doors." The sense of Papa she has sometimes — his arms, his thick embrace — swaddles her and guides her sticky hands. "We'd leave before the tide came and broke them."

Thoughtfully, Jo pats the pile that they've amassed — her eyes bright with a prospector's pride — and bares her first full-blown smile in days. "All right, then. A mudcastle it is."

"Is 'mudcastle' a word?"

"Is now!"

They work in a tumult of mutual invention, hands enmeshed, fashioning their model. A bridge of two twigs spans a pinkie-wide moat; pebbles give a tower crenellation.

So attuned is Frieda to the rhythms of creation that she doesn't fully register the opening gate, or Mrs. Digges's voice raised in greeting. The mud is deliciously batterlike and smooth, as malleable as fantasy itself.

Jo finds a dandelion — sun-faded, but firm — and plucks it for a piece of heraldry. Triumphantly, she plants it on the tower.

"The kingdom of . . . what?" asks Frieda. "What should we call it?"

Jo ponders. "Mudland? Mudrovia?"

"Filth," says a voice from behind them and above. "Kingdom of *Filth* seems more like it."

Frieda turns to face Alice, astonishingly close. "Oh! You're early. Aren't you early?"

"I hardly see how that should make a difference."

Frieda points to her mud-crusted frock. "I didn't even have the chance to change!"

Alice, by contrast, stands clad as if for church in her dress with its prim sash and collar. From Frieda's seated view, Alice looks foreshortened: a pillar overbuilt at the foundation. To make herself even, Frieda stands.

There! Now she sees her as she likes to picture Alice: her lenient chin, her endless eyes. Talking with her won't be half so fraught as she imagined. It's *Alice*, she reminds herself. Not some strange creature. Alice, who has always been so kind.

"Jo," Alice says, but she keeps her gaze on Frieda, "I hope that you'll excuse us if we leave you. Frieda and I have something to discuss."

Jo hunches closer to the castle. She runs a thin finger along the twig bridge — caught, it appears, between gloom and expectation.

Frieda squats down again to touch Jo on the neck. "Stay here, okay? I'll come find you."

Alice turns and walks away in fast, decisive strides; Frieda has to hurry to keep pace. A scent trails Alice — not perfume but something useful: dentifrice, perhaps, or Listerine.

At first it seems to Frieda that they're going to leave the grounds (and her chest goes flitty with delight), but Alice says that that's out of the question. Instead, Alice leads them, improbably, to the guardhouse, which Burnham has abandoned for his lunch break.

Odors of spilled liquor, of squalid cooped-up sweat. Grim light through fingerprinted glass. (It's brighter, though, than the last time she was here.)

Others must have seen them. Won't their sneaking raise suspicions? But it doesn't really matter anymore. Soon enough they all will know of Frieda's special treatment, how Alice intervened to save her skin. (Hers and Jo's, both, if she succeeds.) Maybe they'll be jealous, but admiring, surely, too. Who among them wouldn't take the chance? And haven't they all played a similar game?

"Am I ever happy to see you!" she tells Alice. She holds out her arms to give Alice a hug, but Alice shrinks away against the wall. "Stupid," Frieda says. "I'm all mud! You'd think I might've learned, when I wrecked your other dress. Remember? All that blood? I felt awful."

Alice does nothing to affirm the recollection — no smile, no small forgiving laugh. Her overbite bestows on her a startled, anxious look: rabbity, full of mistrust.

Her anxiousness increases Frieda's own. "Alice," she says, "I have something to tell you. I want . . . or, well, I think that you'll be pleased. Pleased, or, you know —"

"Pleased? You think I'm *pleased*?"

"Proud," Frieda finishes softly.

Now Alice laughs — or makes a sound like laughter, a sudden broken breath from her chest. "The cheek of you. To stand there and . . . the nerve!" She shrinks farther against the guardhouse wall.

"I don't understand. I've been dying for you to come. Dying to have the chance —"

"Stop pretending! It doesn't become you, Frieda. Truly not." Alice, from the sleeve of her crisp churchy dress, pulls out a folded piece of paper. She thrusts it forth like something on fire. "Here. This just came. The morning mail."

Frieda takes the letter and holds it near the window, in the foul glow of which she reads its words. *Her* words: *dear Felix; heaps of love.*

Her hand shakes. "He . . . he sent it to *you*?"

"Someone did, yes. I'm not sure who."

She could tattle on Rattigan, tell Alice what he did — how he bullied her, right here, in this hut — but it's pointless, the damage has been done. "It wasn't," she says faintly, "meant for you."

Alice makes her broken noise again. "And that's just it, now. Isn't that just it."

291

"But I'm finished with all that. With Felix. For good this time." She tries to give the letter back to Alice. "That's what I was getting around to saying."

"Which is just the kind of thing you've said already. What girls like you are always bound to say."

Girls like you. The snub of it stings Frieda.

"Here I was, ready to give you everything," says Alice. "And you . . . you go behind my back, go running to that man." Alice grabs the letter, which she crushes in her fist, then raises like a weight to brain Frieda, or herself. "Did you even have the decency to mention me to him? Not once. As if I don't exist."

From Alice's raised arm comes a sharp funk of sweat, overpowering her antiseptic scent. Frieda should be reaching out to soothe, to beg forgiveness, should stroke Alice, or speak her name at least. But she's past begging, past soothing, everything's too late. Everything she planned has come undone.

"Frieda," Alice says, with what sounds like some effort. "I could get you sent away. You know that? 'Defectively delinquent' is no stretch: pattern of deceit, heightened sex drive." Gone is the shaky, jilted pitch of her outburst, replaced by a hard official tone, as though she's reading phrases etched in marble.

Defective, thinks Frieda, but she's lost track of its sense: Is saying *yes* or *no* what makes her sick?

"Some of your *friends,*" says Alice (as though friends are a shameful thing), "will be moved to the Sherborn Prison shortly. Believe me, there's plenty of extra room." She plucks up the girdle of her dress and twists it slightly so the knot is more evenly centered. "In your case, I'm still inclined, against my better judgment . . . inclined, I guess, to spare you that fate. Instead, we'll let things fall as they may."

Queasy with the stink of Alice's sweat, the sound of *prison,* Frieda has to ask her what that means.

"It means you can forget about any plans we made. I don't intend to see you again, Frieda."

"But where will I . . . what will happen to me?"

In the dim, tarnished light, Alice's eyes are leaky. "If your mother still wants you, you're hers now to bear with. And good luck is all that I can wish her. A shifty, selfish girl is what you are."

Again Frieda thinks of reaching out. *Please forgive me.* But for what? What part of the blame in this is hers? Is it her fault that Alice wants her (now she can't deny it) in just the way that she herself so badly wanted Felix? Must she apologize for being wanted?

Alice, after lunch, meets a group of girls together: all those who were resident when Frieda and Flossie came. Mrs. Digges shifts the parlor sofa to make space, baring dust that spores into the air.

In her holier-than-thou dress, Alice stands. Frieda can't look at her, but also can't not; the sight of Alice makes her insides molten. All the hopeful loyalty, the dreams she's been amassing, pent up in her core with no outlet.

The sight of Jo, too, rattles Frieda. An hour ago, when Frieda found her, head-to-toe with mud, she couldn't even manage to say "No" or "Jo, I'm sorry"; all that she could do was shake her head. How could she admit she hadn't even *asked* Alice, that the helping touch she'd promised was now toxic?

Jo, shyly smiling, said, "I saw her leave the guardhouse," then nodded resolutely. "Saw her leave." At once, as if some burden of decision had been lifted, she lunged with girlish zeal at the mudcastle. Fervently, she dug her fingers in.

Coolly, now, Alice asks for quiet and receives it. The dusty light gives the parlor an air of culmination, like a funeral home's thick, hazy hush. Now that their cohort is generally healed, it's time, Alice says, to move on. "For each girl, we've drawn up a scientific plan, based on the tests we've been conducting — Binet age, intelligence, cognition — with social factors, too, accounted for. First-timers we've designated differently from repeaters. Employment and family histories are remarked."

Frieda pays less mind to the briefing's subject matter than

to Alice's newly firm demeanor: she speaks in the ironhanded "we" of Mrs. Sprague, a "we" that has no place in it for Frieda (just as, in the end, Frieda lost her place with Felix when he sided with his other, former "we").

"Age of lost virginity," Alice adds. "Education. All of this and more is reflected in each plan, which represents our best determination. And this is what we'll give to your trial judge. He's not bound by it, but we think he'll listen closely."

"Trial?" says Flossie. "What do you mean, 'trial'?"

"*Done* our time," says Melba. "Ain't we done it?"

Alice takes a buffeted step backward. "Well, no. No, you haven't, as you put it, 'done your time.'" She sniffs an abrupt, puny laugh.

"Then what the hell've we been doing *here*?" says Yetta.

What the hell? is echoed, and lewder phrases hurled. Mrs. Digges looks too shocked to object.

The Home, Alice tells them, was merely a first step. Did they think *this* was their penalty? No. They came here for their *health*, and now that they've been cured — now they have to answer for their *crimes*.

Alice moves her mouth from pout to frown and back (uncertain, thinks Frieda, if she's the wrongdoer or the wronged). Although Alice keeps her gaze assiduously averted, Frieda feels the burn of it as if it's aimed at her. Did *she* bring this on — this sudden castigation — by frustrating Alice's affections? Will all the girls pay for her mistakes?

"From here," Alice tells them, "you'll go before a judge who will have in hand our recommended plan. Based on that, and the hearing — your answers to his questions — the judge will decide what comes next. Release or reassignment to . . . another institution."

The girls look utterly dumbfounded, sucker-punched. Angelina's cheeks are bright with tears.

"Girls, please," says Alice. "Don't pretend surprise." She holds her palms out to them. "You *knew* this."

"Knew it?" says Hattie. "Knew how?"

"It's there when you're arrested, right there on all the forms. Spelled out in perfectly plain English."

Murkily, it comes to Frieda: the circular in Ayer. *Criminal proceedings against you will be deferred . . .* She was dazed, then. Dead. It didn't matter.

"What a load of bullshit," Yetta screams.

"Yetta," says the matron feebly, "please watch your language."

"Bullshit," she screams again, and storms away.

Frieda expects Mrs. Digges to chase her down and cuff her, to make another show of discipline. *No dinner for you! To your room!* But the matron sits still, looking guiltily bewildered, like a guide who has led her charges up a rugged slope, promising a view as their reward, only to find the view, at last, blocked.

It must be the matron's fluster — was she, too, caught off-guard? — that prompts her, later, when Alice has departed, to misplace her copy of the memo, clearly not meant for patients' eyes. Frieda finds it dropped behind the sofa. The letterhead is from the Section of Reformatories and Detention Homes. *For Immediate Distribution to All Field Agents* is marked beneath a War Department eagle. The author's name is Isabella Pearce.

The memo starts with praise for the rapid establishment of so many "human reclamation centers" but expresses disappointment (if not much surprise) in the high recidivism rates, even among "so-called 'charity girls': those who are not prostitutes but likely will be tomorrow.

"Detention lasting but a few months is of doubtful use," it goes on, "and serves only to embitter the patient without lessening her intentions of resorting to ill habits once released." With this in mind, writes Pearce (who is she, Frieda wonders — someone's daughter? someone's faithful wife?), the Law Enforcement Division is recommending to judges that all girls' cases be reviewed. For those who pose clear risks — to themselves, to men in training — detentions should undoubtedly be lengthened: one to four years in a women's reformatory, or, for minors, at an industrial school.

In cases where mentality is so low as to preclude the possibility of any existence other than one of prostitution, it would be an economy and a humanitarian act to commit such individuals to institutional care for life. They are a far greater menace to the welfare of society than many murderers serving life sentences in our prisons.

Frieda replaces the memo behind the sofa, where she found it, looking to make sure that no one sees. No one does, but still she feels (will she always feel?) collared. Every heartbeat, every breath, a crime.

Twenty-six

———★———

YOU'RE ALL JUST going to *sit* there? Just sit and say nothing?" Yetta pounds the table. Forks jump.

All around the dining room, patients stare down, mesmerized, it seems, by their porridge. Frieda's helping, cooled now to a gummy gray wad, trembles in the wake of Yetta's smash. It reminds her of the way the matron shakes when she berates them.

But the matron, for the moment, isn't giving voice to anger. She, too, avoids Yetta's gaze.

"Lambs off to slaughter," Yetta mocks them. "Just like that?" She's been trying, all through breakfast, to incite a revolution to protest the chance of further jailing. *Double jeopardy,* she's been saying. *An outrage.*

The air thickens with a pall of swallowed silence and the dispiriting smell of burnt toast.

"Cowards!"

Yetta's fist again. Milk slops from cups. Something tumbles, clatters on the floor.

"Yetta, all your beefing doesn't make things any better." It's Flossie, her voice tame, decrepit. She looks as though she's eaten food that's off.

All of them, this morning, have that same poisoned look.

"Tell that to your cousins," Yetta says, "in Ireland — the ones who fought the Brits at Easter time. Connolly and the Republicans? *Beefing?*"

Flossie juts her chin, narrows her dark eyes, as if to say she's tired of Yetta's tricks.

"Or the folks who were slaves down South — beefing? If you were black they'd call you Uncle Tom." Hurriedly, Yetta scans across to the colored girls — anxious, or seeking confirmation? — and all the other patients look, too.

Frieda thinks back to the day that she arrived, entering this room the first time: the girls in grim frocks, the mealy mashed-food odor, and her gut-hollowing fear of the unknown. Again she's void with fear, wobbly and blank, but scared now by a *lack* of unknowns, by the sense that she knows all too well what's coming.

At last Hattie lifts her face, inch by cold inch, her good eye glassy with resentment. "Slaves?" she says. "What the hell would *you* know?" In the angle of her chin and her quick cutting glance, it's clear the question's not meant to be answered.

But Yetta, leaning forward, thumps her chest twice. "I'm a woman. I'm a Jew. *Sure* I know."

"Jew is right," says Melba through a mouthful of porridge but loud enough for everyone to hear.

"What?" says Yetta. "What? Say it again."

Mrs. Digges gets up. "Girls, could you stop? Stop it or I'll have to call the watchman."

Her heart clearly isn't in the scolding. Since Alice's briefing yesterday she's skulked around, an undisguisable dullness in her face. Frieda thinks of Mama's old hollowware tea tray, one of her few treasures brought from Russia, which she buffed so devoutly before Shabbos every week that its silver shine thinned, turned to copper.

Does Mama still display the tea service on her mantel? All too soon, Frieda will find out.

"Stop," the matron says again. "Sniping gets you nowhere."

"*Gets* us?" Yetta says. "We *are* nowhere."

The thud of quiet seems to prove her statement: the girls might be down some dark hole. The hole in which Alice's news left them.

Yetta glowers at Frieda with a look of pleading blame. *Join me,* her eyes implore. *Don't you owe it to me? You who made friends with that woman.*

Frieda turns away. How could she join with Yetta, or with anybody else, when she herself is fissured by despair at losing Alice (and Felix, and all her second chances), the despair of going back to Mama? She doesn't even know how she'll face Jo, who's disappeared — in hiding, Frieda guesses, with her chickens. (Mrs. Digges has given up on making Jo comply: "If she wants to skip breakfast, let her starve." But Frieda can't give up on Jo, has to find her soon. An hour more, and Walter will be here.)

The other girls, stifled, have returned to their breakfasts. Someone, in a whisper, asks for salt.

The matron, seeming tepidly content with the room's hush, with having quelled the skirmish that was brewing, crosses to the front with clasped hands. She might be preparing to sing hymns, or to pray — that's how she looks with her hands fixed together, her spine held so earnestly erect. "Sun today," she announces. "I thought we'd take advantage. The corn could use some tender loving care." The smile that she offers them appears to hedge its bets; her voice is a clear brook gone muddy. "Some of you have meetings with the doctor," she continues. "In fact, he may already have arrived. Frieda, you'll be first, as you're getting your results. Then new girls: Lisbeth, Edith, Bess. You'll find the order posted on my door. The rest can follow me out to the garden."

Results, thinks Frieda, with not a trace of pleasure. All this time she's set her sights on reaching just this juncture,

299

on finally being deemed healthy, freed. But freed to what? To Mama's clasp? To a thwarted life like hers? The doctor may declare her clean (and, bodily, she may be), but Frieda still won't feel that way. She'll always feel sullied: for having come to see the world in all its grubby dealings; for having, herself, trafficked in mistrust. Results? *Those* are the results.

But she will (she should) have her body back, at least. What about Jo, whose body is still beholden: to the baby, and now again to Walter? What will being freed mean for Jo? After her appointment — as soon as the doctor's done — Frieda will go and find where Jo's hiding. This time she'll hug Jo, hold tight and soothe her; this time she'll try to find words.

"Finish up your porridge," says the matron, "and let's go." Her hands unclasp and meet again sharply. "Clean your places. Lots of work to do."

Frieda scrapes her bowl and downs a final gray bite. Filling with the busy clink of cutlery and glass, the room takes on a semblance of vitality — or at least of ongoingness, routine.

Yetta's sudden rising makes a splintering, a screech. "That's it, then? Like that? Like any other day? 'Lots of work to do' and tra la la?"

Mrs. Digges looks givingly impatient. "Now, Yetta, you know you're just frittering time away. We move forward. It's what we have to do."

"We do, do we? What if . . . if we *don't*?" She grasps at the air with a stony-knuckled hand, as if seizing the haft of some blade.

For the veterans, the sight of Yetta riled is nothing special, but the new patients haven't ever seen this. Sitting at their table — the table for fresh cases, still infectious — they trade glances full of leery hope. Frieda can detect in their squeamish, widened eyes the same confusion she herself once felt: will a tantrum like Yetta's gain a foothold on their freedom, or cause the roof to topple down and trap them?

Bess — still ailing, with addiction's canceled look — says, "What? What's she asking for?"

Next to her, Lisbeth makes some joke that can't be heard, and all the new girls shake with private laughter.

"Sure," says Yetta, "laugh. Laugh! It's one big joke?" Her anger shifts its aim to easy prey. "*You're* the ones who need help most of all."

Lisbeth says, "This place. *That's* the joke."

"So *do* something. Do something about it!"

"Yetta," says the matron, "please don't set a bad example. I know that you're upset, but calm yourself."

"But we *are* bad examples, right? Isn't that the point? We're bad and always will be, that's the message. Fine, then. How do bad girls act?" She grabs a bowl of porridge, lifts it high in her right hand: a lampoon of Lady Liberty. "Like *this*?" With a nimble snap, she casts the bowl down. Shards of stoneware blast across the floor. "Or how about this?" She hurls a glass against the wall. "Or this?" She upends the whole table.

Crockery and mush and jagged, shattered glass join in a terrifying racket.

"Bad!" Yetta screams, amid the clang and smash. "Wicked, hopeless cases, right? Let's show 'em." With a look of manic triumph, her storm-cloud hair asunder, she cocks her foot and kicks a fallen knife.

Wet, everywhere. Wet and sloppy. Sharp.

Frieda's scared of Yetta. Of joining her. Of not. Waiting to see who else might rise.

The girls beside Yetta stand up but back away, shaking off detritus from their boots. The knife skitters, jangles to a halt.

The matron pushes forward, breakneck, eyes bulging. She's calling out for everyone to stop, stop this instant! To move away from Yetta. *Not* to move. All mixed up with panic. Wheeling arms.

Clearly she is terrified the girls will join together in defiance; she'll be badly outnumbered. All along, the girls have held this possible advantage — every day they could have overwhelmed her — but somehow she has managed to keep order. Now the grip she's held them in is broken.

The room is an armory of violent potential: shivs of stoneware, glass ammunition.

Frieda scans the faces of her fellow patients — friends — seeking indications of alliance. Hattie's healthy eye might as well be patched over, so absolute is its glaze of detachment. Flossie, features pinched, wears a cringing, wrung expression: shame indistinguishable from contempt.

The place where Yetta's glass hit the wall evokes a lesion: whitish liquid, slowly oozing down.

No one speaks. No one lifts a hand. Maybe they're too stupefied to picture true resistance; maybe they're too scared of retribution. Or maybe no one adds to Yetta's mess because they know that it's they who, at last, will have to clean it up.

The treatment room door is open by an inch. The doctor waits, thinks Frieda. Waits for her.

She pauses, weakly breathing, remembering: *this is it*. One last time, and then the days of pills and probes are done. No more spreading open, wider, wider. Now perhaps her shame can grow a scar. She knocks softly, listens for his summons.

With sympathetic shivers she thinks of the new girls, whose torment is only just starting. The stripping; the endless, indecent laying open; and the doctor with his finicky gloved fingers always poking, searching for some long-vanished virtue.

Again she knocks, this time more forcefully: two raps. No response, still, but her knocks jar the door. An inch. Another. A hand's width. "Dr. Slocum?" she says to kill the quiet.

Through the gap she sees it, then: a foot.

A foot in a small scuffed boot, attached to an unseen leg, but limp — *too* limp — flopped aside.

"Doctor," she says again, barely more than breath. "Doctor?" She lunges through the door.

Jo is sitting, slumped against a cabinet, on the floor, her frock up to her waist, legs apart. Her thighs form a dam to check the black-red leach of blood that seeps, slick and polished, past her knees.

"Jo?" says Frieda. "Someone help me. Help?" Looking to the doorway — it's empty; where's the doctor? — she sees the busted lock, its hasp wrenched.

Jo is still alive, maybe. Maybe not quite dead. Vapid eyes. Shallow rattled gasps. Strewn about her cheeks and her neck are fingerprints that call to mind a scattering of roses. Her right hand — her only part remaining firm with will (or is that firmness death's encroaching rigor?) — holds one of the doctor's steel probes: glistening, a blood-adorned baton. She could be a band leader, lost in song.

Frieda's not aware of rising, leaving Jo untouched; not aware of running from the room. "Mrs. Digges!" she calls. "Dr. Slocum!" (Only later — always — envisioning Jo's last breaths, will she think, *Should have stayed and held her hand.*)

Now she's down the hallway, through the parlor, on the porch. Girls stand in the garden, where the glary morning sun makes them appear ghostly, almost see-through.

"Help," she says, or thinks she does. "It's Jo."

No one seems to move, not fast enough at least. No one understands what she needs.

The Ton Truck is parked in its barren patch of yard. She heads for it, thinking — not thinking, really, *feeling* — that this is what she's meant to do, to help. Put Jo in the seat or the bed somehow and take her . . . where? A hospital? Away.

Now the girls have noticed and are gathering about. Bolting for the truck, she ignores them. Up the muddy running board. Inside. It doesn't quite make sense — first she should fetch Jo — but sense comes from the mind, and hers is spent.

Away, thumps her charging heart. *Away.*

The key is in the switch. Of course — why would they hide it? Girls can't drive a motor truck: they're girls. Frieda can. Her hands and feet can. Here and here and here. Heel on starter button, hand on brake.

The engine makes a blackened noise, empty, disobliging. She tries again. Nothing but a cough.

"Do it," Frieda urges, "do it, do it"—stomping on the starter three more times.

Mrs. Digges appears through the windshield's grimy pane, shaking her pink fist, screaming something. Above the engine's coughing, Frieda can't hear words, only the stern cadence of a warning.

Burnham, looking focused, leaves the guardhouse.

Again she tries, and the Ton Truck, with a quick convulsion, starts. There! She tweaks the choke. The engine snarls.

The matron shakes and screams, barrels closer.

Then, unaccountably, the gate begins to open. It swings— Burnham's moving it, he's going to let her through! Why would he help Frieda? No one does.

Jo, she thinks. *Jo.* On the floor, in her own blood.

The gate swings wider, daring her to drive.

She foots the low-speed pedal, and the truck heaves past the matron, who stumbles and falls aside in fright. Frieda feels the Ton Truck's battered power: life enough within it, still, to sail. Heading for the opening, she tugs the big round wheel, picturing herself as a gifted sea captain, steering toward some undiscovered passage.

Only as she turns does she see the coming car: a low-slung Maxwell, aimed for her. Frieda slams the brake and lurches forward, hits the wheel. Her gut burns with hard, barren pain.

The Maxwell, too, stops short to foil a crash. Climbing out its door comes Dr. Slocum. "Of all the—! *What* could you be thinking?"

It's unclear if his fury is directed at Frieda or at Burnham, who stands between them, pleading: "Didn't see her! I was opening it for *you.*"

The Maxwell sits directly in the middle of the exit, blocking any chance of driving past. She could ram it. She could back up and gather ample speed. The Ton Truck is big enough. She might.

Burnham and the doctor close in on her, shouting. The matron, too, is up again, enraged. The ache in Frieda's gut overcomes her. If she made it past the doctor's car, where then would she go? What would happen next? She can't imagine.

Twenty-seven

*T*HE MURK OF MAMA'S FLAT. Its overboiled smell: cabbage and meat bled of flavor.

Frieda sits and watches Mama, eager to see her go, eager to be left by herself. It's the tenth of September: less than two months later, but it might as well be twenty months, two hundred. That's how Frieda feels, that she'll always be the same now—not, perhaps, in circumstance but in spirit. Less than the sum of all her parts.

Mama, though she planned to leave an hour ago, still futzes, gathering one thing, then another. The Ten Days of Awe are a time for introspection, but Mama, in her penitential frenzy, scarcely hesitates long enough to glance into a mirror. *Teshuvah, tefilah, v'tzedakah,* she keeps muttering—repentance, prayer, and charity—these are what will seal her in God's book before it shuts, five days from now, on Yom Kippur. She's spent the week rushing from the orphans' home to shul to the house of every neighbor she has wronged. Giving aid, asking for forgiveness. She hasn't asked Frieda, not in so many words—nor has she eased her restrictions — but she hasn't mentioned Hirsch, and for Frieda that's a start. An admission, a wiping of the slate.

It's 2:30 exactly: Game Five's starting time. Frieda longs to be there, among the Fenway crowd, to hear "The Star-Spangled Banner" played. Of course she can't. She wouldn't even ask.

Mama says she'll likely go from errands straight to *minchah*. "Watch that carp, Frieda — don't want that he should die. There's carrots on the shelf, and prunes, to make a tsimmes. By when I come back, it will be made?"

"Yes," she says, thinking not of tsimmes but of nuts. Peanuts in their hairy shells. Pistachios.

She wouldn't even know the World Series was in swing — a month early, the season war-shortened — if she didn't happen to hear some boys talking of the opener four days ago, on Rosh Hashanah eve.

Mama had let her out — the first time in all these weeks — because, she said, every Jew must hark the shofar's sounding, must answer its summons to atonement: "*This* year especially, Frieda. Listen." Frieda meant to revel in her transitory release, but all that she could notice on the hurried walk to shul was the city's sharp brickwork, its crowding. In shul, the atmosphere was too much like at Mama's, clotted up with sweat and veneration.

Afterward, when Mama was distracted by well-wishing, Frieda stood against a wall, hiding. Next to her stood two boys, hiding also, clearly, to keep mum the wager they were settling.

"Serves you right for betting against Ruth," said the winner, counting up his bounty of new coins. "Told ya. Didn' I tell ya? Ruth's the man."

"Nah, it's just one game. Need *four* to win the Series. Cubs'll come back quick, watch my word."

When Frieda asked the boys to fill her in, they gladly did; every day since, she's been itchy for an update, praying that the Sox have won more.

Frivolous, isn't it — desperate — this caring? How would a

team's winning help *her*? Or Jo, in her fresh grave? Or anyone in need? Not at all. It wouldn't help. And yet.

It's not that she still pines for Felix. Thinks of him sometimes, yes. How could she not? But never as she used to, never wanting. What she misses most is the way she felt beside him, the Frieda that his spotlight set agleam. And so, without wanting *him*, she lets herself want *this:* this victory that Felix and she together hoped for, what's left of their briefly joined ambitions.

Frieda watches Mama now, gathering her things — her purse, a tin of beef to donate — and wonders what, if any, ambitions she has left from her early days of union with Papa. (The notion that Frieda herself might embody those ambitions forces her to temper her ill will.) And what of Mama's hopes from her courtship with Leo? *Was* there even ever such a courtship? Frieda's thought of asking Mama to talk about Leo, about her own younger, freer self. But she guesses that the questions she would ask in compassion would actually, to Mama, seem cruel. As cruel as if someone asked Frieda about Felix. About her long list of crushed dreams.

"The carp," Mama reminds her, heading for the door.

"Yes," Frieda says, "I remember."

Finally Mama goes, locks her in from the outside. She's alone but the slightest bit less lonely.

She gets up and peers into the galvanized tub. The fat black carp curls darkly through the water, its tail tracing a slow question mark. A day before Shabbos, Mama will club the fish, grind its flesh, and poach it for gefilte.

She hates the carp: its plaintive curve, its ignorance of fate; without it, though, she'd never have found out today's news, so she touches its fin, superstitious. The fishmonger's boy, when he lugged the carp up from his store (two doors down the street), gripped it in this morning's *Boston Globe*. Later, Mama stepped out to visit the *downstairsikehs*, bringing them her annual amends, and Frieda grabbed the paper from the trash. It was crumpled and wet, and stank of fishy doom, but its front page filled her with excitement (not the bold type about the Allies gaining ground, but next to it, the smaller sports headline): "Sox Win on Wild Chuck to Merkle." The team was now leading by three games to one. A win today, and they would be world champs!

It's past three o'clock — two innings finished, surely. Frieda makes her way to the apartment's front window and pulls back Mama's old-sheet drapes. She leans over the sill into sunlight. The light, the bright green — Fenway's grassy splendor — Frieda well remembers how it feels: the buzz of such close-packed aspiration. She's missing it. Missing out on everything, as always. She leans farther out the window, anxious. How will she discover how it ends?

Not until days later, when she reads a news account, will she know that, at the moment of her most anxious wondering, the players weren't even on the field. Not yet in their uniforms. Striking.

She'll read of how the owners had halved the players' profits, and the teams pressed for a more equitable deal before they'd play. The only people uniformed at Fenway, she'll learn, were the batboy who hustled out and tried to charm the crowd (*her* batboy, with the soft blushing cheeks?) and dozens upon dozens of soldiers: a grandstand contingent, just back from overseas — wounded boys who got their tickets free — and, on the field, a Camp Devens detachment, working full-tilt to keep the peace.

It was the soldiers who finally made the difference, the paper says. The crowd was going nuts, hurling beer and insults ("Slackers!"), and it looked like a riot would erupt. Thinking fast, the band started playing "Over There," and the fans, abandoning for the moment their complaint, rose to applaud the injured vets. Then, from his seat in the dignitaries' section, Honey Fitz Fitzgerald, Boston's former mayor, rose. The players, he announced, still believed that they'd been swindled, but they'd play, nonetheless, "for the sake of the public and all the wounded soldiers in the stands."

It's later, still — almost twenty years — while reading another account (in a book on what, by that time, is called the First World War), that Frieda will come upon a thought-provoking theory linking the Series with the great Spanish flu. (By then, of course, she'll know that the Sox won that Series — and that they haven't, in the decades since, ever won again.)

Some soldiers from Devens had the bug — so goes the theory — which they'd picked up from sailors, earlier in the month, at Boston's Win the War for Freedom march. The soldiers, mingling with civilian baseball fans, unknowingly spread the disease (just as others would, another two months hence, in the hoopla of Armistice parades). Sox fans brought the flu to families in Boston, Cubs fans brought it to Chicago; soon the whole country was engulfed. But think how much worse, the historian mused, if the Series had been better attended, if war hadn't cut the season short.

Reading this passage, Frieda won't linger on the numbers (ten thousand sick at Camp Devens in just two weeks) and not on the scientific details. The fact that will give her pause is this: also in the dignitaries' box at Game Five, near Honey Fitz, sat Senator Weeks. Was Weeks accompanied by his friend Meyer Morse?

Morse, she knows, got sick — it was in the news back then. He didn't die but got sick enough that he dropped out of his race. (So even if Frieda had decided to take his bribe, he never, in the end, would have paid her; this knowledge didn't soothe her, it just deepened her bereavement.) Or maybe it was grief that made Morse quit. The article about him that Frieda clipped and saved included the following sentence: "Mr. Morse's son, a private at Camp Devens, succumbed to influenza last month."

The first time she read those words, Frieda was not surprised; instead she felt a certain shameful — no, not satisfaction. A better word, she thought, was confirmation: the un-canny, almost alleviating rightness when the world offers facts to match your mood. *Felix. Dead. Of course.* She might have been equally unsurprised (if this were possible) to scan through the casualty lists and find her own name.

But now, all these years later, reading of Senator Weeks, wondering if Morse sat beside him, she'll be shocked and dis-traught at the thought of Felix dying. Full of sudden agitating questions: Was Felix at that game? Unwittingly infectious? Was *he* the Devens soldier most to blame? It's not hard for Frieda to imagine.

Felix, still favoring his barely healed ankle (do the fans guess he took fire in France?), leaves his position with the peacekeep-ing troops and limps to the dignitaries' box. Men pound the dugout roof. "Greedy sons of bitches." "Outta there, you lazy slackers. Play!" Felix spies his father, who says how proud he is, a sentiment that's echoed by the senator, the ex-mayor. A fine boy, they agree. Country's finest! Felix steps up, reaches out to shake their hands . . .

Stop, she'll think. Don't! Don't touch them! But she knows that it wouldn't have mattered. Even if Felix really was there, was contagious, stopping him would have stopped nothing. You can't put the world in quarantine.

A year after the plague, she's on her own. It's near the end of 1919.

Frieda herself never got the flu, not a sniffle — saved, it seems clear to her, by Mama's stringent rules, by the fact that Mama kept her inside. (Frieda stayed healthy then, and will for many years; healthy, or stubborn enough to make it look that way. Only twice again will she ever see a doctor: once for the birth of her daughter, Joan, and once for a scare about her lungs.)

She'd planned to run away — break the lock, if she had to — but Mama, in the end, let her go. "Frieda, you're eighteen. What more can I do? What more without you should hate me?"

It was a late-winter day. The air that leaked inside bore a fruitful smell of melting. "But no, I guess you hate me already."

Mama's voice was so fragile, so full of hurt desire, that Frieda saw her clearly as the girl she must have been, nervous she would never find love. (But she *had* found it, hadn't she? Might have lost it, but she'd found it.) Frieda, who hadn't touched her, not once, since coming home, was moved to put a hand on Mama's shoulder. "No," she said. "No, I don't hate you."

She stayed a week longer, while she made new arrangements. A week that felt not at all so bad. And now, in the intervening months, she's even visited two or three times, to share supper. With her earnings, she's bought Mama groceries.

She's working seven smoky nights a week as a "dance instructress" — a job that Lou procured for her (it's Lou's job now, too), for which no further reference was required. Thank God that Lou never moved from her old building, that she took Frieda in, all forgiven.

The Honeybee Ballroom, being deemed a "closed hall," doesn't allow female patrons entry. To dance, a man has to hire one of the hall's pros: a dime for each ninety-second spin, of which the pro pockets three cents.

"Instructress?" Frieda balked when Lou proposed the work. "I don't know a thing about teaching."

"Frieda, don't be dim. Ain't your teaching that they pay for. A warm body is all. And a smile."

It's not until Sheldon Kalb's third dance of the night, when he asks if he might purchase all the rest, that Frieda even bothers taking stock: a decent face, rigid with strenuous good will; sturdy hair like something thawed then suddenly refrozen. Shel's in town — his first trip east, he says with flattened vowels — for the National Hardware Sellers' yearly meeting. As a dancer he is earnest, more footwork than finesse, but not without a certain basic balance.

The next night he returns and he buys ten dances straight, remaining until the ballroom closes. Then he walks Frieda home through icy, dark streets, nattering all the while about this year's new products (an egg beater that stands up on its own in any bowl!). Frieda doesn't mind, not especially, his chatter; at least he's not asking her to talk. At her door, she tries to kiss him — to give him what he paid for — but Shel says no; no, he'd like to wait.

A month later, he finds her at the Honeybee again.

"Another hardware convention?" she asks him. "So soon?"

"No," he says, "I'm back in town . . . my business now, you see . . ." And somehow he manages to propose.

Frieda, not certain if she'll get another chance — certain she won't warrant one — says yes.

That will all be history when Frieda, lungs burning, is rushed in her husband's boxy '43 DeSoto to the hospital in Kansas City. It's the end of the next war — Japan's cities have just been melted — and Frieda, despite the spit she coughs up, streaked with pus, won't believe pneumonia is the cause. Who contracts a bug like that in August? Maybe it's some supercharged strain of hay fever, a malady of the vast Middle West. But each day: less air, this buried-alive feeling, her lungs filling inch by inch with mud.

It's Shel's DeSoto, but Joan, eighteen, is at the wheel. Shel will have gone for the week to Cincinnati, to attend, in his new role as bylaws committee chairman, the annual NHS meeting. Their marriage has been tolerable, little to object to, short on any kind of histrionics. When he's gone like this, Frieda doesn't quite exactly miss him, but registers, with just a little measure of annoyance, the altering of her daily routine. Without him there to nudge her, she often sleeps late and starts the day already behind.

He's been a fine father to Joan. Interested, more patient than Frieda; never pushed her one way or the other. Nor did he push Frieda to have a second child (it's been ages since he bothered her in bed). Frieda, after holding out for seven or eight years — worried about what kind of mother she would make, and, too, if her history of disease might harm the child — had

313

relented and given him Joan. But that was it, she'd made good and sure. The girls at the Home had taught her all the tricks; her time there hadn't been for nothing.

Only six months licensed, Joan's a woeful driver — rides the clutch, jerky on the brake — as timid at the wheel as she is in everything, terrified of making any move. But Frieda, wheezing, vision dark and frayed, can't manage driving on her own. They wend past water towers painted with town names, past hog farms whose earthy smell she's never gotten used to. Joan is too nervous to focus on directions, so Frieda has to waste a precious lungful of her breath to huff out, "There. To the right."

But Joan misses the turn, has to back up, stalls the engine.

"Jesus, Joan. Gas. Give it gas!" How could a child of Frieda's be so hopeless in a car?

"Sorry, Mom, I'm . . . don't you know I'm trying?"

You shouldn't have to *try*, Frieda wants to tell her daughter. You should *know*. This should all be instinct.

Frieda vowed to treat her child better than she was treated — and she has, certainly she has — but the thing that's still toughest for her, after all these years, is remembering that to force her sense of boldness on Joan would be just as bad as Mama's having forced her to suppress it.

Years ago, when Frieda and Jack got caught together, Mama said it's harder than you think to love a child. Frieda's come to see that she was right in this at least. It's hard — hard especially when you still can't love yourself.

Finally they make it to the hospital. Emergency is hushed, shades drawn against the sun, only two other patients there: a teen boy whose forearm got mangled in a baler; a woman big with twins, scared she'll lose them. Frieda looks away. She can't bear these ghastly places. She feels she might drown in her own fluids.

They take her back and listen to her chest, make an X-ray, while Joan, useless, waits by the entrance. Two long hours later, a new physician comes. "Mrs. Kalb? Hello, I'm Dr. Miller."

Yes, he says: pneumonia, quite advanced. Why did she let it go this long?

He's her age, a bit older. Bespectacled. Intense. A Star of David hangs around his neck. Could it be? All these years later? No, of course not. She's oxygen-deprived. Delusional.

"Mrs. Kalb, have you had any trouble like this before?"

"No, I'm . . . my health has been fine."

It's such a common surname. But a doctor? In Missouri? Wasn't that where Miller said he came from?

"No bronchitis? No history of infections?"

Frieda — Mrs. Kalb — shakes her head.

That Miller, the single time she saw him at the Home, was skittishly regardful, like this one. But his eye. His lazy left eye. This Miller's tender blue eyes both stare straight. Is it possible that his glasses now correct it?

"Ma'am, I'm sure you're frightened. Who wouldn't be? *I* would. But the thing to be frightened of is *not* being seen. We have treatments now. There's no need to suffer."

She's seen so many die, untouchable, alone. Papa. Sweet Jo. All those corpses back in '18.

"I'm going to give you a shot of a wonderful new drug. Should have you feeling better in three days."

"Three days?"

"I should think. If not sooner."

"What is it?"

"Believe it or not, a mold. From a moldy cantaloupe in Peoria! It's what we sent over with the boys on D-day, and it saved . . . we can't *count* how many lives. Works against everything from septicemic wounds to . . . to what some folks call the wages of sin."

Yes, she thinks. It *is* him. It must be.

Thinking that this man is the same who saw her then, she might well be stricken by disgrace. She might erupt with bitterness long brewing. All she feels, in truth, is short of breath.

"It's too bad."

"Too bad?" he says. "What do you mean, 'too bad'? It's fantastic. A magic bullet, really."

"No. I was thinking: too bad that only now —"

"Oh, yes. Yes, of course. I see your point."

The doctor (who, it turns out, is not the same Miller; he tells her that he's never been to Boston) will come to seem impressed by Mrs. Kalb. He'll say she's quick to grasp implications. They'll talk, as he treats her, of the war's atomic finish, of ends that might justify means. He'll recommend a history of the First World War's conclusion and the Spanish flu: "Full of striking theories."

After, he will walk her to the waiting room, to Joan. "Your mom," he'll say, "is one smart cookie, right?"

But for now, she's still Frieda and knows nothing of penicillin, nothing of atom bombs or influenza. For now she's still leaning from the sill of Mama's window, waiting for the World Series news.

She calls out to passersby, asking for the outcome, but no one from this neighborhood has been to Fenway Park. Peddlers and housewives — who bothers?

The late-summer sun falls fast across the sky, dips behind a cloud. Frieda shivers. Mama's due back soon, but Frieda doesn't care. All she cares about now is the score.

Finally, Frieda sees the boy from Rosh Hashanah: the braggart, the winner of the bet. That time, he reminded her — his zeal — of Jack Galassi, but now he looks helpless, half-drowned.

"Hey," she says. "Hey, kid, what happened?"

"Awful. Unbearable. Got killed."

The boy is so distressed-looking, flexing his bite with anguish, that Frieda for a moment thinks he might mean the war: the Germans have reversed the tide and crushed us.

"Didn't just lose," he says. "A shutout. Three-zip. They looked like *nothing* out there. Like girls." The boy spits and scuffles down the street.

Frieda pulls herself inside and lets the drapes fall, so Mama's flat is shrunk again by darkness. The fated smell of carp fills the air.

Tomorrow, she thinks, *maybe* — but cuts herself short. Sickened to be yearning, still. Her sickness.

AUTHOR'S NOTE

Charity Girl and its characters — even those whose names can be found in old newspapers — are entirely imagined; the novel's context and most of its historical references, however, are factual.

During World War I, driven by an unprecedented alliance between military efficiency experts and antiprostitution activists, the United States government detained some thirty thousand women; more than fifteen thousand, found to carry venereal diseases, were incarcerated for months at a time. Because it was practically impossible to distinguish the criminal from the merely adventuresome, the government's crusade targeted women indiscriminately. They were arrested and taken into custody for the "crimes" of dressing provocatively or walking through certain neighborhoods without an escort. Only one-third of the arrested women were ever charged with prostitution; the majority were detained without having been charged with any offense. To accommodate this sudden population of quarantined women, the federal government funded the construction or improvement of dozens of detention homes, some of them in refurbished brothels.

For dramatic purposes, I have freely altered some details of geography and chronology. Readers curious about the novel's factual basis might want to consult the following scholarly works, whose guidance I gratefully acknowledge: *Making Men Moral,* by Nancy K. Bristow; *No Magic Bullet,* by Allan M. Brandt; *Purity and Hygiene,* by David J. Pivar; *The Response to Prostitution in the Progressive Era,* by Mark Thomas Connelly; *Uneasy Virtue,* by Barbara Meil Hobson; *Cheap Amusements,* by Kathy Peiss; *The Lost Sisterhood* and *The Maimie Papers,* by Ruth Rosen; *Counter Cultures,* by Susan Porter Benson; *Their Sisters' Keepers,* by Estelle B. Freedman; *Delinquent Daughters,* by Mary E. Odem; and *The Year the Red Sox Won the Series,* by Ty Waterman and Mel Springer.

ACKNOWLEDGMENTS

Thanks to my father, Abraham Lowenthal, and stepmother, Jane Jaquette, for the use of their inspiring home, and to the rest of my family, especially Janet Lowenthal, Jim Pines, and the editorial whiz Linda Lowenthal. For research and logistical support, I'm grateful to Michael Borum, Dr. Jack Mayer, the Interlibrary Loan department of Boston College's Thomas P. O'Neill Library, and Evan Ide, curator of the Larz Anderson Auto Museum. I am indebted to the Hawthornden International Retreat for Writers, the St. Botolph Club Foundation, and the Bread Loaf Writers' Conference for generous fellowships, and to Brian Bouldrey, Phil Gambone, Elizabeth Graver, Rachel Kadish, Jayne Yaffe Kemp, and especially Vestal McIntyre for reading drafts. My agent, Mitchell Waters, and editor, Heidi Pitlor, provided help beyond measure.

Special gratitude to Scott Heim.

Charity Girl

by

MICHAEL LOWENTHAL

"Lively and illuminating . . . [Lowenthal] has accomplished the difficult feat of marrying the facts of history with the details that make a fictional life come alive . . . nothing short of a gift." —Anita Shreve, *Washington Post Book World*

About the Author

© Neil Giordano

Michael Lowenthal grew up near Washington, D.C., and graduated from Dartmouth College, after which he worked as an editor at University Press of New England, where he founded the Hardscrabble Books imprint. He is the author of two previous novels, *Avoidance* and *The Same Embrace,* as well as short stories and essays that have been widely anthologized. The recipient of fellowships from the Bread Loaf and Wesleyan writers' conferences, the Massachusetts Cultural Council, and the Hawthornden International Retreat for Writers, Lowenthal teaches creative writing in the MFA program at Lesley University. He also serves on the executive board of PEN New England. He can be contacted through his website, www.MichaelLowenthal.com.

For Discussion

1. At the center of the novel hangs an ethical dilemma, where the rights of the few are weighed against the health and safety of many. Would you consider the government's moral crusade reasonable, given the circumstances of wartime? In what other way might the need to maintain a healthy army have been addressed? In what circumstances do we face similar choices today? What modern relevance does Frieda's story have?

2. How would you describe Frieda Mintz's personality, and how does Lowenthal bring her to life? Does she seem particularly rebellious or attracted to danger, or is she more a regular girl trapped in a series of bad situations? Did you find yourself sympathizing with her, identifying with her? Were you ever frustrated by her actions? Placed in her situation, would you have made the same choices that she did? How does Frieda change during the course of the book?

3. *Charity Girl* opens in Boston in 1918; at the time, employment choices for women were limited. Why does the prospect of being a shopgirl at Jordan Marsh so appeal to Frieda? Aside from her wages, how does her job benefit her?

4. Frieda moves to a boarding house in the city as a form of self-imposed exile from her mother and their Russian immigrant community. What other instances of banishment and displacement—self-imposed or otherwise—are found in the novel? How do these instances resonate with each other?

5. Frieda's friend Lou explains the rules for the dance: "Getting treated when you pick up guys is one thing . . . and we're lots of us charity girls. But it's never just for money, straight out." Why did the shopgirls like Lou and Frieda note such fine distinctions? Why was it important to them to set up such boundaries? What irony is there in the fact that Frieda was incarcerated nonetheless? Do you agree

with Mrs. Sprague's assessment that the so-called 'charity girls' are more a threat than prostitutes? Were these 'charity girls' exploited, do you think, by their employers, by their suitors?

6. Did you find Felix an honorable character? What clues does Lowenthal give about his true regard for Frieda? Why does Frieda hold such unwavering belief in the rightness of his actions?

7. Frieda meets many vivid women at the Home. Each of her fellow detainees—Flossie, Jo, Yetta, Hattie, Melba, Fleur—has a different response to incarceration. What factors contributed to these diverse reactions? With which woman's response did you identify most? How do you think you might have responded if you had found yourself indefinitely detained?

8. Though the rounding up and subsequent detention of thousands of women like Frieda seems appalling from a modern vantage, some of the characters in the book earnestly believe they are performing a public service by participating in the government's program. What motivates Mrs. Sprague or Alice Longley or Dr. Slocum to be party to the situation? Is their participation defensible?

9. Biology doesn't support Mrs. Sprague's notion that women are more to blame than men for spreading disease. Why do you think only women were targets of the government's detention efforts?

10. The novel is infused with themes of trust—and betrayal of trust. What are some instances of trust being misplaced? When is trust abused? What are the consequences of the many betrayals in the book?

11. Set during a time of intense, perhaps overbearing, patriotism, the novel explores questions of identity and group belonging. Consider Frieda's Jewish upbringing and her relationship to her religious identity. Felix is also Jewish, but from a well-to-do, assimilating family; does Frieda have more in common with him, because they're both Jewish, or with the gentile girls she works with, because

they're all similarly impoverished? Yetta perhaps holds out another model of Judaism, that of an agitator for social justice. Frieda seems both drawn to and repelled by her. Why?

12. The novel's epigraph reads: "Charity causes half the suffering she relieves, but she cannot relieve half the suffering she has caused." What do you think this means in the context of the novel? In the course of the story, who gives what to whom, and what, if anything, do they expect in return? If charity comes with real or perceived strings attached, can it be true charity?

13. Why do you think the author chose to write about the book's subject matter as an imagined story rather than as a nonfiction account? What information does historical fiction provide that may be absent from works of history or the official record? How is the experience of reading Frieda's story different from reading nonfiction accounts of the time? How, if at all, does the novelist's modern perspective color the way he portrays historic characters and events? What draws you to historical novels?

14. Why do you suppose the historical episode on which the novel was based, which saw some 15,000 women incarcerated, remains so little known in America today? Which, if any, events of our times are in danger of being similarly lost to posterity?

15. Do you think, in the end, that Frieda finds redemption? What do you imagine her life is like after the War? What does the final sequence tell you about her fate? Is it an ending you would have wished for her?

MARINER BOOKS / HOUGHTON MIFFLIN COMPANY

For information about other Mariner Reader's Guides, please visit our website, www.marinerreadersguides.com.